Lilly Inkwood always wanted penned (literally, with a pen) he grade. It just took her much to fantasy, above all things.

She also writes historical fiction as Patricia Adrian. Her novel *The Bletchley Women* is a *USA Today* Bestseller.

Lilly's interests also include history (especially women in history), skulking around social media for much longer than she should, and reading, particularly when she's on a tight deadline and should be writing instead. Originally from Eastern Europe and now living near the Black Forest in Germany, Lilly has always loved the old European folktales she grew up with.

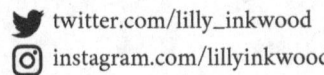

twitter.com/lilly_inkwood
instagram.com/lillyinkwood

THE KINGDOM IS A
GOLDEN CAGE

THE RED KINGDOM
BOOK ONE

LILLY INKWOOD

One More Chapter
a division of HarperCollins*Publishers*
1 London Bridge Street
London SE1 9GF
www.harpercollins.co.uk

HarperCollins*Publishers*
Macken House, 39/40 Mayor Street Upper,
Dublin 1, D01 C9W8, Ireland

This paperback edition 2023
1
First published in Great Britain in ebook format
by HarperCollins*Publishers* 2023

A catalogue record of this book is available from the British Library

ISBN: 9780008526047

This novel is entirely a work of fiction. The names, characters and incidents
portrayed in it are the work of the author's imagination. Any resemblance to actual
persons, living or dead, events or localities is entirely coincidental.

Printed and bound in the UK using 100% Renewable Electricity
by CPI Group (UK) Ltd

For N.

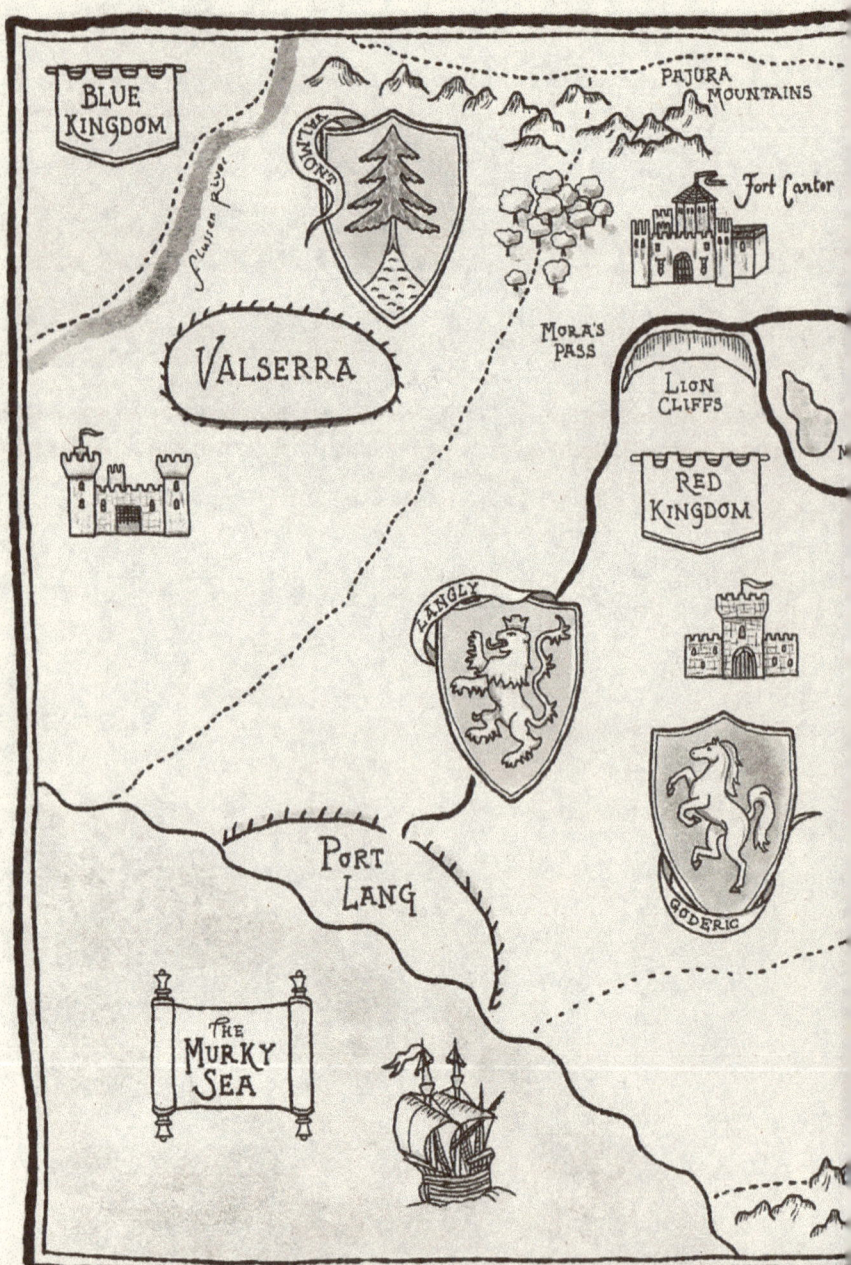

PAL MOUNTAIN

RAID

LANGVILLE

PENERIG

King's Fief

BENCIFERT

bencifert
Castle

LAFALA

THE
GLITTERING
SEA

ARNAULD

GREEN
KINGDOM

HALLOWED
FOREST

REEN MOUNTAINS

LIST OF CHARACTERS

CELINE, Princess of the Red Kingdom; once a powerful Water-Twirler, her main occupation nowadays is pretending not to understand her father's insinuations that she should finally find a husband at the 'advanced' age of twenty-three.

KING MIHIEL of the Red Kingdom, Celine's father; keeper of many secrets, described by his daughter as 'the least magical person that she's ever met.' Rather obsessed with his lineage, and its continuation.

PETIT-MIHIEL, five years old, Celine's brother and heir to the throne; sadly, more often to be found in his sickroom than playing in the corridors of the Royal Palace in Lafala. Celine isn't sure if he has the Gift—that is, any magical ability; this isn't a subject she ever breached with her father, though she wanted to.

CELINE'S MOTHER (died in childbirth), a powerful Illusionist and a doyenne of the Golden Pavilion (the most prestigious magic school in the Three Kingdoms) before becoming Queen.

MAËL, Fifth Duke of Langly, but the fourth person to occupy the seat. Best known for hosting the most enticing revels (read: orgies) in the Red Kingdom (and, perhaps, beyond); otherwise, quite loud and rather unconcerned with what everyone makes of him, and quick to take offence in a fight.

MAGALI, mother to Maël; a Princess of the Blue Kingdom; very concerned with what everyone makes of her and Langly; a very wise advisor and able ruler, in her own words.

FREDERIC (deceased), father to Maël, Second and Fourth Duke of Langly. His rule of the Duchy was interrupted by his brother's rule of seven years, while Frederic himself had been presumed dead. Hailed as the victor at the Siege of the Twins. Remembered as quite short-tempered. What no one knows is that he was the one that had taken his mother's disappearance the hardest among the siblings, and that he was drawn to Magali (whom he later took as a wife) because, with her manipulative ways, she rather reminded him of his mother.

THE LION, The First Duke of Langly, father to Frederic, Kylian and Isabella. Not many people can think of a single nice thing to say about him. Since he was born in poverty, the seigneurs of Langly always made a point to gossip behind his back about what they judged to be his shortcomings. Sadly, this was all anyone thought to prattle on about when his name came up.

THE LION'S WIFE, The First Duchess of Langly, mother to Frederic, Kylian and Isabella; remembered as a powerful and somewhat discreet Light-Cantor—whose songs could bind light and make it do quite interesting things—and generally a role model for the ladies of the Red Kingdom.

ISABELLA OF LANGLY, firstborn of the First Duke and Duchess of Langly; whom nobody actually sees much of.

HUGO, son of Kylian, cousin to Maël; Celine's first love; presumed dead, actually bound into the shape of a cat for the past five years.

KYLIAN, Third Duke of Langly. A wise, smooth, cunning ruler, according to some people; a backstabber and a plotter, according to others. Fate after the Siege of the Twins – uncertain, and no one seems very concerned about it, which lends truth to the saying that memory tends to be quite short, sometimes.

MESSERE PHILIPPE BENCIFERT, heir apparent to Maël of Langly, younger half-brother to Seigneur Louis Bencifert. Would have been rather bookish and leaning towards philosophical examinations, but at the age of seven, he was taken out of the library at Castle Bencifert by his parents and thrust onto a nearby farm. He continues to have many thoughts about social inequity, but mostly does so while tending to the fields or his animals, instead of doing it in the company of seigneurs at tables heaving with more food than they'd be able to eat.

SEIGNEUR JULIEN BENCIFERT (deceased), Fourth Seigneur Bencifert. One of the last Magic-Binders—a rare Gift that permits the binding of various forms of magic. Used to be a close friend to King Mihiel, until he began fostering the fugitives Isabella and Magali of Langly, during Kylian's occupation of the Duchy.

SEIGNEUR LOUIS BENCIFERT, elder half-brother to Philippe; the Fifth Seigneur Bencifert. Very little inclined towards philosophical examinations, but rather polished manners.

COUNT GODERIC, the Warlord of the Duchy of Langly; his main occupation in times of peace is not to show what he truly makes of any given occurrence or situation; he's quite skilled at this.

MESSERE FABIEN GODERIC, the third son of Count Goderic; only known for the propensity with which he participates in the soirees organised by his friend, Maël, Duke of Langly; this is much to the painfully concealed displeasure of his father.

THE FALLEN COURT, a secret society with a powerful influence extending widely through two of the Three Kingdoms. There are members of the Fallen Court among this list of characters. Even if Celine doesn't know it.

PROLOGUE: QUAKE

CELINE

I'm alone in my chambers at the Royal Palace, yet again, while my fate is being decided in another room.

This is the life of a princess.

Staring into the distance, through the open doors to my terrace, at the light breaking over the Glittering Sea, while my father presides over my future.

There's a soft tap of paws over the blue and gold marble, and the cat hops lightly through the doors, and into the room.

A blue-grey cat with a red pouch on its back, tied by fine golden threads.

It's the eyes that arrest me. Eyes the colour of the deep sea, with a circle of gold around them.

My breath catches for so many reasons.

'It is done,' the cat says, stopping a few feet from me. Sad, so sad. 'Your father has betrothed you to Duke Maël of Langly.'

I do not have words, not even tears for this.

Duke Maël, that ogre-like man, with paws like a bear's, whom I have done my best to avoid. Too loud, too vulgar, simply too much.

My husband-to-be, in spite of my protests.

But this is what my father sees when he looks at me – just someone who can secure the future. My little brother is just five years of age, and sickly, and women may not inherit in our kingdom.

Not duchies, not thrones. But the law says that their male children may inherit, and my father wishes for nothing more than for me to produce an heir.

As if I were all womb and no feelings.

'No,' I say, barely a whisper.

And that I should sink so low as to have a cat spying for me, to tell me about the conclusions that my father and the duke have reached.

The cat dips its head. 'I'm sorry, Celine. It's true. Though they will not announce it for a while. Not until the matter with the duke's mother is settled.'

I chuckle, bitterly. 'The "matter"? Do you mean the fact that Maël threw out his own mother, Magali?'

Oh, the powerful Dowager Duchess, Magali. That a woman I loathe so much should be in the way of their plans is one of the ironies of fate.

'Yes,' says the cat. 'They would not want to make waves. Not now. So this will be kept a secret for a while.'

I clench my fist. 'Do you suggest that this might be kept even from me?'

The cat closes the distance between us, touching the hem of my skirts. 'Possibly.'

A man who threw out his own mother from Fort Cantor. And this is who I am to wed.

The call of my Gift is a song in my blood, a whoosh in my ears, deafening me, making me dizzy. I used to be powerful, twirling water to my desire. I could have driven a river to wipe clean an entire village, I could have raised cataclysmic waves from the sea.

But now, it is almost nothing. A call without an answer, clenching over my senses when I am angry or close to tears. I feel both now and I can hear nothing but a roar, nails digging deep in my own palms, the glass of water on the low table spilling, its contents rippling, rippling, rippling.

They won't even tell me, not even me, as if this doesn't change the course of my entire life.

I look to the sea, begging it to obey, begging it to carry me away.

Anything, so I would not have to marry that man.

There's a pull on my skirts and I look down, and there's the cat. As I pick it up, the roars in my ears quieten and I hear him calling me softly. 'My dove.'

I stroke its fur, from the top of its head to the base of its tail, and the feeling is nothing like it should be. It's soft and velvety, cut by currents of magic under his skin.

This is not his skin.

Underneath it, the love of my life is trapped into this shape, has been trapped for five years, cursed to walk the kingdom as a cat. Trapped by Magali, the Dowager Duchess, and her accomplice, Seigneur Julien Bencifert.

The only reason why he is here, today, with me, is that Julien Bencifert has fallen gravely ill, and his spells have started to fray.

Spells.

Since the powers of the mages in our kingdom have waned, only Spell-Lore remains, for those who are ready to use these forbidden, foul practices.

But what has ever Magali stopped at?

Like mother, like son.

I shudder, again.

'Are you all right, my dove?' says the cat. Hugo. Hugo who is now the cat. Hugo, who is Maël's cousin, nonetheless.

'How will I ever be?' I ask. 'How could I?'

The cat lays a paw on the embroidery of my bodice. Such rich ornaments for someone who has no power over her own fate. 'My dove,' he says. 'What do you want?'

I can't even look at him. Not as he is, not in this form. 'No one can give me what I want.'

Because all I want is him.

He strokes the side of a paw on my jaw, my cheek. 'Please tell me. You can always tell me.'

I realise he's been wiping away my tears. 'I don't want this. Any of this. I don't want to marry him.'

Hugo stares into my eyes, while concern is stamped in his. 'Celine, listen. I have to go now; I've been away for too long. They might realise something is amiss if I don't come back.'

I know who he means. Bencifert and Magali, who have yet no inkling that Hugo, even though trapped in this shape with the help of a binding object, has begun to remember who he was.

And came to seek me.

'I promise you this,' says Hugo. 'I will find a way. I will find a way, and I will come for you.'

I promise. I promise.

I remember a promise he made to me five years ago, which he hadn't been able to keep.

But I rein in my tears, hold him close before he leaves.

Because if I learned something, it is that I should never take for granted that the people I love would come back.

That I would ever come to see them again.

PROLOGUE: FAIRY TALE

CELINE

*L*et me tell you a story.

In the time of my grandfather, the rightful king and ruler of the Red Kingdom, the first Duke of Langly married a beautiful, quiet princess. She was a mage, a Light-Cantor, whose songs could bring light forth even from the depths of the sea, who could make fires burn brighter and stronger.

Together, they built a stronghold, Fort Cantor, and turned it into a place of learning and merriment that even rivalled the Royal Court.

They had three children: a girl, Isabella, and a set of magnificent twins. Dark-haired Frederic was strong and stubborn, like his father, while Kylian's hair was the colour of rich honey, and his words just as sweet.

But the first duke – also called the Lion – and his duchess had differences beyond the fact that she possessed magic, and he did not.

As time passed, the duchess began to disappear more and more often from the ducal table. Until, one day, she was gone without a trace. People whispered of her husband's violent nature.

People whispered how he might have murdered her.

Yet the whispers remained just that – whispers – which did not touch the powerful duke.

And then, by a whim of cruel fate, when Isabella was nineteen years of age, the duke vanished, as well.

Isabella, undaunted and unmarried, took on the guardianship of the duchy until her brothers came of age.

Frederic took an ambitious young woman as a wife, a princess of the Blue Kingdom. Her name was Magali.

His brother, Kylian, married for love, a girl of the people, who was warm and bright like a summer morning.

They say the twins struggled for power, when the time came. They say that Isabella herself happened to favour the cunning Magali, and the matter was soon settled in Frederic's favour.

They say that when the duchy passed into his hands, the sisters-in-law gave birth to their children, less than a month apart.

It so happened that Maël, Frederic's son, came into the world as heir to the greatest duchy in the Red Kingdom, the Duchy of Langly.

It so happened that Hugo, Kylian's son, came into the world as the heir of nothing.

One would be inclined to think that the matter of the inheritance would be thus settled between the cousins.

One would be wrong.

MAGALI

Let me tell you how it was.

In the times when my mother was a young girl with her head

full of dreams, a ruthless outlaw called the Lion carved himself a duchy, from the ruins of the principate of Anselme.

In order to strengthen his position, he married a cunning, manipulative mage, a princess of the kingdom. Together they ruled for many years in lands that should not have been theirs to begin with.

Their marriage was blessed with children: a girl and a set of twin boys. And because the Lion and his duchess thought they could control anything, even fate, they never told anyone else which of the boys, Frederic or Kylian, came into the world first. They wanted to be the ones who decided which of them inherited the duchy, which of them proved more worthy.

But the first duchess could not settle for what she already had. And in her insatiable hunger for power, she disappeared, while pursuing even greater ambitions.

The Lion went mad. For as long as he lived, he never gave up looking for her, obsessed by this quest so much that he met an early end, before he could settle the matter of the inheritance.

This became the task of the eldest sister. Isabella was wise beyond her nineteen years and could see the ill influence that Kylian's wife exerted over him. She could see what a backstabbing, scheming woman she was, who, on top of it all, possessed a dangerous Gift. In order to spare the duchy from her devious ways, she settled the inheritance upon Frederic.

You would think that the matter of the inheritance would be laid to rest after Frederic and I, his wife, took the reins of the duchy. After our son, Maël, came into the world.

You would be wrong.

PART I

THE UNLIKELIEST OF MATCHMAKERS

TIDELINES

CELINE

*I*n my hands, I'm holding a man's fate.

I squeeze the document that Hugo has stolen in my left hand, sweat glistening on the dry parchment. It's not the heat, though the fire is blazing in my chambers in our house in Langville on this late spring day. The windows that look towards the town have been sealed, and I made sure to lock the door before casting on my desk the meagre contents of my satchel: a piece of blank parchment, ink, quill. And, most importantly, the seal I have stolen from my father.

The cat leaps on my lap, sensing my hesitation. I stroke its blue-grey fur, perhaps to reassure myself, more than anything, though it is less than reassuring. I shouldn't feel this when touching my lover. I barely remember how he felt when he was still a man, while we were still everything to each other, five years ago, when he left to challenge fate itself and more than two decades of wrongs against his side of the family.

'It's the only thing we can do,' he whispers. 'If you don't want to find yourself married to him.'

Maël, the stuff of my nightmares.

Though not only mine, it seems.

Hugo returned yesterday, while my father and I were attending the yearly fair in Langville. He told me, 'There might be a way.' My heart leapt, but I tried not to lean too much into this feeling.

I know better than to hope, by now.

Hugo told me, 'Magali seeks to replace Maël, her own son, at the helm of the duchy.'

I felt like I couldn't breathe. 'With whom?'

'With his cousin, Philippe. My cousin, too.'

I frowned. 'Philippe?' I hadn't even heard of him.

'He's a modest boy, the only child of Isabella of Langly. Had nothing more than a farm to his name, for all his life. He's a bit of a dolt.'

I chuckled at this. 'The only child of the firstborn of the first duke? A farm?'

'There was a scandal some years ago, if you remember, my dove. When Isabella of Langly married a widowed seigneur who already had two older sons from a previous marriage. Seigneur Julien Bencifert, if you recall.'

I was so shocked, that I could barely find the words. 'Julien Bencifert? The man who did this to you? And Magali seeks to replace Maël with his son?'

'Magali and Bencifert seemed to have worked well together in the past, haven't they?' I knew what he meant. What was done to *him*. 'But there is a way,' said Hugo, 'to kill two birds with one stone.'

The same thing that my father is trying to do by marrying me against my will with Maël: to force my hand to produce that heir, and end once and for ever the struggles for power in Langly.

I suppose my father never thought that this dove might have

some plans of her own. He hasn't even informed me about my betrothal yet.

I look at the golden cage that has been deposited in my chambers. A tool, Hugo said, that he snatched—with help—from under Magali's nose.

A tool that she would use to bind Maël to an animal form, just like Hugo has been.

'We need time,' Hugo told me. A few more days. So I can do *this*.

I look at the parchments. Once I lay the royal seal on the new document I've written, once I throw the one in my hand in the fire, the course of a man's life will be changed for ever.

'There is no going back after this,' I whisper, my finger tracing Hugo's spine, to the red pouch fixed on his back. My skin tingles with the possibilities, my heart swells with a red-hot glow.

I shudder.

'It's the only way,' says Hugo. 'The only way to prevent Magali from using Philippe as her pawn. You would save him from it. Do you enjoy being a pawn, my dove? Is that what you want for him?'

I could almost laugh. I don't even know this man – but...

But.

'What is it that you want, my dove?'

'You,' I say.

Hugo burrows his head in my shoulder. 'And we will be together. Again. Soon.'

Because there is something else that Hugo has found. A way to release himself from the spell. All we have to do is go to Fort Cantor, and search for the binding object. But someone else will be there: Maël.

'Do you think we will succeed?' I say, when I mean to ask, *Is there any way that I can wrench back my own life from my father's hands?*

'We will, if we do this.' He looks at the parchments. 'I will be there,' he adds softly. 'At Fort Cantor. With Philippe.'

To make sure that, after we do this, Magali would hold no sway over him. To make sure that Philippe escapes her before she can hold him too tight in her grip.

And this is how I know.

What must be done, must be done.

It will be for Philippe's own good.

My hands tremble as I roll the other piece of parchment, the forged one. I drip red wax on it, the stain spreading like a pool of blood. But Hugo's presence steadies me, so close, after years when I thought I'd never see him again. My fingers are sure as I press my father's seal into the soft wax.

A mould. Something that can be whatever I want it to be.

Shaping my life, from this moment forward.

Hugo leaps down from my lap. 'You are so strong, my dove.' His voice is trembling with emotion. 'I knew that, if there was someone who loved me enough, who could forge our future anew … so it can be what it was always meant to be … that person is you.'

Not yet.

I'm not done yet.

I swallow my tears and toss the stolen document into the fire. It burns with a hiss, embers glowing. Only the one we forged together, in the gauzy light of this tepid afternoon, remains. And I still can't believe that the future I always dreamed of might still be within my reach.

'I will see you again at Fort Cantor, in a few days, my dove. And soon, everything we ever wanted … it will be ours.'

HEIR IN THE WATER

CELINE

*Y*ou would think that after nearly a week of revels at the tournament in Langville, my father, the King, would be pleased. Perhaps even happy, as we weave our way towards Fort Cantor, where the betrothed I don't want awaits.

You would think that he'd be lulled into half-sleep by the gentle rocking of the royal carriage.

He is not.

My father is prone to sighing today. 'Do you intend to be a bit more forthcoming towards Maël during this stay?'

My heart pounds in my chest. I'm not sure if what Hugo and I have done will be enough for me to escape my fate. And I cannot believe that, of all people, I have to rely on Magali to save me from a future I don't want.

'Celine?' says my father. 'Did you not hear me?'

'It depends what you mean by forthcoming,' I say tartly. 'It depends where you draw the line.'

I look to the white ground-stone road, snaking around the

mesmerising Mermaid's Lake, bordered on the side by slate-grey cliffs, like the rims of a polished bowl. There's a boulder at the end of the lake, and a sharp bend in the road. Weeping willows hunch above the boulder, patches of reeds rustle in the wind.

So much, hidden from sight.

And only a day's travel until we reach Fort Cantor. But, at least, Hugo should be there, waiting for me. Giving me strength.

'Are you all right, Celine?' says my father.

'What?'

'I beg your pardon,' he says. 'Not what.'

I look at him with the crazed expression of a deer being cornered by a pack of wolves. 'Your father should never suspect a thing,' Hugo told me. 'So much depends on him.'

'Isn't this lovely?' I say in a meagre attempt at conversation. 'I wonder why they call it the Mermaid's Lake. Did Mermaids ever live here?'

'Mermaids?' guffaws my father. 'I rather think not. Perhaps Shape-Shifters.' A frown creases his brow. My father hates all sorts of magic, but he despises Shape-Shifters the most. 'In any case, there is something I wish to discuss with you.'

I shrink on my padded bench. By Sabya's Morningstar, not this. I have feigned ignorance about my betrothal for so long, and I wish I could do so for a few more days.

It's as if *not* speaking about it makes it less real. As though my engagement is less of a given, where my opinion wasn't relevant.

Perhaps, perhaps something absurdly good will happen to me.

Perhaps, for once in my life.

'Maybe you remember how much trouble the inheritance matter in the Duchy of Langly has brought to our kingdom.'

Oh, no. Please, no.

Not this. The Siege of the Twins and all that.

'I am aware of the historical details,' I say.

Air. I need air. The carriage engages in the hairpin curve just as I try to stick my head out the window, and I'm tossed back into my seat. Not before I spy a silhouette ahead, on the boulder.

A cat with a red pouch on its back.

Hugo? I wonder. He shouldn't be here.

He should have reached Langly, ahead of us.

The cat brings a paw to its heart and bows. My heart pounds so loudly in my own ears that I can barely hear what he says. 'Oh, merciful and great king of our lands! Please, could you come to our aid?'

Hugo gives me a sideways look, and I don't know what to read in it. Has something happened? Are things amiss?

Expressions swim on my father's face, from surprise mixed with a sort of delight, to concern.

It's a fraction of what is happening in my soul.

My father says, 'My, my. A magical cat. I thought your sort had vanished from our lands.' He taps with his cane on the roof of the carriage and everything comes to a sudden halt, even the knights who accompany us.

Enchanted animals scattered to all corners of the Red Kingdom after the last beast whisperer in the Arnauld counties died – singing dogs and talking bears and all manner of creatures of this sort.

I think, *My father must not suspect who is standing in front of him.*

Or else...

'Everything but, Your Majesty,' says Hugo. 'And woe to my master had I not been here. Brigands have stolen his mount and his clothes, and I managed to chase them by calling out from the rushes. But now he has nothing to put on, not even a single piece of cloth.'

Brigands? His 'master'?

I think, *Perhaps one thing has gone right, and Philippe is with him, and not at Castle Bencifert, where Magali would drip poison in his ears.*

The cat's moves are quick and lithe, a reminder of what they used to be when he inhabited a different form.

I stare into his eyes, gripped. Eyes that have haunted me in my dreams for five years, dreams that were, until today, at the tips of my fingers.

What happened?

My father stretches his head through the open windows of the carriage. The pressure in my ears increases. Then he laughs. 'They took all his clothes? How did they manage that?'

'They took them from the bank, Your Majesty, while my master was bathing.'

My father grows red in the face with the effort of holding back his laughter. He has no idea who he's talking to. 'Please. Show me to your master.'

I sneak out after them, trying to piece together what happened. With my father present, Hugo can hardly tell me.

Next to a group of tall reeds, I spot a young man. Wet, dark curls fall in disarray on his forehead. He hugs his broad chest with thick arms, the water reaching above the line of the muscled planes of his stomach. When he sees us, he bows in an odd curtsy, still shivering slightly.

My cheeks are ablaze – this borders on indecency in more ways than I can count. There's a tug in the depths of my belly. It's improper to stare, but I can't look away. I take in the angle of his jaw, every ripple in those arms. And just like that, his gaze snaps to me, brushing against me, from the top of my dark hair, pinned in a half-braid, to the red-and-gold velvet dress that I'm wearing today.

Assessing me, as if I were the naked one, and not he.

I turn my head away, blushing.

Hugo did mention the man is not so well-mannered as the sort of young men I usually rub shoulders with – or, better said, I'm trying to avoid.

My father inclines his head and asks the cat, 'And does your strapping, forlorn master have a name?'

'Of course, Your Majesty. This is Messere Philippe of the Benciferts.'

Messere. Yes. The appropriate title to address the son of a seigneur.

Good, I think. So this is, indeed, Philippe. And he is with Hugo.

'Your Majesty, if you don't mind,' calls the naked Messere Philippe from the water. His voice is deep and raspy, but I make myself *not* look. I think I've seen quite enough. 'Might I borrow an item or clothing or two? If you would be so kind.'

'Of course, of course, Messere Philippe.' My father makes to call for the pantler-botler, but he rode ahead of us, preparing our chambers at the inn where we'll spend the night.

'I'll do it,' I say, even though I'd much rather dally at the edge of the lake and listen.

But the man needs clothes.

And he's helping us.

And he's a distraction from whatever Hugo might have planned, standing naked in the water as he is.

I head for the cart with supplies, tossing at our head of guards a request to borrow a set of clothes from him. I find a shirt and a pair of breeches, but I need a nicer surcoat. After all, this man, Philippe, is the heir apparent to Maël, even if *this* hasn't been apparent until a few days ago.

I throw a quick look at my father, who is smiling at something that Hugo is telling him, and clutch a black velvet doublet from the King's own trunks. It might be a tight fit for Philippe, but we'll see.

Once I almost reach the edge of the lake, I see my conundrum – I can't get so close as to hand the clothes to Philippe himself.

I have seen more than enough as it is, so I shove them in the arms of one of the guards. 'Give these to him.'

'*Merçi*, Princess,' says Philippe in that raspy voice of his, and I have no choice but to look.

He seems amused.

I am not.

I stalk back to where my father is conferring with Hugo, eager to find out more about why they are here, and not already at Fort Cantor.

'What leads you here? You are quite far away from home,' asks my father.

'My master lost his father recently,' the cat says, dropping his voice.

This clangs through me. So Seigneur Julien Bencifert has expired. And Hugo is still a cat. We need that binding object from Fort Cantor, we need it so badly.

'My condolences,' says my father. 'We all regret Seigneur Julien Bencifert.' He scrunches his brows. 'I take it that Messere Philippe's eldest brother is now the new Seigneur Bencifert, then?'

The cat leans in conspiratorially. 'Yes, that would be Seigneur Louis, Your Majesty. Messere Philippe's half-brother.'

My father's face lights up as he turns to watch the young man in the water. He is catching up to who he is.

My father says, 'This means that Messere Philippe is—'

'Isabella of Langly's only child, yes,' says Hugo.

I look behind, just to check if I can recognise any of the Lion's stark features on his face. Philippe is just pulling on a shirt, his powerful arms snaking through the sleeves. The hem is already soaked. But he meets my gaze with raised eyebrows and I glance away instantly.

He must be a knight, with those arms. In our kingdom, the firstborn sons inherit, and the younger brothers have to make their way in life with a sword and whatever small income that is bestowed on them. A farm, in Philippe's case.

'We were, in fact, on our way to Fort Cantor,' says the cat airily. A-ha. There it is. 'Messere Philippe wished to visit his cousin, Duke Maël.'

My secret betrothed. On the inside, I gag.

'Is that right,' says my father, flatly.

Philippe stands bare-footed on the shore now, struggling with the laces on his breeches.

I plaster a smile on my face and turn to the cat. 'What a coincidence. So are we.' I tilt my head, hoping that Hugo understands the silent question. *What do you want me to say?*

'I'm sure Maël would be pleased to see his cousin,' says my father.

The cat chimes in. 'The cousins used to be very close indeed, as children.'

My father scratches his beard. 'I'm sure they were.'

I look to Philippe and notice that he's struggling to get into the surcoat, his back turned to us, his elbows at an odd angle.

Too tight, indeed.

My father turns to say something to the head of his guards, and Hugo hisses. 'Get him here. Quick. We need to come with you, to Fort Cantor.'

I set myself in motion even before I realise what I'm doing,

21

pulling the surcoat from Philippe, tilting the right sleeve towards his hand. 'Easy,' I say. 'One hand after the other.'

He slips his right arm, and I arrange the other sleeve, so that it would be within his grip. 'I always struggle with coats,' he mumbles, his back still turned to me. 'My shoulders are too broad. My mother tells me they're the shoulders of a farmer.'

'Right,' I say, noticing the painful angle in his left elbow. I bunch the fabric, helping slip it up his arm, then stretch the surcoat. He's so tall – I need to rise on my toes to drape it over his shoulders, patting the velvet straight.

The coat strains on his arms.

'Did I upset you?' he says. 'I'm sure my mother does mean it as an insult, but I don't see why the seigneurs should look down at the farmers.'

His shoulders *are* broad.

And hard.

He says, 'Is your father a farmer or a farmhand? I didn't mean it as an insult, really. I always see it as a compliment.'

Sabya's Morningstar. He has no idea who I am, who is helping him. He must think I'm a chambermaid. My cheeks are ablaze, but I manage to mumble, 'There you go.'

'Thank you,' Philippe says, and turns his head towards me.

His eyes, a warm green-brown, I notice from so close up, widen and he stumbles forward. 'Mothers of the Forest.' He twists towards me. 'Princess, what are you doing here?'

I open and close my mouth, but can only come up with the obvious answer. *Helping you.*

Philippe goes on, 'You shouldn't sneak up like that on people.'

Lucius' Flaming Finger. 'Maybe you should learn to get dressed by yourself.'

He opens his mouth, then frowns. 'Of us two, I'm not the one who has an army of servants to help them get dressed. I manage just fine by myself. When the clothes fit.'

'Do you often wear clothes that don't fit, then?'

'Let's say I don't make a habit of bathing naked in lakes, and then having my clothes stolen.'

He has breached so many rules of etiquette within just a few moments, but I don't even know where to begin. 'You should greet the King,' I say. I remember Philippe needs to impress my father. So that they can come with us. As Hugo said. 'Properly. By taking a bow.'

Philippe brushes his damp locks away from his forehead and follows me. 'Thank you, by the way. I'm sorry about what I said. It might have all come out backwards, but you gave me a fright.'

'*Is your father a farmer?*' I mimic him. Then snort.

He blushes to the tip of his ears and is still a bit discomposed as he bows, indeed, to my father. 'Your Majesty, thank you for the clothes.'

'You are most welcome,' my father says magnanimously, looking from me to him. Perhaps seeing us blush, but not for the reason that he thinks.

Any lingering look, and my father is always inclined to ask if I could be tempted into marriage.

'I heard that brigands stole your horse,' says my father.

'Indeed, Your Majesty,' says Philippe. 'We'll probably have to walk to the next inn, so we can secure another mount.'

By the way Hugo frowns, I can tell that's *not* what Philippe was meant to say.

But my father chuckles. 'There will be no need. We have enough room in the carriage. For Maël's cousin.'

I should be pleased when Philippe climbs into the carriage and takes a seat on the bench across from me, next to my father.

But there's something unsettling in the way my father invited him to join us.

I pick up Hugo, lay him across my lap. Like a shield.

I suppose we turned this around, but there's no way I can know what happened, what has changed.

All I have for now is the mild inconvenience of Philippe's knees knocking against mine, when the carriage jolts.

BLOOD LINES

MAGALI

THAT SAME MORNING

*a*t the end, when it is all said and done, only the two of us are left on the cliff, just as planned. The stableboy and the lioness. Two unlikely allies, two old enemies, for now united by the same goal. I lick the blood around my snout, nothing more than a feint to show him my sharp teeth and repeat my request.

The stableboy protests, a growl about what we did and did not agree upon. 'Will there always be such a lack of trust between us, Magali?'

I stretch out one of my bloody claws to point him to the lonely tree, behind which the chambermaid's clothes are hidden. On the plateau below us, the horse caught in the hedges finally falls quiet. A red sunrise cracks from behind the clouds. On the opposite cliff, the white stone of Fort Cantor begins to glow in the sunlight.

In the centre of it, the tower rises like a challenge.

Distant guards who look like toy soldiers patrol the battlements. In the inner yard, the kitchen maids must already be fetching water for the master's breakfast.

What would they say if they knew where their master is now?

At the top of the cliff, we strike a new agreement. 'Hurry,' I say, 'or they will soon be upon us.'

Reluctantly, the stableboy steps behind the tree and places what I told him to in my pocket. I glance towards the lower plateau where the battered body of the destrier lies, deep gashes in his belly where I struck him. The boy murmurs something about having been lucky that the horse didn't fall all the way down the cliff and alert the guards before we made our escape.

We dance as within a dream, the stableboy and I tiptoeing around each other, as he weaves his way towards the path that leads downwards. There are no goodbyes, no professions of goodwill as I make my way towards the tree to slip into the form – and the clothes – of the chambermaid. Gone is the lioness. Only a few traces of the horse's blood remain on the tips of my fingers.

I wipe it off on a few rotten leaves. This will have to do for a few more days. No one is suspicious of an ageing chambermaid – this skin has served me well for weeks, helping me hide in plain sight. I pull on the drab clothes, so different from my usual fare of silks and satins, garb fit for the dowager duchess.

But soon I will return to my rightful place.

I pull on my surcoat, guilt weighing heavily in my pocket, where the stableboy had placed it.

In the valley, the stableboy crosses the bridge and breaks into a run towards the gates of the castle. I survey the surroundings one last time before I make my way towards the farm at the foot of the cliff. The ridge looks precisely as it should: as if a terrible battle has taken place.

As I descend, I touch the ring hanging about my neck, the ring that made all this possible. I tuck it underneath the chambermaid's tunic, hidden. Like I have been in the past few weeks at the castle, while my son, Maël, has been looking everywhere else for me.

When I reach the bottom of the meandering path, I save a few thoughts for Philippe. I wonder where he is now. What he is doing. If he'll rise to the challenge. If he'll know better than to place his trust in Hugo.

I stop, watching. The stableboy is pounding at the gates of Fort Cantor. Probably screaming something about a lion and how his master, Duke Maël, has been killed.

I duck out of sight and make for the farm behind the cliff.

Guilt weighs heavy in my pocket.

INNS AND CROSSROADS

CELINE

*W*e stop for the night at a crossroads, at the Griffin Inn. As soon as we step down from the carriage, my father confers with Gaston, our botler-pantler, while Hugo leans in towards Philippe and tells him he must slip out.

I'm sure the comment is meant for my own ears, as much as for his, but I don't miss the slight panicked grimace that Philippe makes. He was rather quiet on our way here, leaving most of the conversation to Hugo, who regaled my father with tales of magical beasts.

He told us a story about a young lady who charged on a bear's back in a battle long ago, during the Year of the Red Maiden. I'm sure the tale was meant less to entertain and more to dull my father's suspicions that he could be a Shape-Shifter.

Though that isn't completely accurate, either. If Hugo could change his form at will, we wouldn't be here today, would we? And because he is trapped in this cat skin, we are all trapped.

Philippe looks caged, too, as we enter the dining hall, his steps stiff, and he throws me a few furtive glances. There have been some of those in the carriage, too, full of curiosity and awe.

Maybe he's embarrassed about our previous exchange.

Rough manners, indeed.

The owner of the inn has cleared the dining hall of its usual customers, strewn fresh rushes on the floor – though that still cannot cover the miserable smells. He has even arranged a sort of dais, three seats around this not-quite-so-royal, weather-beaten table.

Philippe and I sit on either side of my father, and the men-at-arms and the rest of our suite take their places on low benches.

What must be the inn's best fare is placed in front of us: hare stew, freshly baked bread, hot meat pies and what looks like a sort of tough venison in a red sauce. Philippe starts scooping helpings on his plate, ignoring my warning glances.

This is not how it is done at the Royal Table—everyone who has dined at least once at the Red Court knows so. My father, however, ignores this trespass completely, and breaks a piece of bread, finally signalling the beginning of the meal.

But a sliver of the same thought seems to pass through my father's mind, because he says, 'I do not remember seeing you at the Royal Palace.'

Philippe lays his large, callused hands on both sides of his plate. So much strength seems to be coiled within them. These are certainly not hands meant just to hold a quill, or twist a fork. 'No, my father usually sent my elder brother if our presence at Court was necessary.'

'My condolences,' says my father. 'We all regret Seigneur Julien's passing.'

'No one more than me,' says Philippe.

I can imagine he has more than one reason to do so, and I must be so callous for not being able to feel the same regret.

It's because of the man's death that we even sit at this table.

And after what he and Magali have done to Hugo... It would be impossible for me to feel any compassion for them.

My father toys with his wine goblet. 'I don't remember seeing much of your mother, either, in the past few years.'

Me neither. This seems at least strange, come to think of it. 'I heard she was often unwell,' I say.

'Unwell? No,' says Philippe. 'But she liked to travel often.'

My father knits his eyebrows in that way that tells me that he finds it quite hard to believe what he has just said. 'Are you well acquainted with Fort Cantor, then?'

'I used to visit there as a child.'

'But not at first, of course,' says my father.

I'm not sure if this is a question or a statement. He must refer to the turmoil in Langly. During the first ten years since Isabella first bestowed the inheritance upon Frederic, the duchy passed from one twin to the other, and then back again to Frederic, in a chain of events that's too complicated for me to begin to untangle now.

'How old are you?' I ask. I can't quite tell. Isabella must have had him after the duchy passed back to Kylian, Hugo's father.

'Twenty-two,' says Philippe.

Ah. Just one year younger than me, then.

'You grew up at Castle Bencifert, then?' asks my father.

Castle Bencifert. I shiver to hear the name. I could see it from the Golden Pavilion—the magic school perched on top of the Opal Mountain. Built in white marble with golden threads, which glowed in the purest light at sunrise. The place where I met Hugo, and where I spent the best four years of my life.

And across the valley, Castle Bencifert. Brown edges of stone on top of a hill. The place where Hugo had been kept as a prisoner, in his form as a cat, for the last five years.

I throw Philippe a sideways glance as I realise something.

Isabella was a mage, like her mother. But Philippe was never a student with us, at the Golden Pavilion.

I wouldn't be amazed if he didn't have a Gift. After all, his grandfather wasn't magical, and perhaps he does take after him.

Philippe toys with his spoon, still considering how to answer my father's question. 'Not quite. You see, my mother didn't... She was at the castle a lot, of course, but she insisted that I should be taught responsibility at a young age. And my place. It isn't common that a second son should inherit a castle. Even less likely for a third son, like me.'

'No, it is not. This is most unfortunate for the parents,' says my father.

He means that if a second son inherits a castle, the first one has expired.

But it's almost ironic that this younger brother of the current Seigneur Bencifert is the heir apparent to the greater fief, the Duchy of Langly. I suppose this is the thing with genealogy: it is full of ironies, if you look close enough. One might even call it blunt sarcasm, at times.

And I suppose it's not unusual for men to have children by different women. In the end, my father had Anne-Mihielle by a woman who wasn't my mother.

I can never bring myself to think about Mihi without a pang. What she might be doing now, the kind of person she might be. It's not as if she's replying to any of my letters. Even if Mihi was a child born out of wedlock, it doesn't excuse my father hiding her in another kingdom.

Thoughts of my half-sister make me miss the rest of Philippe's reply.

'A farm?' says my father.

'My mother always thought that I should live according to the place I'd have later in life,' replies Philippe. 'Nothing to do with the Red Court. So as soon I was seven, she gave a farm into my care. And that's where I grew up.'

'On a farm,' I say.

The farm.

I'm painfully reminded of what Hugo and I have had to do.

It was for Philippe's best, I tell myself. So that he wouldn't become Magali's pawn.

'Yes,' he says. 'I learned all about sowing and reaping and manning a plough from a tender age.'

Ah.

This explains the off-hand comments about farmers, today.

So Philippe is not a knight, but rather closer to a farmer. Quite peculiar, for someone who is Maël's heir apparent, as long as Maël remains unwed, and without children of his own.

And I want nothing more than for Maël to remain unwed.

Or perhaps for him to marry someone else.

I'm sure my father is preparing to comment on what Philippe has just said, when a messenger barges into the room. I recognise him by the tight-fitting livery, the crumpled white cape with a red lioness embroidered on it.

A messenger from Langly, then. He's a thin boy with dishevelled hair, and coated in dust. By his short, quick breaths, he must have hurried here.

'Your Majesty, if I may,' he says panting. 'Fort Cantor sends word urgently.'

'Of course,' says my father, extending his hand.

But the message the boy has … well, it's not in writing, that's for sure. 'Your Majesty, Duke Maël is gone. We have reason to believe he has perished.'

The tips of my fingers grow numb.

No, this can't be.

It's too soon, too unexpected. We haven't found the binding object, we haven't released Hugo from his form.

This means that—

My father's head snaps to Philippe at the same time as mine does.

The—presumptively—new Duke of Langly is utterly frozen, his eyes widened in blinding surprise.

MAGALI

The word of the day is 'disquiet.' The castle staff is like a writhing hydra, in that moment suspended in time when a head has been severed, and the replacement hasn't quite grown out.

The steward of Fort Cantor steps in. Organises search parties, of two or three. In the skin of the chambermaid, I take part in one of them, calling Maël's name, pretending to search for him.

CELINE

I lie on the bed, putting the finishing touches to my little drawing. Alone, in my chamber, while my father is conferring with Philippe.

Another essential conversation I have been shunned from.

My fingers are still trembling.

I trail them across the sketch, detailing the ancestry of all the lion cubs, the three cousins. I cross out Maël's name from the family tree.

It seems that I won't marry him after all, but this is the only sure thing in a sea of uncertainties. What Hugo predicted is coming to pass, but too fast, much faster than it should, and I'm frightened that the hopes I'm hanging onto so hard will disappear in a puff of mist.

I draw a circle around Hugo's name, sighing.

With Maël gone, it's Hugo who should be the new duke.

If Hugo were more than a cat.

If Hugo wasn't presumed dead, as he has been for more than five years now.

It should have been Hugo. It has always been Hugo for me. Hugo and me, me and Hugo, since our days at the Golden Pavilion.

When we were students, the buildings were still splendid, a symphony of towers, turrets and hanging balconies, all sculpted in the most beautiful white-and-gold marble. A place held together by magic, of course—the oldest magic school in the only kingdom in the world that could still wield that power, though not as much as it did before the Year of the Red Maiden.

I remember one of the early days, when Madame Hirondelle, the doyenne, made me practise in the central piazza of the Golden Pavilion, by the fountain. It was never hard to conjure my Gift—I used anger and tears to prod my powers. I only had to think of the day they took Mihi away from me, to send her to the Green Kingdom.

The waters in the fountain swelled in a pointed dome, as high as the highest tower of the Pavilion.

'That will be enough, Celine,' Madame Hirondelle, the doyenne, said.

I thought of nine-year-old Mihi, with her scraggy dark hair, and her dresses always ripped at the hem. Restless, cheeky Mihi.

I thought of Mihi in tears, while one of our nursemaids dragged her away.

I thought of my mother, standing with her arms crossed, telling me to get a grip on myself.

The water dome exploded in a splash, soaking Madame Hirondelle and all the students around us.

'I said stop, Celine. When will you learn how to stop?' She wrung out her drenched cloak and asked for a bucket and a set of rags.

So that I could clean up my own mess.

After she left, a group of students approached, Hugo at their core. Even at fourteen, every girl wanted to have Hugo's attention, and every boy in the school wanted to be him. But he said nothing, just looked at me from the depth of his mesmerising eyes.

Princess Delphine of the Blue Kingdom snorted. 'What an embarrassment you are,' she said. 'You don't have a grip on your Gift.'

'At least I have a Gift, and I'm not here just because my mother is queen, like you,' I said, scrubbing.

Delphine flinched. 'If your mother hadn't been the doyenne before, you would be shipped back home instantly,' she spat.

That was when Hugo stepped forward and I cringed. I'd been sweet on him since I started studying at the Pavilion, but never dared say a single word to him. 'Oh, I'd pay a lot of coin to see that again,' he drawled. 'Madame Hirondelle, drenched. That look on her face.' The group around him started to chuckle and my heart raced.

Hugo was taking *my* side.

My side, and not Delphine's. He gestured towards one of his friends. 'Can't you fix this? It's getting dull, and we have to get to the Refectory.'

The older boy nodded. 'Can you move aside?'

I took a few steps towards them, and that's when the boy threw a whoosh of fire all around the fountain, the puddles hissing as the water evaporated.

A Fire-Blazer. 'Oh. Thank you,' I said, dumping the rags in the now incandescent bucket.

Hugo started marching toward the central building of the Pavilion. 'The Refectory, then.'

Everyone else followed.

And then, the most impossible happened, conjured, in a way, by my Gift. Hugo turned towards me. 'Aren't you coming? Your chore is done, you can join us, you know.'

That was the beginning of me and Hugo.

And the end...

I don't care to remember.

Not when so much hinges on what would happen tomorrow.

I pace the narrow length of the room, a knot in my belly. I say a silent prayer.

Mothers of the Forest, if you are listening to me, please, please, don't allow Hugo to fail again. Please, please, help us make our dreams come true.

The floorboards creak under my steps. I wonder what my father is discussing with Philippe. What a farce. Maël is gone, and Philippe and Hugo aren't at Fort Cantor, like they were meant to be.

I rest my forehead on the shuttered window, and I hear voices carrying from the inner courtyard.

I could never mistake Hugo's lilting tones. His words, spoken too low for me to make them out, are a call, pulling me to wherever he is.

I toss a thick cape on my shoulders and nod at the two guards in the corridor. 'I'm going down for a bit of fresh air.'

They make to follow me. 'I'm just going into the inner courtyard of the inn,' I protest.

'King's orders,' says the captain, closing the distance between us.

I sigh.

I need to speak to Hugo, to find out what's truly happening, but the chances that I could have done so were always slim, in any case, in Philippe's presence.

'If you must,' I tell the captain, already sulking.

This day, this blasted day.

The courtyard is like a box, surrounded by the inn's stone-and-wood walls. It's a clean but old building, the beams already sinking here and there, especially on top of the dining quarters.

Plenty of windows around us. Plenty of ears that might be perked.

I must tread carefully with what I say.

Philippe and Hugo are conferring on a log, set underneath the only tree in the courtyard, a young linden.

It's Philippe who notices me first, falling quiet, tilting his head towards me. The moon slices through the rich foliage of the tree, revealing his eyes, red-rimmed, burning. He shifts in the surcoat I gave him, as if he isn't yet comfortable wearing it, even after almost a full day.

Hugo turns to see what has silenced Philippe.

I say nothing, taking them both in, waiting for a cue from Hugo.

What does Philippe know about me? I didn't think we'd be so soon in such close quarters.

Such a debacle, and I can't have Hugo a few moments to myself. Not when so much hangs in the balance.

Hugo rises on his hind paws and takes a deep bow. 'How wonderful of you to join us, Princess Celine.'

Formal then. Like strangers. I repeat the lie I told my guards. 'I wanted some fresh air.'

'Ah, but so did we, did we not, Messere Philippe?' Hugo's eyes slide to his companion.

Philippe digs his heel into the moist earth. My guards hover a few feet from us, probably having ascertained that we're the only ones in the courtyard.

I wonder how I could ask my burning questions. I can hardly say, *So what did my father tell you? Will he support you?*

We had taken into consideration that this might happen. That we wouldn't be able to find the binding object, until Magali moves.

Sabya's Morningstar and Lucius' Flaming Finger. The complications are endless.

What a fix.

So I settle on, 'I'm sorry to hear about your cousin. I wager you were eager to see him.'

Philippe shakes his head, still staring at his boots. 'I'm shocked. I can't believe it.'

I exchange a quick look with Hugo, unsure what to make of this statement, if it's genuine or not. Hugo's eyes widen, and I'm not certain what he is trying to convey.

'Will you still be … joining us on the way to Fort Cantor?' I ask, carefully.

'Your father said that I could hire a horse now from the inn,' says Philippe bluntly.

'Was my father so coarse, indeed?' I ask, unable to believe this. That he would not offer Philippe a place in our carriage, which is also headed to Fort Cantor.

That he would refuse to make our entrance together.

'He was not,' says Philippe. 'He wrapped it up nicely, of course. But what he said amounted to that.'

Mothers of the Forest, the manners of this man.

Or lack of them.

Hugo quips, 'The King has certain doubts when it comes to Messere Philippe's identity.'

If he spoke this way to my father, no wonder. 'Is that so?' I ask. 'But why?'

Philippe fixes me with a blazing stare. 'For the obvious reasons. Hardly anyone knows me, do they?'

By Sabya's Darkblades.

That my father should have told Philippe as much, so openly. But if I hadn't known the story from Hugo, wouldn't I have doubted, as well?

The heir apparent to Langly, who spent his life hidden on a farm.

If my father rejects Philippe's claim, if he favours other suitors, all will be lost before we have even started taking the first steps.

All will have been for nothing.

My palms are covered in a moist sheen.

This can't be, this can't be. What a nightmare.

'Aren't there ways to ascertain this?' I direct my question more towards Hugo, hoping he will understand.

He does. 'We showed the King the minor seal of the Duchy of Langly. Isabella's seal. But not even that seemed to have swayed him completely.'

'How?' I ask. 'I thought Messere Philippe's clothes were stolen.'

'We had taken precautions,' says Hugo. 'It was stored in the red pouch on my back.'

Ah. The pouch, then. I'd been wondering.

'Of course, your honoured father thinks it rather suspicious that an heir should be found in a lake, with no horse, no clothing, no other servants to accompany him,' says Philippe in a low grumble.

'You are always this straightforward?' I say, before being able to stifle the impulse.

That Philippe should say such a thing is astounding.

'Don't misunderstand me, Princess. I would do the same.' I can't quite read the expression of Philippe's face. Sadness? Disappointment? Crushed hopes? 'I can't blame the King.'

Hugo says, 'It is still most unfortunate that he does not believe us.'

Unfortunate. I read enough in Hugo's words.

He did not count on this.

As I feared, nothing is as it was meant to be.

I take a few steps towards Philippe. 'And are you who you claim to be, Your Grace?'

He meets my gaze, unflinching. 'What do *you* think, Your Highness?'

MAGALI

A messenger boy from the Griffin Inn cleaves through Fort Cantor, through the hush of whispers, the raised voices in the Great Hall.

The King is coming.

Tomorrow.

The steward sags with relief, and the voices rise higher.

The King, the King is coming.

Poor fools, they don't even know there is still a question to be answered.

Will he come alone, or will he be accompanied by a certain heir?

LORD OF THE CASTLE

CELINE

I am up before dawn, unable to sleep.

My future is, yet again, slipping away from me.

The air inside my chambers is stifling, so I throw open the shutters. Not the window towards the courtyard—I can't bear to look at it—but the window carved in the outer wall.

I'm met by the misty silhouette of Fort Cantor, in the distance.

So close, and yet farther than it seemed yesterday.

Oh, Hugo. If only we could speak, in private.

He and I, he and I.

And then, I remember.

While the world was still full of magic, we had dreams.

Five years ago, on our last evening together, we spun them. Frederic, his uncle, had expired a few days before, and Hugo was getting ready to claim what was his from Maël: Fort Cantor. From the Night-Walker's Tower, we could see that imposing silhouette, though from a different angle than the one I have now at the inn.

In the times of my grandfather, Langly had been called the Light of the West, rivalling in splendour the Royal Court in

Lafala. While the first duke had employed the finest soldiers, the first duchess had used her wealth to support history writers, scholars specialising in all forms of magic, poets and the finest travelling singers.

And those that had come after them, in the grapples for power that had plagued Langly in the past twenty years, carefully demolished, step by step, what its first legendary leaders had built.

We wanted to be the Lion and his princess. A beacon of light, a beacon of learning. I wanted people to see me for who I was, just like Hugo did, and not like some prized cattle on the marriage market.

'Believe me, Celine,' said Hugo. 'I want nothing more than to be like the Lion. Except the part where he kills his wife.'

I punched him in the shoulder.

I took him in, from the button nose, his dark blue eyes with their golden edge, the well-shaped lips. He read my thoughts, my feelings—he was the whole of my feelings—and he leaned into me and we melted into a kiss that was the beginning and the end and a road and a fluttering in my heart, and heat darting through my chest, pooling in my belly.

How different things have turned out, for all of us, from what we had expected them to be.

This time, I will not stand aside, motionless.

Hugo is here, so close, though not himself at all. And there's nothing I wouldn't do to have him back.

I quickly put on a travelling dress and go to see my father.

* * *

WHEN I'M ADMITTED into his chambers, my father has just awoken. He sits in an old chair, while Gaston is arranging the clothes he will wear for the day.

'What brings you here, Celine, at this hour?' he asks in the solemn voice of His Majesty.

There's no point in tiptoeing around it, and I have no idea where I find the courage to say, 'The travelling arrangements.'

'How so?'

'I spoke to Duke Philippe last night, in the courtyard.'

'I know,' says my father, interest sparking in his eyes. He waves off the servants and they understand the message. They leave us, alone, without another word. 'I saw you.'

'You did?' I say, my cheeks blazing.

I shouldn't be surprised. Every single person who slept at the inn last night could have seen us. 'I needed to stretch my legs.'

I don't quite know what to say from here, but fortunately, for once, my father is helpful. 'He complained?'

I frown. 'No, I asked. He does not strike me as the sort of man to complain.'

'You would know so much after exchanging a few words? You seem to show a certain ... interest in him.'

There's a knot in my throat. I can see what he's implying. It's his most ardent wish, after all.

'He suggested that you do not believe he is who he claims.'

'Did he, now? And you believe him?'

I wring my hands. I will not lower myself to pretend that I am interested in him in ... other ways. My father's mind must be whirring with the possibilities. If the Duke of Langly I was betrothed to—in secret—has expired, perhaps there is a way I could be given in marriage to the next duke.

But I have my integrity. I will not let myself be pulled into this. 'Does it matter what I believe or not? What if you reject his claim, and he is, indeed, the heir presumptive? Can you imagine in what a fix we would be then? Can you imagine all the distant relatives who would stake a claim, if you do not act quickly?'

My father seems to hesitate at this. 'His identity will need to be confirmed.'

'Then do so,' I say. 'Magali will perhaps be at Fort Cantor.' This mere thought makes my stomach tighten painfully. Hugo will need to hide, before we arrive. He won't be safe within her presence.

'Why should she?' says my father. 'She and Maël have quarrelled.'

I can hardly tell my father that, if something happened to Maël, Magali is probably the one behind it. So I say, 'Then one of the seigneurs is bound to know his face. But the longer you hesitate, Father, the more people will think that something is amiss. The more people will see it as an opportunity. Hesitate, and they will think there's something off about him even before you've had time to ascertain the truth. You said to me yesterday that you wanted to avoid unrest in Langly. Why would you lay the foundations of that unrest?'

I may have said too much because my father's eyebrows knit. I'm so used to saying nothing that when I do speak my mind, I tend to get carried away.

And I'm not even finished.

My father says, 'I hope you do not presume to teach me how to rule, Celine.'

'I do not. I was simply trying to advise.'

I expect him to tell me that it's presumptuous to even give advice to him. Instead, he says, 'We don't even know if Maël has truly perished.' My father's fingers skim his beard.

Ah, that. So he hopes that it might not be true. That my betrothal still stands.

I blurt, 'Then what would he think if we were not hospitable to his cousin?'

My father's eyes flash and I may have hit the mark. 'I shall have to think on it.'

I understand the quiet dismissal and take my leave. When I've reached the door, he says, 'It is not good for you to forever hide in my shadow, Celine. You know your mind. The time is ripe; it has been so for a long while. You're meant to have a household of your own.'

I take his words as a warning. As an order. I have thoughts on that, as well, but I shove them back down in a corner of the mind I'm supposed to know so well.

What good would they do to anyone, anyway?

MAGALI

I lose myself in the crowd of bailiffs, servants, scullery maids, fruiters, candle makers, laundresses and bakers gathered in the Great Hall of Fort Cantor, come to greet the king and the heir apparent. In my form as a chambermaid I don't draw attention—they think they know who I am, even though they don't.

Shock ripples through the castle staff. It's scarcely been more than a day since the stableboy returned from the cliff with the news of Maël's demise.

Guilt weighs heavier and heavier in my pocket, grows stronger. The binding spell is waning, and it needs to be bound to the object that has been prepared in advance. I scan the crowd for the cat, but there is no trace of it.

The King and his retinue enter the Great Hall by the side entrance, and the murmurs quieten. Earlier today, there were voices that said they would chase away the new duke if he dared enter through the gates of the castle. Saying that there was no need for a new duke, since Maël's body had not yet been found.

But even those voices are silenced in the presence of the King himself and his retinue of knights in full armour, ornate swords glinting in their scabbards, chainmail clinking as they arrange themselves at the foot of the ducal table. The knights build a wall between them and us. They hold their lances like so many threats.

The King does not take his seat on the dais—he stands and so do we. Not even after all these years can I look upon him without the old anger flaring in my belly.

I look at the princess, her eyes shifting about the room, taking it all in. Undoubted interest is written on her face. She is quiet and observant, as always. Much cleverer than everyone else has ever given her credit for, but not all have known her since she was a child, like I have. As slippery as water, when you try to grab it with your fingers.

For how long has my son Maël tried to bring her within these walls, make a duchess out of her?

But where Maël has failed, perhaps Philippe might yet succeed. He watches the faces of the staff gathered here, the peeling walls of the hall. He sweeps his gaze over me, no trace of recognition in it.

A pang of fury stabs me. This hall deserves to be returned to its former splendour, and how long have I insisted that it should be so? But Maël saw fit to spend the duchy's riches elsewhere. What a long way he has come from the boy who helped me hold fast my grip on Langly such a long time ago.

Look where that has got him.

In my pocket, guilt thrashes and pounces.

For too long have I allowed Maël to keep Philippe away from Langly. There had been a bond of affection between the two, forged during their time at the Castle Bencifert, while they were children. But of late, perhaps Maël feared that the seigneurs might see the kind of character that Philippe possesses. Perhaps that might have given them ideas—the same idea I have had.

The King clears his voice. 'Inhabitants of Fort Cantor, I greet you. The gravest and most upsetting of rumours has reached us. Even while we seek to ascertain the course that events have taken, I bid you to welcome Maël's heir, Messere Philippe of Castle Bencifert. And please assist him through these difficult times.'

Murmurs fly around in ripples.

An heir, then. The King does not introduce him as the new duke.

So, so.

People call, turn to one another. They do not know the heir, a man they've barely heard of. In my pocket, guilt scratches at the seams, trying to find its way out.

Had I been firmer with Maël when it came to inviting Philippe to Fort Cantor, had I been firmer when it came to everything else... Phillippe's face twists in a disappointed grimace. The people reject him.

With my gaze, which he doesn't catch, I beseech him not to give up.

It is the princess who leans forward, across the table, and pats the shoulder of one of the knights, making a sign. The men then proceed to tap the butts of their lances on the floor, loudly. Again and again and again until the crowd quietens. 'You will allow your king to speak,' calls the head of the guards. 'Ten lashes for any man who interrupts the king.'

This is enough to bring even the loudest of the men and women to silence.

'I should like to ascertain the efforts that have been made to find Duke Maël.' The King lifts the goblet in front of him. 'But before that, I decree we should all feast.'

The crowd meets him with a feeble assent. And yet, the King, he is no fool. He knows that the best way to stop rumours and gossip is to fill the clamouring mouths with food, so they will have little room for stray words.

I tiptoe out of the hall. Guilt weighs heavier and heavier. It will soon be too strong for the confines of my pocket.

CELINE

If there is some comfort in this awful day, it is that at least Magali isn't here. But there was no time for me to seek anything—the ripples of disquiet have been too strong.

There are few here who know Philippe. Fortunately, Magali's chambermaid has stepped forward and greeted him underneath my father's watchful eyes.

Of course the chambermaid would know him, close as she was to her mistress. I must do my best to steer clear of her.

And yet, another small favour done to me unwittingly by Magali.

But Philippe is fumbling—he can't even find his way around the castle.

This would have been so different if Hugo had been in Philippe's shoes.

There's a pad of soft steps through the creaked door, and Hugo drifts in, hops on my bed. The pouch on his back hangs to one side, and I straighten it.

Hugo brushes his head against my cheek. 'My dove?'

I wanted to scold him. Where has he been? What was he thinking, to drag Philippe into this, with his complete lack of manners?

I wanted to tell Hugo how, had my father not been here today, Fort Cantor would have swallowed Philippe whole, ground him between its stones and spat him out in tatters.

But none of that comes to mind. Instead, I say, 'What do you make of it?'

'For one, I never expected Magali to make good on what she told Julien Bencifert. To go against her own son. Thank the Mothers of the Forest that Philippe is with us now, and not with her.'

Ah. Philippe. 'This wasn't how it was meant to happen. What do we do now?'

'We make the best of it. The first step would be to have Philippe declared the new duke.'

A cold arrow darts through my chest. 'It's just not right.'

Hugo slides under my palm, and the wrongness of this strikes me again. We have been too slow. We should have reached Fort Cantor, and found the object that keeps him tied to his shape as a cat, before something happened to Maël. Hugo could have then made his claim on the duchy, which is rightfully his.

'It's fine, my dove,' he says. 'We assumed things might happen this way, or else Philippe wouldn't have been with us, would he?'

There's a difference between taking something into account, and hoping that it will happen otherwise. 'How do you know that once he sees himself as the duke, he won't do everything in his power to cling to that?'

Hugo sighs. 'Believe me, being the duke is the last thing Philippe wants.'

'What does he want, Hugo? Why would he do such a thing for us?'

'He has nothing left.'

Uneasiness clenches like a fist in my stomach. We have done this to him.

49

Philippe had grown up on a farm, which was his.

Until it was his no more.

Hugo says, 'I have promised to make him steward once all is said and done. Once we step up and claim our rightful places.'

'As the Duke and Duchess of Langly' is what he doesn't say.

'A steward,' I repeat. I do hope he isn't wrong about Philippe. I will have to see for myself what kind of a man he is. 'Do you trust him, then?'

Hugo says, 'To a point. I … I don't want him to know we're looking for the object. I would trust no one with that task but you. Only you, Celine.'

Hugo leans into my touch, and I pull my hand away.

'Also, I'd refrain from suggesting to him that you and I are in cahoots,' he says, dropping his voice. 'So he doesn't suspect anything.'

Anything about a certain afternoon at the Royal Palace, a fire and a stolen seal.

This is why Hugo and I were forced to behave like strangers, yesterday, in the inner courtyard of the inn. Tears clog in my throat. Our dreams, which seemed so close to being within our reach, are now so far away again.

Hugo says, 'I gathered that your father is conducting an inquiry tomorrow. As to what happened. And he is summoning the seigneurs to witness his judgement.'

Another obstacle to overcome, another point where everything might go wrong. But at least Hugo is here. There is nothing that I dread more than being alone again.

This brings me to another thought. 'What do you think happened to Maël?' I ask.

'Who knows, my dove? Perhaps we will find out soon.'

The stories that are going round, about lions on the top of a cliff and great pools of blood, are too fantastical to be believed.

But I dread what my father might find out.

'We have time,' says Hugo. 'We have time to find the object.'

If Maël isn't found. If my father agrees to support Philippe.

'Keep your ears open tomorrow, when the stableboy gives his confession,' says Hugo.

'I will.'

Hugo rises from the bed and pads towards the door. He says, as an afterthought, 'Oh, and don't allow Magali's chambermaid anywhere near you.'

'I wasn't about to,' I say, even though my own chambermaid is still at the Royal Palace with a twisted ankle.

'Clever girl,' says Hugo. 'That woman is a terrible gossip. We must not forget Magali.'

I sigh. I have no idea how my own mother could have been such close friends with that woman. Magali is the sort of person who waits for the right time to pounce and strike.

Just last week, on the day we forged the document, Hugo told me that she had left Castle Bencifert for Port Lang or Langville. That this made it possible for him to sway Philippe, by telling the truth about what she'd done to him.

But where will Philippe's loyalty lie once she returns? And how could something have happened to Maël if she wasn't here?

Her shadow looms above Fort Cantor, threatening to consume anything Hugo and I might achieve.

There is no way in this world that we could forget about Magali.

QUESTIONS OF FEALTY

MAGALI

The word of the day is disquiet. Not that anyone dares say a single word to the King, even a whisper in his presence. They reserve the rustle for the servants' quarters. For the scullery, the stables, the stores and the pantry. The questions they have. The doubts at the speed with which everything is happening.

But in the solar where the King, Philippe and Celine are having their breakfast none of this is expressed. They are quiet as I serve them their dishes and withdraw into a corner of the room. I study the way the princess moves, how she glances covertly at me. She refused my help as a chambermaid last night, adding to the many small insults she has offered me throughout the years.

How far I have fallen, to skulk around in the shadows in my own castle. But not for long. I will have to find a way into the princess's quarters. I only have to speak to Philippe about it.

There's a knock on the door and the steward, Jacques, drags in the stableboy who was on the cliff with me. We exchange a quick look, and I wonder if he is who I think he is. Who he should be.

The steward asks for a private audience with the King.

Weariness plays on the king's face. The old codger should have his hands full. And yet he makes an inviting gesture with his hand.

Philippe pushes the cold mutton and eggs onto his plate and my heart aches for this quiet boy who was perfectly content with his farm. But sometimes, we can fly higher than we think. And Philippe had to be set a greater challenge.

The princess watches, as always. Her dark eyes move little, but I can still read the interest in them. She says nothing. But she is the definition of quiet waters that run deep. And treacherous. She takes in the stableboy for a beat too long, and I wonder if she, too, knows who he is.

The steward clears his throat. I remember. How I helped him rise from the position of a clerk to the High Steward of the duchy. How much he owes me. I also remember how he kept silent in the last few days that I spent here as Magali, when I quarrelled with my son.

How much less a woman's word matters, compared to a man's.

'Is this the boy, then?' says the King.

'The events he has to recount await your judgement, Your Majesty,' says the steward.

The judgement.

The King's judgement.

It might alter the entire course of events. If he decides to keep searching for Maël...

By Sabya's Morningstar, he must not. The stableboy must see to that. All our work cannot be ruined within a few moments. It cannot.

The King eyes the boy now, up and down. What has he heard? What does he believe? I squeeze my hands together to prevent myself from moving. So much depends on what is about to happen.

The steward starts speaking. 'We tried to send men to recover the body of the destrier. But we could not do so, Your Majesty. The lower plateau is sloped. It would have meant their deaths,' says Jacques, talking faster. 'We searched every corner, every nook, every cave for where the lion might have taken the duke—'

'The boy,' says the King, drumming his fingers on the table. 'Is he the one?'

Jacques nods.

And then the King does the most surprising thing. He turns to Philippe and asks him to show the castle to the princess. Annoyance plays on Celine's face, but they both make their exit in a clatter of chairs. Not a word passes between Jacques and the King until Philippe and Celine have left the chambers.

CELINE

I'm so irked that my father threw me out of the room, again, when things were beginning to become interesting, that I don't even notice that Philippe is leading me to the battlements, nor how close we are walking together, his strong arm pressed against mine.

A glance up and it strikes me how much he towers over me. I take in his smell, like something that has just broken out of the earth.

This is much too close for my comfort, and I take a step aside, pretending to admire the surroundings, while I mull over what that stableboy might be telling my father.

At least Philippe came here with us. This has been an endorsement in itself from the King. But the man at my side has no clue that he has anything to be thankful to me for. He takes in the battlements with a wary look.

There are too few men-at-arms—many of Maël's followers are still in Langville, after the fair, and not an insignificant portion fled when we arrived the day before.

'Isn't it beautiful?' says Phillipe.

Fort Cantor? With the cliff embracing it from behind and the western side, and two rows of fortifications, it is said that the Lion built his residence so that it could never be taken by storm.

But I wouldn't call it a thing of beauty.

'I'm not sure if it's beautiful.' I doubt he ever saw the architecture of the Golden Pavilion, or of the Royal Palace, all arches and laced marble, a dance of colours, woven with gold. Symphonies of blue and golden and red rooftops, of different heights. 'But it's supposed to be strong. Though it did fall once, during the Siege of the Twins, if my memory serves me.'

Philippe smiles. 'I didn't mean the castle.'

In the distance, a day's ride away, I can make out the walls surrounding Langville, the red rooftops, the tallest among them belonging to the Guild Houses. The town is the meeting place for traders from the west and the east, and where the largest fair takes place every year. There are yearly tournaments, and even knights from neighbouring kingdoms come to compete for the great purse of money. Maël has been winning consistently for the past few years.

Had been winning?

Philippe watches me, amusement crinkling the corner of his eyes.

I am clever and mannered and I have no idea what he finds so amusing. I'm under the impression he's half-mocking me.

And I certainly hope he wasn't calling me 'beautiful'. Though he doesn't know about me and Hugo, does he?

'I wouldn't call Langville beautiful, either, though the Guild Houses on the riverbank are interesting.' But the smells within Langville, especially in high summer...

Urgh.

Philippe is now smirking. 'Mothers of the Forest, we really aren't looking at the same thing, are we?'

'Explain,' I say, a bit morose.

'The valley,' he says. 'There's no more beautiful view from Valmont to the Glittering Sea. And the lands, they're the most fertile farming lands in the kingdom. With the appropriate crop rotation, and perhaps introducing a few modern irrigation techniques...'

He trails off, perhaps noticing something on my face.

By Sabya's Morningstar.

I take in the expanse of flatlands, the fields of wheat and rye and barley, extending on both sides of the pass. The roads are golden ribbons that someone dropped from above, dotted by lonely farmhouses.

'It is, indeed, the most coveted fief in the kingdom,' I say. 'So much power.'

So much power, and it will be, possibly, bestowed into Philippe's hands.

For a while.

'Interesting,' he says.

'What?'

'When people look at Langly, they see the power. You see the castles, walls you can hide behind. Unbreakable fortresses. What would there be to hide from?'

I say, 'Perhaps from other people who grapple for power? Isn't it important to want to be safe?'

Philippe leans into one of the crenellations, looking downwards. 'There are plenty of people who would covet this sort of power, you're right.'

Does he covet this sort of power, I wonder? In spite of what Hugo told me last night?

He says, 'But doesn't it strike you that most people covet that power for the sake of power itself? Not for what they would do with it?'

He is mocking me. I can't help but think that this is sort of a veiled criticism. Addressed to Hugo, perhaps? But we know very well what we would do with that power, thank you very much.

It's not as if I would tell *him*.

Though his bluntness is refreshing, in a way, this reminds me that I probably shouldn't be dallying, carrying on pointless conversations, when I'm on a mission. A mission that aims precisely to grapple for that power.

I take in the seemingly careless way with which he leans forward, how he's not even looking at me.

The easiness with which he moves, like a man fully in control of his body, and of what he does. From what I spoke about with Hugo, we barely rescued Philippe from becoming Magali's puppet.

'I'm sorry, I must be boring you,' says Philippe, straightening himself. He is now towering over me again, and I have to tilt my head upwards to look into his eyes. I can't quite grasp what is in them. 'I'm, in fact, a bit nervous about meeting the seigneurs tomorrow.'

He offers me his arm, and I take it this time.

I have an object to seek today, and what better way is there to explore the chambers than hand in hand with the heir, or even possibly the new duke?

Even if his manners are quite odd.

'Why would you be nervous?' I lead him towards the corridors of the Inner Keep.

'Are you asking if I'm fretting about meeting a bunch of men who have been accustomed to wielding power for years? And who have to submit to me, a man who has been merely the owner of a farm until a few days ago?' Philippe raises his eyebrows in a cheeky way.

A challenge of sorts.

I smile, in spite of myself. His frankness is refreshing. I debate whether to tell him this or not. Instead, I say, 'Will you please show me the rest of the castle?'

SEARCHES

MAGALI

*L*et me tell you how it was.

I had been married a little over three years and had a child of two when Frederic and Kylian went to war in the Green Kingdom. A backwater, with their expansive woods and antiquated ways.

I was young and powerful, and nothing could touch me, the Duchess of Langly, so I did not worry. Not when Frederic did not send word. Not when Isabella, my sister-in-law, started asking questions. Not when Kylian's wife scooped up little Hugo and hurried to visit some relatives, far away, in Valmont.

What did worry me was to hear that my husband had fallen in battle.

What did worry me, even more, was to see the entirety of the Langly armies marching upon Fort Cantor.

Isabella and I watched from the battlements, Maël given into the care of his nurse.

'You know what this means, don't you?' I told her.

Isabella's dark green eyes turned into a storm, and she coaxed her red plait over her shoulder. 'You presume the worst about my brother.'

I did not presume the worst about Kylian until then, but perhaps I should have. 'I think I have enough reason to.' I trusted, yet not blindly. And I knew what had gnawed at Kylian ever since the inheritance had been settled upon my husband. 'He thinks he has a right to rule.'

'Do we wait or do we leave at once?' she asked, and again, as she had done so often before, she spoke directly to my heart. Of what was in it.

'The Fallen Court?' I asked, more out of the habit of seeking advice there than anything else.

She frowned. 'The Fallen Court will not interfere in the matter between the brothers.'

'I would be a fool to hope.'

From an open window, a child's giggle erupted. So loud, so intense, as if he were choking on his own laughter. Everything was always more, harder, faster with Maël.

That he should lose his birthright even before he would know what that is... That he should lose his father before he could even remember him...

'We have hours, at most,' said Isabella, glancing at the sky. 'Perhaps there is something I could yet do, to gain us some time.'

I grabbed my skirts, nudged by a feeling to go and embrace my son. To see him to safety. To run, and perhaps wait for the day when I would be able to strike back.

There was nothing left to strike with at Fort Cantor. The men had gone to war with Frederic, only to return in Kylian's tow.

Isabella and I made for a dark spiralled staircase. 'Where to?' I whispered, leaning onto my sister-in-law in this time of great need.

Because I knew that her brother would not want her here more than he would want me.

'The Blue Kingdom?' Isabella asked in a whisper.

I shook my head. No. I would not return home with the tail between my legs. 'Closer,' I said, thinking of keeping my goal within my reach.

'There is someone from a family that still owes a debt of blood to the Fallen Court,' said Isabella. 'Someone that not even the Duke of Langly could touch.'

'Who?'

My head was pounding.

Widow. Coward. Fugitive.

Mother. A mother, who had to see that her son would live.

Anything.

Anywhere, as long as there was still hope to one day take back that which we had not yet left, that which had already been lost.

Isabella said, 'Seigneur Julien Bencifert.'

CELINE

Because Philippe knows nothing of Fort Cantor, it's easy for me to guide him where I want us to be. We find ourselves in the blink of an eye in Magali's chambers. The best chambers in the castle, I think, looking at the battlements, the towers and the valley beyond. My own chambers, which used to be Isabella's, face the small courtyard to the side and the cliff.

Not altogether an enticing view.

Magali's quarters consist of three chambers linked to one another, and I run through all of them, dragging Philippe after me from one room to the next, my fingers tight around his arm. It's best to make the most of her absence, as long as it blissfully lasts.

We reach the dressing room first. It has carved armchairs and an ottoman covered in velvet on the other side of a massive, sculpted table. Two ornamented chests line the walls, which are covered in fine tapestries, draped silks. This room is all softness and luxury, so different from anything else I've seen in the castle so far.

The bedchamber next to it looks airier by comparison. An escritoire, a bed and a fireplace are all the furniture within it. A fireplace! I nearly squeal at the sight. Finally, a modern invention.

The last of the three chambers is a surprise; it houses a giant bronze tub and next to it a group of low stools. The walls are lined with shelves filled with jars and glass bottles. I pick up one of them and uncork it. It's dry lavender. It smells of freshly dressed pillows, the touch of scrubbed sheets on my skin, of a light breeze ruffling my hair.

'What are you doing?' says Philippe, catching up with me.

'Exploring,' I say.

Not quite. I'm here to ensure that, unlike five years ago, Hugo's plans will not fail.

Let me tell you a story.

Once upon a time there was a princess whose betrothed went on a quest. The princess lingered in the school of magic they both studied at, confident that it would all work out for the best.

She heard rumours from Lafala. Her betrothed had brought his cousin before the highest court in the land, contesting his right to the inheritance that had been unjustly bestowed upon him. And, as expected, he was stirring a riot.

The people had had enough of the oppressive rule of this cousin's ilk.

The princess was pleased. Her betrothed had been right to set himself upon this path.

A few days later, the princess was called to the Royal Palace. Her mother had died in childbirth, leaving behind a frail baby, her little brother. The heartbroken princess slipped into her mother's shoes, took the reins of the castle's household and did what had to be done for her mother's funeral.

Seigneurs from all across the duchy came to pay their respects, and even monarchs from the neighbouring kingdoms. Only one person was missing, vanished before the day he was to appear at the trial where his inheritance was disputed: her betrothed.

The princess searched, and searched, and searched, but no one could tell her where to find him.

The princess was heartbroken, again.

She decided to return to the magic school and wait for his return there.

But her father, without even the hint of a warning, destroyed the Crystal of Power that fed magic throughout the kingdom, while the doyenne herself wrecked the school's buildings, for obscure reasons.

The princess, depleted of her magic, was heartbroken, yet again.

There was so much heartbreak that the princess wondered how she might be able to continue.

And moreover, with the princess now at the Royal Palace all the time, her father pressed her to marry someone else.

So the princess did the only thing she could do: she withdrew to the shadows. And she waited. The only beckon of light was a bunch of peacock feathers that she sometimes found resting upon her pillow.

A message. A call not to lose hope.

The princess will not falter this time. She will do what she has to: she will find the object that will release her betrothed from the shape of a cat.

Philippe says, 'I don't think Magali would be too pleased to know that you are touching her things,' bringing me back to the present.

I'm sure she wouldn't. But Philippe shouldn't stand in my way. 'You call the dowager duchess by her name?'

I glance around, hoping to find what I'm looking for, though even I'm not sure what that might be, exactly. An object. The thing that ties Hugo to his feline form.

I might not have much of my Gift anymore, but I have will. Plenty of it, bottled in the years when I could do nothing.

'Of course,' says Philippe. 'She was a frequent guest at Castle Bencifert.'

This is why Magali's chambermaid seemed to have known him so well. And why Magali herself intended to use him as her pawn. 'Ah. Are you close, then?'

Philippe shifts. 'I'm not sure what you mean.'

I open a jar. It's filled with a creamy substance that smells of fennel.

'Are *you* close to her?' he asks, drifting closer to my side. I can sense that smell of his again, like grass and rain and new beginnings. 'So close that you can ransack her things?'

'I'm not ransacking. I'm just looking around.'

'Some might think that ill-mannered.'

'Oh? How many princesses have you met before, to judge what is considered ill-mannered or not for them?' I run my hand over the shelves, around the contours of the jars and bottles. I pull them aside, looking for secret compartments behind them, then get down on all fours and check under the bronze tub.

'Do princesses usually get on their knees in front of men they've just met?'

This isn't just blunt, this is coarse. I pull myself up, blushing from the root of my neck to the tip of my ears. 'This has nothing to do with you,' I hiss.

He cocks his eyebrows, a cheeky smile on his face. I must concede that it suits him. 'What is this, then?'

'If you must know, I'm examining the finishing touches of the tub,' I say. 'I'm passionate about all sorts of innovations, especially when it comes to enhancing personal comforts.'

I draw a hand under the tub, searching for anything solid. Any object. Philippe's gaze sears me as I crawl on the ground and we lock eyes for a moment. 'Stop looking at me,' I grind.

'Stop acting strangely.' His eyes don't let go of mine.

He doesn't seem as awestruck as yesterday, the way he was in the carriage. 'I think we should go.'

This time, I agree. It seems there's nothing for me to find in this room. I turn away from him, march into the sleeping chambers.

I fiddle with the escritoire, but the drawers are locked. I knock on the wood, looking for hidden compartments. But to be frank, I'm not sure what that would sound like.

'Do you often go into the rooms of people you don't know, in the company of men?' says Philippe.

He stands by the window, arms crossed, a half-smile on his face.

Mothers of the Forest, he has a point. How this must seem. Should someone have seen us, how I dragged him into someone's bedchamber, what would they think?

I put more distance between us, walk up to the bed, feeling the spots between the down mattress and the leather springs. 'I told you, I do know Magali.'

'I still don't think you should go through her belongings,' he says.

'Some might say that these are your belongings now. Since you're the duke.'

'I'm not yet the duke. This depends on your father's judgement, remember?'

My fingers strike something hard and cold. I clench my hand around it and pull at it. The object proves to be a metal chain.

My heart flutters. Perhaps this is it. Perhaps she left in a hurry when Maël chased her away and she wasn't allowed to take anything.

'And even if I was, I wouldn't have said that all of this belongs to me.'

I roll my eyes. Apparently, on some points, Philippe can be more of a prig than even me.

But I need to see what I have here. Perhaps, with a bit of luck, this is it.

I point my chin to the window. 'Are you sure you don't want these chambers for yourself? Look at that view. Strategic advantages and so on—whatever a *duke* might care for.' I put enough sting in the title for him to turn his eyes away for a moment.

Barely enough for me to drag the chain out and slip it into my pocket.

But he has had enough, too.

He strides over to me and lays a hand on my elbow. 'Let's go, strange princess. How about we explore other rooms?'

I would argue with him out of principle, but I also think we're done here. Still. 'I don't think so.'

I'm curious what he will do. Drag me out of here by the arm? Throw a tantrum?

He turns his head towards me, a wide smile on his face, as if I've just given him a great idea. 'Would you like me to carry you out of here? In my arms?'

Mothers of the Forest and Lucius' Fire.

That's the very last thing I need. As if what's happening already isn't enough of a scandal. I let him lead me out of the chambers.

We are done here for today. And I have something.

SCALES

MAGALI

*I*n the solar, there are four people left: the King and the steward, the stableboy and the invisible chambermaid —none other than me.

I'm no more than a silent witness to the King's inquiry, who braces himself, intent on everything.

Except me.

How unaccustomed I am to being overlooked.

'What happened, boy?' asks the King.

'We were riding out, Your Majesty,' says the stableboy. He keeps his head bent, as he should. 'And when we reached the cliff, the lion caught up with us.'

'Why were you riding out so early in the morning?' asks the King.

'The duke, he wanted to catch the lion, Your Majesty.'

Guilt stirs in my pocket.

'The lion?' says the King.

There are no lions to speak of in our kingdom, except the lioness on the Duchy of Langly's crest and the one who has sporadically plagued the duchy's lands for the past twenty years, though much less often since the Crystal of Power at the Golden Pavilion was destroyed.

'Yes,' says the steward. 'It has been sighted on our lands again, killing cattle, but cunning enough to keep its distance from men. It has only been seen from afar. The duke was furious when it appeared again. Obsessed, may I say, with catching it.'

Of course he would be. These men would also see the sense in it, should they know precisely why.

'Ah, yes, I seem to remember something... Go on, boy,' says the King.

The stableboy covers his face, as if he can't bear to remember the terrible events.

I must say, he plays his part as well as I could have expected him to.

'It came for us, Your Majesty. The Mothers of the Forest save us, I've never seen anything so frightening. There isn't much to say. The beast took the horse down with a slash of its claws. And then I clambered up a tree. This is how I saved myself. But Duke Maël, no, he wasn't the man to clamber up a tree. He drew his sword... That was the end of him, the last I saw him.'

This is good. It sounds distressed, and not too well rehearsed, though I wonder how often he must have practised, in fact, this little speech.

Guilt thrashes in my pocket, maddened and aggrieved.

'You saw Duke Maël being killed by the lion, then,' says the King. 'With your own eyes.'

Here, the stableboy hesitates. He has told this story so many times. What is there to think about? 'Yes and no,' he says. 'The lion took the duke down with his claws and then he carried him away between his jaws. I heard a snap of bones. And the duke's arms and head were hanging limp from the lion's mouth.'

This part of the performance doesn't quite rise up to the rest. Why leave room for doubt, then?

The King takes a moment to clear his voice. He turns to the steward. 'What was found at the site of the events?'

'Great pools of blood, Your Majesty. And the duke's sword.'

The King scratches his beard. 'Have you been scouring the spots where a lion might hide with his prey? Caves, abandoned buildings and such?'

The testimony done, the stableboy sinks again into irrelevance. Good.

'We have, Your Majesty.'

'Very well, then,' says the King. 'I have heard the facts. I will soon provide you with my judgement. Now I need some time to think.'

Guilt weighs heavy in my pocket.

CELINE

When my father summons me to his chambers before dinner, before I've even managed to arrange my hair—at least, as well as I can in the absence of a maid—I know it can't be good.

When he pours wine for both of us in matching gold-gilded goblets, I'm certain that I should dread what he means to tell me. My father thinks young women shouldn't drink wine, that it's unbecoming, and for him to feel the need to fortify me before he proceeds… My stomach tightens in knots.

Perhaps he wants to discard Philippe after all; but why, in my father's opinion, should that make any difference to me?

To be fair, it wouldn't have made any difference to me if Philippe went or stayed, if it weren't for Hugo. If we hadn't been tossed together on this path that is taking quite a sordid turn.

I take a seat in one of the armchairs, my limbs heavy. Every hour of every day, I'm waiting for that blow that will destroy our hopes, again. That will make what I want most in the world impossible.

My father takes a sip of wine, staring at a frayed patch of carpet.

'It's good of you to join me, Celine. I wanted to ask your opinion on something.'

I almost bowl over, taking my seat with me. My father wants to ask *my* opinion. If there was something I would have never expected, it was this.

'I assume it has transpired what has been discussed today?' he continues.

'Servants talk,' I say, but the story I heard is quite absurd. It has something to do with a lion, who ripped Maël to pieces.

Not even I would have wished for such an end to him, to keep him from my bed.

My father just nods.

'Is it true, then?' I ask. 'Do you think Maël died?'

My father swirls the wine in his goblet. A drop lands on his wrist. 'I have reason to think so, yes.'

In this instant, I don't even know if I'm breathing. I would ask if he means to confirm Philippe as the new duke. If I could utter a single word.

'You spent some time with Philippe today,' he says, his eyes set on me. Gauging every slip in my features, every gesture.

I'm used to these looks. This is why I'm so skilled at keeping my feelings tucked away, under the weight of his expectations.

My father asks, 'What did you make of him?'

I riffle through all the possible answers in my mind. I'm not sure what he'd like to hear. If my father comes to think of Philippe as someone who is up to the task, if he endorses him, if he asks the seigneurs to swear fealty to him, then Philippe would be the new duke.

But also, I carry something in my pocket that might mean that it's not necessary. That we would need Philippe no longer, and Hugo could finally take his rightful place.

If only I had seen Hugo today, before I met my father. If only I could have spoken to him.

If only I could have asked for his advice.

The tips of my fingers grow numb.

'Celine?' says my father. 'What did you make of him? Do you think he is ... suitable?'

And there it is. Blood rushes through me, pounding in my ears.

Did it not always come down to this? Isn't this the only thing my father sees, when he looks at me?

Someone who must find a suitable man. The one reason that, to my father, justifies my existence.

I rattle the chain in my pocket. If it is not what I hope it will be, a wrong word from me, and all that Hugo and I wanted for ourselves will be doomed.

My mind races through the maze of possibilities, travelling from dead end to dead end, until there is only one path left.

'I think he's an honest man,' I say, meaning *blunt*. 'I'm not sure whether he isn't afraid to speak because he doesn't realise what he is saying, or because he hasn't learned to be guarded.' Like the high seigneurs of this land, like most people I know.

'Is that so?' My father scratches his pointed beard. 'What did he say to you?'

Do princesses usually get on their knees in front of men they've just met?

Mothers of the Forest. I remember the smug face that went with that comment, the way his eyes twinkled.

'Nothing that's worth repeating,' I say. 'It's more of a feeling.'

'Do you think that would make him a good duke, or a poor one?'

But doesn't it strike you that most people covet that power for the sake of power itself? Not for what they would do with it?

I answer, honestly this time, 'I don't know.' Not that it would matter. He's not here to hold on to the seat. He probably wouldn't want to, either. It's not his world, that much is clear.

The seigneurs would eat him alive, if he didn't have help.

'Fair enough,' says my father, staring at the wall. 'But you still haven't answered my question. He is handsome enough, I suppose. He seems gentle. What more would a young seigneur need to be suitable?'

I find that, at this point, I can't look at him. I understand what he's asking, what he's implying.

This is the price I need to pay today.

A promise.

A compromise, of sorts.

No one will ever have to know, I suppose.

I hold tight to the chain as I say, 'I think, yes, he would be suitable enough.'

'Good,' says my father. 'I have my answer. We will make an announcement, then, tomorrow.'

MAGALI

The King summons all the castle staff, early the next morning, in the Grand Bailey. The rumour spreads like wildfire in the kitchens and the stables, the storerooms and the pantries.

We all answer the summons. It is not every day that a king wishes to speak to the servants.

He appears after we have all gathered, his knights building a shield around him. The King is a man who has made many enemies.

In a quick speech, he booms at us that he has investigated the matter of Duke Maël's disappearance carefully, assisted by the esteemed steward of Fort Cantor. This is a cunning move, because the steward is a man who is respected and loved. Willingly or not, he has just put his stamp on the King's announcement.

The red velvet mantle lined with fur and the thick golden chain on top of it dazzle the audience. The King has taken pains with his royal attire and as someone who has taken on so many forms in their life, I have to say that appearances do matter a great deal. I don't receive even half the respect I'm owed when I take the form of a chambermaid rather than that of Magali.

And Magali never received half the respect or the affection that was bestowed on Frederic.

'There remains no further doubt in my mind,' the King says, 'that Duke Maël has expired.'

Only a faint gasp follows this statement. Memories are short and the people are already growing accustomed to Philippe's face.

The King says, 'And while I mourn with you the loss of Duke Maël, I sincerely hope you will join me in supporting your new master. My daughter, Princess Celine, can attest to his wonderful character. Please welcome Duke Philippe as warmly as we have.'

Their new master. Duke Philippe.

I exhale noisily.

So it is done.

The princess, tiny and irrelevant, curtsies. The staff watches in awe. What is there to admire about someone so faded, so quiet? I tried more than once to show her the ways of the world, but she's as stubborn as a mule.

With the promise of a celebration for the newly proclaimed

Duke Philippe, the King dismisses us so we can return to our work.

But on their way to the bowels of the castle, the clamour of dissatisfaction among the staff grows. If a farm boy can become a duke, why not a bailiff, a marshal?

No, as much as I loathe it, Philippe needs someone at his side to strengthen his claim, especially after the King leaves.

Someone like Princess Celine.

CELINE

Hugo catches up with me in the library, while I'm up on the sculpted ladder, roving through the books. I've never seen so many tomes about magic in a single place, but I think that the first duchess liked to be informed.

As far as I've heard, the Lion couldn't even read.

All thoughts about ancestors fade when Hugo hops onto the small table in the corner. I rush down to greet him, my hand already going to my pocket, where I'd hidden the chain. It's still warm, after I've carried it around all day. 'I found something.' I'm not sure I dare hope this is what we need.

Hugo sniffs it. 'Yes, it's a chain, and what of it?'

He sounds rather morose today. I thought he'd be pleased. 'I hoped this would be … you know, the thing that keeps you bound.'

Hugo sniffs it again. 'I'm sorry to disappoint, my love, but this isn't it.'

I let the chain fall. Did I dare even hope? Really? I suppose this was why I told my father what I told him, last night. 'No matter, we have enough time to look.' A thought crosses my mind. 'What if Magali took the object with her, though?'

Hugo considers this. 'You are so clever, Celine. Magali might have it, indeed. I saw no sign of it; I can't be certain that she doesn't have it. I always assumed that I would have felt the ripples of power if she had it upon herself, but now I'm not certain of anything anymore.'

He seems defeated. Exhausted.

I pause to rearrange my thoughts. Magali, of course. Would Magali leave something like that behind? In how much of a hurry could she have left?

'This could take longer than we might have first thought,' says Hugo. 'And it's much more complicated. Langly is stirring; not all seigneurs agree. It smells like turmoil.'

'No matter, we still have time.' I slide down into one of the two sumptuously embroidered armchairs.

'Yes, you've said that, but do we, really, my dove?'

I become still at this. 'What do you mean?'

'Your father confirmed Philippe as the duke today.'

'I thought you'd be pleased.' I had gone so far as to push the matter in this direction the night before, hadn't I? 'What if my father rejected Philippe's claim? What of it then?'

'Your father is already calling for the seigneurs to swear fealty. Once that is done, you have no reason to dally here anymore, Celine, don't you see? You will be gone from Langly. Who would look for the object then?'

No, no, no. Not this. Not me and Hugo, parting again, before we can set things right. 'Not all will swear fealty,' I say in a low voice. 'My father is leaving tomorrow for a few days, to visit these seigneurs in their homes, to persuade them.' Whatever that might entail. 'At least, Count Goderic will come.' Langly's warlord. And he *will* swear fealty.

Hugo says nothing.

I bite my lip, so hard that I almost draw blood. 'It's my fault. My father asked me last night what I made of Philippe.'

Hugo tenses at this.

My throat feels tight. 'I'm sorry, I didn't know what to say. If I knew this would happen ... I would have told him that Philippe isn't suitable.'

'*Suitable*? Is that what you called him?'

I can't even look at Hugo now. He understands, too, what my father implied. 'That was what he asked. I was afraid that...' My hands are trembling. I've made a mess of things. 'I'm sorry. I'm so sorry; this is all my fault.'

Hugo leaps into my arms, brings his head to my cheek. 'No, my love, no, you couldn't have done otherwise. You couldn't have told your father anything else. But it's just that we're in a bit of a fix right now.'

I hold onto Hugo, tightly.

'If your father leaves to tour the duchy tomorrow, he will take you with him.'

'Yes,' I breathe.

'We can't afford that; we don't have enough time. You must persuade your father that you have to stay here. So you can seek.'

I pull my head away. 'How do you expect me to do that?'

Hugo's eyes are tinged with sadness. The only human aspect still about him, except his voice. I can't even bear to look at him. I have failed him. Failed us.

'Is there anything at all you can tell him to convince him you have to stay here? With Philippe?'

My heart shrinks. There is one thing I could tell him. One thing that could persuade him. But this would mean... 'I can't, Hugo. I'd have to tell him I'd rather stay and help Philippe.'

Hugo looks at me. 'Is that what you're concerned about? Don't be, my dove. I love you to the ends of the earth and back. Nothing you say could shake my belief in you. Say whatever you need to say. It's all for us, in the end.'

'What makes you even think that my father will agree?'

Hugo blinks. 'Have you really spent such a long time making yourself small? Have you forgotten how powerful you are, what you can do?'

I want to say, *You have no idea. I'm not powerful anymore. At all.*

'I know you, my dove. How you bottle it all in. And when you erupt… It's the power of the sea, unleashed, wiping it all away. Be the sea, Celine. Remember who you are.'

PEEPHOLES

MAGALI

*T*he dinner is loud, as loud as it has ever been in the good old days of Fort Cantor. The days when I had a say. And this isn't the sort of raucous clamour that would have sent any decent woman scurrying for a way out, like the final weeks when Maël was a duke.

It's the sort of noise that comes from relief, at the end of a good, useful day. I wish my son understood how far he strayed from the right path, from what the duchy and Fort Cantor should have been.

Guilt weighs heavy in my pocket.

At the ducal table, Philippe, the King and the princess sit in the middle. The men look pleased. The princess seems exhausted. Around them, the seigneurs, the ones who swore fealty to Philippe today, are seated in the order of their rank. They take turns to toast the new duke—and each takes a moment to mourn the unexpected demise of Maël. But no true sadness lives in their eyes.

They always feared him more than they respected him.

They never loved him.

Out of habit, I gaze towards the peephole, hidden in the roof of the Great Hall. The one that opens directly into my chambers. The candles in the room flicker and the peephole flashes blue, with a ring of amber.

I know who is watching. Who is behind the peephole.

The seigneurs might not have trusted Hugo, either, but they could have learned to love him. Five years ago, binding him into the shape of a cat was good riddance.

But now I play a game more dangerous than the ones with fire, allying myself with my enemy.

Needs must.

At the table, Philippe clutches his goblet. His gaze washes over the princess's face and he leans forward, the laced cuffs of his chemise landing in the broth on his plate. He tells her something but she gazes into the hearth at the foot of the ducal table and sips her wine, not deigning to reply.

This little self-sufficient princess.

She'll never know a good man when she sees him.

Her father then calls her and she shudders, as if woken from a dream. She turns to Philippe, who now stands, offering her his hand. She takes it hesitantly as he helps her up.

They walk together to the side entrance, the one that leads into the small courtyard at the side of the cliff. Every pair of eyes in the room is watching. And why would they not? Who would not admire Philippe's tall, broad frame next to Celine's plump but graceful silhouette? They'd make the most extraordinary couple in the kingdom.

I can almost make out the stories they'll tell in my mind.

The third son who married the princess.

The farmer who married the princess.

The princess who refused to marry any nobleman for years and years, and eventually married a farmer.

The legends growing around it.

Philippe opens the side door and they disappear from my sight.

CELINE

I gulp for air as we reach the side garden, nestled between the castle and the cliff. It's the small courtyard I can see from the windows of my chambers, filled with rosebushes and whatever herbs the kitchen might need, a few apple trees and vines. But I can't make out any shapes of flowers in the half-darkness and, perhaps because of the wine, the images blur and dance before my eyes.

'I thought you might need some fresh air,' says Philippe.

I become aware of the way I press my shoulder into his arm, leaning into the hard flesh underneath, of how he has clasped my hand with his to steady me. It's large and warm and covers mine entirely. I look up and there's something like worry etched upon his face.

This is where my father wants me to be. This is why he agreed to let me stay, while he leaves tomorrow, in order to consolidate Philippe's position.

He does this for *me*, for whatever plans concerning me and the new duke he has hatched in his mind, whatever hopes he has threaded around the two of us.

I free myself from Philippe's touch and wobble towards the nearest bench. 'I did. Thank you.'

He hesitates, then walks towards me, keeping the distance. 'Are you all right? You looked so pale at the table.'

Am I all right? How I can be? My darling Hugo is still trapped in his feline form; Magali is nowhere to be found, and I might have made a mistake yesterday. And my father is pushing, pushing, pushing me towards Philippe.

I don't even know where to begin.

'Celine?' he says, the first letters of my name soft on his lips. And I look up at him, even though I don't want to. I remember the way we watched each other yesterday, when we were in Magali's chambers, and feel that pang of discomfort again. Of getting too close.

I take in a few calming breaths, like we were taught all those years ago at the Golden Pavilion, during the Morgen Movements. In and out. Gather it all in. Throw it out. Let the world do with it what it can.

I remember the words of the Golden Pavilion.

I am the master of myself.

I am the master of my own power.

'Everything went well with the seigneurs today?'

At least it seems that way, judging by the good disposition of everyone inside.

All these people are here for *him*, I remind myself.

Philippe stands straighter. 'I think there is still much work to do.'

He is right. But I'm still not sure what happened behind closed doors. The fact is, Philippe is now the new duke. And we don't know yet when he will be able to step down, to allow Hugo...

'You could be a bit more forthcoming with the details.'

'What would you like me to tell you?' says Philippe, gently.

I roll my shoulders back. They feel so tight. 'Anything that you'd tell any of your friends. Don't worry, my mind can wrap itself around the complicated connections between the Duke of Langly and his seigneurs.'

Philippe comes closer, takes a seat on the other end of the bench and laces his hands together. 'Good, because I can't. Perhaps you'd care to explain them to me.'

I chuckle, and this time I'm honest. 'Everyone seemed rather pleased with the outcome at dinner.' I caught quite a lot of what was being said during the meal, in spite of my blinding headache. It's a skill.

'Your father, he is magical,' says Philippe.

'Hardly.' Magical is the last thing that my father is. He's the most anti-magical person I've ever known in my life. I can never forget how his life's work had been to banish magic from our kingdom.

'No, you should have seen him today. The way he spoke to the seigneurs. The way he coaxed them. The way he made veiled threats.'

'Did you truly have nothing to do with it, then?'

Hugo called Philippe a dolt. And he was surely awkward in the crowded hall, but my father wouldn't push his daughter towards a man he deemed unworthy.

Or would he?

'Do I have anything to do with everything that's happened since my father died? It's as if I'm riding a wild horse that's beyond my control.'

I may have something to do with all that. Yet for now, I am beyond guilt. Philippe might have lost the farm he grew up on, but he has gained a duchy. As long as Maël doesn't reappear, I remind myself. I shudder when I think of him. 'You chose to come to Fort Cantor when you lost everything. There were a dozen other paths you could have taken, couldn't you?' One that led directly into Magali's clutches, nonetheless. 'Yet here you are. The duke. I find it hard to pity you.'

'Are princesses always so blunt?'

'Did your father not expect you to inherit the ducal seat, should something happen to Maël? For years, you have been the only possible heir to Langly. Why did he not raise you at the castle, prepare you for the task?' In the stillness of the night, it feels like I can see more clearly the shape of things. And some aspects haven't been handled sensibly.

If anything, it's as if someone had taken pains to hide Philippe.

'How do you think Maël might have liked that?' he says, with equal bluntness.

That brutal honesty again.

If my father saw me, he would be horrified. I suppose these aren't the sort of conversations a young lady ought to have with a potential suitor. Though, to be frank, I haven't been a maiden for quite some time.

And I remember what Hugo said about the power that I keep hidden in me, beneath the surface.

I wish I could believe him.

Philippe says, 'I'm sure you will disagree on this point, but, in fact, nothing could have prepared me better to lead a duchy than running a farm. It's the same, isn't it? But instead of one farm there are many, and each one has many more tenants. But it's no more than farming land, and selling harvests, and managing the fiefs.'

'I wouldn't say it's quite the same.' I try to remind myself to be nice to him. He chose to help Hugo and me, after all. But there is a line I must not cross. I have to avoid being so nice that it would give him ideas of the sort that my father has.

Mothers of the Forest, the very thought that my father might have broached that subject with him makes me cringe.

I make myself prattle on. 'First of all, the food supplies for all the people who live in it, from servants to men-at-arms. Then there's the matter of managing the taxations in Port Lang. And the Guilds' rights, which have become so much more complicated since your grandfather's time. Then, there are the fairs, the markets, other taxes. Maintaining security and managing the knights, rallying them occasionally, and maintaining the merchant roads from Port Lang to Langville and Lafala. And, and, and.'

Philippe laces his hands on his knee, grinning. His entire face lights up. I might be tempted to think that he's quite nice, on the whole. Thoughtful. He asked what I thought, and listened to the end.

He says, 'You sound an awful lot like Magali.'

'I surely hope not.' He must be aware of what Magali did to Hugo, or else he wouldn't be here today.

He must not have realised this. I wonder, now, how close were they as he grew up? He must have looked at her in awe.

How skilfully must Hugo have pleaded our cause, for Philippe to turn his back on her.

This is why Hugo is precisely the sort of man Langly needs at its head. Someone who can convince others to work with him. To follow him.

All his life, Hugo never lacked followers, did he?

And Philippe and I, we are allies of sorts, I suppose. We were so before we even met, I realise. He is my ally and he did nothing to disabuse me of this notion. Not even when I brazenly searched Magali's chambers yesterday.

A long moment of silence stretches between us. He seems about to ask something, then changes his mind. 'You would certainly be fit to rule a duchy. Maybe you could show me how.'

I swallow, hovering over my words. I find none. Suddenly I'm not sure if he means what I think he means, but he doesn't know that my affections aren't his to take, because I've given them to someone else a long time ago.

It's all the more the reason for me to feel ashamed. So I jump to my feet and tell him, 'I think it's awfully late. Don't you think we should return to the hall? I'm sure everyone must be asking themselves what we are up to.'

I am the master of myself, I try to chime. But it surely doesn't feel like it.

MAGALI

I clean the bedpans in the chamber that Philippe calls his own, ignoring the thud of my own heart in my ears, the pangs of guilt in my pocket. Everything is so chaotic, and the Fallen Court is bound to interfere soon.

I am certainly *not* looking forward to that.

I will have to be ready to face them.

I nearly jump out of my skin when Hugo slips into the chambers, as a cat. 'This is what I like to see,' he says, eyeing the bedpans.

How little he is privy to my life. About how much of it has been clearing up someone else's droppings. 'I begin to think that Julien and I were too generous. I always thought we should have turned you into a worm, and not a cat.'

Hugo swishes his tail, displeased, and adds that he remembers what we spoke about in his presence, all those years ago.

I don't need to be reminded of *that.* 'Where's your princess?' I ask.

'Waiting for me, I suppose.'

As much as I loathe him, he never ceases to surprise me. 'How did you even manage to persuade her to be a part of your scheming? Is she so gullible?'

'No,' he says, 'but she loves me.'

'What a fool,' I say.

Hugo freezes at that.

There it is, should I need it. The soft spot. The only one I could ever find, except his blind faith in his own abilities. I wonder if the princess truly knows what happened five years ago.

He wants me to believe that he does all of this for power, but I'm certain that in the depths of his dark, twisted heart, he loves her, in the only way he can.

Guilt nibbles at the seams of my pocket.

Had Julien and I not acted all those years ago, confining Hugo to the body of a cat, I don't want to even think about what might have happened. Never had a scandal shattered and divided our kingdom in such a way. Everyone was waiting for the King's judgement on the matter of the inheritance in Langly. They were like a heap of twigs, waiting to catch fire.

I even half-expected the Mothers of the Forest to emerge from whatever cave they have been hiding in for the past decades to come forward and try to sort through that tangle.

Hugo narrows his eyes. 'Never mind. It's time you give me what you swore you would.'

I cannot show Hugo my relief—the creature grows too strong against the spell. It needs the object to bind it. I reach into my pocket, feeling for it, mindful to avoid its little teeth. It squirms and tries to hide, but I grab it by its middle and pull it out.

Its beady eyes are full of hate.

Hugo turns around. 'Put it in the velvet pouch. It will have to hold for now, until I can make other arrangements.'

'I thought we'd made these other arrangements already,' I say. The creature thrashes and I have no choice but to drop it into the pouch and close the mouth with the golden string.

'Dear aunt,' says Hugo, 'do you truly not trust me?'

'Oh, but I do. As soon as you deliver on your part of the deal. Talk to the princess, it's time to proceed.'

CELINE

When I return from the garden, Hugo is waiting for me in my room, perched on top of my bed.

'My love, I've been expecting you,' he says.

'I've been out in the garden. Walking with Philippe.' The exchange still unsettles me for some reason I can't pinpoint. When I gave him a piece of my mind about the duchy, he grinned in a way that...

He asked me to help him.

I swallow.

'Excellent. I have a gift for you,' he says, signalling me to open the pouch.

I pull at the threads to bring out a small creature, wriggling in my palm.

'Quick, quick, the cage,' says Hugo, and I leap off the bed, one hand squeezing around the mouse, one hand trembling around the golden cage's opening.

The cage I brought here, the cage that was delivered to me in Langville.

The small creature thrashes, and I try to hold tight, without squeezing hard.

'What is this?' I ask, pulling the small golden lever shut. The mouse stops, frozen in the middle of the cage, then charges towards one of the bars.

Its fur is blue-grey, and it's absolutely demented with fear.

Hugo sighs. 'This, my dear, is Maël.'

'What?' I'm utterly frozen. No words come to me.

'We were right, my dove. Magali must have acted, though something went wrong.'

I watch the mouse, numb. 'She's not here, is she?'

'Many things could happen when speaking a spell like that.'

I shudder.

'But I felt the ripples of power coming from him when I roamed the castle. I know what it feels like.' Hugo's voice fades at this and my heart fills with sorrow. He *would* know because he had gone through the same. 'I knew I had to catch him, to put him somewhere safe. He was even lucky that we found him first. Magali will be looking for him.'

My head is numb. 'But where is she?'

Hugo roams around the cage, while the mouse stops, twitching its whiskers. Then it charges at the bars once more, completely feral.

I've never seen the likes of it. A mouse, attacking a cat.

'Who can say what she's planning, my dove?' Hugo stops. 'Listen, Celine. We are running out of time. Your father will be gone for a few days, but I'm afraid this won't be enough to do what we need to, not by far. There is too much unrest in Langly.'

We did this. We are the ones who did this.

And if we don't find the object by the time that I have to leave... I don't even want to think about that.

Leaving here, leaving Philippe as the duke, as a possible prey to Magali.

She might yet turn him, convince him to do her bidding.

Hugo says, 'We might need Philippe to fill the duke's shoes for a while longer.'

'What? Why?'

'He will need a bit of time to establish himself. Though I could tell this morning, in the Great Hall, that the seigneurs like him.'

'You were in the Great Hall this morning?' I ask. Maybe gaping.

'I'm a cat. I can go anywhere I want.'

'Well, I can't.' How humiliating. To be excluded from all matters of significance.

It must have been different for Magali when she was a duchess. I think she was the one who attended this sort of gathering when Frederic wasn't here. When he was ill. What must it be like, as a woman?

'Do you truly think the seigneurs will listen to Philippe? He has neither the upbringing nor the manners of a duke.'

'Nor did the first duke,' says Hugo.

'But Philippe isn't like that,' I find myself saying. 'He isn't ruthless. The seigneurs will eat him alive.'

'The seigneurs will be happy not to have to take sides. And this will work to our advantage.'

I'm still taking in the mouse, completely baffled. That Magali should do such a thing to her own son.

Simply remove him.

And still there is no trace of her.

'My dove, Magali is brewing something.'

That, at least, is becoming more and more obvious to me.

Hugo goes on, lowering his voice. I can see what he's about to say pains him. 'I'm not sure you're aware of this. But I can't quite rise from the dead and be entrusted with the duchy instantly. It would have to be passed on to me. By Philippe. And it will be so much easier if, by then, Philippe is somewhat established. If we don't have to handle this ... turmoil.'

I can see how this would be a sensible course of action, but... 'What are you trying to say?'

'I think, my dove, that you should marry Philippe.'

I feel as if the ceiling has been dropped on my head.

'What? You can't possibly mean that.'

Hugo clambers onto my belly and I brush a finger against his fur.

This is so wrong.

This isn't us; this is him, but it isn't him.

To be so close, and yet so far, it drives me nearly to tears.

'My dove, this is the last thing I want. But if we ever want to be reunited again... My heart is breaking. But I see no other way. You have to stay here. And it will be just for a while.'

I understand why—to guard Langly, and Philippe, against Magali. But Hugo can't mean this, he *can't*.

All my life, I've only wanted to marry one man: Hugo.

The mouse stops, as if he's watching. 'Does he understand what we're saying?'

'I think not,' says Hugo. 'Before Seigneur Bencifert died, most days, I was just a cat. I lived and thought like a cat. I think Maël will forget soon that he ever was anything else.'

This seems so fantastical, perhaps even more fantastical than the fact that the love of my life just asked me to marry another man. 'The cage,' I say. 'Why did she proceed without the cage?'

'Perhaps she was running out of time,' says Hugo. 'Perhaps part of the spell turned against her. Weakened her. She'd left for Langville when Philippe and I stole the cage. Perhaps she came back and decided to proceed without it.'

I gasp. 'Philippe helped you steal the cage?'

'He tried to keep his cousin from the fate I had been destined for, being trapped in an animal form.' Hugo pauses, while I still struggle to take this all in. 'We can trust him, my dove.'

But once we are married, can I trust him not to want more? 'What if he wants to ... after we're married.'

Hugo gives me a look brimming with love. 'But you are so strong, my dove, as I've told you. Don't make yourself small. And he's not the kind of man... He will do nothing that you don't want him to do.'

This task, this task that has been set before me. It seems more impossible than anything else.

In this story, it seems, the princess will have to save her prince.

Hugo says, 'I need you at the helm of the duchy. To work with Philippe, to smooth the way for us. I would trust no one else.'

My heart skips a beat at this. It is this that I have been dreaming of for years. For someone to trust me to steer a duchy. To free me from my lonely cage. And Hugo would trust no one else to pave the way for us.

And yet, I was never the girl who wanted to carve a path for herself. No, that was never me. I had enough of being on my own in the years at the Royal Palace, since my mother died.

All that I ever wanted was to build something with someone. To build something here. With Hugo.

I was asked by him to build. And I am here, working with him.

The role that I would have to play…

A peacemaker in the duchy. A chatelaine.

But what would I have to sacrifice for it?

'My dove?' says Hugo and I still can't find the words.

He is not giving me away to Philippe. He wants to me to be the one who paves the way for us. It seems that I would be, indeed, the princess who rescues her prince. And Philippe could be my partner, my ally.

I take a deep gulp of air.

'If Philippe marries, Magali will have to show herself,' says Hugo. 'She has no choice. And it will be too late for her, by then.'

'I'm not sure I can do this,' I say. 'You ask too much of me.'

'Don't be afraid.' Hugo's voice softens. 'Don't be afraid to be what you were always meant to be—the lady of this castle. The choice is yours, my love. Think about it. And we'll do whatever you think is best.'

CALCULATIONS

CELINE

*A*fter my father has left on his quick tour of the duchy, I debate whether to make good on my word to help Philippe, or just try to avoid him.

My father wants me to marry him. As absurd as it is, my love wants me to marry that man, too.

My first instinct is to shy away, studded into me by years and years of avoiding coming close to any man who isn't Hugo.

Philippe is in the steward's tower, and I take the long way, via the stairs that wind around the Great Hall and the oriel where I've heard Magali liked to take her breakfast on sunny days.

It's with fresh eyes that I now look upon the rotten rushes strewn on the floor of the Great Hall. I don't think I want to find out what lies beneath them. I note the torn tapestries, the damp walls. Ideas whirl and swirl through my head like so many dancers. About transforming smoky hearths into comfortable fireplaces, about scattering the floors with clean rushes and fragrant herbs.

The freedom I always dreamed of is so close. It's so close I can taste it.

It's not that I don't have qualms about what happened to Maël. That poor mouse in the cage… I should have some compassion; I should hate cages more than anything.

But didn't Magali do the same to the love of my life? And I shudder to think of all the horrible things that Maël has ever done.

Will it be all for nothing? I find myself standing at the foot of the steward's tower, unresolved. I suppose I'm itching to have a look at those ledgers, as well. To see what I'm stepping into, as the chatelaine.

I make my way up the winding stairs. I suppose being in the same room with Philippe doesn't amount to the same as marrying him, does it?

I take a deep breath and knock on the steward's door.

'Yes?'

There's little furniture in the room—merely a large oak table with four chairs grouped around it—but upon it are stacked piles of thick leather-bound ledgers.

Philippe and the steward—a middle-aged man with a round belly—sit face to face. I remember the man from the day before, when he approached my father at breakfast. There's a feather dipped in a bottle of ink in front of Philippe.

They rise to their feet with a clatter of wood scraping on stone. 'Your Highness,' says the steward.

'Princess, what a surprise.'

I curtsy with all the grace I can muster. 'My father told me I might find you here.'

'You wish to speak to me?' says Philippe. I notice the circles under his eyes and wonder what has prevented him from finding sleep. Perhaps the knowledge that his cousin has been turned into a mouse to make room for him?

I wonder if he knows, and what kind of man this makes him.

'I wish to help you.' I draw myself up a chair, since the men seem too dumbfounded to do it for me, and sit down at the new duke's side.

He follows me with a questioning gaze that wraps me from the tips of my fingers to the hem of my blue velvet dress. 'You wish to ... help me?'

'Yes. I'm not sure if you're aware but I've managed the household at the Royal Palace for the five years since my mother died. I'm very, very good with a ledger.' And ruthless, also, when it comes to expenses or rooting out those who steal from our stores. 'If I may?' I say, looking from Philippe to the steward.

'I appreciate your offer, Princess,' says Philippe, 'but in spite of what you might think, I'm very good with a ledger, also. I might not have had the finest tutors, like you, or even reasonably fine ones, like my half-brothers, but I've learned enough to be able to make simple calculations.'

Stiff today, then. Prickly.

'I didn't mean to offend,' I say, 'but since I have more experience with larger households...'

'I'm not offended,' he says. 'I suggest, instead, you make a nice day for yourself, and do whatever princesses do all day. Not that I have met many princesses before, as we've established.'

I feel the sting in this. The challenge.

I am the master of my own power.

And ledgers are my greatest powers, lately. Like the one which the steward is just examining. I stretch across the table and pinch it.

'You might be surprised to hear that this is precisely what princesses do. At least those whose mothers are gone.' I trace a line of expenses with my finger. There are an awful lot of them. 'You may hear about the carriage rides and the balls and the state dinners, but this is a bigger part of my day than anything else.

Someone has to organise them—in conjunction with the botler and the pantler, of course.'

My heart warms when I think of Gaston, our botler, and his gentle hand that guided me in my duties when I was eighteen. 'One has to consider where royal guests must be seated so that no one takes offence, and what they will be fed, and how the Royal Palace will pay for all that. So whenever you are invited to one of our royal events, Duke Philippe, and when you are lodged in one of the beautiful chambers at the Royal Palace, think that there's someone behind it all who has worked hard to make sure, every time, that everything will be perfect. And more often than not, that person is me.'

Philippe leans back, a restrained smile on his face. His hand is carelessly draped across the armrest of his chair. It seems to communicate that he isn't intimidated by all these ledgers. Or by me. In fact, he seems more comfortable in this room than he did at the ducal table last night.

'By all means, then,' he says. 'I didn't know this.'

'There is plenty you don't know about me.' Like the fact that I can make the water in goblets dance and bubble without even touching them. But this is none of his business. 'The expenses are exorbitant,' I say, following the rows in the ledgers. 'So much wine imported from the Green Kingdom. Figs? Olive oil? Spices? Where did this all go?' I make a note to inspect the goods in the castle's storerooms.

'Duke Maël … entertained guests often,' says the steward, lowering his eyes.

'Oh,' I say. Wild dinners, if the rumours about Maël and what happened at the castle are to be believed, and hunts that went on for weeks.

I tap my finger on my lips, examining the lists, leafing through the pages. 'And actresses? Why so many actresses? From this you would imagine that Maël was the greatest lover of theatre in all the kingdom,' I say.

The steward averts his gaze, mumbling. I look at Philippe. 'What did he do with all the actresses?'

'I think you'll also see plenty of dancers in that ledger,' he says, meeting my gaze. Then he chuckles. 'It would be quite inappropriate to explain to you what he did with all the actresses and dancers. I think many of them weren't actresses, as such. Is that right, Jacques?'

The steward blushes to the tips of his ears. And then I remember. The women who were invited here. How Maël sometimes brought not only courtesans from our kingdom, but from the neighbouring kingdoms through Port Lang.

'Oh,' I say. 'Apologies if I was indelicate. Though I suppose Maël was the indelicate one really...'

The steward looks as if he wants to disappear under the table. Philippe just grins.

'Fine,' I say. 'But the expenses are exorbitant. How did he pay for all this? The revenues from the duchy must have been fantastic.'

'Extortionate, you mean to say.' Philippe tosses me the ledger on which he has been making notes. 'If you're so passionate about administration, then maybe you'd like to look at this.'

I leaf through the pages documenting the taxes collected from the people in the duchy, both commoners and seigneurs.

I'm more and more scandalised as I read on. There are taxes still being collected here that have been obsolete in our kingdom for decades. Like the tax on smoke and the tax on rainwater.

Rainwater.

And the share that Maël collected from the farmers who were working the ducal lands is hard to believe. 'How did these people have enough left to live through the winter?' I say, turning the ledger towards Philippe.

He shakes his head. 'I don't know. This is the first thing that must be amended.'

'Yes, perhaps quickly, before the spring understandings for the crops are sealed,' says the steward.

The spring understandings are agreements that the seigneurs and their vassals enter into every year, setting out the share of the crops that the landlord is to receive from the farmers. It's mostly a formality, but with Philippe intent on changing the rates, it will be the work of days and days. Perhaps weeks.

'You have your work cut out for you,' I say.

'Ha. Do you think so?' He ruffles his hair towards the back.

I fold my hands in my lap. 'But if the first thing you do when you take over the duchy is offer more reasonable terms to the farmers, they will absolutely adore you.'

'Thank you for pointing out the obvious,' he says.

'I thought it was very clever, that's all.' And, of course, worrying—for me, at least. And for Hugo. If Philippe moves fast, he'll secure the people's allegiance, which might not be so good for Hugo, once we release him from his feline form.

We all exchange quick glances. And when I start examining the ledger again, I can still see from the corner of my eye that Philippe's attention is entirely fixed on me, his gaze that of a person who has come upon a simple row of numbers that don't make sense when they start adding them up.

I turn a leaf. 'In any case, the household expenses should decrease sharply,' I say. 'I hope there's enough in the duke's purse until after the harvest?'

'Oh, yes,' says the steward. 'The duke and I were just about to see to that. Duke Maël always kept a purse of money for his entourage. His followers.'

'Do you mean the wild minions he used to hunt with for weeks in a row? The so-called friends he would invite to those dinners with the actresses?'

'Yes, precisely.'

'Ah, yes,' I say. If I remember correctly, Maël didn't go anywhere without his entourage. A bunch of thugs and thieves and mercenaries and the debauched second and third sons of his seigneurs. His personal guard, he called them.

'Where are they now?' asks Philippe, his spine stiffening.

'Some of them were still here, at Fort Cantor, when they heard that the King was approaching,' says the steward.

So this is why, perhaps, my father chose to spend the first night at the Griffin Inn after he heard of what happened to Maël, instead of rushing to Langly. To allow for the rumour to spread that he was approaching. To allow people to get out of the way.

'And the rest?' asks Philippe.

'Some of them would have been in Langville, at the annual fair,' says the steward.

So much has happened since a few days ago, when we watched Maël compete in the tournament. And not only him. His minions, as well, such as Count Goderic's third son.

I wonder where *his* allegiances lie.

'And the others would be in Port Lang, awaiting the festivities of the Spring Festival.'

Ah, the Spring Festival. Another pretext for the townspeople of Port Lang and the noblemen of our kingdom to drink wine for days and gorge themselves on food.

'Or to find another employer,' says Philippe.

'What do you mean?' I say.

'Jacques, do you have a ledger in which Maël kept track of the … gifts he made to his followers?' asks Philippe.

Jacques nods and hands him a thin ledger, bound in soft red

calfskin. Philippe opens it in his lap and tilts it so that I can look at the entries, too. I crane my neck, leaning my elbow on the armrest of his chair, grazing him slightly. He doesn't shy away from the touch.

I think, *Perhaps he wasn't upset with me* and then wonder why I would even think such a thing. Why would it mean anything to me?

'Maël spared no expense when it came to spoiling his entourage,' says the steward.

And I can see it in the list of gifts: gold, expensive silks, perfumes, spices, rings and silver chains.

'This is extraordinary,' I say.

'That is precisely what I thought,' says Philippe. 'Or, better yet, what he let slip. Maël continuously bought the trust and the allegiance of the people around him.'

'You seem to know an awful lot about Maël,' I say.

He shifts, his arm now pressing into mine. 'You seem to forget that he was my cousin.'

'I didn't think you were close.'

I reach out my hand and pluck the ledger from his hands. He offers it up with no resistance. I get comfortable in my chair, the book open in my lap.

'You could say we used to be close.' Philippe follows the movements of my fingers as I leaf through. As if he'll find some kind of answer there. 'What surprises me is that he kept such an accurate account of his expenses.'

The steward says, 'Duke Maël always liked to know how much he was owed.'

'Well, *that* is consistent with the impression I have of my cousin.'

Cousin. Cousins.

Philippe has two cousins, not one. I must tell Hugo about this ledger. Not only that all these people would certainly rush to Maël's side again if he reappeared, but these are people whom Hugo could buy, when it comes to it.

'Do you think they might attempt something?' asks Philippe, taking me completely by surprise.

The steward isn't surprised at all. 'This is something that, of course, we might have to take into account.'

'Who could rally them?' wonders Philippe.

There's a pit in my stomach. As long as my father was here, with the royal guard, no one would have dared challenge Philippe. But my father isn't here anymore, is he?

'Frankly?' says the steward. 'Whichever third cousin twice removed of Maël pays most.'

Philippe grips the armrests, idly moving his knees. 'I will need a small army.'

'First of all, you need to pay the guards. You can use Maël's personal pouch for that.'

'A few people I trust are arriving tomorrow,' says Philippe. 'From my farm.'

I think, *This man is cleverer than I thought.* Replacing Maël's people with others he can trust is exactly what he should do.

'But you might need to pay for a few mercenaries,' says the steward, 'before you form a guard of men-at-arms from the duchy. These things take time. And the same goes for Port Lang and Langville. Fort Cantor is nothing without its two cities.'

'I know,' says Philippe.

'You're very … prepared,' I say. I'm nothing if not shocked by his presence of mind and his spirit. He might be less skilled when it comes to his table manners, but he seems to understand perfectly well how a duchy works.

And Hugo couldn't have taught him all of this.

'Are you surprised? What did I tell you last night, Princess? A duchy is naught but a larger farm. Wherever we are, we're all just a bunch of thugs fighting for influence.'

Sabya's Morningstar. Last night, and what Hugo asked of me.

Philippe chuckles, then turns to the steward again. 'Can I afford the town guards in Langville?'

'Not for long, I'm sorry to say.'

'Humph,' says Philippe. 'And how do I find more gold? We've just agreed to reduce the taxes.'

I could tell him what the obvious answer would be. What so many have done, before him. Which is, marrying a girl with a nice fat dowry.

But I can't bring the words to pass these lips of mine.

TRAPPED

MAGALI

*S*ome days, I can't walk along a dark corridor without bumping into that awful cat. And when I need to find it, it's nowhere to be seen. I don't catch sight of that swishing tail until midday. I'm preparing Goderic's chambers—he is to come to Fort Cantor to spend the night while the King is touring the duchy.

'Hugo, come here, you wandering rascal,' I hiss at the cat.

It follows me into the chamber and takes in the perfectly made bed. 'I think you're becoming quite skilled at what you do.'

The irony isn't lost on me. 'We must all do things that we dislike, if it serves our purposes.' And anyway, I will not keep this form for much longer. In fact, it wouldn't be advisable, not with all the people who are asking more and more questions.

'I'm not commenting on the form you chose to take.'

I snort. My mother would be appalled if she knew. But fortunately, she never will. And I hope that Isabella will never find out, either.

'Hugo, I'm not here to listen to your snarky comments. The King will depart soon and so will the princess.'

'Philippe and Celine spoke yesterday with the steward in his chambers. Are matters not advancing quickly enough for your taste?'

'No, not by a long way.'

However, other matters are advancing too fast. The King has taken a liking to Philippe and is assisting him. Perhaps too much. Perhaps he thinks he will be a more manageable duke than Maël. And as much as I loathe it, I must see Philippe married to Celine. And soon.

'You suggest we handle it in some way?' The cat paces the chamber on the tips of its paws.

'Correct.'

'I've just spoken to her, two days ago. She needs some time to get used to the idea.'

That princess and her fancies. She's so weak. She doesn't have the strength to do what needs to be done.

'We don't have the luxury of that time,' I say.

Hugo fixes me with his cold glare, but I know he agrees. 'I might have an idea. Philippe and the steward are worried about Maël's minions, the ones that are still in Langville. They fear that they might foment unrest amongst the people.'

'Then help them cause it.'

'Humph,' says Hugo. 'I could find a form that could serve these … purposes.'

I picture the layout of the castle before my eyes, just like the lines in an open palm. I tell Hugo about supply carts, and the side entrance to the kitchen.

In the quiet chambers, we forge yet another plan. A diversion.

It irks Hugo to have to give his princess as a wife to another.

Good.

There aren't punishments cruel enough for what this man deserves.

But until I achieve what I want, I suppose I will have to be content with whatever allies I can find.

CELINE

On the third day when we're in charge of the castle, I offer to help Philippe put together an inventory of the kitchens, drafting plans for the meals in the following days, and he agrees with the look of a man who hadn't even realised how much he needs my help. I'm more than happy to saunter about the place and play Lady of the Castle.

I still have hope, I still search for the object, when no one is looking, and Hugo does the same. My father will return two days from now, and we are bound to leave the day after that.

And there is still the matter of bringing peace to the duchy, and perhaps finding Magali.

Time is running out, but I'm still not ready to do what Hugo asks of me. Giving my hand to Philippe ... it feels like parting for ever with the only bit of me I ever truly kept to myself.

The household, however, seems to have slipped effortlessly into a comfortable rhythm under its new master, but by evening, we receive tidings of stirrings in Langville. While the servants of Fort Cantor might be easily silenced, it isn't the same with the gossiping folk of the city. And it only takes a single spark to light a fire.

The atmosphere at dinner is quiet. A few of the local farmers are sitting at the table. While my father is gone to Port Lang, Count Goderic has ridden out personally to join us and is spending the night at the castle, with a small guard of his own. Somehow, instead of making me feel more settled, this disquiets me.

If Count Goderic thinks he needs to ride here himself, and bring his own guards…

'Have you had a pleasant time in Langly, Princess?' asks Count Goderic, patting his pointed salt-and-pepper beard.

'Of course,' I say, picking at a roasted leg of goose. 'Two days ago, I helped Philippe get to grips with the castle ledgers. It's been quite interesting.'

'Has it?' replies Count Goderic.

Philippe rips the flesh clear off a bone. 'Most interesting. If I hadn't seen it with my own eyes I'm not sure I'd have believed it. Duke Maël let the farmers starve so that he could gift expensive jewellery to his minions.'

I wince at Philippe's indelicacy. This isn't something that one says to a seigneur. Especially when Maël was his cousin.

He still is, I think. The mouse in the cage.

In spite of everything, I feel sorry for him. I gave him a few crumbs before I came down today. 'What would you like to eat, Maël?' I whispered. 'I wish there was a way you could tell me.' I touched the cage's door. I thought, what if I let him run around the room for a bit?

But who knew if there were holes in the walls he could crawl into? We cannot risk it, not when so much is at stake.

Not when agitators in Langville are stirring.

I looked around to see if there was any trace of Hugo.

But again, I haven't seen him all day.

'Do you disagree with me?' asks Philippe, raising his eyebrows.

I think, *He must have been looking closely, if he noticed that I don't agree with him.* I'm not sure how this makes me feel. We had been unexpectedly comfortable the past few days—Philippe makes a surprisingly pleasant sparring partner.

But tonight he says, 'Does the plight of farmers not affect you?'

So. The little lion has begun to grow teeth. 'No, I'm shocked at your bluntness when we have an honoured guest who has joined us.'

'I wish I could say I'm shocked,' says Count Goderic. I'm not sure if he refers to Philippe's coarse opinions or to Maël's husbandry.

But Count Goderic has always been sparse with his words. This is the sort of man who Philippe also needs to be, if he wants to keep his grip on the duchy.

At least, until Hugo replaces him.

A guard barges in. 'Riders approaching!' he cries.

There's a great deal of disquiet in the hall. Men jump to their feet.

'By Lucius' Flaming Finger!' curses Count Goderic. 'Close the gate!'

'To the battlements,' says Philippe.

Count Goderic nods.

Philippe is quickly at my side. He lays a hand on my shoulder, guiding me towards the stairs. 'You need to go to your chambers. I'll post a guard at the entrance to the tower.'

My eyes meet his. I know why he is worried. I remember what we spoke of two days ago, in the steward's room. 'I will do no such thing,' I say. 'I want to see for myself.'

Philippe opens his mouth, as if to say something, then shakes his head. His hand drops to my waist, twisting me gently towards the door. I feel the restrained strength of his arms. The warmth of his body, covering half of mine.

My heart starts thumping in my chest. We're coming closer and closer, it seems.

He says, 'You need to go. It will be safer.'

If only he knew. If only he knew what I could do with my water magic even five years ago, how I could have faced a small army by myself.

Well, at least if I was close to a river.

'Princess,' says Count Goderic. 'It might be wiser to do as the duke says.'

Wiser, indeed. There's nothing I can do for them here, today. But I wonder, if Magali were here, would she hide? I think she would not.

There's something pleading in Philippe's eyes and I can't stand to see it anymore. I turn my head away and free myself from his grip. He calls to the two guards at the doors. 'Please guide the princess to her chambers. See that she's safe.'

MAGALI

In the afternoon, I speak to the steward and tell him I've had news of a death in the family and that I have to leave. This is the last time he will see the chambermaid, but he doesn't know that yet. I gather my belongings in a patched satchel, along with the new clothes I'll need as of tonight, and beg a ride in an empty wine cart that's returning to Langville.

I will be just in time to join the others who have come from the farm to Philippe's aid. In my clean but old chemise with the scrubbed apron, I look the part of the girl that I'm meant to play from this day forward.

When, I wonder, will the day come when I'll be able to slip into my own skin, to put on my own clothes? They must be gathering dust and moths at the bottom of the trunks in my chambers, but after tonight, I shall have opportunity enough to see about their state.

The men have travelled from afar and they are dusty. Their

mounts—strong carthorses—are not fit for travelling distances at great speed. 'How is the duke faring?' asks one of the boys with a smile. He is one of the most reliable farmhands that Philippe has worked with.

I pull a face. 'I couldn't say. So far, Philippe has only asked me to take care of some business in Langville.'

'I hope he isn't too high and mighty now to share a jug of ale with us,' says one of the older men.

'I think not,' I say. 'You all know Philippe.' My heart aches when I think of how he is struggling with the task that has been set for him. But we must learn to rise if we want to climb to the peak of a mountain.

I stop by the farmhand and signal to him to get down from his horse. 'You can ride double with one of the others.'

He pulls a face. 'Why don't you ride double with me, Aurelie?'

'She's too high and mighty now,' roars the older man.

'Get down,' I tell the boy with a wink and he finally complies. I take the reins and settle into the saddle. 'I'll show you the way,' I say. 'And we should make haste. Langville is stirring.'

CELINE

I walk from bed to window, from window to cage and back, like a trapped lioness. I have only faint noises to tell me the story of what might be happening outside. The great iron gate is dragged shut. There are the shouts as men give orders. I hear the clank of boots on the battlements across the Grand Bailey. I wager the view is far more revealing from Magali's former chambers.

I make a note to take possession of them as soon as I'm the lady of the house. But that can only happen as soon as I'm married to Philippe, and if Maël's close circle finds him…

I sit down on the bed, take a deep breath. I don't want

Philippe harmed. No, we are partners, we are allies. We have shown well enough these past few days that we can work together. And without Philippe here, now, there is no future for me and Hugo.

I lean against the carved headboard of the bed, trying to shut out the sounds. I tell myself my favourite story.

The story of how the princess came to hope in droves again, after five years of hope in small increments.

Hope fed by peacock feathers on her pillows, the only sign of life, until a few weeks ago, when a beautiful blue-grey cat was waiting for her on those pillows.

A cat who told the princess his story, until the princess started crying, and more. And after her tears had dried, they left behind a large seed of hope.

The cat told the princess about a cunning woman who would have done anything to cling to the duchy she thought belonged to her, even using the foulest of spells, forbidden magic. He told about the help that woman had from a seigneur, his fief at the edge of that duchy. He told her the long and short of it, and he told her that now that the spell was waning, there was hope for them.

He told the princess that he had a plan.

If only she still loved him, if only she would listen.

Footsteps resound in the corridor. I jump up from the bed just as the door is opened and Philippe comes into my chambers.

My heart almost leaps out of my chest.

He's followed into the room by a tall, stout girl with a wide, pleasant face.

'Celine,' he says. There's so much joy on his face. 'No need to worry. Reinforcements have arrived from the farm. And I wanted to … well… You still don't have a maid with you, so I was wondering if you'd like Aurelie to take care of your … whatever princesses need assistance with? As long as you're here. She's very skilled with braids, I'm told.' He ruffles his hair, visibly uncomfortable.

The girl lowers her eyelids but I can feel that she's observing me. There's a great bond of intimacy between a lady and her chambermaid. He wouldn't know anything about this, or how important it is that I can trust someone in this position. How much my chambermaid would be privy to the most intimate details.

And yet … I'm so relieved, and the gesture is so kind, that I can't refuse him. 'That's so thoughtful of you,' I say. 'I'd be delighted.'

He nods, obviously pleased. 'You'll like her, you'll see. Would you like to come down, then, to meet the rest of my … retinue?'

I take his arm for the descent, keeping him at a distance with my elbow. Aurelie is trailing behind us—I feel her gaze at my back. It won't be for long, I tell myself. When things are settled and my maid recovers, I'll fetch her from the Royal Palace. And I'll find a way to seek alternative employment for Aurelie without offending Philippe.

As we return to the Great Hall, I search in vain for a following of knights and soldiers. At the lower tables I can see only farmers. Philippe leads me straight to them and introduces them by name, as they rise to their feet and bow or curtsy.

'Delighted,' I say, over and over and over again, but I'm certainly not.

If Philippe wants to keep the ducal seat, he'll need more than a handful of labourers to defend a castle.

Hugo would know all this.

And, perhaps, after everything we've spoken about over the last few days, I can give Philippe credit that he knows this, too. That he only needs time to get the matters settled.

He is not so bad, as partners might go.

We go back to our places at the ducal table, picking up the dinner from where we left it before news of the threat came. What would we have done, I wonder, if Maël's thugs had indeed come to the gates of Fort Cantor? How could we possibly have defended ourselves? With pitchforks?

I sip, sip, sip from my wine, the hunger all gone from my belly. How easily Philippe's position can be toppled by a gust of wind.

I glance towards him. We need to be stronger, though I'm not sure there even is a 'we'. Or what that entails.

MAGALI

Let me tell you how it was.

Isabella had come on one of her rare visits to Castle Bencifert and the two of us were conferring in one of the damp chambers on the first floor. Below us, in the inner bailey, the children were playing battle, their shouts and cries travelling to us through the open window.

Maël, now almost ten years of age, was on the same side with Philippe, as always, fighting against Philippe's older half-brothers. What they both lacked in size—though Maël not so much so—they made up in terms of sheer will.

'Seven years,' I told Isabella. 'It's been seven years.' Since I gathered my skirts around myself and fled. Since Kylian had set up court in *my* castle. Since Kylian had taken it upon himself to rule what was mine, by marriage and birthright. 'I think this is quite enough.'

'Is it?' said Isabella.

'I am waning here,' I told her. 'I cannot live like this anymore.'

'One would not think that, looking at you,' she said, as blunt as always. 'Does *he* believe that you are waning? Did you tell *him* so?'

Julien Bencifert. Oh, Julien Bencifert and the endless complications around him. Which I had not expected when we had first come to this place.

Nonetheless, I gave her a sharp look. 'It is time to claim what is ours. What is his,' I said, tilting my chin towards the courtyard.

Isabella knew I meant Maël. 'But he is so young.'

'He is also ready for the task we have set ourselves. He must be.'

'Did you think about the sacrifice others will have to make? Did you think what it would mean for—'

'I will take steps,' I said. 'I will care for Philippe's safety. He will lack nothing.'

'I disagree.' Isabella's tone softened. 'What he will lack, no one will be able to make up for.'

In spite of myself, my eyes were stinging. In spite of myself, my chest tightened. 'He has his father. You understand, Isabella, that we cannot live like this for ever. It's as good as having a target on our backs. It will not be long until Kylian will turn his attention to us. If I want us all to survive, I must strike first. For us. For the children.'

Isabella hid her hands in her heavy cloak, musing. 'I would like to tell you how I disagree, but just as you'd stop at nothing for Maël, Hugo's mother would stop at nothing for her son. What an unfortunate tangle. I wish I had more wisdom all those years ago, when I agreed to the twins' marriages.'

I smiled at this. 'You would not receive me into the family, if you were to do it all again, Isabella?'

She pursed her lips. 'You know very well what I mean. As things turned out … it has been a recipe for disaster.' She sighed. 'The Fallen Court will not like this.'

'The Fallen Court may shove their dislike up their arses. And I doubt they'll interfere.'

Isabella chuckled. 'I think you might be right. Well, then, I suppose we're getting ready for battle.'

'Yes,' I said. 'Yes. Ready for battle.'

CELINE

The hour is late, and that applies to a number of things in my life.

'You are quiet, Princess,' says Count Goderic. 'Is anything the matter? Were you frightened?'

Philippe also turns to watch me. 'I didn't think you could be so easily scared.'

'No, I wasn't frightened, but I think that, were it a real menace at your gates, we would be in deep, deep trouble by now. You must do more to defend the castle.'

'At first light tomorrow,' says Philippe, 'Count Goderic rides to Port Lang to gather a handful of mercenaries.'

'And until then? My father doesn't return tomorrow. What will happen to us if Maël's men stir up trouble?'

'I've sent for more men-at-arms, Princess,' says Count Goderic. 'To man the walls until I return.'

'But I appreciate the concern,' says Philippe, arching his eyebrows. He's surprised. Maybe a little amused. 'I didn't know that such matters are so close to your heart.'

If he only knew.

As the evening draws to a close, I take another sip of wine. It has already made its way out of my belly and into my feet and head. I hear the chatter of the people in the Hall as if through water.

And time is running away from me. I seem to have spilled it, toppled over by a careless move, as if it were no more than my goblet of wine.

114

I have failed at finding the object. And Hugo wants me to stay, anyway. With Philippe.

I feel a touch on my wrist. It's warm and steadying. Philippe leans in towards me. 'Princess, are you quite all right?' he asks. A dark lock falls onto his forehead. I stifle the impulse to brush it away with my hand.

'I think I'll retire to my chambers. I feel suddenly rather tired.'

Philippe nods and gets up from his chair. I mean to tell him that I wasn't asking for him to accompany me, but he's already following me as I step down from the dais. And so is Count Goderic.

Suddenly there is a cry from the corridor. Before I realise what's happening, there's the stamp of feet and more than a dozen men march into the room, men wearing hoods and helms. Men in chainmail, men with their daggers drawn, herding in a few frightened guards and the scullery maid.

Philippe takes them in with a cold gaze as they create a half-circle around us. 'What is the meaning of this?' His fists open and close.

'We heard you were here,' says one of the men, a tall one with a dark red cloak. He's in the second row.

'And? You came to pay your respects to the new duke?' demands Count Goderic. His eyes are alert, going from the band of thugs to the wide-eyed farm boys on the side benches. Calculating, probably. Seeing how the odds can't possibly be on our side.

'Count Goderic,' says the man, who is probably their leader. 'I wasn't expecting to see you. We come to ask Messere Philippe to wait for Duke Maël to return before he lays claim to the duchy.'

'Sadly, Duke Maël is dead,' I say, finding my voice. 'My father, the king, declared him dead.'

'But there's no body, is there? He might yet live, for all we know.'

'I dread to think where that body may be,' says Count Goderic, 'and in what condition, based on the witnesses' account. But, in your own way, you are right. We have no solid proof of Duke Maël's death.'

I shudder and shiver. Count Goderic tilts, tilts, tilts, never revealing which side he is on.

And they want to harm him. They want to harm Philippe. I watch him from the corner of my eye, his spine stiff, taking them in wearily. These are men who wouldn't flinch to drive a knife through his belly.

Blood drains from my face just to think of it.

I can't let that happen.

'Princess, how unexpected,' says the leader, turning to me again, as if my presence here has just sunk in. 'I thought you were travelling with your father.'

Philippe shifts, moving closer to me, as if looking to protect me. How silly. He's the one who needs a shield.

'I've taken quite a liking to Fort Cantor,' I say. 'And its people.' I hold the thug captain's gaze.

Because suddenly I understand something. There is a reason why the man addresses me. If there is anyone in this room who can shield Philippe and his farmers, it is me.

Only me.

'May I ask who invited you inside at this hour?' says Count Goderic. 'As far as I'm aware, the main gate is closed for the night.'

'Oh, we didn't need the main gate. There's a special little entrance to the side.'

Ah, I think. They must have come in through the delivery

door that faces the kitchens. This explains the presence of the scullery maid.

Perhaps it was pure accident that it hadn't been barricaded.

Then again, perhaps not.

'We don't want to be a bother,' continues the leader. 'Our business is with Messere Philippe and Messere Philippe only.'

The men inch forward, encircling him.

'I think the correct way to address him would be Duke Philippe, and not Messere, Captain.'

'Princess, if you'd step aside. You too, Count Goderic,' says the leader, the thugs already stepping in to cut him off from us. His eyes flash at me and I see that they're the coldest blue.

He motions to the others, and they come even closer to Philippe. They are almost touching him.

And those daggers…

My breath catches. My chest is too tight, far too tight for air.

I am the master of myself. I am the master of my own power.

Think fast. Land on your feet. Like a cat.

I can't let them harm him. Hugo's plans and mine aside, Philippe doesn't deserve this. He doesn't deserve what these thugs have in store for him. If Philippe is here today, in this Great Hall, facing this threat, it's partly my fault.

If something happens to him, I'll never be able to forgive myself.

No, I don't want him injured, or worse.

'Yes, they have nothing to do with this,' says Philippe. He stretches out his arm, pushing me aside, towards Count Goderic.

To get *me* out of harm's way.

My hand darts out, catching his. I wrap my fingers tightly around it, and I pull myself closer to him again.

I am the one shielding him now. There is only one sort of

power that I have left: my name. 'Are you implying that you have a quarrel with my husband-to-be?'

Philippe blinks fast, then snaps his head to mine. His lips part and I squeeze his hand hard, willing him to keep quiet. To just shut up and follow my lead.

I try to remember the way the power used to crash inside me. The way it could have concentrated the waters of a river into a single devastating wave that could have swept away an entire settlement in the blink of an eye.

I ride the wave—I am the wave, and I will destroy anything in my path.

'I am Celine, daughter of your King. Touch either me or the duke, draw one single drop of blood, and there will never be a safe place for you in this kingdom for the rest of your lives. We will hunt you down and kill you.'

My wave crashes down on them and uncertainty starts to bleed into their eyes.

Count Goderic strokes his pointy beard, but doesn't utter a single word.

The thugs look to their leader.

''Tis true, then?' The captain directs his question to Philippe.

I squeeze his hand again, my eyes still on the thugs, focusing all the unleashed power of that wave towards them.

I feel Philippe hesitating, and then he says, 'Yes, it is. I am to marry the princess.'

THOSE WHO ARE PREPARED

CELINE

*L*ater, after the thugs have cleared out of the Great Hall and the kitchen door has been safely barricaded, Philippe accompanies me to my chambers.

'Could I come in?' he asks. 'Just for a moment.'

The wine has cleared from my head—the events of this evening have seen to that. As I close the door behind Philippe and take a seat in the armchair by the window, I can look with unclouded eyes at the situation in which we find ourselves. I have taken that step, crossed that chasm and made it to the other side. And because it had to happen so fast, I forgot to be afraid. And I'm not afraid, not even now. Things are just what they are meant to be.

All I can feel is a tide of relief. Hugo's plan and mine is on the course we have set.

The only thing that remotely disquiets me is the way Philippe stares at the tip of the silk slipper that emerges from under the hem of my dress. As if he can't quite face me.

'Yes?' I say, placing my hands in my lap.

For a moment, I wonder what he makes of all of this. If this is what he wanted, too.

'About what happened earlier … thank you.' He drives his hand through his hair, ruffling it, then puffs his cheeks. 'No one has ever done such a thing for me.'

'I should think not. Or else you would have been a married man by now. Unless you already are and never told a soul about it.'

He blinks twice, then guffaws. 'No, not that I know of.'

He paces the room, clearing his throat. I shiver, thinking about what nearly happened in the Hall earlier. What could have happened, had I not stepped in. I'm not sure how I summoned the courage to do such a thing. Looking back, I'd be too ashamed to do it again. Years of manners and what is proper and what isn't have been drilled into me mercilessly.

What I did, it had nothing to do with all that. It was a surge of an animal instinct, like the surge I used to feel in my Gift when I felt happy or cornered.

I could not stand aside while Philippe tried to push me out of harm's way.

I wonder what this says about where we are now. I wonder what Hugo would say, if he saw the way I took Philippe's hand.

This was quite an unsettling evening, to say the least, and matters between Philippe and me aren't anywhere near settled.

'Could you please sit with me?' I say.

'Sure.' He slips down onto the edge of my bed. 'Well.'

'Well.'

A long, quiet moment passes between us.

What we say to each other tonight will change the course of my entire life. What I did in the hall, telling the world that we are to be married—it was a momentous decision. It is only starting to catch up with me.

I stare at my nails, watch him from the corner of my eye. How he laces his fingers, twisting them. He feels it, too, the weight of what I have just done.

But on the inside, I'm still. The wave has settled within itself. I'm not trying to extricate myself from this, and the realisation helps me breathe easier.

This gives me the courage to look into his face fully. Mothers of the Forests, when he's ruffled like he is now, he is so handsome. I suppose he'll cut quite a fine figure at my side, in the time when we'll be married, and this makes me terribly vain, but this is nothing I don't know already, which is that I'm a very, very vain person.

I smile inwardly. 'Quite the day, was it not? Besieged and betrothed in the course of a few hours.'

'Yes,' he says. 'I wanted... I'm not sure how to ... release you from your obligations.'

I sigh. He can't possibly mean this.

Can he? 'You want to break off our engagement?'

He gives me a piercing stare, so unsettling that I have to will myself not to look away. 'I can't quite tell if you're joking or not.'

'A betrothal is not a matter to be taken lightly. Do you take it lightly? The entire duchy will be speaking of it by first light tomorrow.'

'Yes,' he says. 'True. This is why it's essential to find an explanation—to stifle the rumours as soon as possible.'

It would be easy to slip out now. I could hold on to hope that Hugo and I will find the binding object.

But that wouldn't be the point, would it? Even if Hugo does turn up tomorrow, risen from the dead, wouldn't that put more dry twigs on the small fires that are burning around Maël's disappearance? Wouldn't people think that, just as Hugo has reappeared, Maël might do so, too?

Especially since the last duke is very much not-dead.

And I only have to think about tonight to realise what a scandal that would be, how ruffians like the ones that have just attacked us might turn up in droves.

No, we need to bring peace to the duchy. I wonder if Hugo dared suggest to Philippe that he should try to win my hand. As callous as it may sound, it would have been the clever thing to do.

I make a note to ask Hugo about this, when I see him. 'What do you think the rebels will do then, as soon as they realise that they've been cheated? Also, do you think you have enough men to repel them? I wager they can do more damage than they have shown us tonight, if they're given time to rally.'

'What do you suggest?' He's half smiling now. As if...

As if he were hopeful.

Something tightens in my chest. 'Really, Duke Philippe, is the prospect of a betrothal to me so terrifying?'

He smiles in such a way that his eyes light up. My cheeks grow warm, for some reason. 'Not at all, Princess. I can't imagine making a better match. There is none in the kingdom.'

'Then, why do you ask such a thing?' I almost laugh. This conversation is so absurd. And so much depends on it.

'I don't,' he says. 'But ... you rejected so many suitors, it seems unbelievable that you'd settle for me. I wanted to save you the trouble.'

I take in the room around me, the dusty draperies, the mouldy walls. 'I've always had a soft spot for Fort Cantor.'

'Fort Cantor? Is that all there is to it? You could have been the chatelaine of Fort Cantor a long time ago, if you'd wanted to.'

'Honestly, if you were a woman, would you choose to lie with Maël?'

Philippe snorts. 'Is this a compliment, then? That you find me more ... palatable than my cousin?'

He shifts his arms, setting his hands behind him on the bed. His powerful body is open. I wonder if he expects me to kiss him. I wonder if this is how things are done when a farm owner finds a girl he likes and asks her to marry him. This is certainly not how it's done between noblemen, but what we've done tonight is a far cry from how things would have gone if he had never lost his farm.

The farm that should have been bequeathed to him, according to his father's last will.

So much taken away from him, including this. I wonder if he had ever imagined this moment when he pledges himself to someone in marriage, and it is so far from what it should be.

It will be only for a while, I remind myself, and then I'll set him free.

But, perhaps, in exchange for taking this, too, I should take care of him. Be kind, kinder that I have been so far.

So I can give him this much—I say, 'I think we'll be just fine.'

Something shifts in his face, and he gets to his feet. 'Celine, I think we're fine already.'

MAGALI

I wait for Philippe in his chambers, which used to be Maël's until last week. He seems surprised to see me, even if this was what we had agreed upon—that I would covertly come to find him in Aurelie's form when he is settled.

He kisses me on my cheek. 'Dear aunt, I'm so pleased to finally see you. I take it that you have travelled well?'

'As well as the circumstances allow,' I say. He is bright, I see. Smiling. 'You have made good friends with the princess while I was gone, I gather.'

Just as I wanted. Just as I pushed him to. He needs the little brat, even if for a while.

To my undiluted horror, Philippe seems nervous. He chuckles, then ruffles his hair in that gesture that is only his. 'Who would have thought, Magali? Who would have thought?'

Well, I, for instance. I know what Hugo has told him, what Phillipe thinks he will come out with after all of this is done.

What he doesn't know is what Hugo and I are truly up to.

Something that would change the way things are done in this kingdom, from their very rotten foundations.

CELINE

My father returns the next morning, hastily called back from his visits to the seigneurs by the good news. We confer in my chambers—just the three of us.

'It is true, then?' my father asks, like everyone else.

Just like Hugo asked early this morning, when he hopped onto my bed to wake me. When he delivered congratulations on my betrothal, with more than a trace of irony.

As if I weren't doing this for us, in the end.

I asked him if he needed to be unnecessarily cruel about it, if that wasn't what he wanted. What we must do.

'I'm sorry, my dove,' he said, remorse dampening his voice. 'I can't help but be a bit jealous.'

I almost flinched at this. 'But you know that I love you more than anything or anyone in the world. Why would you be jealous?'

He lowered his head. 'I think the dolt might be falling in love with you a bit.'

By Sabya and her Morningstar. This turned out to be, well, an unnecessary complication. 'But did you suggest to him that he propose?'

'I reckon he has some strange ideas, in the end.'

That's quite a mild statement, knowing Philippe. 'What kind of ideas?' I asked, perhaps a bit sharply.

'He wanted a sign from you, I suppose.'

A sign. Well. If didn't show him clearly enough where I stand—

So when my father asks if the rumours are true, all I can do is nod.

Philippe raises his hands. 'Your Majesty, we might have discarded a certain ... etiquette. My apologies. We were in a fix last night. We had to reveal the news before we had your blessing.'

'I hope you don't mind,' I tell my father. 'It was the only way I could see out of that tight spot. Those ruffians didn't want to anger the King.'

'But the engagement still stands?' asks my father, rubbing his beard. I can tell he's nervous.

'Yes,' I say.

'Of course,' says Philippe at the same time.

My father looks from one to the other, taking us in. This is precisely what he wanted. Precisely what he wanted to hear when he returned to Fort Cantor, after having left me here. 'Well, then,' he says. 'The matter is settled.'

Wonderful. I have one more question. 'Should we fetch my little brother for the wedding, too?'

'No, I should think not.' My father rubs his beard. 'He is only five years of age. I don't see how the ... event should be in any way relevant to him.'

Of course it is relevant. My brother, the heir to this kingdom, should be present at my wedding.

Yet I understand what he implies. That my brother's health is fragile as it is. That he does not want to risk it, by compelling him to travel so far, making him attend a ceremony with so many people.

But isn't my poor brother half-forgotten most of the time, confined to his chambers at the Royal Palace? Even I, his sister, barely see him.

Enough has been said on all matters, then, so far. There is something I will *not* say to my father. I will certainly write to Anne-Mihielle, ask her to come, though the Mothers of the Forest know that I don't hold onto hope when it comes to seeing her at my wedding.

My wedding.

I get to my feet, hoping to evade further questions. If my father subjects me to close scrutiny, I'm not sure for how long I'll be able to keep up the lies. The deceit. He's wont to guess where this path I have set myself upon is leading.

Because my father is a man who understands other people. There was a reason I stayed out of his way for years. Why I chose a life in the shadows.

Because he knows which questions to ask.

'I will allow you to arrange the matter of the dowry between you,' I say. 'This is not a conversation fit for a woman's ears.'

'It's not?' says Philippe, caught off guard. There is much I have yet to teach him.

'No,' I say. 'And we wish to marry as soon as possible.'

'We do?' says Philippe. He cocks his head in amusement and surprise. I answer with a smile of my own.

'You do?' says my father.

'I see no reason why we should return to the Royal Palace,' I say. 'I think things could be arranged much more elegantly from here.'

'You wish to marry here?' says my father.

'Yes, why not? In a fortnight? Do you think that gives us

enough time? I wouldn't want to keep you away from your business in Lafala for too long, Father.'

My father scratches his head, which implies a level of confusion far beyond the usual scratching of his beard. 'But why the hurry?'

'Why waste time?'

'People will talk,' says my father.

Philippe ruffles his hair in that way of his again, which shows me that this isn't quite what he was expecting, either. But it stuns me, all the while, that he doesn't even try to dissuade me. I think about what Hugo said, that he might be sweet on me, and I feel a sudden urge to avert my eyes. He doesn't even try to oppose me, and as nice as it might feel to be able to hold the reins for once, what does this make me? It's as if I'm tricking him.

A day of reckoning will come, when we will lay bare our expectations, and I'm not sure how it will end.

Again, I'm taking something away from him.

'People will talk anyway,' says Philippe. 'Celine is right, let's be done with it.'

I think, *We are partners.*

I think, *Matters might have just become a little more complicated.*

MAGALI

I spend two days in the princess's service before I decide that I dislike her savagely. There is nothing in the castle she leaves untouched in preparation for her wedding. The first thing she does, out of funds that I doubt Philippe even knows exist—but oh, the woe of not being able to read Jacques' ledgers—is to hire half a dozen workers to erase all traces of the hearth in the Great Hall and replace it with a fireplace made of burnt bricks. Holes are being drilled in the thick walls for a chimney.

I trail after Celine during the day, doing her small errands.

I think I would have much rather mucked out the stables. One week before the wedding, while the banging and hammering still goes on, I have a question. Masonry dust flies all around us, crunching under our feet.

'Do you think it will be finished by the wedding?' I ask.

Celine crosses her arms, admiring her work. Bare walls, half-painted. A building site. And many people have to dine in this chaos every evening. 'Oh, it will,' she says. 'Can't you just see it? A large, modern fireplace. With an iron grate. I have studied them. They use the opposite wall to store the heat; this is why I've decided to place it there. And no more smoke. So thrilling, isn't it?'

She seems so proud of herself. So self-sufficient. And I can't say a single word to guide her. Nor to advise.

The day when I can finally slip back into my own skin can't come soon enough.

CELINE

This business of arranging the wedding certainly seems to take more time that I would have thought. I forsake completely looking for the object, but Hugo is away for varying lengths of time searching for it, and he assures me that marrying Philippe is the best thing I can do for us, anyway.

Nonetheless, I was the one who insisted on a short engagement, and the amount of work needed to arrange everything is staggering. Between sending out the invitations, drawing up the lists of guests and gathering all the supplies—we need to feed such a host of noble faces and their retinues for a few days—there is no time left for anything else.

My father seems not to notice that I avoid him, or perhaps he also has much to do, flattering and coaxing the noblemen, swaying them in Philippe's favour. Seigneurs of the Langly duchy come to feast in the Great Hall—the Goderic, Champy, Peneric provinces are well represented within our ranks. And the noblemen are hungry not just for the famed blueberry pie that the cooks at Fort Cantor prepare, but also to hear the details of my surprising betrothal. And to see the man who will finally bind me into marriage.

It's just that they're looking in the wrong direction. They stare at Philippe while Hugo stands on the table, entertaining those gathered with tales from Sabya's time.

It is this that we had agreed on: that Hugo should appear as a sort of court jester, allowing him to keep his eyes peeled, observing everything that's happening.

What a cruel joke for the love of my life, but if he can bear it, we will make it up to each other, for every single indignity we have had to suffer.

One evening, when Hugo is absent on one of his quests to discover the object that binds him, Philippe comes to my chambers. Aurelie, the girl whose services he kindly offered, is just about to undress me.

'May I speak with you?' asks Philippe.

So polite. I think he is indeed trying to rise to the challenges of his position.

I glance at my maid, considering whether I should tell her to leave the chambers. Then I remember the way he sat on the bed the last time we were in this room. How I was slightly tempted by him. 'If you don't mind, I'd prefer that we are not alone. There is too much talk as it is on the matter of our hasty marriage.'

Philippe closes the door softly behind him and strides into the room, stopping at a chair next to the fireplace. 'As you wish.' He fidgets with the pin securing his mantle.

'Are the agreements with the farmers coming along well?' I'm left to handle *all* the logistics of a hurried wedding, while he travels around the duchy and shakes hands with the farmers.

Partners, I remind myself.

The wedding might be a headache now, but it *is* vital to secure the allegiance of the common people by simply showing his face —they don't know him. They'd barely heard his name before that fateful day at the Mermaid's Lake.

'As well as can be expected,' he says. 'The people are … suspicious of the duke and his family. And fearful.' He shakes his head. 'I'm afraid that my loyalty and my affection to Maël are being tested.'

Behind me, Aurelie undoes my hair and begins to brush it. Long, wavy strands fall down my back.

I pull together everything I remember about Philippe's childhood. 'You grew up together, didn't you?'

He shudders, looking at a point behind me. I turn around to see what he's staring at, but there's nothing there except Aurelie and a wall. 'We grew up at the castle together, yes. When Maël and Magali left the Bencifert lands, I was sent to the farm.'

I think, *When Magali and Maël left, the Siege of the Twins took place.*

But I say nothing because it's my turn to avoid his gaze. The farm had been his home, for almost all his life. And in a single blow, when Julien Bencifert expired a few weeks ago, he found himself without a father and without a home.

'I'm sorry,' I say, so softly that I'm not sure he hears.

Philippe has a faraway gaze.

I can't bear to look at him now. 'Did you mean to tell me something?'

'Ah, yes.' Philippe shifts in his seat. 'I wanted to ask … you seem quite besotted with the cat.'

I shudder. Questions about Hugo, even before the wedding... I hope Philippe doesn't suspect what we have done. Even if it was for his own sake. Of sorts.

Aurelie pulls hard at a strand of my hair. I wince. 'That hurt.' She isn't much of a chambermaid when it comes to styling my hair, but she doesn't ask many questions. If Philippe sent her to my chambers so she can spy for him, she isn't much of a spy, either.

'Celine?' says Philippe. I notice how he always lowers his tone when he says my name. How the first letters roll off his tongue. My cheeks feel warm. It must be the fire, blazing too high.

'Don't feed the fire when you leave, Aurelie,' I say.

'You want me to leave, Your Highness?'

'Oh, no, that would be terribly improper.' I glance at Philippe from the corner of my eye, hoping he'll take the hint.

'I'll leave right away,' he says. 'I just wanted to ask about the cat.'

'What about the cat?'

'You like the cat.'

I make myself stare at my reflection in the small mirror in my palm. I notice that Aurelie watches me, as well, from underneath her lowered eyelids. I wonder how much she knows about the cat, since she lived on the farm, as well. Or in the castle. That part isn't clear to me.

'It's just a cat. I like its grey fur. It's so sweet with that red pouch it carries on its back.' I sound like a child, but with that sad gaze he threw me a few moments ago when he mentioned the farm, I must admit that the ground is slightly slipping from beneath my feet. 'Also, it tells these incredibly daft stories. And its fur is so grey that it's almost blue.'

Philippe exhales loudly. 'Yes, you mentioned the cat is grey.'

'Well, then, I suppose that's all there is to say.' I place my hands on the sleeves of my dress, trying to show him that I'd like to take it off. Soon.

Surprisingly, my betrothed takes the hint. 'If that's all there is to it.' He stands up, casting a large shadow on the floor in front of the fireplace. He bows clumsily and takes his leave. 'Good night then, Princess. Celine.'

There it is again, the way he says *Celine. Ssseline.*

Urgh.

Aurelie helps me slip out of my embroidered surcoat and tunic, and for a moment, as her fingers drag across my back, I imagine they are Philippe's. I shake my head, hard, hoping to escape these thoughts.

After helping me slide on a fresh chemise, Aurelie starts braiding my hair. She takes a long time and all I want is to get into bed. 'How long have you been a lady's maid, Aurelie?' I ask. She's not particularly skilled, nor swift at what she does.

'Not long,' she says.

'Ah, I can always tell when a maid is experienced in these matters. Though Duke Philippe says you assisted his mother at Castle Bencifert? Or at the farm?' I never seem to remember precisely where she was.

'Yes,' she says. 'Whenever Madame needed me.'

'But I would have thought she needed you a lot?' I remember what my father said about Isabella of Langly having been unwell and spending a lot of time at the farm. 'I have yet to meet my future mother-in-law. Did Philippe not send for her, when all of you came?' It's as though thoughts succeed themselves like a flock of starlings and fly out my mouth the second I think them.

She lowers her gaze, concentrating on my braids. I can tell this is an effort for her. 'Aurelie?'

'Yes, Your Highness?'

'Tell me, did my husband not send for his mother when you all came to Fort Cantor? The people from the farm?'

'That I could not tell you. I'm not privy to the duke's plans.'

What a peculiar girl, I think. She grew up on a farm, taking the odd jobs, as far as I can tell, and yet she chooses her words so carefully.

'But was his mother still at the farm when you left?' Then I realise that she must have lost her home the moment that Philippe did. 'Did she leave when Philippe lost the farm?'

Aurelie shifts behind me. 'No, the duke's mother wasn't at the farm when I left. The new tenants had already taken over. When Seigneur Bencifert expired, the farm was passed to his eldest son, Seigneur Louis, with the entire fief.'

'This is odd, though, isn't it? Isn't there any affection between the brothers? Why didn't Seigneur Louis allow Philippe to stay on at the farm, as his tenant?' This small fact seems to soothe me, to realise that I wasn't the only one who was unkind to Philippe. After all, his own brother could have chosen to allow him to stay on.

'That I cannot tell you, Your Highness.'

I hum, displeased. 'You certainly don't seem to know much, for someone who used to live there.'

'I'm sorry, Your Highness. Will you be needing anything else?'

I try to make my voice sound light. 'I thought you could help me know my future husband better, Aurelie. That's all. I'd like to find out more about his upbringing.'

'I'm afraid I'm not as close to the duke as I'd have liked.'

I think, *What a strange comment this is for someone to make*, but shrug it off. An odd girl, indeed, but in the midst of all this wedding madness, I have no time to look for someone more suitable to play the part.

'Very well, then,' I say. 'That will be all.'

A ROYAL WEDDING

MAGALI

'The girl asks too many questions,' I tell Philippe, the day before the wedding. 'Far too many.'

I catch him again in his own chambers, pouring himself some ale.

'Perhaps we should tell her who you really are, Magali,' says Philippe. 'I feel bad that we have to lie to her this way.'

'I think we should brush these outbursts of ... conscience aside,' I say. Philippe and his morality. I had forgotten how tiresome he can be at times. 'It would not be clever at this stage.'

'But perhaps if you show yourself at the wedding as Magali, you would be doing us all a favour? The seigneurs are starting to wonder where you are.'

'No,' I say. 'Out of the question.' I remember my agreement with Hugo. As long as Celine thinks that they're all looking for me, our plan stands. Then let it be this way. 'I'm as anxious as you imagine to leave Aurelie's form behind, but needs must. For now.'

CELINE

Hugo arrives in my chambers just as Aurelie sets a crown of flowers in my hair, the final detail before I am ready. I watch in the mirror as he jumps onto the bed and settles on a mountain of pillows, a flowing, distorted silhouette. A Hugo made of shadows.

'Thank you,' I tell Aurelie. 'You may go.'

My chambermaid curtsies, watching both me and the cat. 'Will you need anything else, Your Highness?'

I run my hands over the cloth of gold fabric of the dress, across the beads sewn in with gold thread. It is the most precious dress I own, fetched in a hurry from the Royal Palace. Now it will be my wedding dress.

'That will be all, thank you, Aurelie.' I prod at my hair. It isn't what I pictured it to be but there we are, another detail that is far from perfect on my wedding day.

Aurelie closes the door softly behind her. I stare at a patch of mould on the wall. I will have to take care of that. Soon.

'How do you find her?' says Hugo.

'Quiet,' I say. 'But I'm glad of it.' At least, she doesn't bother me much. She doesn't ask questions. Just watches. 'Do you think Philippe might have asked her to spy on me?'

'I would be wary, if I were you,' says Hugo.

I turn around to face him. 'This isn't how I imagined this day at all.'

Hugo leaps from the bed and pads over to me. 'Nor did I, my love, nor did I.'

'Don't,' I say. 'Please.' I can't bear to touch him today. I smooth down my dress again. 'Are there many people gathered below?'

'The Great Hall is full to bursting,' he says. 'Seigneurs have arrived from all across the kingdom. From Valmont, Langly,

135

Arnauld, the King's Fief. I think I even saw a few faces from the Blue Court.'

'I know. I had to arrange accommodation for all of them.' It wasn't easy, at such short notice. Some have to stay as far away as Castle Bencifert, which isn't even on our land. But at least putting together the wedding has provided some sort of distraction. 'I can't believe this.'

'Nor do they, love. They had to come from all across the kingdom to see it with their own eyes.'

'Don't be a pig,' I say.

'I'm not. I'm a cat.'

I smile. And then I don't. 'But the one person I didn't have to arrange accommodation for is my future mother-in-law. Don't you think that's strange?'

'Why don't you ask Philippe?'

'I did. He avoided giving me an answer.'

'I think he might be hurt, love.'

'You think?' I bunch the lace on my sleeve in a fist. 'You knew her. Didn't she live at Castle Bencifert while you were there? For five years? What happened? Where is Isabella?'

'I couldn't say, my dove,' says Hugo, sitting on his hind paws. 'I didn't see much of her. I assumed she spent more time on the farm.'

'But...' I pause to gather my fluttering thoughts. They're everywhere today. 'Where was she when Philippe was told that he had nothing left? That he had to leave his farm?' I thought about this last night, as I lay awake in the darkness. How can it be that a woman such as Isabella of Langly, a daughter and a sister of the duke, would see her son stripped of everything, and say nothing?

'Darling, you know what everyone says. Isabella has been unwell for a very long time.'

'I don't care what they say. I care what you have to say. I asked you.' I stare straight at Hugo.

I'm not so good at judging a cat, but I believe he softens his gaze. 'I'm sorry, love, it's hard for me to remember. Everything that happened before Seigneur Bencifert died... Well, I was a cat, remember? I looked like a cat. Thought like a cat. I can't remember much that's useful.'

Hugo is so sad that it breaks my heart. He told me about all this.

I pet his head and he turns it in my palm. Even after all the time we've had since he came back, it's odd to feel fur under my touch, and not the burn of his skin. 'I'm sorry,' I whisper.

'It's not your fault,' he says. 'But together, we can work for the future we want. And it starts today.'

'I know,' I say. I don't feel shy, like I thought I would. I'm not frightened. What I feel is ... determination. For too long have I wandered through the hallways of the Royal Palace. Alone. Waiting.

Today will be my first day as the duchess. And I can rule as I see fit—I can't imagine that Philippe will put up the sort of resistance that my father has. No, the battle will come from an entirely different quarter.

'It's not just Isabella that I worry about, though,' I say.

Hugo's eyes are still closed. 'Oh?'

'Magali,' I say. 'Do you think she might be waiting for the right moment to ruin all of this for us?' And what better moment is there than a wedding? 'Do you think she might spoil our day?'

Hugo dips his head. 'I think, even tonight, it will be a bit too late for her. She won't be able to do much harm.'

Indeed. After the wedding, Philippe's fate will be tied to mine. By sacred bonds.

I slide down onto the cold floor, cradling my knees with my arms. 'I don't know.'

'Don't tell me you're afraid of her,' says Hugo. 'Besides, that was what she wanted. To see Philippe in the ducal seat.'

Yes, but a Philippe she could control. After today, the tide will turn for ever. 'But when she sees that Philippe is my husband—'

'What will she do? Claim the ducal seat for herself?' says Hugo dryly.

That's impossible. Even for someone of Magali's reputation. And if she had wanted to do it, she could have done so a long, long time ago. When her son was young, her husband was presumed dead, and someone else was on the ducal seat: Hugo's father, Magali's brother-in-law.

Would that Frederic had never returned, as horrible as that may sound.

Then none of us would be standing here today.

Then things would have turned up quite differently, for all of us.

'We should go,' says Hugo. 'I'm sure they must be waiting for you.'

* * *

IF THE REALITY of marrying Philippe didn't strike me in my own chambers, it does when we're in the Great Hall, hand in hand, waiting to open the dance at the wedding feast. I don't know if it's because so many people are staring at us, or because the hall is so packed, with too small a space available for dancing, or if it's because Philippe and I are husband and wife after a ceremony that passed like a dream, but I can't breathe.

We were married before a raging fire, according to a custom dating back to Sabya's time. Many people in the kingdom have returned to worshipping the Mothers of the Forest, like they do in the Green Kingdom, and even more overtly in the past few years. Since the Crystal of Power was destroyed, fewer and fewer people have upheld the old traditions connected to our gods.

But we are mages.

We are royalty.

The old stories, the legends, they matter to us.

And when my father spoke the last words, binding Philippe and me together as husband and wife, the servants shuttered all the windows, letting darkness take over the Great Hall.

A single candle was lit in the hands of a woman with a hooded face. It does not matter if she is young or old, short or tall, among the rich or the poor of our kingdom.

All that matters is the voice.

And that voice filled the hall, above the hush of so many people who had gathered to listen to the ancient words, devoid now of meaning.

Her voice rose and fell, like a sword in battle. Like a screech, like a clash, like a call, and when it reached the end, the darkness flickered with the promise of light to fill it.

Even the night trembles before that voice, before that song.

Those last notes still resonate in my bones as the servants let light fill the hall once again, the singers string their instruments, and Philippe's clammy hand grasps mine.

This is not how I had imagined this day to be because I'd been allowed to dream that I would have a choice. My mother, the most powerful woman in the kingdom at that time, had also chosen her husband.

But standing before me is not the man I chose.

The first merry sounds tremble in the air and Philippe stumbles through the steps that begin the dance. If Hugo were here, we would glide seamlessly across the floor, our bodies effortlessly responding to each other. Instead I am in the arms of my new husband while Hugo is nowhere to be seen.

Just for a while, I tell myself.

Just for a while.

The Hall isn't what I had imagined it to be either. I did as many repairs as I could, but the tapestry behind the dais is patched, most of the wall is still cracked, and it's so hot and stuffy that I can barely breathe. But the worst thing is that I orchestrated this tangled web.

But I wasn't on my own, I remind myself. It was me and Hugo. We did this together, and though the thought should warm me from the inside, it somehow does not. I can't help wondering if, in aiming to do something beautiful, to right the wrongs, we have done unspeakable things on our way.

We led my father on our journey across the kingdom; we got him to be precisely *where* we needed him. At Fort Cantor. And before that, I did something terrible. Something I shouldn't have done. Something that forever changed the life of the man I'm dancing with right now.

It wasn't an accident that Philippe was destitute when Maël vanished.

It was my hand that signed the papers, the forged papers, that left Philippe without the farm after his father died. Perhaps this is why I'm always so uneasy when I am with him. I can never forget what I have done.

My husband breathes hard and his eyebrows knit in concentration, as if he doesn't remember whether he has to spin me left or right. I look around at all the faces studying us. No sign of Hugo. No sign of Magali, either.

Nothing that gives me hope.

Philippe stumbles through a step, breathing hard. He is not enjoying a single moment of this. Not at all.

And *I* did this to him.

It was me.

He wasn't the one I wanted, but I did this.

And this is when my heart fills with something. I level my chest with his, feeling a trace of his heartbeat even through all the layers of cloth beneath us. We are closer than the dance should allow. I gaze up at him, willing him to look up from his feet and into my eyes.

He stiffens in my arms.

His eyes lock onto mine and there's so much wonder in them that, for a moment, I forget what I had meant to do.

He blinks.

I push harder against him, push with my whole body, leading the way.

And he follows me.

He follows me, step by step, spin by spin. Until we are both dizzy with it.

Until the others join us.

MAGALI

I watch the two of them, stumbling through their first dance. Philippe never learned the proper manners suited to a boy of his birth. More than once had Julien questioned my decision. And with Isabella gone, I have been left alone to fight this battle.

But I was adamant. The proper upbringing could not be put before Philippe's safety. And the way he was raised, I like to think it brought out the best in him. The very absence of his mother hardened him. I must only look at Maël to realise that, perhaps, it was better for Philippe to receive a different sort of education, without someone constantly fretting over him, smothering him.

At least, this is what I tell myself.

I can't help but notice the princess. That silly girl … the looks she gives him. She blushes like a maiden on her wedding night, but it has been a long time since she was a maiden in truth.

She doesn't even know what a good man Philippe is.

And when the King invites Countess Goderic to dance, my heart tightens in a fist. It is I who should have been his partner on this day. It is I who should have shone at the ducal table.

Needs must.

CELINE

The moment of truth comes when the wedding guests lead us to the duke's chambers, give us a good shove inside, and close the door behind us. We're left standing in the middle of the chamber, not quite sure what to do with ourselves. My heart is racing.

He stands, his eyes set on my face. His arms hang by his sides, as if he's waiting for a cue from me.

Something twists in my gut. I remember how, when it came to the matter of marriage, Hugo said that Philippe was waiting for a sign.

Hugo, I remind myself. I did this all for Hugo.

'Wine?' I ask, nodding towards the heavy table.

While he fills the goblets, I lean out of the window. The view of the valley is gorgeous from here. The farmhouses look as if they're made from gingerbread, the roofs glazed in the soft light of the moon. 'Nothing for me, thank you.'

Isn't it beautiful? he asked me once.

I tell myself, *He should be happy with what he has.* With what he received out of our understanding.

There's the clink of metal on wood, but I don't turn to look. I run my hands over the surface of the shutters. 'These need fixing.

'I'll draw up a list tomorrow of the most urgent repairs around the castle.'

He says nothing. There is only the sound his footsteps, softened by the carpet. And then, faster than I can begin to brace myself, before I can dissolve the knot tightening my throat, I feel his warmth beside me.

I can't look. I dare not look.

I remind myself to inhale and exhale, in that way we learned at the Golden Pavilion.

Then there's his breath in my hair and my heart starts drumming wildly. I move just a fraction, but it's enough for me to lean into him, into that strong chest, and his arms close around me.

And it feels so nice that I could cry.

'What's wrong? Are you scared? I would never hurt you, Celine.' *Sssseline.*

I turn my head and we're face to face. So, so close. There's so much tenderness in his gaze and it warps something in my chest.

I can't resist the sudden urge flowing through my blood, steeling me on the tip of my toes. Before I can stop myself, my lips brush against his. He answers my call right away, his lips opening, and it's as if not just my mouth but my entire body responds to him, as if I'm aware of every point where we touch.

I twist to face him better, a hand going up to his shoulder. His fingers draw a symphony of tingles in their wake on the back of my neck, and heat spreads across my entire body, concentrating between my legs.

When his tongue brushes my upper lip, I moan and he pulls me closer. I can feel his hardness pressing against me.

My intimate parts throb, tightening.

And I remember.

I remember where all of this will lead.

And I can't.

I break the kiss and take a step back, putting as much distance between us as I can. His face crumples, just as his hand reaches for me.

'I can't,' I whisper. 'I just can't.'

There's so much disappointment in his eyes that I can't bear to look. He lets his hand drop and takes a step back as well. I'm terrified he will ask why. What will I reply?

I can't tell him that I will, but on another day.

Never.

I should never.

I must think about Hugo.

So I must slice into him, deep and hard. Now. Right here. I must draw a line in the sand, define the borders of what we will and will not do in our marriage.

'Just because I married you, don't expect... I barely know you.'

'Then why did you agree to marry me at all?'

'To lend you a hand.'

His eyebrows shoot upwards. He clears his throat, the sound vibrating with his disappointment. 'I wasn't under that impression.'

'I saved you,' I remind him. 'Anyhow, you can take my dowry as a consolation, since you already seem to have so many plans for it.' He told me a few days ago how he intends to go to Port Lang and buy a new sort of plough that drives deeper furrows—or something of the sort.

'Why are you being so tart?' he says.

'You're the tart,' I say.

He winces, takes a few steps around the room, then ruffles his hair. 'Are you afraid? Is that it? Because I can—'

'I'm not a maiden anymore, thank you,' I say. 'And I'm certainly not afraid.'

Philippe takes a large gulp of his own wine and pours himself more. 'You're not a maiden anymore? Now, this is interesting. I had no idea.'

I am taking him apart, piece by piece. Ripping to shreds everything that he thought our married life would be.

And I hate myself for every moment of this. For putting him here, in this room, today.

But I must. So much is at stake. Everything I've ever dreamed of. 'There's plenty you don't know about me. And I about you.'

He has no inkling about Hugo and me, I remind myself. And it would be for the best if he doesn't find out.

'This is nothing at all like I'd imagined it to be, Celine.' Philippe stands in the frame of the open window, the light of the tallow candles playing on his face.

I grit my teeth. There was always going to be a price to pay, and I knew the day would come when I would have to do this. I just didn't expect it would hurt so much. 'Well, if it's any consolation, this isn't what I thought it would be, either.'

PART II

MARRIED LIFE

INQUIRIES

CELINE

*I*t's been a few weeks since our wedding and already Fort Cantor feels like home. After all, I've been imagining myself here, in this place, for five years. And Hugo accompanies me with every step when it comes to choosing the tapestries or changing the furnishings.

The best parts of my day are the moments when Hugo and I go to the upper rooms to look for hidden treasures—and, of course, the object that might return him to the body of the man I love. Even though I honestly doubt that Magali would have hidden anything in these spider-infested chambers, it's so joyful to see Hugo's eyes light up when he recognises a piece of furniture that his mother especially loved. Like when I reconditioned her escritoire and placed it in the library or exchanged my own bed for the intricately sculpted one that Kylian used in his time as a duke.

More than seven years had Kylian ruled from Fort Cantor, only to be unjustly removed from the seat. The order in which the twins came into the world had always been disputed. On that last day when I saw Hugo in his human form—his true form—he had taken it upon himself to set everything right at the trial in Lafala.

He was about to bring forth a witness who had been there, in the room, on the day the first duchess had given birth.

Bygones, I tell myself.

Wrongs that have been righted.

What matters now is the twinkle in Hugo's eyes when he sees his parents' furnishings now returned to their rightful places. How pleased he is.

As for Philippe, that's a different story. He might have won the farmers to his side, but the truth is that the farmers can be easily coaxed into submission—this was a lesson Maël learned early on. Not so much the seigneurs, or the other disruptive elements in the duchy's territory—like Maël's band of thugs, who are roaming around Langville causing trouble.

The last straw is the moment when Count Goderic arrives, accompanied by his third son. The son who has been so close to Maël. I'm supervising a few workers painting the walls in the Great Hall when they join me. 'Your Highness,' says Count Goderic. 'Apologies for the unexpected visit.'

'It's always a pleasure, Count Goderic,' I say, watching the famed third son, Fabien. He's tall and lean, like his father, with vivid eyes that take in everything that's happening.

He bows so low that I almost think he's mocking me. 'Lovely to see you settling in so well at the castle, Your Highness. This hall looks quite different from how I remember it. Is this … pink?'

'Lilac,' I say. 'Certainly more tasteful than chipped paint. Alas, there was only so much time before the wedding.'

'Surely this colour would be more appropriate for chambers where women gather in order to finish their embroideries, than for the kind of … feasts that used to take place here until recently,' he roars.

Count Goderic seems slightly uneasy at the comment.

'Oh, we're trying to turn the castle into a home after our own taste,' I say.

'I'm sure the dowry you brought is … helpful,' says Fabien.

'Oh?' I say. 'I doubt Maël was short of the means to do this. If I'm not mistaken, he simply chose to spend his budget differently.'

Fabien chuckles. 'I wasn't aware that the duchess was so spirited.' He has slippery eyes and also no shame. Quite a partner to Maël. Fate has been merciful, indeed, by not making this man Count Goderic's heir.

'We were, in fact, looking for your husband,' says Count Goderic, slicing through our conversation.

'He must be at the farm.'

Showing off the new equipment or discussing the deals or whatever he does. I do my best to stay out of his way. And even if he wanted to catch me in the early days, I put a stop to that. I told him that we inhabited different spheres in the castle.

It might seem unkind, but, on the whole, I think I'm doing him a favour by not allowing him to get the wrong ideas. He seemed put off for a while, but then I explained to him that, amongst the highest ranking people of our kingdom, this was what a successful marriage meant: the women minded their business inside the castle and the men minded the business of the lands.

'I'm not allowed to come inside the castle?' my husband said.

'No, of course not.'

He raised his eyebrow again in that infuriating way of his that always makes me think he's mocking me. 'I'm to sleep outside?'

'No, I meant of course, the castle is all yours.'

'Except for the times when you have business within the castle.'

'You have such a way of spinning what I say,' I told him.

'Every single day since we've married, you've made me feel like you've tricked me.'

I bristled at this. Because, of course, he was right. He's anything but the dolt that Hugo made him out to be.

But he will be rewarded, according to what he does for us. After all is said and done, Philippe will be able to continue at Fort Cantor as a steward.

I must admit I'm a bit sorry about Jacques, when he will have to leave his position, but Philippe excels at what he does. I like to think we work well together: me when it comes to the castle itself, and him when it comes to matters relating to the duchy's lands.

Honestly, we complete each other so well, I'm secretly thrilled that we'll go on to be partners, when all this is over.

I only wish I could make him understand that.

And not push for more. 'I promised you nothing,' I said. 'Except for my dowry. And that, you received.'

I discovered that when it comes to the wealth I brought into the marriage, Philippe withdraws and says nothing. Because, of course, he brought only himself into this agreement. Everything else has been done by Hugo, my father and me. So for now, I have managed to guide him into an uneasy distance.

But Fabien's presence here is nothing less than a threat. I send a guard to fetch my husband. 'Where should I look?' the guard asks me.

'Perhaps the farm outside the castle walls,' I say softly, so that the Goderics wouldn't hear me. 'Or better yet, ask the steward before you go.'

I turn with a pleasant smile towards my guests. 'Should I show you the changes we have brought to the castle, so far?'

I lead the most important seigneur of the duchy to the library first, where I've created a corner for writing letters under one of the windows. The books have been rearranged and I've moved the ones about magic higher up the shelves, where they won't be so visible.

'Impressive,' says Count Goderic.

'I've also ordered painted glass panels for these two walls,' I demonstrate. 'From glass artists in Port Lang. I've commissioned my husband with ordering them—I can't wait to be surprised.'

In fact, it was less a matter of trust and more one of refusing to travel with Philippe. Being cooped up in a carriage for hours with him, and then, perhaps, having to share a bed.

I wouldn't want to give him ideas, not when we're finally finding a comfortable balance.

'I haven't seen much of the library,' says Fabien. 'And I've been here quite often.'

'I don't think Maël saw much of the library, either,' I say.

'I think you might be surprised.'

I'm taken aback by this. 'I never thought him to be a man of letters.'

'Ah, yes, not that. But he was a man who liked to improve his craft.' Fabien examines the shelves that stand right across from the entrance. The ones where the books about shape-shifting and magical objects had stood. He gives me an odd look. 'Have you been rearranging?'

'I thought you never saw the library,' I say.

'I never said never.' He gives me a sly smile.

'Allow me to show you the sitting rooms,' I say, an odd feeling clinging to my shoulders. As if, through the sheer curtain of jokes, I'm being watched.

* * *

PHILIPPE CATCHES up with us as we prepare to sit down in the Great Hall. I had hoped to keep my guests busy with eating. My husband is in a pair of worn trousers—ducal-looking only in their embroidery, so at least there's that—and a shirt unlaced at the neck under a dusty mantle. His hair is ruffled and by the state of his nails I can tell he's been digging them in the earth again.

I'm livid.

This is no way to show himself when our most distinguished seigneur visits. And, most of all, not in front of someone who obviously came here to pry. He greets them rather coldly and takes his seat beside me.

'My apologies,' he says. 'I wasn't expecting you. I was speaking to the people on the farm; I'm implementing a new system of crop rotation.'

No, no, no, I think. You do not bore the seigneurs with such matters. This is for the stewards to take care of. I find it rather sweet that Philippe is concerned with the fate of our farms and farmers and that he is intent on increasing their harvests—which I have to agree is a very profitable business, in the long term—but this is definitely nothing to speak about with the man who commands the largest army in the duchy.

If Hugo were here, in his seat, he'd know what topics to converse with Count Goderic about, how to handle him.

'I think Count Goderic meant to discuss something specific with you,' I interrupt before Philippe launches into a detailed account of his plans for the crops. When he starts one of these conversations with the steward, I could lay my head on the table and fall asleep. But of course, I'm too polite to show any of that.

'Am I boring you again, Celine?' says Philippe, half-sharply, half-smiling. He bores his eyes into mine as if, should he try hard enough, he might be able to see inside my head.

He often gives me this sort of look. As if I'm something he has to untangle. 'I think my noble wife has heard about this too many times. We've spoken about it quite a bit in the steward's quarters.'

'In the steward's quarters? Well, isn't it very comforting that the princess is so committed to the matters of the duchy?' Yet again, I can't quite tell if Count Goderic is mocking me or if this is genuinely a compliment.

I decide to believe the latter. 'Thank you so much. I do my best for my people.'

'If you could please excuse me,' says Fabien, rising from the table, slowly. 'I need to visit—'

'Spare us the details, Fabien,' says Count Goderic.

I can tell now, at least, how he looks when he's irritated. How his eyes flash.

'Your Highness, there's a reason why I wanted to come to you today. Old friends of Maël have been gathering in Port Lang for the Spring Festival.'

'We know,' I say.

Count Goderic tilts his head. 'After they finally woke up from their drunken debaucheries, they started asking questions about Maël's whereabouts. This would normally be the time when they'd return to Fort Cantor to hunt and indulge in other sorts of entertainment.'

Philippe lowers his head. 'Do go on, please.'

'You can well imagine that they're a bit ... aimless now.'

'And penniless, I suppose,' I intervene.

Count Goderic turns to me, surprised.

'We've spoken to the steward,' I say, looking to Philippe. 'Many of them were paid directly by Maël. We assumed they might look for new employment.'

'We hoped so, at least,' says my husband.

'Well, your hopes weren't wrongly placed. Except that the timing isn't ideal,' says Count Goderic. 'They don't have anywhere to go. The waters are quiet in the kingdom and around it.'

'So they just dally in Port Lang?'

'Worse,' says Count Goderic. 'They seem to be trying to stir up trouble by themselves.'

Philippe rubs his chin. 'I can tell you this much: if I were an unemployed thug, that's what I'd do. Stir up trouble, cause strife, so I could create ... opportunities for myself.'

Count Goderic nods. 'That is right. But they're asking questions. Spreading rumours. About Maël's death and how uncanny it is.'

Then why did you bring Fabien here today? I want to ask.

And then I think, *where* is *Fabien?*

Out of the corner of my eye, I catch movement. Hugo is approaching us at a slow pace, jumps onto the table, and slides himself under my hand.

'How are you?' I coo.

Hugo climbs up onto my neck, nuzzling my ear.

'You're tickling me,' I whisper.

'What do you think we could do about them, Count Goderic?' says my husband.

He nudges me with his boot, as if commanding my attention. I scowl. *I know, I know. It's important.*

Hugo whispers, at the same time, covering the reply, 'You need to come. Fabien is asking around at the stables.'

I get up with the speed of a storm, almost dropping Hugo. 'If you'll please excuse me,' I say and hurry to the famed stables.

Fabien is inside, his hand on the shoulder of a stableboy, his head bent and whispering. I paste a smile onto my face, although it makes my cheeks ache. 'Messere Fabien, may I help you find your way back into the castle?'

He whips his head up, then grins when he sees me. 'Your Highness, I just wanted to see if you still had that white destrier. I need a good warhorse.'

'Do you now?' I say and wave the boy away. 'I'm afraid that particular horse perished with poor Maël.'

'Poor, indeed,' he says, still grinning at me. So much shame-lessness irritates me endlessly. That he should come into my house and trudge around, as if he has any right.

'I could ask the stableboy what you were really prying into. Or you could tell me yourself.'

He lifts his hands in the air. Hugo is at my foot, glued to my skirts. Watching.

'You caught me,' he says. 'I just wanted to speak to that groom who was there the day Maël disappeared.'

'Died, you mean.'

'As you wish.'

'I'm told he isn't here anymore.' In the whoosh of the wedding, and the events before and after it, I didn't spare many thoughts for the poor stableboy. And when I said I wanted to question him, Hugo told me he had gone to Port Lang. That he wanted to forget the horrible events of that day but he couldn't, because people were still assaulting him with questions. 'You might have better odds finding him elsewhere.' Where the bulk of your army of thugs are, I think.

'Hm. That's the problem. It seems he's nowhere to be found.'

I shrug. 'That is none of my business. He was free to do as he chose.'

'Odd though, isn't it, that the boy should disappear?' he says, searching my face.

'I wouldn't know,' I say.

'I think you know much more than you let on.' He crouches and stretches his hand towards Hugo. 'What do we have here?' he says. 'Is this the famous talking cat? Why don't you purr me a story?'

I pick Hugo up. 'You are mistaken. This is just my cat.'

'Very unusual eyes.'

'You seem to think that everything around Fort Cantor is unusual these days. Perhaps it has to do with the change in leadership?'

He laughs and rubs his belly. 'Could you please escort me to the Great Hall? I'm starving.'

MAGALI

Hugo approaches me while I'm bringing some of Celine's chemises to the laundress. I also take her sheets—not creased, not bothered by the writhing of two happily married people. And even though he busies himself from dusk until dawn, I can feel Philippe's quiet anger, his pain whenever he sits at the ducal table with Celine.

'We need to speak,' says Hugo.

'Fine,' I say, pulling him into my former chambers out of habit. Celine promises that she will exchange her quarters for those that were once mine, but she keeps deferring it. Good, very good. I can tell by the way she speaks of me, the way she says my name, Magali, that she fears me.

She has every reason to.

But Hugo seems impatient, his usual cool gone out the window, along with this heatwave. 'When do we start?' he says. 'It's time. It's time we set our plan in motion.'

He has told Philippe he would make him his steward. He has perhaps told Celine something that amounts to the same.

But to me, oh, he said something entirely different. Because he knew that I wouldn't want Philippe just a steward, he knew what I wanted for him.

Nothing less than the ducal seat.

The truth is that much blood will be spilled if we set our plan in motion, in the way we designed it.

The truth is that Philippe is already on the ducal seat. Not a single step we might take, starting from today, will benefit him in any other way.

Except, perhaps, to rid him of that bothersome princess. And the King… Everything he has ever worked for, it would crumble before his eyes.

Turned to dust.

Humph.

This is something worth considering.

Tilting, tilting. This side and that.

A dark web of secrets we know about each other is the only thing that keeps Hugo and me tied together. He is afraid I would tell the princess the truth about his *real* plan, and I'm afraid he will spill into the world the deepest, darkest secret I have, prised from me in his long years of wandering about Castle Bencifert.

Perhaps we shouldn't have kept him with us.

Perhaps things were always meant to be this way.

The truth is that going forward with that plan would mean letting go of that precise secret. And what would Hugo hold against me then?

The truth is that, in the pockets of my tunic, there is a certain phial.

The truth is that, should I use its contents to make away with Hugo, this would cost me my magical powers. No mage can kill another mage without losing their Gift.

I'm not sure if I'm ready to pay that price.

159

My Gift, it is the only thing I have always been able to rely on in my darkest hours. And there have been many of them.

The truth is, it might be time to let my Gift go, if I don't want to endanger everything we have achieved so far.

If I don't want Hugo to ruin it.

If I want him forever out of my way.

The truth is, if I lose my Gift, the curse I put around Hugo's mother will be gone, and the door to this kingdom will again be open to her.

And I'm not sure that we are ready.

We must be. We must. As far as she knows, her son has been gone for five years. Opening the door now to what Hugo means to achieve… It would reveal to the world that he was always here, hidden.

Tilting, tilting.

This way and that.

'Magali?' says Hugo. 'Are you listening to me?'

'Get on with it,' I say.

He bristles. 'Count Goderic's third son was here. Looking for the stableboy. Asking questions.'

Tilting. More towards one side.

It might be time.

'So?' I say, trying not to show how I might make up my mind, one way or the other.

'No matter,' says Hugo. 'It's enough. I've had enough of this fur and tail and paws. It's time.'

Oh, yes. It might be time.

I have had quite enough of him, myself.

But he doesn't have to know this.

'Yes, you might be right. It's time.'

'Good. I'm glad you agree.' Hugo seems soothed.

The fool.

But as he prepares to walk in the opposite direction, he stops in his tracks. 'Oh. One more thing. Philippe has been asking questions about Maël.'

Ah, Philippe, dear, silly boy. He shouldn't ask questions if he doesn't want to know the answers. Nonetheless, I inquire, 'And what did you tell him?'

'Nothing.' Hugo averts his eyes. 'Nothing at all.'

CELINE

After the two have left, Philippe takes me aside. 'Why did you leave me alone? Count Goderic thought you weren't interested in what he had to say. Celine, the matter with Maël's minions is serious.'

There is no warmth in his words. I have taken care of that, bit by bit. Perhaps too well.

No, there is certainly no warmth between us. 'I don't need you to berate me for my manners, thank you. I was looking after another serious matter. Fabien, one of the minions you mentioned, was poking around the stables, asking after the stableboy who was with Maël when he disappeared.'

Philippe takes a step back. 'This isn't good.'

'You think? And out of all his sons, Count Goderic chooses to bring *him* here today.'

'But he came here to warn us,' he says. 'He meant well.'

'Who knows what sort of games Count Goderic plays? When the matter of succession between Kylian and Frederic arose, he was the one who always came out unscathed. Who always knew how to choose the right side. Things with him are never simple.' My nerves are in turmoil from this day. I need some space. I need to be able to think clearly.

'I'll be in the garden if you need me,' I say. 'I want to ask Aurelie to read to me a bit.'

THE SMALLEST FUGITIVE

CELINE

*W*e sit in the small side garden, between the castle and the cliff. Aurelie reads aloud and her words melt in the whoosh of wind, in the clink of the brook flowing at our feet. I could never concentrate on poetry, anyway—my mind always wanders.

For instance, it fails to distract me from Fabien and my fears that he suspects something. That someone else knows what we know. About why he came here asking questions.

I shift on the bench, uneasy. We have made our bed and now we must lie in it. With or without the rats.

'Are you all right, Your Highness?' says Aurelie. 'You seem ... worried.'

I turn around and look into her wide, open face. I still haven't decided if she's Philippe's spy or not, but what could she tell Philippe about me? How I like to wear my hair?

I chew on my thoughts for a few more moments in silence. In the end, what could Maël's minions really do to us? Try to find and release the mouse if it comes to it? They'd have to get past the guards. And we have hired more men-at-arms since the wedding—it was one of the first things we did. Along with making sure the side entrance was always locked when we wanted it to be.

The only one who can truly harm us is Magali, I suppose. Whenever I think of her, a sense of unease grips my entire body. She is an uncanny sort of woman, and, oh, my, can she be uncomfortable.

And she thinks far too well of herself.

This warm, early summer light, the smell of salt in the air, it takes me back to a day like this, more than five years ago. I chanced upon my mother, her pregnancy already visible, and Magali, sitting in this very garden. A falcon, its eyes hooded, was perched on Magali's wrist. She was speaking in a low voice, and my mother's gaze was clouded, directed at the cliff.

I always loathed this sort of whispering between the two old friends and found it drove an even deeper wedge between my parents. I've never been close to my father—he'd always been too keen to replace me with a boy—but I always sensed a sort of tension between him and my mother whenever Magali was nearby.

My dear mother took such a liking to her. They'd been great friends ever since Magali had been her student at the Golden Pavilion.

But on that fateful morning Magali and my mother disagreed. I could feel it in the air. In the butterflies that were flying erratically like wounded birds, mismanaged illusions, children of a distracted mage.

'Have you had word on the matter from the Blue Kingdom?' said Magali as I arrived, then fell quiet, looking at me. 'Do you need anything, child?'

'I wanted to sit in the garden,' I said. My chambers were built directly into the cliff—only a narrow shaft allowed a little light inside. It was stifling. And I'd come from the Golden Pavilion to see my mother while she was visiting; I was tired of libraries.

My mother patted the bench where she was seated. 'Come to me.'

'Child,' said Magali.

'My name is Celine.' I was eighteen years of age, and she still treated me like a little girl.

Magali said, 'Do you know that the falcon, the hunting falcon, like this one here, is always female? The males, they're considered … lesser hunters. Do you find that hard to believe? I do not.'

'Magali,' said my mother. There was a sort of warning in her tone.

'I like to hunt with a good falcon,' said Magali, chuckling. Her eyes were directed at my mother while she spoke to me. 'Would you like to hear how they train a falcon, child?'

'No,' I said.

'They sew her eyes shut and tie her down. And then they starve her. For days on end. The falconer walks her around, and then he feeds her, and pets her, and walks her around and feeds her again. And when the falconer brings back some light into her life and begins releasing her, bit by bit, the falcon, she thinks the falconer is her friend.'

'Magali,' said my mother, raising her voice.

'But he is not, in truth,' said Magali. 'He is just her captor.'

My mother took my hand and stood, dragging me towards the side entrance to the castle. 'Celine, I'm hungry. Should we go to the kitchens and ask for something to nibble?'

How that scene haunted me in the months and years afterwards. What Magali said, it was like a bad omen. Like an ill-fated prophecy. How I chewed on what she said, over and over. I could never forget it.

That was the last time I saw my mother alive.

'Aurelie,' I say, 'did you know that the hunting falcon is always a female, never a male?'

Aurelie shuts the book. 'Why do you mention this, Your Highness?'

I think about trapping. How my brother's fate will never be decided by whom he chooses to marry—but that lies far, far away in the future. He is only five for now, and he is more the master of his own destiny than I am.

And yet my mother managed to be the master of her own fate, at the Golden Pavilion, but then she chose to relinquish her liberties. I think about keeping prisoners captive and sewing their eyes shut, and how when they fly, even on a leash, they would mistake it for freedom.

I say, 'I think I should visit the mews.'

'Are you interested in falcons, Your Highness?'

'No. I think we should release them.'

'I hardly think that you should do them a favour.' Aurelie winces. Quite odd.

'Is falconry a theme close to your heart, Aurelie?'

She puts the book aside and arranges her tunic, taking a few deep breaths. 'Some creatures … perhaps they don't belong back in the wild. Maybe they belong in cages.'

Cages. Creatures. Fabien.

Cold shudders run down my back.

I haven't checked on Maël since this morning. 'Aurelie, will you do something for me?'

'Of course.'

'Could you please go to my rooms and look after the mouse? I don't think I've fed it today.'

Aurelie straightens. 'I just saw to it before I came down.'

'Please,' I say. 'This is very important.'

She nods and steps quickly towards the side entrance. I leaf through the book, not seeing anything of the intricate illustrations, the wonderfully crafted handwriting. We should have asked someone to guard my door. But then, might that have drawn too much attention, perhaps?

I'll have to speak to Hugo later, when I find him. Ask him what he would do.

I stare up at the window to my bedchambers, waiting for a sign from Aurelie.

Waiting for a sign. It seems that is all we do these days. I'm tired of waiting. The matters of the duchy seem to be heading on a straight course, and yet Hugo and I haven't come very far with our searches for the binding object.

I honestly doubt that it is here, at all. If Magali had been at Fort Cantor, even briefly, to bind Maël to his shape as a mouse, then perhaps she took the object with her. Wherever she might be.

I think, *She can't harm us anymore.* Not like she could have, before I married Philippe.

Perhaps it's time to do more to find her, if she won't come to us.

Aurelie appears in the frame of the window. I breathe out. Yet she looks anything except reassuring. 'My lady, he is gone. By Lucius' Flaming Finger, the mouse is gone,' she cries.

MAGALI

We are wild with the search, Celine and I, and even Hugo has crawled out of the holes he hides in during the day and goes hunting for traces of Maël. Only Philippe isn't here, having returned to his farming activities long before we knew the mouse was gone.

The Mothers of the Forest have blessed us, in that sense. He doesn't know about Maël, what we did to him, and if he could see how frantically we are searching, perhaps he would have more questions for us.

Hugo examines the cage, then smells around it. 'Nothing,' he says. 'It's as if he vanished into thin air.'

I take a few steps and slam the door shut. Anger churns in my stomach in waves and I'm wild with it. And the fear. Not only of what Maël might do once released, but of what might have happened to him.

Who might have taken him.

And what they plan to do.

He was meant to be safe. Caged, but safe.

This is my punishment for plotting against my own son. My own flesh and blood. Everything I've ever done to protect him no longer matters. It turned around to bite me when he cast me away from my home, from the castle I secured for him. And when I try to make amends by supporting someone else because I realised that Maël was undeserving of all that I had bestowed on him, when I try to right all my wrongs, this is what happens.

He is gone.

I never wished Maël any ill. Never. Never. When all is said and done, I'm still his mother.

I storm in towards the cat. 'Did you take him, you scoundrel? You sewer cat? Is this another of your ploys?'

Hugo jumps and hisses, arching his back. 'Why would I do that, when we are so close? When it's all going so well?'

'Who took him, then?' Who would want to harm Maël?

Who knew he was a mouse?

Who needed him, as a guarantee to protect himself? The answer is right before my eyes.

Hugo.

'Let me tell you something. Until my son is found, until he reappears, there will be no moving forward with the plan.'

'But—'

'I don't want to hear it. Not a single word. And if I ever find out you had anything to do with this, believe me, as I stand here before you, I will twist your neck.'

CELINE

It's late in the evening and Hugo returns to my chambers from his hunt. He looks wild with surprise. 'I searched every nook and every corner and still no sign of him.'

I sit down on the bed, which we've yanked out into the middle of the chamber. We've searched every possible hole in the wall, pulled all the furniture apart, but the mouse seems to simply have disappeared.

'This isn't good,' I say.

'You think I don't realise that?' snaps Hugo.

'And we haven't got even an inch closer to finding the object that sets you free.' I nibble at a nail. 'Do you think Magali might be behind this?'

'I'm not sure,' says Hugo. 'I certainly wouldn't put anything past her.' He jumps onto my armchair, also pushed to the middle of the room. The cage stands empty on its high table.

'He could be anywhere by now,' I say. 'He's a mouse. And this castle is so vast. Not to mention that he might be well beyond its borders.'

'Someone must have taken him. Someone who could slip through the castle unobserved.'

'Isn't it somewhat of a coincidence that Fabien came here on the same day the mouse disappears?' He could have spoken to anyone. 'But how would he know about the mouse? Perhaps we should find that stableboy. To make sure that Maël's band of troublemakers don't find him first.'

If that happens... The Mothers of the Forest have mercy. Everything we have achieved so far would be blown to pieces.

'I wouldn't worry about the boy,' says Hugo.

'Why? He's the first person I'd worry about. Don't you realise? What if Maël's minions find him? Fabien was looking for him. The stableboy could start a riot. If he says anything... If they have Maël...'

'We don't know who has him, though. And the binding spells would have to be broken first.'

I bury my face in my hands. 'This is the last thing we need.'

'I agree, my love,' says Hugo. 'But what can we do? We'll just have to wait and see.'

For the first time since we found each other again, we fall asleep together, curled up in the bed. I'm too afraid to ask if this means that our future, the one we dreamed of, is again slipping away from us.

THE REVENGE OF THE SKIES

MAGALI

I seek out Isabella in the place where she's been hiding for years. Trust her to be happy in an empty place. Trust her to be happy with just a bunch of old books and scrolls for company.

But she is also happy to see me, even though she does not show it. A person would need to know her well to spot the signs of heightened emotions: the repeated tucking of her hands in the sleeves of her robe, the way she offers me the finest treats in the pantry. I settle for the vintage Arnauld wine she stores in the caves.

'Maël is gone,' I tell her.

'I've heard,' she says, the light on her face dimming. 'Our Marchionessa is mad with worry. She's been looking everywhere for him. She says, she can't believe he is dead.' Her gaze sharpens. 'Do you happen to know more about this?'

Then the Fallen Court doesn't suspect. For a moment, I thought they would have been the ones to have taken Maël.

Those who have protected him.

I can say many things about the Fallen Court, but I could never say that they don't look after their own.

I tell Isabella the bits of the truth that I can part with. 'I don't think he's dead, either. I would feel it. But this isn't the time to mourn. Langly is stirring. I need your help. They have to look up to their new duke. He needs to be their hero.'

Her expression tightens. 'You want me to do something for you.'

'Think of it as something that would benefit everyone, including the Fallen Court. The last thing they want would be more disruption in Langly right now, would they?'

Isabella seems to ponder.

We were the closest of hearts once, but time has mercilessly ripped into this, as it has into everything. That bond of trust between us has been frayed.

By my actions, perhaps.

But would I be wise, indeed, to lay my trust, as well, on someone of the Fallen Court? Isabella has cradled and locked enough secrets of my own.

She is still their guardian.

'Isabella—' I say, and I know that in my voice is what we used to be to each other, what we once were.

She looks away. 'Tell me what you need.'

CELINE

It's not enough that we're confronted with the matter of a missing mouse who is, in fact, the true Duke of Langly. In mid-June, the heat comes. And with it, the drought. Rumours spread in Langville like wildfire: that this is a punishment for what happened to the last duke.

As if they knew we had something to do with it.

I wander through the empty chambers of my castle, looking for somewhere I can cool down. But there is no place where I can hide from the heat.

Everything is stagnant: the very air around me; our searches for Maël and for the binding object. Hugo is flighty and in poor spirits, and I barely see him.

We have decided to look for Magali, to ferret her out from wherever she is hiding. I have had enough, and Hugo thought it a splendid idea. He left for Langville, and the Duke of Langly's residence there—one I have yet to see with my own eyes, such has been the state of the duchy—in order to seek traces of her.

I lift my heavy skirts above my ankles, sweat dripping down my back, tickling me. My tunic is stuck to my skin. It's ridiculous to have to wear so many layers of clothing, but with so many seigneurs and farmers coming into Fort Cantor to beg for water, it's impossible to change into something more comfortable.

I turn towards my old chambers, the ones nestled in the shadow of the cliff. The chambers that I occupy now, the ones that used to belong to Magali, are mercilessly scorched by the sun. And I can't stand its glare anymore.

There is no hiding from it except inside, no haven provided by clouds. The servants who can are hiding in the cellars.

The clear sky weighs on us, day after day.

As I prepare to open the door to my chambers, a scuttling noise in the corridor makes me turn. It's Aurelie, running after me, breathless. Her cheeks are a vivid pink with the heat and sweat gathers above her eyebrows.

'Your Highness, Seigneur Champy is waiting for you in the Great Hall.'

I snap out my fan but it doesn't help. It just shifts hot air from one side to the other.

'Where is my husband?' I say. 'Why isn't he here?'

Philippe and I have done well to manage this crisis, I believe. Until now. Until fate and weather began spinning well out of our control. We have divided our duties so we can cover all fronts: he is responsible for managing the farmers and the seigneurs, and I'm in charge of the household.

So my husband needs to be here, to handle this. There are limits to how much the seigneurs would listen to me, as a woman.

'Tell Seigneur Champy I'll come,' I say, and step into my chambers. I need a few moments for myself, a few moments of stillness. I didn't come all the way up here just to go back down.

My mind drifts towards Hugo, in Langville. Even if we find the binding object, it would mean no further steps towards Hugo claiming his place at the helm of the duchy—on top of the drought, a new pretender to the seat is the last thing Langly needs.

Greats herds of cattle and sheep are being driven across the plains towards Bencifert River at the border of the duchy. There are many among the beasts who would not survive the journey without water.

I would like some solace from Hugo, a haven from the quiet horrors encroaching upon us. A brush with his true form, if only for a while. If the duchy is thirsty, I am starved for affection. If Philippe's arms around my waist, the touch of his lips, had felt so good on the night of our wedding, how would it be to touch Hugo again? How would it feel?

I crave, yes, I crave, in *my* hour of need.

I have never lived through such days, and my exhaustion comes not only from the heat. It's finding ways to spare water. It's pacifying the high spirits, a pyre waiting for a spark.

Someone is telling the seigneurs and the farmers that we have water hidden in the cellars of Fort Cantor, which is absolutely absurd. Where would we keep it? But as more and more people come and ask the same, about the water that we have supposedly ferreted away, I'm starting to wonder if someone isn't keeping this rumour alive on purpose.

If someone isn't trying to turn the tide against us. Someone like Magali.

Of late, magic had been spoken of rather little in our kingdom. Even before the doyenne, Madame Hirondelle, reduced the Golden Pavilion to a pile of rubble, it had been decades since the mages were called by their Gift's name.

But if I remember correctly, there were rumours.

That Magali had been a Storm-Caller.

Perhaps it might be time to investigate in the library.

* * *

I BRUSH my hand across the spines of the books. They're dusty, except for the section about magic. I read the titles. *Secrets of Fire-Blazing. The Dangers of Water-Twirling. Storm-Calling – Consecrated Tricks.* And many more titles that include the word 'Shape-Shifting' than I'd ever care to read.

Hardly a surprise, considering so many members of the ducal family are Shape-Shifters. Frederic, Maël, Hugo.

I leaf through a set of books, filled with family trees and tales about ancestry. There is the Fire Line, said to be born of the union between Lucius, the Flaming One, and the Golden Mother, who had justly ruled upon our lands in Antiquity. Their descendants are the Valmonts, among other families, like the one that ruled our kingdom for almost six hundred years, before the crown passed to the Earl of the Edge. My great-great-great-grandfather.

The Shadow Line.

My eyes skim through long passages about the Confluence,

when a Valmont girl married a king descended from the Earls of the Edge. According to the book, two children resulted from this union: the powerful, just King Etienne and a frail sister, with 'failing wits.'

Someone has circled the girl's name and her description and written 'Ha!' beside the entry.

This isn't at all what I've heard. I turn the book, to realise that it had been written during Etienne's rule, shortly before the Year of the Red Maiden. Perhaps Etienne even commissioned it.

No wonder, then. This explains the gross exaggerations and inaccuracies.

I don't think I'll find answers here. I lay down the book, wondering what sort of magic Isabella possesses. What kind of Gift my husband would have inherited, if he'd had one at all.

I know for sure that Seigneur Bencifert was a Magic-Binder, a peculiar sort of Gift that relies on absences.

I wonder what Philippe and I would have been to each other if we had ever met at the Golden Pavilion. If he would still be here today, helping us. I wonder if having a Gift would have shaped him into someone different.

Having all that power, it can do something odd to a person.

I sigh, selecting a book about magical enhancers. The Crystal of Power was the mightiest of them all.

Let me tell you a story.

In ancient times, when the Romannhon still ruled an empire, the gods still walked the world. Some lived lives longer than most, and some did not, but they were honoured among our people as warchiefs and kings.

There were gods among the Romannhon who were more powerful and long-lived than all the others, and they grew old and cruel and bored and began tampering with powers even more ancient than they were, at the borders of the empire, in the regions that had once belonged to the Mothers of the Forest.

Once, the Red and Green and Blue Kingdoms were one, thrown under the Romannhon yoke, filled with people who bowed to the same gods and spoke the same language. They called themselves the People of the Forest—the Waldemannen.

It happened that the Romannhon awoke what should have never been awoken, in their unquenching thirst for power—the Dark Mother and her terrible Nightdragons, their wings dark as tar, breaths as foul as Death, falling upon Romannhon and Waldemannen alike.

The Mothers wept and sought for a champion. And that champion rose, in the shape of a young girl with a beautiful Gift, capable of weaving the light and shadows into weapons with the power of her song.

The world's first Light-Cantor.

Sabya was her name and, to this day, it is her that we honour most. Now, the story is long, and filled with twists and turns, and seems to focus—worryingly—on Sabya's involvements of a more romantic nature, but the long and short of it is that Sabya defeated the Dark Mother and created the Crystal of Power, hiding it deep in the heart of the Opal Mountain and raising the Golden Pavilion on top of it.

Scholars argue that this is why the mages of the Red Kingdom held on to their Gifts much longer than anyone else in the world, but I never had patience to look very much into the still-raging argument.

What I can tell you is that the world around us changed, slowly, and magic faded from it.

The people changed, too. The warchiefs of old became seigneurs—most of them. There are few to this day in the Red

Kingdom who do not have the Gift, but there are some, like the Goderics of Langly.

And the people began to resent them—us—for our Gifts. The noblemen, and the King. And in the Year of the Red Maiden, great rebellions shook our kingdom to the core. It was in defeating one of those rebellions, at the foot of the Opal Mountain, that the Lion rose as the Duke of Langly.

But the story has me in its clutches and it pulls me away from the point.

Which is this. The people feared, and the seigneurs began to fear, too. Since my grandfather's times, what had once been honoured and cherished began to be spoken of in hushed tones. We did not display our power anymore.

And slowly, we forgot what we could even do.

And yet, the people grumbled, of what is now considered unnatural. A quirk of nature.

We had already turned away from our magic, but there was one who sealed our fates. There was one by whose orders the Crystal of Power was destroyed, and our powers leaked, in a crushing blow.

That would be my father, the King.

* * *

AFTER I'VE HAD an embarrassing conversation with Seigneur Champy, doing my best to persuade him that we aren't hiding water from anyone, I turn the castle upside down looking for my husband. It's not enough that it's so searingly hot outside, now I'm burning on the inside, too.

Where. Is. My. Husband.

I ask every servant I can find. I go to the kitchens that are steaming hot with everything that's being cooked. Soups, stews, braised pork. Water clings to my skin, dripping down my body. 'Has anyone seen the duke?' I ask.

The footmen and the kitchen helpers shake their heads.

I raise my hands above the clamour of pans. 'No more cooked dishes at the ducal table until the drought passes.'

The head cook, a wiry woman with quick hands and deep wrinkles stares at me. 'Yes, Your Highness, but why?'

'We need to save the water,' I shout above the clatter. At this rate, we won't have enough water for us to drink in a few days, if the rain doesn't come.

I don't even want to consider when I last took a bath. 'So just cold meals for now. And bake bread, if you must. But I don't want to see anything more elaborate at my table.'

The head cook runs over to me and grasps my hands. She then gets hold of herself and curtsies. 'Yes, Your Highness, thank you, you are most kind.'

I am not, I think. I should have put a stop to this nonsense days ago. The kitchens use heaps and heaps of water and it's so hot in here that I wonder how people don't faint.

Maybe people do faint, and they just don't tell me. In any case, with the wells dredging up barely more than wet mud and even the spring at the side of the cliff having dried up, we literally have days until we run out of water.

I don't even want to think about the poor animals.

And then I realise, the animals. That is where my illustrious husband might be.

MAGALI

Let me tell you how it was.

After Frederic's return, we roamed the duchy faster than Kylian could catch our trail. The seigneurs started to revolt. It was my husband's birthright. His ducal seat. Kylian—and his wife —should have done well and made room for us, the rightful rulers. That was what they all said.

Especially that his wife should step aside.

Oh, the people of Langly, seigneurs and common folk, they did not like the changes she had brought about.

No, they would a thousand times rather have had me.

We rode, we rallied, we gathered.

At the gates of Fort Cantor.

We gathered, too, after a few weeks' siege. Me, Isabella and Goderic. As often since he had re-emerged, we told everyone that Frederic had been taken ill, confined to his own tent. So it had fallen to the three of us, as it would in the many glorious years when we ruled the duchy, to make the hard decisions.

'They can hold out for months, maybe years,' said Goderic. 'With all the supplies they have.'

Isabella nodded. 'My father built Fort Cantor so it could not be taken by storm.'

Yes, yes, the legendary first duke.

Murderer. Thief.

Carved himself a duchy from the ruins of the grand fiefs of Anselme. And that—

Isabella gave me a sideways glance.

I said, 'We could set it on fire. Smoke them out like rats.'

Goderic pinched his chin. 'It would send a message, and I'm not sure it would be the right one.'

'What kind of ruler sets fire to their own dominions, so that no one else could have them?' said Isabella. 'Is that who you wish to be?'

I tapped my fingers on the map between us. A woman or not, I wanted to be the kind of ruler who wasn't afraid to do what was necessary.

But no, fire was not the answer. I watched the frail brook that flowed at the foot of Fort Cantor. Its meandering course towards the river.

I thought, *If not fire, then water.*

Yes.

'No setting fire to anything then,' I said. 'But perhaps there are other ways.'

Isabella nodded. And understood.

And, on that day, Goderic did, too.

CELINE

Philippe isn't to be found at the stables, but a groom points me towards the farm, the one that is within immediate reach of the castle. He offers to prepare a carriage for me, but I ask him for a horse.

'Which one would you like?'

'Whichever can survive the journey,' I say.

The palfrey the stableboy brings me looks exhausted. And this is the horse which they say is in best shape. How easy it would be for Maël to knock us from the duchy right now if he came leading even a tiny band of misfits. It would be enough for him to say that we are guilty for what happened to him and that the drought is punishment for our deeds.

The people would eat us alive.

That's what I'd do. Spread the rumours. But this degree of calculation is beyond Maël.

Magali, however, is clever. I wouldn't put this past her.

My palfrey stumbles in the blistering heat.

Oh, the pains my husband puts me through.

But nothing is as bad as the scene I stumble upon at the farm.

A boy directs me to one of the cow barns. My eyes slowly grow accustomed to the darkness.

Five farm hands are gathered around a farmer who is kneeling with his back to me. In front of him, a cow lies on the ground, its eyes closed. The shirt is clinging to the man's back and his sleeves are rolled up. I notice those strong forearms, flexing, and the way he holds his broad shoulders.

I know it's Philippe. I just know.

The stench is so unbearable that I could gag, but I just open my fan, watching him.

'Duchess!' The farm hands bow low when they notice me.

'Duchess?' He turns, annoyance stamped in his tone. His hair falls in sweaty strands over his forehead, and the front of his shirt is stained. I can only hope none of our seigneurs has seen him in this state.

'Could everyone please leave the stable,' I say flatly. 'It's too hot. It can't be good for the ... cow.'

The men glance at each other, indecision rippling through them, but they start moving towards the door. I mutter a quiet *Thank you* that Philippe hasn't tried to stop them.

'What are you doing?' I hiss when they have all gone.

'I'm trying to save the cow,' he says.

I walk up to him. The stench of rancid piss and gone-off cheese is stifling. 'You should try to save the duchy,' I say. 'The seigneurs are furious. Someone has been telling them that we have stockpiled water at Fort Cantor and that we refuse to share it with them.'

'I think you can handle that better than I can. If you don't mind, I have to see to this cow. She's dying, in case you're too annoyed with me to notice.'

He lays his hand on the cow's body and closes his eyes. He

breathes deeply, in and out. The animal flutters its eyes, then closes them again.

'Do you even hear me? We have a colossal problem on our hands.' Especially since Maël has vanished.

'I know we have a problem on our hands, Celine, and it's not just at Fort Cantor. It's everywhere.' Anger creases his forehead. 'Now if you don't mind, I have things to do.'

I think about putting up a fight about what's more important: the cow or the fate of the duchy. I think about asking him what he is doing. Instead, for a reason I can't quite fathom, I kneel and touch the cow, as well. Philippe closes his eyes again and his breath slows down.

And then I feel it. This surge of raw magic going through the cow's hide, like a tide, flowing into my fingers. I snatch my hand away, as if it's burning.

It can't be. Animals don't have this sort of magic, not even talking ones.

But this is a feeling I'm familiar with.

A Shape-Shifter, keeping hold of a foreign skin.

'What is it?' asks Philippe, his eyes wide.

I jump to my feet.

'Philippe, I think you should step away from that cow.'

'Why?' he says.

I pull him up, tugging at his shirt. What if the cow is Maël? Or some other Shape-Shifter? They might be all around us, circling us. What if Maël had other shapeshifting minions who have infiltrated our castle?

Philippe gently unclaws my hand from his shirt. 'What is it with you?'

'You mustn't touch it,' I hiss. 'It's—' I'm frantic to find a good explanation so that he'll leave the cow alone, but I can't. 'The cow. It's magical.'

Philippe touches the back of his neck, and his shirt sleeve hitches even higher. Mothers of the Forest. The amount of sculpted flesh on his arms. 'Why do you say that?'

I shift uncomfortably. I have never talked about magic with Philippe, which is silly, considering both his parents had a Gift.

He scoffs then grabs my hand, wrapping it in his. The calluses on his fingers tickle my palm and I want to snatch it back. And then I feel the surge again. But it's stronger now, a prickling liquid fire burning through my veins, making my blood come alive.

I look to the hand, my tongue unable to form the words. And then I rip it free. 'Sabya's Morningstar! You have a Gift. Why didn't you say anything?'

A thousand thoughts fly through my mind. Why did I never see him at the Golden Pavilion? Why did he never say a word?

I wonder what he intends to do with the cow.

'What are you?' he says, trying to look unimpressed. But I can read interest in the way his eyes scan my face. He is trying to look into my head again.

'I used to be a Water-Twirler,' I mutter. 'You're a Growth-Mage. I can feel it.' There were Growth-Mages at the Golden Pavilion and this was what their magic always felt like. This tingle that made me feel like I could do anything.

'How can you tell?' he says.

I turn and swish away. 'Let's go outside.'

He grips my wrist, but gently. 'If you're water, then why don't you help me?' He points at the cow.

'I don't do that anymore.'

'What? Help?'

'Ha ha,' I say. 'No. I don't use my Gift.'

'Why?'

'You don't know how it is. If my father finds out—'

My father could feel me, I swear, even after I left the Golden Pavilion. He didn't like it when I used my magic in the Royal Palace. And after a while, after many confrontations, I gave up. There was no point in persisting. My powers were fading anyway, and there wasn't much good they could do.

'I don't see your father anywhere near us,' he says.

I shift uneasily. He still holds my hand. And then he starts sending that tingle up it. I snatch my wrist away. 'Stop it.'

'You don't like it?' he says.

I love it, but I can't tell him that. It makes me feel strong again. Powerful. Like I can do anything.

The words come unbidden. *I am the master of my own power.*

The waters within me stir and foam, begging to be released.

It's as if he can sniff it. 'Help me. Please. This cow, she's dying.'

'I can't,' I say.

'Show me what you can do.'

'I'm sorry,' I say, and prepare to flee.

'What about the seigneurs?' he says.

'I can handle the seigneurs.'

'You've changed your tune.' I can hear the suppressed laughter in his voice.

'I'm flexible,' I say. I stop in my tracks. In my ears purrs the flow of a river, rushing over rocks.

No, no, no. This is a catastrophe. I can't.

'By Lucius' Flaming Finger, you really are heartless,' he says. 'You can save her.'

'Lucius has nothing to do with this. I'll see you later at the castle,' I say.

'Do you really mean to say that you have the Gift to wield water and yet you haven't lifted a finger to help our people?'

It dawns on me as it dawns on him. I turn around. He stands with his legs spread wide and his arms crossed.

He is challenge itself.

'You don't know how it is. I'm useless,' I say.

After the Crystal of Power was destroyed, I had but a fraction of my magic left. I worked so hard for years and years to learn to channel it. To what end? Now I can do much less than I could when I was but a girl, starting to study at the Golden Pavilion.

'Show me.' He pauses. 'I only need a fistful of water for the cow. Can you conjure it?'

'I can't make water out of thin air,' I say. 'I'm not sure what you know about water magic, but that's not how it works.'

'Then call it,' he says. 'Make it come to you.'

We lock gazes for a long, long time. A thousand thoughts go through my head, but I can't grasp a single one.

'What's the harm in it?' he says.

Indeed. What would be the harm in it?

I have been trying so hard, for such a long time, to draw as little attention to myself as possible, that I gave up attempting to channel my Gift.

I walk back over to the cow and crouch beside it. My dress will be soaked and dirty, but what does it matter now? I put my hands to the floor and try to concentrate on the tiny beads of water in this room, in the air, try to draw them to my own hands. At first, nothing happens. I hear the flies buzzing and Philippe's strained breaths behind me.

'I can't,' I say, tears in my eyes. 'It's been so long … and I can't do it anymore.' I think about the years and years when Madame Hirondelle pushed me harder and harder at the Golden Pavilion, to do better and better. To learn to control my Gift, to use it in increments. All of that has amounted to nothing at all.

'That's fine,' he says, laying a hand on my shoulder.

Without warning, he does it. He sends those tingling waves crashing through me. Everything around me is blurred, as though

I am looking at my surroundings through a mist. And then I feel it, the water, crawling slowly towards me. Driblets and droplets, summoned from all corners of the stables, wherever it has taken itself to hide. Soon, they gather to coat my hands in a flowing shield, thickening.

'Stop it,' I hiss, wrenching myself away. The shield falls in a puddle at my feet.

I want to sob. To howl. My hands are shaking after exercising a power I didn't even know they still had.

'I'm sorry,' he says. 'I was trying to help you.' He pauses, crouching next to me. 'Can't you pick it up? If we could give all that to the cow, it would make such a difference.'

I watch his face and there's nothing but concern and tenderness in it. 'Can't you try?'

'I can't do this,' I say, close to tears. 'It's been so long... And my Gift has been almost nothing since the Crystal was destroyed.'

Philippe wipes his face with his forearm, smearing dirt on his cheek. I feel an urge to lean in and wipe it down, but restrain myself at the last moment.

'I didn't want any of this.' He sits, his long legs apart, letting his strong arms fall between them. He looks just as defeated as I feel.

'When the opportunity was ... presented to me,' he goes on, in a low voice, 'I wouldn't have accepted it, if I hadn't been left with nothing. I'd lost the farm I'd grown up on. I'd lost everything.'

'I know.' I hide my face in my sticky hands. I can't bear to hear this. What I've done. How I've defeated him.

'And when I arrived here,' he continues, blissfully ignorant of the role I played in all that happened to him, 'and I saw how little the people wanted me as their duke, I honestly thought to turn my back on it all. Just go.'

'Where would you have gone?' I ask, breathlessly, unable to imagine what that would have meant to Hugo and me.

And that Philippe should have struggled so much with the role he had to play. With no one to talk to.

It strikes me how similar we have been, with regard to this.

How lonely we were, the both of us.

'I don't know,' he says. 'Away.' He shakes his head. 'But I didn't want to give up, not so fast. And then, a few days after we arrived, I went to the steward's tower. And when I began looking at the ledgers, and I saw that I could make sense of them, I thought to myself, for the first time, maybe, just maybe, with the right people at my side, I *could* do this. Rule a duchy.'

I remember that day. The first day when I felt, as well, that I could be the chatelaine of Fort Cantor. If I tried hard enough. I never thought that what he felt all this while was a mirror held against my own feelings.

Something hollow resounds in my chest.

'And then you came in,' he goes on. 'And suddenly, everything was so bright, so clear. And I remember myself thinking, between the two of us, we could master this. We could climb this mountain. You and I, we are so different, Celine.' *Ssseline*. 'But we complete each other. I have my blind spots, and you have yours. But together—it feels like there's nothing that we can't conquer.'

There's a stinging in my eyes, because he knows, because even if we never spoke about it, he feels it, too. 'We are partners,' I say. 'We fight on the same side.'

'Really?' he says with a small smile. 'You certainly do your best to convince me of the opposite sometimes.'

I chuckle, in spite of myself. What he says is true. I catch myself keeping him away at times, and not even *I* am sure why I do so.

'I'm sorry.' I'm sorry for so many things that I can't even begin to tell him.

But mostly, I'm sorry for not being a good person, like he is.

'The point is... What I'm trying to say...' He stops for a moment. 'I forgot what the point was.'

He buries his face in the nook of his elbow and I think, *No, no, let him not be upset about this. I never wanted to upset him so much.*

I stretch out my hand and brush the taut skin of his forearms with the tips of my fingers. He looks up, surprised, and emotion clogs my throat.

I clear it away. 'Perhaps what you were trying to say was that we shouldn't fight each other anymore. But that we should fight alongside each other.'

His eyes glimmer and I think, *Yes. Yes.*

He uncoils his arm, touching my fingers, tentatively, watching my face for my reaction.

I think, *Yes. Yes.*

His skin is rough and warm at the same time. I close my hand around his and it feels like things will be right again.

Eventually.

He tilts his hand gently, as if settling into my touch, just as much as I settle into his.

His skin is burning, but so is mine.

I blink. 'I suppose we could...' I sink into the sensation, into the way his hand feels, covering mine.

I forgot what I meant to say, but now I can hear the pained huffs of the cow in front of us. I extract my fingers from his.

'I'll try again,' I say. 'Keep your trickle of power steady. You don't need to distract me with jolts.'

Before he can reply, or he can show any sign of surprise, I touch the soaked surface of the floor.

Madame Hirondelle used to say that I was so talented and

surprisingly hard-working. And there were things that I could do … like conjure water from the ground. Direct it towards me. Build water shields. Put out fires with just the water I could summon from the air.

I used to feel so … protected. And my mother, she encouraged me to use my magic. She taught me how to channel it. She always told me, *Celine, be strong so you don't have to rely on someone else to be strong for you.*

I've let myself forget.

No, it wasn't that. After so much heartbreak, I *made* myself forget what I could do with my Gift, because it didn't feel like my Gift at all anymore, after the Crystal of Power was destroyed; because so many bad things had happened in the space of a few weeks, my entire life fell apart, and my Gift had been of no use then to make things right.

I pick up the moist dirt in my hands and Philippe lays a hand, gently, on my shoulder. There's a faint thread of power coursing through us where we touch, a fine current that stirs the Gift from where I had locked it up and hidden it for so long.

I breathe in, breathe out.

I am the master of my own power.

The Gift thrums and sings within me, calling my name, calling for me to wield it.

I close my eyes, my fingers drawing circles on the ground, trying to remember. Drawing. Pulling. Towards me. Drawing. Feeling the tingle in my palms. Water crawling its way to me. Water. I am water. I feel water. I draw water.

I am the master of myself.

Philippe's power is like a ray of sunshine in the morning, awakening me with a warm and soft caress. I feel the soft thrum of the shield, growing around my hands, but I don't open my eyes. Next to me, Philippe's breaths quicken.

And when I look, there's a thick layer of water, curling up towards my wrist. 'Open her mouth,' I say. 'I don't know for how long I can hold this.'

* * *

WE RETURN TOGETHER to Fort Cantor. Philippe drags the exhausted horse behind him. 'You shouldn't have brought the palfrey,' he says.

'Yes.' I swallow, but there's nothing except grit in my parched mouth. 'I can't wait to have a cup of water at the castle,' I say.

He doesn't reply. For a while, we walk in silence. There are no words for what we did—we'd spent them all in the dark inside of that stable, just like we spent our powers. The lacy shape of Fort Cantor profiles itself against the grey cliff, the blue sky. The image shimmers in front of us with the heat. My skirt whooshes on the dusty path, my shoes clap.

'How can you stand shoes in this heat?' he says.

'Believe me. I'd like nothing more than to strip to my bare skin.'

He gives me a quizzical look.

I say, 'Don't even think about it.'

He shrugs, but seems in a good mood. 'I was thinking,' he says.

'I was afraid of that.'

He guffaws. 'Can you call water from underground streams? Fill the wells and things of that sort?'

'I used to be able to but I don't think I can anymore. And I can hardly run around from well to well, replenishing them. My father will hear about it.'

'You will let the people of the duchy die of thirst rather than upset your father? I was wrong about you.'

I can see what he's doing. He challenges me. Again. Like he

has, day by day, ever since I met him. 'People have been wrong about me in the past.'

He hums. The quiet settles again between us. Then he says, 'You're certainly more than I bargained for.'

'What did you bargain for?' I remember the day when he not-quite-proposed. The thugs. The fear I felt for him then. Our conversation in my room afterwards, and the disappointment in his eyes on our wedding night.

'You,' he says.

'And what did you get?'

'A chatelaine. A large dowry. A Water-Wielder.'

'The correct term is Water-Twirler,' I say. 'And it seems you got *more* than you bargained for.'

'I wanted a wife.'

I scoff. 'Why? You have so much more now.'

He wants more, I realise. Hugo told me as much, that he thought Philippe might be a bit sweet on me, which seemed impossible, but now…

I remind myself of what Hugo has promised him. That Philippe would stay on as a steward. But on the other hand, when Hugo suggested that Philippe should marry me, he never told him that I am not his to take.

He didn't draw a line in the sand because he didn't want my future husband to suspect what we had done.

He relied on my husband's kindness and sense of honour, and we exploited it like a weakness.

Somehow, this leaves a bitter taste in my mouth.

I shudder when Philippe speaks again, following the course of his own thoughts. 'It wouldn't have to be every single well in the duchy. Just one. A stream. Under the cover of darkness. Enough to silence the angry voices, to keep everyone alive, until the rain comes.'

MAGALI

I watch them return to the castle, two silhouettes in a field of scorched wheat. Their shoulders almost touching. Dipping their heads while they exchange words, Philippe turning away to smile. I can't hear what they are saying, but I hope she won't ruin this for him. His first great moment as a duke.

As I watch them walk down that path, I remember what Isabella told me. *Do not dismiss Celine. She is stronger than she makes herself out to be.*

But I see no strength. Just a little girl, strutting about as if this castle is hers. Moving the furniture and painting walls and styling herself a duchess.

If she only knew what I had to do for a duchy.

If she only knew how easily I will undo all that she has done, once she is gone. I will leave no trace of her. None at all.

And that she disregards Philippe, of all people... I want to slap that self-sufficient little face every time she sneers at him.

I have no idea how he puts up with her.

Let her. Let their marriage not be consummated—once all of this is over, and once we are rid of Hugo, it will be easier for Philippe to set her aside. Annul the marriage. Or choose another way.

The day will come when we will no longer need her.

And soon, soon, I hope, once Maël emerges, one way or another I will have again my rightful place.

CELINE

Aurelie helps me slip into the chemise I sleep in. Every evening, she brushes and brushes my hair until it's as smooth as silk. But tonight, I can't stand the way it sticks to my moist nape. 'Please, just take care that it doesn't touch my face. Or my back,' I tell her.

Thoughts are whirring in my mind. The last conversation I had with Philippe, for instance. After we arrived at the castle, he was possessed by the idea he'd had.

'And what would be the harm in trying?' he said. 'What will you have then? Bruised pride? But think, just think, what would happen if we succeed. Some water to help us through a few more days.'

'Do you realise,' I whispered, looking around to make sure no one was listening, 'if we succeed, people will be arriving from all corners of the duchy with their buckets. There won't be enough to give them all water.'

But that would not be the worst thing that could happen. The worst would be to try, and to fail. The worst would be to lean into this crashing feeling rising inside of me, the feeling that I am more, that I could be more, only to be disappointed.

Only to become again a powerless princess who has to cling to the shadows.

Philippe said, 'It won't be enough to save them all, but we'll save some. And it will be enough.'

'It won't make a difference, in the grand scheme of things.'

Philippe stopped in front of me, his legs spread wide. 'You may be able to recite by heart the names of twenty different kings and their years of reign, and know the perfect way to address anyone, and everything might seem a bit like a game to you, but it is not. Those water supplies you're rationing and distributing within a village? It can make the difference between someone cooking a dinner, or not. A family being fed. Between someone having enough water for their goats, or letting them die. Our people, they are not numbers in your ledgers. They are just like you.'

I recoiled at this, trying to say something, but he went on, 'I have been on the other side. And I can tell you that if you can make a difference, even if it's for a mother and her two children, then you should do everything in your power to make that difference. Because everyone matters. Every single person. Why do you think you're more important than them?'

He stared me down, a sort of fire in his eyes that I had never seen before. 'I told you I didn't want this. But I am glad I'm here now. Because I'm not spoiled. I know that I have to fight every single battle I might win. Because it might matter to someone. And it is my duty, as the duke, to care for everyone in Langly. For every single soul.'

For once, it was him shutting me up with his words. Making me uneasy.

He was right, and I wasn't afraid to concede it.

Of sorts. 'I'll think about it,' I told him, a bit frightened that he could start to wield such a power over me.

And that he could try to use it, try to use my Gift for his purposes.

As Aurelie's hands trail in my hair, I wrap my nightgown tighter around me. He wants to use my Gift, but the purposes aren't *his*.

Not really.

He wants me to use my Gift for what he believes in.

And, perhaps—

'Where's the cat?' asks Aurelie, startling me.

'What cat?' I reply.

'The talking cat. Your favourite.'

The question takes me by surprise. I shrug, trying to feign indifference. To pretend I don't know that Hugo is in Langville. 'How should I know? Around the castle, I suppose.' And then I think there might be a point to her question. 'Maybe you should ask the duke. It's his cat. He brought it with him.'

My reply seems to throw Aurelie off. She purses her lips.

And then I try to turn the tables, putting her under the light of the torch. 'How was Philippe as a landlord when he lived at the farm?'

'Landlord?' asks Aurelie.

'I'm sorry, didn't you see him as that? Was his mother the one who had the affairs of the house more in her grip?'

Aurelie stares at me through our reflections in the small mirror in my hand.

'Well?' I say.

'No, I suppose not. We didn't see much of her.'

'How come?'

I'm genuinely fascinated by the aura of mystery surrounding my mother-in-law, whom I have yet to clap eyes on. Especially since the reports I hear about her seem to contradict themselves. I don't remember ever seeing her at the Royal Palace.

'I don't know,' says Aurelie, arranging the brushes on the table. 'I didn't see much of her. But I didn't live much on the farm itself. My parents lived in a cottage.'

'So did she spend much time at the castle, with her husband?' I wonder what kind of mother would leave her young son at a farm and go to live in a castle. What was she hiding? Perhaps the fact that Philippe is gifted. And it seems she went to quite some lengths to conceal that, by not sending him to train at the Golden Pavilion with the rest of us.

Or perhaps she didn't care. My chest tightens at this because all evidence seems to point this way.

He is so good, Philippe, good in ways I have never been. He deserved more than a mother who ignored him. More than a wife who will not let him come close to her.

I wonder, for a moment, if my reluctance to help him tonight has to do with the walls I've built around myself.

'I wouldn't know, Your Highness. Why do you ask these questions? I'm just a farm girl,' she says simply.

I shift in my seat. I have the feeling that she's hiding something from me.

'We've been married for months and Isabella of Langly hasn't come once to Fort Cantor. Which is quite strange, don't you think? Considering that she was born here. Raised here. And that her son is the duke.'

Aurelie busies herself with my pomades. 'I have learned one thing, and that is that nothing seems strange once you know the reasons.'

'Oh? And what are the reasons that might make all of this seem less strange?'

'I wouldn't know, Your Highness. I'm just a farm girl.'

TWO HANDS, JOINED

MAGALI

*L*et me tell you how it was.

After many, many years when the duchy enjoyed peace, my son became restless. It had been so long since the Siege of the Twins, he said. He had come of age.

'It's time for me to rule,' Maël said. 'In my own right.'

What he meant was, it was time to finally be rid of Frederic.

I knew what it would mean to me. Maël was growing harder to control, wiping away the wise advice I was dripping into his ears.

A few more years, I told myself. That was what he needed. He was a child at the stormy age when his blood frothed with rebellion against those who had brought him forth into this world, who had guided him.

The age when he wanted to carve his own path.

'Just a bit longer,' I told Maël, but he threatened to spill our secret, anyway.

So I had to concede.

What I didn't count on was my nephew, Hugo. That he had a

thirst of his own, threatening to lay waste to all of the duchy, to all that I had ever built.

What I didn't expect was the uproar in Lafala, our capital, and in Langly when he came forward to challenge Maël's rule and his right.

'Don't you remember Kylian's rule?' I wanted to spit, but they would not listen. Time had glossed over the failings, as it tends to do, when people are tired and looking forward to change, no matter what it might bring.

No matter if it were to take them through the eye of a storm. All they had was hope, weary of the course their lives had taken. A sliver of mad hope, clinging to an unsuitable alternative, just because there seemed to be an alternative at all.

And when Hugo produced that witness, that wet nurse, the woman who claimed that it was not Frederic who came first into the world, but Kylian, I knew I had to act.

I turned to my old ally, the one who had stood by me in my direst hour of need.

I turned to Julien.

And to make sure that we could not fail, I turned to the King, too.

CELINE

I toss and turn in bed, unsure what do to. Attacked from so many sides. Tomorrow, the battle with the drought will start anew, and it will be a battle we'll carry well into the winter, if the crops are ruined.

People all across Langly will be close to starvation, so helping just a few, tonight... My Gift twinkles inside of me, sloshing, disquieted. Aching to be touched and moulded and used as it had not been in years.

Aching to dance alongside Philippe's.

I cover my face with my pillow, my cheeks flushing at the memory of today. I cringe when I think that I would have to tell Hugo about it.

With a jolt, I realise, *Why should I be ashamed? I didn't do anything.* And I'm free to do with myself as I please, am I not? My father isn't here anymore, pressing to do one thing or the other, though I can wager he'll start sniffing soon and ask about that heir.

I can't give anyone what they want, but with my brother's health as frail as always...

There's always Anne-Mihielle, I think bitterly. Though she hasn't married anyone. How easily we forget about her. How we want to, and my soul aches for the half-sister who was my constant companion for the first years of her life.

I was never alone, since she began walking at my side—which was at about the same time that she began taking her first wobbly steps—accompanying me everywhere in the Royal Palace. Not until they sent her away. I consider the gaping hole she left behind, the hole I still feel, like an old ache, when I returned to the Palace after Hugo's disappearance.

There were two of us, I remembered more often that I would have liked to. But when I asked about bringing her back to the Red Kingdom, my father always dismissed me.

I wonder what kind of person she is now, and if she remembers our childhood as fondly as I do. Perhaps not, considering that she barely replies to my letters these days.

There's a loud tap on the door to my chamber and I jump out of bed, tightening a nightgown around me. Standing there, in just a shirt and a pair of ridiculously tight trousers, folded halfway up his muscular shins, is Philippe.

'You shouldn't be here,' I whisper.

He cocks an eyebrow. 'Why? Are we still courting?'

I snicker at this. I feel an impulse to ask if he would like to, but I push it back.

By Sabya's Morningstar, Hugo has only been gone a few days and I'm up to mischief.

'What do you want?' I say.

'You know what I want.' His voice is low and playful and, for a moment, I realise, *Perhaps I do want to play with him, too.*

But just as partners in ruling this duchy, of course.

Fine, fine. He knows, perhaps. That he persuaded me with his little speech. That I have no reason whatsoever not to try.

Not a good one, at least.

'I was just coming to meet you,' I say airily.

He eyes my nightgown, laced together by a fine thread. 'Were you now?'

My heart begins thudding and I push past him. 'Let's go. We don't have much time until dawn.'

* * *

DEEP in the black of night, Philippe and I exit the small bailey through the side door. I take in the herb garden in a corner, the rose bushes. We haven't been here, together, since before that day when my father gave up Maël for dead.

Since before Philippe became my betrothed. He is my husband now, I remind myself, though I'm always so ready to brush him off. I scan his lovely face, his eyebrows knitted already in a concentrated frown.

What does a man like him feel, forgotten and ignored by his mother, to be pushed away by his wife? As if there was something wrong with *him*? There's a pit in my stomach and something must have changed on my face because he turns to me. 'What?'

'Nothing,' I say, trying to focus on the matter at hand.

I step forward on the chalky alleyways, towards the wall of the cliff.

At its foot, there used to be a stream that surrounded the small bailey on two sides, which then rolled down the cliff in a waterfall, creating a small pool where it landed. Then, the stream used to coil around the fort towards the farm, finally joining the river that flows a few hours' ride from us towards Castle Bencifert.

The plan is simple: to make the stream flow again.

As if it's as easy as that.

I wonder what Hugo would tell me about all this. I wager he'd have a few useful tips at hand. I think, had he been unbound of his form as a cat, and had he been free to use his Gift in the years since the Crystal of Power was destroyed, he would have never allowed the grip on his own Gift to slip, like I did.

He loved too much to wield it.

Perhaps he would still do, once he is unbound of this form.

Hugo was always so ambitious. So certain of what he had to do, in a time when I was still grappling with desires that had not taken shape.

It makes no sense, but I'm suddenly afraid, both of what I can and can't do anymore. Perhaps the people are right. Being able to wield the Gift, it gives one ideas. About one's place in the world, about pushing boundaries.

'You seem distracted,' says Philippe, once we arrive at the cliff wall, its surface a slate grey in the clear night. There are no clouds in the sky but this is hardly surprising. When did I last see a cloud?

I touch my hand to the surface of the rock. Philippe shifts closer to me and I see shadows play on his face. In the moonlight, I'm almost shocked by what a pretty man he is. He searches for something in my eyes and seems a bit startled by what he finds. 'Do you need help? Should I—' he says, shifting his hand.

I tighten the grip on myself. 'No,' I say, feeling the surface of the cliff.

'Have you … started?' he says. 'Is this how it's done?' I frown and he takes a step back. 'No, no, I didn't mean to bother you. Go ahead. I just don't know.'

'Philippe, right now, you're being a bit of a bother,' I say. My head is a jumble. 'I haven't started anything. I'm looking for the hole through which the water used to flow. I can't conjure water from nothing. It would miss the point of what we're trying to do.'

'Oh, let me help, then.'

Our hands search the surface of the rock. 'You should have brought a torch,' I say.

'I thought you didn't want to draw any attention.'

I move my hands more frantically. Of course he's right. Worse than failing tonight would be to succeed and for the people to realise what we've done.

We are not quite favourites in the people's hearts, since the unfortunate drought that has befallen us all shortly after we married. It is looked upon like an omen that will define our rule.

Perhaps it's not an omen at all, but a metaphor. For what's happening inside our bedchambers.

In any case, making people aware that we wield Gifts, I doubt this will make us more popular. I remind myself of how they rebelled during my grandmother's time, in the Year of the Red Maiden. When the Golden Pavilion had been almost destroyed, had it not been for Philippe's own grandfather, who exploited the unrest to make himself the first duke.

The Lion, indeed; and perhaps there is something of him in Philippe, after all, in the way he pursues what he thinks is right. My husband might have chosen a different battlefield, the one of lowering taxes and introducing new agricultural techniques, but what good is paying less tax if there will be no crops?

My hands scan the surface of the rock and they suddenly find something warm beneath them. The sensation shocks me before I realise it's Philippe's fingers. I pull away, still tingling where we touched.

'Stop it,' I hiss. 'It's not time yet.'

He cocks his head. 'But I wasn't doing anything.'

'Right,' I say. 'You know what, we're in each other's way. Maybe it's better if you look for the hole.'

I have to admit I'm not sure what I'm searching for. I wouldn't tell him that, though.

Not long after, Philippe says, 'Here.' He takes the tips of my fingers and guides them to a small cavity in the rock. We hold our hands laced for a moment too long. He clears his throat and pulls away. 'I'll leave you to it, then.'

I try to remember what I have to do. I've read a fair bit about it today. I even tiptoed down to the library at midnight to look for a book that might help.

And, because of how well the library is stocked, I found what I was looking for. Locate the source, the book said. That is, try to feel the water. I close my eyes, focusing hard. I move my body to the side of the cliff, trying to feel if there's any water at all, deep inside.

I try to see it with my mind's eye. I try to taste it. I call it. But nothing.

I am the master of myself, I shout at my Gift, anger simmering within me.

For the first time in years, I am the master of my life. I am the chatelaine of Fort Cantor. I am in the open. Fighting.

It seems I have to battle myself today. My Gift twirls inside of me, I can feel it. If I could only bend it to what I want it to do.

I can't believe I've allowed myself to forget.

'Can I help?' says Philippe.

I sigh. 'I'm bringing the water into focus.'

'Fine,' he says, pursing his lips. 'I won't say another word.' It comes out muffled.

I roll my eyes. 'Patience. I need patience.'

I try to concentrate again, but all I can think of is Maël, at the head of his small army of ruffians, coming to besiege Fort Cantor. I wonder if the servants would open the doors for him, if they saw him in the flesh. I wonder what he'd do to Philippe and me, if he finds us. I wonder if Hugo has discovered traces of Magali or Maël in Langville. I wonder if Maël has found Hugo first and taken his revenge.

I'm so tired. So, so tired. The strain of always looking over my shoulder, of hoping for Hugo, of avoiding Philippe ... it's exhausting. And there's this drought, this bloody drought.

'Are you all right?' says Philippe, laying a hand on the small of my back. He's warm and close, his shoulder brushing mine.

How silly, I think. I don't need to avoid him. The dice have been cast in such a way that we have cast them together.

Regardless of what Hugo and I have planned, for now, it's Philippe and I who are at the helm of the duchy. It's us whom the people see.

Not just me.

And for once, I feel that I am not alone. They see the pair, the ducal pair. Sharing the blame between one another, sharing the burden.

Not alone. I lean my forehead against the surface of the cliff, the stone still warm after the scorching day. And then I hear it. The faint murmur coming from the cliff. 'It's there,' I say. 'The water is there. I just have to find a way to pull it out.'

MAGALI

I wake up, the call of magic pressing heavy on my chest, like it did in the old days when the Golden Pavilion was still standing. Before I carried the weight of having to be two different people at once.

The Gift, my Gift sings to me. A summons, an answer. A hand, reaching in the dark. And then, it stops. It must have called me from another time, another age, from a strongbox in my own head that had been locked for a long, long time. I strain to listen to it again, but all I hear are the snores of the cook and the two kitchen helpers with whom I share my chambers. I'm drenched from head to toe in sweat.

I turn angrily to the other side. It might be time for Maël to reappear. And even if it isn't, I've had enough of sleeping on straw in dirty, smelly quarters.

It might be time for me to do something.

CELINE

After almost an hour, I still can't find the way to make water come to me. I try all the methods of concentration that I learned at the Golden Pavilion. I call it. I whisper to it. I almost scream.

I'm so tired I could cry. Again. 'I can't do it.'

Philippe says, 'Then let me help you.'

I give up and direct Philippe to lay his hand on top of mine. I shake off the exhaustion and concentrate on the pull. His magic flows like a river through me, bringing everything to life.

I remember.

Mihi, being dragged away from me.

Leaving no stone unturned in Lafala, looking for Hugo.

The cat, who was in fact Hugo, telling me that it was done. That my father promised me to Maël.

A dome of water and a blast of icy drops.

The clink inside the cliff builds up to a thrum and the stream of Philippe's power courses through me, tingling. My Gift sloshes and froths, snarling and growling, and it's a stir in my blood. It makes its way into my limbs, which start quaking—

Philippe's voice is the whisper of a wave. 'Easy, Celine, easy. Easier.'

I look away from the cliff and notice that his eyes are on me. Steadying, calming. Worried.

Too late.

A dam bursts, and my powers come rushing through.

I feel the ripple start in my chest, a shiver going through my limbs, and into the cliff.

I am your master, I shout at them in warning. *You are not the master of me.*

I take a deep breath, as if trying to keep my footing in the face of an approaching deluge, but it's too late to put a lid on anything, and my Gift, a clawed beast with sharp teeth now, leaps with everything it has. It takes it all from me, takes all that Philippe has to give, and unleashes itself upon the water in the cliff.

There's a sudden quake in the rock and I feel the stream rising up. Rising like gall. Rising like the blood in pulsing veins.

'Stand aside,' I tell Philippe.

'Why?' he says, but by the time I push him away it is too late, and the water streams from the cliff, drenching us both.

* * *

I'M SO exhausted after this that I don't even want to clap my hands and stare at the water filling the empty riverbed.

'Let's go,' I say. The sky is a deep purple and the night is nearly over. 'Someone might see us.'

Philippe watches me, perhaps noticing the way I can barely hold my eyes open. He offers me his arm. It would be wiser to refuse him, but I'm too tired. 'Let me help you.'

I avoid his gaze, unable to face what I have realised. As we sneak through the garden, he keeps looking behind him. 'Sabya's Darkblades! I can't believe it. You did it. We did it.'

I'm so, so drained that I can't even jump up and down about it. 'Well,' I say, 'I don't know for how long it will flow. So hold your horses.'

'We've done it.' He pushes open the side door to the castle. 'I'll weave some growth magic around the stream after I get you to bed,' he says. 'Maybe this will keep it flowing for longer.'

I make an effort to put one foot in front of the other as we crawl up the stairs. I draw a line at him carrying me into my own chambers.

He keeps giving me glances from the corner of his eye.

'Stop staring,' I say. 'I'm fine.'

He bites his lip. 'Are you? It was rather … intense,' he says. 'As if there was a tight lid screwed on top of something, and it simply blew off.'

Yes. I always found it hard to control these outbursts. Even more now, after not using my Gift for so long. But I'm not ready for that conversation. 'It's normal. Maybe this is why people thought mages were dangerous. Because we are.'

And also … it's this emptiness I always feel afterwards. This void of feeling. Of anything, in fact. As if I'd given everything and I have nothing more to give.

I open the door to my chambers and turn on the threshold. This is my boundary. Yet my hand lingers in his.

'I wouldn't know,' he says.

'What?' I can barely speak.

'How it is for everyone else. I was never at that fancy magic school of yours. To see how children of my age wielded their Gifts.'

A lock falls over his forehead and I brush it away.

Of course.

Of course he would have longed to meet others like him. To mingle with them. He was never given the chance, was he?

I can't give him words of comfort tonight, but I have this.

I lean into him, and his arms close around me. It's good, it's so good, simply to tip and fall into this. The wall of his chest, the press of his warm arms. It feels as if I'm doing this for myself, allowing a part of me to finally let go, as much as I'm doing it for him. With my eyes closed, everything around me still swirls. And tonight, Philippe smells like a new beginning.

His hands rove over my back, with only the nightgown between my skin and his. We stand like that, and then I realise we have no business being here; I have no business making him believe I may still offer what has been Hugo's for a long, long time.

'Goodnight, Philippe,' I say and stumble towards my ruffled bed.

MAGALI

It is early morning and the noise from the side garden pulls me to an arrow slit at the first level. I watch Philippe in the small bailey, his feet immersed in the flowing stream, giving out buckets full of water to the men and women gathering in the small bailey. This is a miracle, indeed. But not one he brought about with his own two hands in full view of the most important people of the duchy, like I had planned it.

Had he waited only a few more days…

This is not how events were meant to unfold.

CELINE

When I wake, the sun is shining. It has probably been shining for hours. I roll over in my bed. My fingers ache; they feel almost frozen. It's painful to bend them. Memories of last night come rushing in and, for a moment, it all seems like a strange dream. But the pain in my fingers is real.

Hesitantly, I place a slippered foot on the floor. I was too tired when I got back to even take off my shoes. With a racing heart, I approach the window.

No matter how much I could have prepared myself for what I was about to see, I wouldn't have been ready for this. The small bailey is swarming with people. Young people. Old people. Women. Children. All carrying buckets. The chatter and buzz rise to my window. And in the midst of it all, Philippe is standing in the middle of the stream, filling bucket after bucket after bucket.

The sleeves of his shirt are rolled up, and so are the legs of his trousers. Even so, he's soaked to his hips. But he laughs and swings the buckets, the muscles of his powerful forearms tightening and flexing, playing like snakes under his skin.

And then he stops and looks up, shielding his eyes from the sun. As if he felt that I was watching. He looks up at my window, drops the bucket and starts waving at me, calling for me to come.

I know what he doesn't say. *Come and show them what we did.*

That's where I belong—down, in the small bailey, helping give water to the people. With him.

I slip into a plain dress, and rush downstairs to join him.

THE RUNAWAY

CELINE

a few days after the stream starts flowing again, the rains fall. And when there is hope that the crops could be saved, Hugo returns. He finds me at night, alone in my chambers.

'Look who the cat dragged in,' I say, and it comes out perhaps a bit harsh.

Hugo is dusty and miserable. 'I've heard there was trouble at Fort Cantor.'

'Trouble?' I say. 'I think we're lucky we didn't live through another Year of the Red Maiden.'

Hugo is prepared to jump on my lap, but seems to reconsider at the last moment. 'You were lucky, though. The rains came at the right time.'

'Lucky?' I say. 'Lucky?'

'You're upset,' he muses.

That doesn't even begin to express what I feel. When I see him now before me, completely unfazed, I could scream.

When the tide turned, when the walls began to press me in, he wasn't here, so I could lean on him.

I was alone, again.

Well, not quite. There was Philippe.

Hugo says, 'The townfolk in Port Lang whispered that the Mothers of the Forest themselves protected the duke and the duchess in their hour of need, that they made flow a dried stream. They say you are blessed by the Mothers.'

I prepare to tell him something about what Philippe and I did, when something snags my attention. 'Port Lang? I thought you'd gone to Langville.'

Just a day's ride from Fort Cantor, so close, the reason why I couldn't understand how come he didn't rush to my assistance. He must have known I needed him.

Hugo's eyes widen for a moment, then he says, 'This was what I wanted to tell you. Magali's trail led from Langville to Port Lang.'

My heart skips a beat. 'You found Magali?'

Hugo's mesmerising eyes are tinged with sadness. 'No, it seems she was last sighted in Crane's Harbour.'

Ah. The Blue Kingdom, I think. It wouldn't be a surprise if Magali went there to seek shelter, after quarrelling with her son.

Hugo crouches at my feet, barely touching my toes. In silent supplication. 'I'm sorry that I wasn't here when it all happened,' he says. 'I thought of nothing else but you, did nothing else but try to work towards my freedom. Ours.'

I bend to touch him, but hesitate at the last moment. He left me here, with Philippe. There was no telling what might have happened with the man he encouraged me to marry. With the man he encouraged to marry me. Not that Hugo could do anything in his form as a cat, if it came to it, but...

Hovering above him, I whisper, 'I needed you. When the stream dried, Philippe and I...' I think about the weight of his hand, the flow of his magic, rousing mine. Calling to it. I remember how he held me on that night, a ghost of his touch around my back, following me all day. 'It wasn't a blessing, nor a miracle. I coaxed the water out of the rock.'

Hugo's eyes narrow, then he rises to his four feet again. 'You used your Gift?' There's awe in his voice. 'How much of it do *you* have left?'

'Not much.' I wish I could find the words to tell Hugo how I had to seek the Gift within me, after it lay forgotten for so long. How Philippe helped me. But for some reason, I can't. 'There are enhancers, aren't they? I seem to remember that the first duke procured some for his wife.'

'There are,' says Hugo, pacing the chambers, his tail swishing from side to side.

'One of the ducal seals, with the lioness?' The details come to me through a fog.

'I don't know,' says Hugo, hopping to the window ledge. The red pouch on his back swings with the move. It's not empty, and I wonder what a cat could possibly need to carry.

Sometimes he has the pouch, sometimes he doesn't.

'Would you be able to shift, once we released you from this form?' I ask. Hugo loved nothing more than to shift. I was in always in awe how in the blink of an eye he could become someone else entirely.

'I don't know,' says Hugo. He gazes at the valley below. I must have touched a sore spot. I suppose he would need to get used to the fact that he can't use his Gift anymore. Though after such a long time being caught in his shape as a cat … reclaiming his human body would come as a blessing.

But if we were to find the enhancers again… Perhaps he would be able to use his Gift, after all. I'm startled to realise that I could use an enhancer, too. And what I'd be able to do with it…

I almost chuckle when I think what Philippe would make of it. With the enhancer, he'd probably coax me to create a sort of an irrigation system for fields throughout the duchy, and he'd use his Gift to make the crops grow to yet unseen sizes. They used to do that, in the days of old. The Duchy of Langly had risen from the ashes of the principate of Anselme, and the last Anselme princess, Gisele, always used her Gift that way.

Oh. This diverts my thoughts towards Magali. 'Where are the ducal enhancers, then?' They must have remained within the ducal family. 'Does Magali have any of them?'

By Sabya's Morningstar. If Magali has one… My thoughts get far ahead of myself. She could wreak so much havoc.

There's a pause, and then Hugo leaps down from the window ledge. 'What was that about Philippe? You said something about Philippe earlier. How he helped.'

I think, *The cat's out of the bag now.*

Not amusing.

'Yes,' I concede.

'How?'

He tried, I think. And he convinced me to try, too. 'Philippe has a Gift, too, did you know?'

By the way Hugo stands completely still, I realise that perhaps he hadn't even considered it. 'No. I had no idea. He was never at the Golden Pavilion. I never heard anything.'

'Odd, isn't it?' I lean back in my chair. 'Very odd. But considering how his mother always treated him…'

The blue in Hugo's eyes almost glows. 'Aren't you quite concerned about Philippe's well-being?'

I open and close my mouth, not sure what to say. 'He's a Growth-Mage.' The moment the words come out, it feels like a small betrayal.

Hugo fixes me with his stare. 'Interesting. Crafting an enhancer of your own, then, my dove?'

'I don't understand why you have to be like this. You left me alone to handle a duchy. What was I to do?'

I'm not even sure what we're arguing about, exactly. Hugo swishes his tail again, and it seems so ridiculous that I'm arguing with a cat. What he holds against me. But then, his chest expands wide and he says, 'I'm so sorry, my love. I wouldn't have left if it wasn't for us. I did all of this for us. You know how much I want to be with you.'

This makes me feel as if I've been caught doing something shameful. 'I know. I know.'

We study each other for a beat, and I almost apologise, but I'm not sure why I should.

Hugo turns around then, sagging a bit. 'I'm tired now. Perhaps we can speak tomorrow.'

I wonder if I should ask if he wants to rest in my chambers, but, in the end, I don't.

MAGALI

The blasted cat finds me in my own chambers, now tainted all over by Celine's touch.

That girl.

I swear.

'Did you find anything?' I ask Hugo.

'Fabien joined the rest of Maël's retinue in Port Lang. That is all.'

I plump a pillow, making the duchess's bed. My bed. This used to be my bed.

I give the pillow a hearty punch. My son. Where is my son? I suspect that this blasted cat has him. Who else would it be?

'Aren't you keeping interesting secrets, Magali,' he says.

Surprise bolts through me. 'You never mentioned your little Philippe had a Gift of his own.'

I swing around, steeling my gaze. 'What business of yours is it?'

'Apparently, it is, when you whisk me away, so the princess can join forces with him.'

Someone is a bit jealous, isn't he?

There's no use telling him that it was precisely his beloved princess who clawed her way into my own plans. Because this would mean having to admit that I had plans, in the first place. I say, 'I was just as surprised as you.'

'Were you, now? So the drought was a coincidence.'

I shrug.

Poison.

This man is pure poison.

I can wreck him. Completely and utterly wreck him—I only need to whisper a few words in the princess's ear about what her beloved has truly been up to. About what he truly could and could not do, since he emerged again into her life. I could tell her about that captain thug who barged into Fort Cantor with his band, that night when she thought she saved Philippe by binding him to her.

Oh, I would have so much to say.

But if he whispers a word, he could wreck us, too.

And if we were to carry on with the plans, as Hugo laid them out... I can't deny that perhaps Hugo knew I would agree to cooperate, because I was of the same mind.

That this injustice that has lasted for centuries could be righted. That we could be the ones to do it. And I don't see how it could be done without the simpering princess.

'Find my son,' I say. 'And let's get on with the plan. I think I'm growing quite tired of you.'

He says nothing, but his looks tells me all I need to know. That he feels quite the same about me.

CELINE

It was I who suggested, after the rains came and the pastures bloomed in an off-green, and part of this year's crop had been saved, that we should hold a sort of ball for our faithful subjects. And by this, I had meant the more illustrious seigneurs, like Count Goderic and his family.

But what does Philippe do? At this gathering, to which I invited the choicest musicians from Lafala, the most talented bards I could think of and the most elegant dancers, he invites his farmers.

In droves. And he didn't even bother to tell me. I catch him by the entrance to the Great Hall, as he is shaking their hands, instead of waiting for them to bow, like any civilised seigneur.

He does not understand. No matter how much I explain to him, he doesn't understand that our power is an illusion, and just like it drained my mother to create illusions through her magic, so it drains me every day to maintain this particular one. He doesn't understand that power and status are something you have to work for. Every day.

He doesn't understand the sacrifices that one has to make. How some choices shred you from the inside.

'What are you doing?' I hiss.

'I'm welcoming our guests,' he says. 'What does it look like?'

'You can't stand by the door and welcome guests like this is some sort of village wedding. The duke stands at his table and waits for the people to pay their respects. Since you invited them, in the first place.' I throw a quick glance at the ducal table where Count Goderic sits alone with his wife, sipping our best wine.

My husband does not understand how much appearances matter. How inflamed the noblemen can be by what they might perceive as a slight. The duke is only as strong as the bonds he shares with his seigneurs. I can tell him about kings that have been unseated, robbed of their thrones, not even very long ago and within my own family.

With the help of the very man who raised these walls around us.

I could tell him how respect is more valuable than coin, and it should not be traded so easily. But all that Philippe has for me is an angry flare in his features.

'Since I invited them? Darling wife, who bore the brunt of this drought? Whose cattle died? Who had to worry about feeding their children this winter? Who had to wait hours at their lord's wells to draw two buckets of water? I promise you, it wasn't the petty seigneurs.'

I'm not sure what he means by petty, but the tips of my ears are burning. What a catastrophe it would be if all the people who are here catch on that we're squabbling.

We have been squabbling a lot, of late. I think, since Hugo came back, I'm much more mindful of how I am around Philippe. So he doesn't grab the wrong end of the stick.

I can't allow him to come too close.

And, on the other hand, Hugo would understand this … this dance we have to perform in front of our guests. Philippe was wrong to say last week that he completes me. He does cover my blind spots, as he said, but it's Hugo who is the perfect match for me. And tonight painfully reminds me of this.

The ducal table has been arranged at the very end of the hall, on the dais. Two rows of tables have been set, lining the walls, so as to form a U-shape, and to allow enough room in the middle for the artists and for dancing.

The hall is already crawling with people, knights of all standings in their velvet mantles, farmers who have put on their cleanest shirts and their smartest tunics, which are often ill-fitting and much too worn. The farmers' wives cluster in groups and examine the fruit arrangements on the table and the colourful tapestries that are hanging on the walls.

Right behind the ducal table, there's a scene in which the first duke, Philippe's grandfather, accepts the fealty of his most powerful seigneurs and lays the first stone of Fort Cantor. His wife stands beside him; even the first duke must have heeded his reputedly quiet wife, when it came to navigating the world of noblemen and their customs.

Perhaps the first duke understood what Philippe does not: that form matters. Otherwise, why would he have commissioned this tapestry, to remind his seigneurs of their vow of fealty every single time they stepped into the hall? To remind these powerful families, which had been playing politics for much longer than his own, that he was their ruler.

'I have yet to hear a reasonable answer from you,' insists Philippe.

'Stop. People are watching,' I tell him. I feel people's gazes brush over me, over my dress. It's dark blue silk with silver thread, all matched with embroidered slippers, and I am wearing my mother's sapphire necklace—seven stones set on a thick gold chain.

'I'm sorry, did I come up to you to point fingers?' he says. 'A moment ago you were sitting at the table.'

'Where you are neglecting your guests.' Three of the most important seigneurs are sitting with us: Goderic, Claudel and Champy, with their wives. The three who muster, between them, more than half of the forces in our duchy; who own more than half the lands.

I wish I could make him see how important this is.

I wouldn't need to explain this at length to *Hugo*.

'Then go take care of your guests,' he says. 'And I'll take care of mine.'

With this, he turns away from me.

It would be odd to insist now. People would catch on that something is amiss. So I put on a smile and stride back to the table. I take my seat next to Count Goderic. 'Excuse me, but my husband is intent on greeting every single one of our guests,' I say.

'Yes, that's rather … unusual,' he concedes. A deep frown is etched onto his forehead.

I hope he does not take offence.

'We're all just so happy to have rid ourselves of the drought,' I say. 'Most unusual measures for most unusual times.'

'Yes, most irregular,' chimes in Countess Goderic, who sits one chair over, next to where my husband should be sitting.

I swipe a gaze around the hall, but there's no trace of the bloody cat. I am all alone, yet again. I take a sip of the wine. At the lower tables, the farmers and their wives are gorging themselves on the grapes and apples that are set on the tables. The tables will be empty by the time the first course arrives.

Countess Goderic seems to have the same thought as me. 'How barbaric, to have fruit before the dinner has even begun,' she says.

'I suppose they haven't seen fruit in a while,' says Count Goderic.

'I saw a few of them even pocket the fruit,' says Madame Claudel. 'I'd never.'

'They must have children at home,' says Count Goderic, neutrally.

'Yes, broods of them,' nods Madame Claudel. 'These people always have so many children. I can never keep count.'

'Well, they don't have to worry about succession wars breaking out over a farmstead,' guffaws Seigneur Claudel.

No, they don't, but their fights are just as bitter. They're just as likely to lose children to sickness and hunger as they are to wars. My eyes drift to Philippe, who has opened my eyes of late, and it seems like a small betrayal to my husband to allow the seigneurs to speak like this.

'But that high number of children does seem to come in handy when succession wars do break out, doesn't it? The seigneurs turn quickly to recruiting any free men who can hold a weapon.'

Count Goderic raises his cup to me. 'The duchess speaks the truth. I can't begrudge anyone for wanting to feed their children. We do all want the best for them. You only have to look at the latest ... clashes in the duchy to see parents who wanted to support their children. We're not so different from them, are we? You have to think about how Duchess Magali pushed and coaxed and nego-tiated to get her son the army he needed and the place he deserved.'

'Magali?' I ask. 'I thought it was her husband Frederic who besieged Fort Cantor, and Kylian and his troops within it.'

'Frederic could wield a sword, it's true. But, sometimes, they who can hold the most people in bonds of friendship—or fear— are more powerful.'

'I'm afraid I'm not familiar with many of the details,' I say. 'I was but a child.' The roar in the hall seems to die down for a moment.

'Well, I suppose you know the story, though. How the duchy passed to Frederic, then to Kylian, then back to Frederic.'

'Frederic, who returned from the dead, and besieged his brother at Fort Cantor in the Siege of the Twins.'

Which was ended by a drought, too. Kylian's forces within Fort Cantor had to surrender because they were dying of thirst.

How oddly does history repeat itself.

Count Goderic nods.

'But where was my father when all of this was happening?' I ask. 'Why did he stand for this, when Frederic was presumed dead in the Green Kingdom? No law would have allowed Kylian to become the duke if the son of his brother was alive.'

'No, of course not,' says Count Goderic. 'But the truce with the Green Kingdom was still frail.' Frail, until he sent Anne-Mihielle there as a ward. As a sort of hostage, to guarantee peace. 'The last thing your father needed was for his most powerful seigneurs to be at war with each other. Kylian came back with the army from war, placed it at the foot of Fort Cantor, and that was that. Magali was gone.'

'And so was Isabella,' I say.

'Yes, so was Isabella.'

At the door, Philippe is still clasping the hands of the farmers, who continue to trickle into the hall. It is time we started the proceedings, but I don't want to tell him again what he has to do so I could be rejected, like a humble supplicant.

'So he threw them out?' I ask.

'I believe the women and Maël slipped out in the middle of the night,' says Count Goderic.

'Yes, that's what I also heard,' says Seigneur Claudel. 'Slipped away, while Kylian was approaching. But Magali had too few troops and her Gift could only do so much.'

'What kind of Gift?'

'I think she is a Storm-Caller, if I'm not mistaken,' says Madame Claudel.

Countess Goderic says, 'I'm not sure if that's true. I think Isabella was the Storm-Caller.'

Brilliant. It would have been even nicer to have Philippe's mother with us, then. And one or two of those magic enhancers. The problem of the drought would have been solved much faster. She could have, for instance, called up a storm.

'And then,' I say, 'Isabella married Seigneur Julien Bencifert. To protect herself.'

Julien Bencifert, Philippe's father. The very man who bound Hugo to his shape as a cat for five years. Whose death partly released my beloved.

Perhaps Philippe's mother also had a hand in this, though Hugo never mentioned this to me.

'Yes, that was a bit of a shock to everyone,' chimes in Madame Claudel. 'And then, to shut herself up as she did at the farm. You never—almost never—saw her at the castle.'

'It's not as if we are seeing much of her these days, either,' I mumble into my goblet.

By the sharp look Count Goderic gives me, I fear I may have said too much.

Fortunately—for once—my husband plonks himself down in his seat and raises his cup. 'My dear guests, thank you for joining me tonight. It is wonderful to celebrate with friends when there's so much to be thankful for.'

All the knights and ladies raise their cups and agree with him. The mood seems to lighten towards my husband. In the hall, there's the mild agitation that goes with a large number of people bringing a large number of bowls of food to the table. Our own table seems to fill up of its own accord, with a small number of tiny plates containing the menu I'd selected for us for the evening —blancmange with almonds brought all the way from Port Lang, lamprey, fried goose, roasted piglet—and a worryingly large number of plates of commoner's fare: mutton stew, beans, broth, eggs. I turn, worried, calling for the pantler.

Philippe spills a few drops of wine on the table, in honour of the Mothers of the Forest, then says loudly enough for me to hear, 'I hope you don't mind, but I asked for our table to be filled with the same food everyone else is having and just a few delicacies. This is an evening where the duchy should come together in solidarity, not an occasion to fill our bellies with the finest food.'

This strikes me so hard that I don't even know what to say. My mouth hangs open. Philippe has changed the menu without even thinking of consulting me.

'I mean,' he explains himself, goodwill written in his eyes, 'think what would have happened if the drought had gone on for longer. A simple loaf of bread would have been a treat this winter for most of the families here. I think a bit of gratitude and humility suits us all for tonight,' he says with a smile directed at me.

'Hear, hear,' says everyone else, clinking their cups, saving me from having to say something to save face.

The rest of the evening isn't any less of a disaster. Philippe digs into his fare without the traditional breaking of the bread over his plate, and everyone follows suit, a bit embarrassed. While we eat, the artists I hired graciously perform before us a dance on the tips of their toes, and then the floor is cleared for a flute player. I breathe a sigh of relief as it begins to look more like a civilised ball when the dinner is over and the tables are pushed even closer to the walls. But Philippe's mood plummets visibly as he holds out his hand to me to open the dance. 'Not me,' I hiss. 'Countess Goderic. You open the dance with our guest of honour.'

He stumbles through the opening dance, mixing up his steps, refusing to fall in line when the pairs are switched. He almost knocks me over when we dance in the circle and stays in the middle when everyone catches hands.

But I suppose it's my failing, as much as his, for not teaching him the required dances after our wedding.

How could I, when I was so worried about keeping my distance from him? Worried about not giving him ideas, not allowing him to come too close.

What happened during the drought is proof enough that I cannot always be trusted to set the proper boundaries.

I return to the table with Countess Goderic, making free use of the fan to drive away some of the flush in my face. And it has nothing to do with heat. 'I'm sorry, I'm sure my husband is doing his best to learn,' I say.

'And so I am,' he says, having appeared at my shoulder. He kisses Countess Goderic's hand. 'I hope I didn't make you too dizzy, madam. As my darling wife says, I am doing my best.'

He flashes me an angry look and the heat in my cheeks blazes.

As if conjured by magic—or desire—Hugo slips between my feet, his fur brushing my damp ankles. I instinctively lift him up into my arms. Philippe also throws Hugo a furious look. 'I see,' he says, and stalks away to speak to the master of ceremonies, no less.

And then, complete and utter catastrophe strikes as the elegant music is replaced by a jaunty folk song. The people at the lower tables rise to their feet, the clatter unbearable to my ears. Where there had previously been only a dozen dancers on the floor, within moments it's heaving as men and women join hands and elbows and begin merrily hopping around, no order in it whatsoever. Tears spring into my eyes, and no matter how hard I try, I can't stop them from flowing.

'Let's go,' I murmur to Hugo, and head for my chambers, unable to watch any longer how this might unfold.

MAGALI

I visit Philippe in his chambers after all of the guests have withdrawn. I am seething.

I have watched from the peephole in my chambers.

Her chambers. For now.

'Why do you allow Celine to treat you like this?' I say. The anger burns hot in my belly. 'You are her husband. Put her back in her place, by whatever means necessary.'

'Stop,' he says, retreating and pouring himself some more ale. Too much ale. 'This is none of your business.'

'But it is my business. The duchy's business. It's—'

'You always go on about her flaws, but if you think so little of her, why did you push me to marry her?'

'She's worse than I thought.' I have made mistakes. And yet, this had to be done. I simply didn't take her airs into account.

'She's nothing like you think,' he says. 'Do you know who is much worse than I thought? Hugo. I can't stand bloody Hugo.'

'Leave Hugo.' I will take care of this business, at the right time. Soon. I grow tired of waiting for Maël to appear. I'm beginning to doubt whether he will. 'Stop defending her. After the setback with the drought… Had you waited, Philippe, had you waited for only a few more days… It was meant to be your most glittering moment and she ruined it.'

Philippe fixes me with a strange stare. 'What do you mean? What on earth do you mean?' He slams down his jug on the table. Ale splutters out of it. 'Did you have something to do with the drought?'

The floor is tilting a bit under my feet. He's not as drunk as I expected him to be. But I have never hidden from my own actions and I will not begin today. 'It had to be done,' I say. 'For your own good. For the duchy.'

He shakes his head and I can almost see how comprehension slips in, slowly. 'Are you mad? All the victims. The beasts. The children, Magali! Think of how much worse it could have all been.'

'Don't. I had it all in hand.'

'How dare you! How dare you do something like this? Hurting people. Animals. Did you not even think to consult me? No, you didn't, did you? Because you knew what I'd say.'

'Because I knew what had to be done.' I clench my fist. 'And I had the courage to do it. And do you want to know something? I did it all, all of this, for *you*.'

Philippe takes a step back, disgust written on his face. 'That's what you always tell yourself, don't you? But it isn't that at all, is it, Magali? I dared to ruin your carefully concocted plan and you lost the reins of the duchy. You think *you're* angry now? *You're* angry? I don't want anything to do with the harm you caused. All of this taints me.'

'Philippe.' I open and close my fists. 'You need to rest. You'll see the sense of it tomorrow.' I exit in a rush, before I say anything I will regret.

'Yes. Yes,' says Philippe, his voice trailing me. 'We'll see tomorrow.'

CELINE

The next day, I wake up to the servants still clearing away the remnants of the feast. Food crumbs are growing ripe under the rushes, lavender and mint I sprinkled on the floor of the Great Hall. The tapestries are hanging askew. I did return, eventually, to the ball, even though Hugo urged me to take as much time as I needed away from what was happening in my own castle.

But I had a duty to my guests, and it was good that I returned, because Count Goderic pulled me aside. 'You want to see Isabella,' he said.

Recalling our conversation at the table, I was too embarrassed to even admit that yes, I was itching to see her. So I said nothing, another wave of humiliation washing over me.

'I will tell you this much, then,' he said, with a soft touch on the elbow. 'It is most likely that you'll find her at the Golden Pavilion.'

I wanted to protest, to say that it didn't make much sense to look for her in a ruin, but by then Count Goderic had swept away from me.

I thought I'd untangle this today. That, and prepare for the reckoning with Philippe. For everything that happened at the ball.

Yet this morning he's nowhere to be found. I came down to look for him even before I managed to get dressed for the day, haunting the halls and chambers of the castle in my chemise. He isn't in the Great Hall, nor in his working chambers, nor in his own rooms. With a pang, I realise he must have gone to do something that would really soothe him, like help a cow with her calving.

Later, I think.

I'll look for him later.

MAGALI

'He's gone,' I hiss at Hugo, having met on the cluttered top floor, where my trinkets have replaced those that were Kylian's. 'Philippe is gone.'

'I suspected as much,' says that bloody cat, its usual airs about it. 'Why don't you go and fetch him back? Use your powers of … persuasion?'

I can't tell the schemer that I failed. That I have made a mistake. I have to tell Hugo, instead, what he has to do. So that we won't lose everything we've worked for. I say, 'You need to send the princess after him.'

'What?' Hugo flinches. 'Why would she do such a thing?'

'Because, my darling friend, no one has Philippe's ear more than her.'

I let this sink in. Oh, he isn't pleased. He takes this with more than a pinch of jealousy. 'Why would you say that? They've been horrible to each other since I came back.'

He means, *she's* been horrible to him.

Again.

'Trust me,' I say. 'If you want him to return, send her after him.'

CELINE

He's gone.

Philippe is gone.

He left me without a word.

I sit on my bed, my hands trembling.

I thought that we were allies, I thought that we were partners, and he left me.

Sooner or later, they all vanish: Anne-Mihielle, Hugo, my mother. Philippe.

A small voice inside of me says, *Why would he think he was anything to you? You were nothing but awful to him.*

I was.

I truly was, and I wonder what it was that I did to chase him, what I could take back, so he wouldn't leave.

And then I think, *No, I can't possibly have that much power over him.*

I breathe.

Hugo slithers in. 'By the Dark Mother, he's gone,' he says.

'Don't say that,' I snap. This has been drilled into me since I was a child. We never say those curse words aloud. *She* might mistake it for a call.

'Why?' he challenges. 'Everything we assume about the Dark Mother—'

'Hugo, this is not the time.'

'Someone is in a mood today.'

I gather my hands in my lap, squeezing.

'In any case, I think you should go after him.'

'What?' My fingers grow cold. *Why?*

'He's your husband. We need him here. You need to bring him back.' Hugo fixes me with quiet determination.

Of course. Of course I should go after him. How about all of Philippe's talk on making a difference if he was given the chance? Why throw this chance away when we were finally turning things around?

But.

Hugo thinks I can change my husband's mind. *Hugo.*

'Aren't you eager to send me after him?' I say. 'And where would I even begin to look?'

'Maybe you can start at his farm.'

Other words clang through my mind. *Maybe it's time you find a husband.* That was my father, speaking. And yet, somehow, I don't feel far from that. *Maybe you should do this and that and the next thing.*

'And how far should I go in charming him to come back? Should I speak sweet words to him?' My tone is vicious and cold. I'm so disappointed that Hugo should even suggest this. I wonder if this can truly be love. 'Perhaps let him kiss me? How about letting him touch me? What would be fair game? How should I entice him, Hugo?'

Would Philippe even want me, I wonder.

Why should he, after all?

'You don't need to be vulgar, it doesn't suit you,' says Hugo, his eyes sliding away from me. 'I don't like this, a single bit. But think of how much we can lose. Everything we've ever achieved. Everything we ever wanted, everything we ever dreamed of is at stake.'

I study him, study this cat form, looking for tells. But this isn't the Hugo I knew at the Golden Pavilion, is he?

I close my eyes and try to remember being in Hugo's arms. The real Hugo, not the cat. But all I can think of is the feel of Philippe's hand on mine, when we spoke about how lonely we were. Well, he spoke, and I felt the same.

His smell—something peppery, something earthy. I remember how Philippe held me after we made the stream flow again, as if he was afraid that I'd disappear if he'd let me go.

I shiver the memory away.

Hugo, I think. The man whom my entire life revolved around for years.

Perhaps that isn't the case anymore. I am the duchess, and the duchess needs to... 'I'll look for him.' But not for the reason Hugo thinks I should.

I need to find Philippe and apologise. And see what can be done from there. I can't manage all of this on my own. I need my partner.

My ally.

I need him to come back.

'Celine, we can't give up. We're so close. So close. I love you,' murmurs Hugo.

Somehow, I find this harder and harder to believe.

THE FARMER

CELINE

We arrive at the farm mid-afternoon. I took no one with me, except two mounted guards from the castle. I didn't even bring Aurelie with me, since I hoped to be back home by nightfall.

A summer shower catches us on the last leg of our journey, so by the time we arrive at the farm where Isabella of Langly may or may not have spent the last few years, we're caked in mud and dust.

I expect perhaps something like a proud manor house instead of what the farmstead truly is: a farm like any other, a mix of buildings, constructed partly of stone and partly of wood and dry manure.

Just like any other farmstead, the main house is a rectangular building with tiny, shuttered windows. The contrast with Fort Cantor is even starker here.

How could someone like Philippe, who lived here his entire life, ever feel at home at Fort Cantor, with its stained-glass windows, vast library and Great Hall that could swallow this farm and the low timber buildings scattered around it? Judging by the squeaking and mooing and chirruping that I hear, these must be where the animals are kept.

A woman opens the creaking wooden gate of the farmstead. She holds a piece of stained cloth in her swollen hands. She's neither tall nor short, and has a lined face. But her dress, though discoloured, is clean. 'Can I help you, Messere?' she says, looking at my captain of the guards.

I glance at the stained hem of my own riding skirt, at the dusty gloves, and realise how I must appear to her. But she doesn't look like Isabella of Langly, either. I step forward. 'I'm looking for my husband, Duke Philippe of Langly?'

'There's no duke here.' I turn towards the voice and spot him in front of the largest of the stables, a broad silhouette with his arms crossed. He has a pair of worn trousers and a shirt that might have been white, perhaps even this morning, before he smeared it with whatever is in the stables.

My heart leaps, nonetheless.

I found him.

'Philippe, darling,' I say, and head towards him.

I haven't been the kindest of wives. But I still can't keep away a smile from my lips.

He stalks back into the stables. I follow him briskly but stop at the threshold, stricken by the unexpected darkness. The day is bright and clear but this place looks like a cave. Of course, darkness isn't the only thing that strikes me. It's the stench of manure, which Philippe is shovelling.

'Where are the horses?' I say, surveying the empty premises.

'Out,' he says, 'in the fine weather. We bring them in for the night.' He then shakes his head. 'Why do I even bother to explain all of this to you? You don't care.' He goes on to scrape the manure across the floor with the shovel.

'Good,' I say. 'I worried the drought had killed them.'

He rolls his eyes. 'Celine, what are you doing here?'

'Well, you left.' I take off my gloves, my skin damp and sticky inside them. 'I didn't know what to make of it.'

'Of course I left,' he says. 'You spent the evening sniggering at my expense.'

'Did you have to ride all the way to the Bencifert lands so you could muck out a stable?' I say.

'Apparently, yes. You weren't going to allow me to do it at Fort Cantor. Everything has to be so difficult when I'm with you, Celine. Everything is such a struggle. You always, always judge me, no matter what I do.'

'What a coincidence. That's precisely how I feel when I'm around you.' He thinks I'm spoiled and pretentious, but it's because he doesn't know the rules of this world he now moves in, too.

'What do you want from me? Go away.'

I pocket the riding gloves, undecided. What *do* I want?

I want him back.

And I want to apologise. But I can't quite find the words yet. 'Is your mother here now?' I ask, hoping I haven't made a blatant mistake. But we've been married for two months now and we never speak about her.

Philippe's back becomes rigid, and the scrape of the shovel on the floor stops. He half-turns towards me and all I can see in the dim light is his long, straight nose profiling itself against the darkness. 'What's it to you?'

'I was trying to know you better. We never speak about anything.'

'That might be because we never speak.'

Of course we speak. We spoke when I helped him with the cow. And when he convinced me to help with the stream.

He resumes his work, while I shift my weight from one foot to the other. 'And we also never sleep in the same room. I can't even remember the last time I was in the same room with you, except if we have to entertain guests.'

I think of him, knee-deep in the water of the stream, waving to me at the window. 'Or put an end to a drought,' I say.

'Don't speak to me about the drought.' He wipes his forehead with his arm and even in the dark I can see how thick and strong it is. For a moment, before I stop myself, I wonder what it would feel like to have his arms around me again.

My entire future depends on this encounter, though I wonder now exactly what that future might be. 'You're happier on the farm, aren't you?' This thought comes with a bit of sadness. 'You'll never be happy at Fort Cantor.'

'How could I? I'm alone there. And you're only one of the people who try to tell me who I should be. Who do things in my name.'

I wonder, *Hugo? Did Hugo try to advise him, too?*

And then, something clangs through me. What he just said. He said he was alone. It rips the scab from my wounds. 'So you just left me? I thought you owed me at least an explanation before you left.'

'I don't think I *owe* you anything.'

'I am your ally,' I say, more to convince myself than anything. 'I am your friend.'

'Sure,' he says, not even looking at me.

He doesn't think we're partners, it seems. But this isn't a good moment, either, to call him out about giving up and the little speeches he gave me.

We are so good together, why can't he see that? I might have to show it to him. I haven't been particularly good at it, after the drought came to an end, and that is certainly my fault.

Out of the corner of my eye, I notice the trough, and how a

pipe continuously trickles fresh water into it. This is it. I'm so wild with excitement, that I nearly stumble as I hurry towards it.

I touch the surface of the pipe. Emotions course to me, high and low, and a sort of blind determination, as well as a desperate wish to make everything right. *Shame*, I think. All of this is coated in shame, and I want to let this water wash away my appalling treatment of him.

I am the master of myself.

And water will answer and obey.

I send these words into the water and I don't have to tell it twice, because it feeds off all the feelings churning in my chest. The water shudders and quakes, but it will not bend—and yet it did once, before the rain, when his hand was on top of mine, covering it, giving it warmth; sending much more through the skin that we have ever expressed in words.

'What are you doing?' he asks and turns just in time to see the jet of water splashing through the pipe. It's a powerful stream that strikes him in the chest and sends him reeling, a deluge that filters in no time through the piles of manure, soaking them through and sending them gushing out through the stable's open doors.

But before that, the soaking pile submerges Philippe up to his knees. Surprised by the weight of it, he teeters on his feet. The only thing that prevents him from falling is throwing out a large hand to catch a beam.

I literally snort with laughter. If he hadn't been in an even more ridiculous situation than I am, I would have fainted in shame.

'What are you doing?' he cries.

I take my hand away from the pipe, but the stream still flows strong. 'I'm sorry, I was just trying to help.'

'Lucius' Flaming Finger, make it stop.'

By now, the manure pours out in streams into the courtyard, and I'm doubling over with laughter. 'I'm sorry, I'm sorry, but I don't know how to.'

The stench has become unbearable and I try to go back towards the door, but the ground is more slippery than it was when I came in and I stumble into the trough, laughing.

'Stop it!' he says.

'I can't.'

He wades through the flowing manure to reach my side, pressing my hand to the pipe. 'Do what you did when you started it, but in reverse.' The touch of his hand is nice on mine, even though he's dishevelled and I have no words for the way he smells. My heart starts racing but the deluge of feelings in my chest quietens into a single sensation, and that's the warmth of him beside me.

'What did they teach you at that fancy magic school?' he says. 'It is so like you. To keep something bottled up, giving no clue whatsoever about what you're brewing inside. And then, it comes out, and razes everything off the ground. There's no middle way with you.'

I chuckle. 'That's a gross exaggeration.'

'That's exactly how I felt when you told me that we should get married. I had no inkling that you'd even considered it.'

I look up at him.

He is right, of course. It's the habit of keeping my own feelings to myself.

Until I can't.

I'm preparing to tell him something, when he frowns, his gaze on the pipe again. On our fingers, laced together. There's a deep welling up of emotion in my belly and he must feel something too because he pulls away, quickly.

'No,' I say. 'I think it was just right.'

He presses his body closer to mine, enveloping me from behind and presses my hand with his to the pipe. For once, my thoughts are quiet again. I can't see his face, because his head is level with mine, but I can feel him all around me.

'Easy,' he says. 'One hand after the other.'

I scrunch my brows, unsure what he means, and he gives a low chuckle.

I remember.

This is the first thing I ever said to him. 'Very funny,' I hiss.

'Didn't they teach you at the school how to stop it?' he says. 'Close your eyes. Will it back. Will it back to where it came from. Make your mind still, for a moment.'

A warmth passes from his body to mine again, but it's a warmth that shows me the way to the calm waters of a lake, to still the buzzing of a bee's wings in flight, and then there's that humming in the back of my head, coaxing the water to level itself, finally.

'Breathe,' he says. 'Celine, breathe.' *Ssseline.*

In and out. Deep. Just like during the Morgen Movements. It's hard, with the stench of manure around us, but the stream gradually fades to a trickle. Philippe's chest rises and falls slowly, moving against my back. And then he lets go, bit by bit. Behind us, the water drains into the courtyard.

The magic has exhausted my life force and my knees wobble. I grip the trough with both hands. Philippe takes my arm and untangles me from it and from the pipe. 'I think we should go outside.'

I allow him to support me, dragging my feet through the muck. 'I never properly learned how to stop,' I say.

'That statement can be applied to a number of things, when it comes to you.'

I'd chuckle, but I'm nauseous. The smells, what I've done, the closeness between us … they are suddenly too much for me to bear. And when fresh air and sunlight strike us in the face, I'm overwhelmed.

'Please let me go,' I say. I take a few deep breaths. 'How did you learn to do this? Who taught you to stop?'

'My parents.'

I blink. He's a dark shape in the blinding sunlight.

Philippe says, 'My father was a Binder. A powerful one.'

Hugo did tell me as much. I didn't realise that they taught Philippe their craft themselves, even if my husband has a different Gift.

'You're right,' I say. 'I use my most powerful feelings to spur my Gift on. It becomes hard to control at times.'

Philippe raises his eyebrows. 'I gathered as much. I'm not a teacher, but I'm not sure that's the best way to go about it.'

Hugo always said it was. That he was awed by how powerful my Gift was. But I'm not sure I ever told him about the cost. I wanted to present to him the strongest version of myself, always, so I could feel that I matched him.

A few farmhands and the woman from the gate are approaching from wherever they've been busying themselves, to take in the catastrophe.

Philippe turns around, looking for something. 'I'm sorry,' he cries towards the woman from the gate, who I assume is the new tenant. 'I'm sorry. It was the princess's fault.' There's suppressed laughter in his voice, and then he stops. My eyes now growing accustomed to the light, I see there's someone else, too. A seigneur, by the look of his clothes—well-worn, but good boots with brass spurs, and a lacy collar underneath a blue mantle.

'Louis,' says Philippe, half a smile on his face. 'I'd embrace you like a good brother, but I don't think you'd appreciate that.'

The seigneur has dark, short-cropped hair and a rather severe look. 'Philippe, my boy, I heard you were here. Couldn't quite believe my ears, so I had to see it for myself.'

My boy?

Philippe chuckles. 'I was planning to pay you a visit, after I washed. I'm sorry, there has been a small incident in the stables. You see, whenever my wife tries to be helpful... But where are my manners?' Still holding my hand—which I hadn't even realised—he half-bows, presenting me. 'Louis, please meet my illustrious wife, Princess Celine of the Red Kingdom. Celine, this is my brother Louis, Seigneur Bencifert.'

This is Philippe's half-brother, then. One of the two children Seigneur Julien Bencifert had with the woman who was his first wife. Before Isabella.

I curtsy with all the formality I'm capable of, given the state of me, and that the ground beneath me is quaking. 'Dear brother,' I say, 'this was certainly not how I hoped to meet you.' I don't remember him from Court, nor from the wedding, but of course there were so many people.

The blood drains from Louis's face. He freezes for a moment, then hops down from his horse, slings an arm across his chest and takes a bow. 'Your Highness, what a pleasure.'

'I'd offer my hand, brother,' I say, 'but I'm not sure where it has been.'

Something tightens in Philippe's grip, in his smile. This doesn't escape me, not even with the heaps of manure around us.

For a moment, none of us is sure what to say. I'd love to sit down to rest; not a single thought settles in my mind. For a moment, it seemed like Philippe and I were sharing something very precious, but now that the spell has been broken, I can't find my footing.

'I'm sorry,' says Philippe, addressing the tenant. 'As I've said, there was an accident. I'll take care of it.'

'No, no, Monseigneur,' she says. 'No bother. The men will clean up.'

It seems as if Philippe is about to insist, but I catch the critical gaze his brother throws him. It's unfit for a duke to shovel manure; even my husband must see the sense in that. I squeeze his hand, willing him to understand. I think he does, because he falls quiet.

Louis clears his voice. 'So, will I have the pleasure of seeing you at dinner tonight at the castle?'

'Of course,' I reply, before either Philippe or I have time to think. It would be good to dine with his brothers. Or, at least, I think it would be. I can see for myself the sort of family he comes from. I've been married to this man for months and I barely know a thing about him, like why he is the way he is when his brother seems perfectly capable of behaving properly.

'Wonderful,' says Louis. 'And, if I may, where are you spending the night?'

'Here,' says Philippe hurriedly. 'There is a spare room.'

I pout. A single spare room. It's obvious what this will mean. After the dinner I just agreed to attend, it will be too late for me to ride back to Fort Cantor.

'Nonsense,' says Louis. 'You must stay with us, at the castle. We have plenty of room there.'

I have a choice between spending a night on a farm—with no potential accommodation for my two guards—and a night at the castle. It's no choice at all. 'We'd be delighted, wouldn't we, Philippe?'

My husband throws his brother a frozen grin. 'Surely.'

'If it's not too much, we have two men accompanying us. And a few horses.'

'Of course, Duchess. Anything you need.'

I curtsy, pleased. For the time being, I need a bath, and the fresh set of clothes that are bound in a sack to the saddle.

MAGALI

There are smooth days and there are days of struggle. Today is one of the latter.

I can't control the Gift anymore, can't force my body to keep the shape I have taken on. I touch the ring tied to a chain around my neck and take a few deep breaths.

Like we were taught at the Golden Pavilion. In and out. In and out.

Throw it out into the world. Let the world do with it what it can.

I am the master of my own power, I roar at myself.

They never tell you in all the Shape-Shifter books how absolutely exhausting it is to keep all these different shapes; how it drains you. But there is worse. I remember the times when I had to slip often between different shapes, and how it sapped me of my strength. I remember what it did to the inside of my head, and how on some days I didn't know who I was speaking to anymore, and which of the people I was impersonating might have told them what.

I shudder to think of it.

There's nothing I wouldn't have done for the duchy.

Nothing I wouldn't do for my children. And this little witch thinks she can outsmart me.

What would she say if she knew Hugo was working with me?

It is a great circle of lies. Celine lies to Philippe; Hugo lies to Celine.

And I stand in the middle of it all.

Let me tell you how it was.

A few weeks ago, the life I had carefully constructed for myself had fallen apart: I had quarrelled with my son and left Fort Cantor to rally; Julien was dying and Hugo was so close to being released from his shape. Julien had no alternative, five years before, but to tie the spells binding Hugo as a cat to his own life— and the spell, as well as that precious life, were fading.

You would think Hugo was the least of my problems, especially since we had taken precautions to confine him to a room, for when the time would come.

You would think that I could have solved the problem quickly —it doesn't take much to strangle a cat, does it?

The problem would have been the cost. Such a smooth, simple gesture. And yet, the cost—my Gift.

What would I be without my Gift?

I went back and forth in my mind, ever since Julien had fallen ill.

Hugo, oh, Hugo. That eternal thorn in my side. After the binding spell broke, the restraining spells we had woven around him to keep him in that chamber were strong. But Hugo was always cunning, and we could not risk it. Not for long.

The price, I had to pay the price.

Hugo summoned me through the servants, as if he knew. Those smug features, those odd eyes, his mother's and his father's at once. An arm carelessly slung across an armchair. Radiating arrogance.

Awful, despicable Hugo.

He had to be taken care of.

Yet the first words he spoke to me in five years were, 'Dear aunt, I know what you want to do. But listen to me, please.' He paused at this, straightening. Smirking. 'Do you think it is fair, in our kingdom, that women are passed over when it comes to inheritance?'

Laws. Inheritance. A dull pain thudded through me. I couldn't help but think about that which should have always been my mother's, and then mine.

I paused to listen, in spite of what I knew that I should do. Said nothing.

Hugo pushed. 'What if I told you there was a way? What if I told you that I had a plan?'

CELINE

We take a bath at the farmstead. The tenant, Albertine, heats some water for me, which she pours into a wooden tub that's probably also used to scrub the laundry. It's better if I don't think about that. I peel off the layers of dirty clothes all by myself and sink into the clear water. At least there's water.

I think, *What a surprising day.* How odd it is to see Philippe outside the confines of Langly.

I'm slipping into a clean if wrinkled chemise when Philippe barges into the room. He's rubbing his hair with a clean cloth and the shirt he's wearing is clean, too. 'You'd barely arrived, and you had to escape to the castle,' he says, grinning.

'The man offered. I couldn't refuse your brother's kind invitation.'

'Sure.' Philippe's shirt is yet unlaced. I can see his well-defined chest underneath. 'It seems I'm the only man you *can* refuse with a clean conscience.'

I think, *How direct.* Here, at the farm, we are on a different footing. 'Where did you bathe? The pig trough?'

He frowns. 'Don't be mean.'

'I'm not, Albertine is lovely. I was just wondering.'

'I think she's scared of you.'

'Why?' I ask, turning my back to my husband while trying to

pull my tunic over my head with as much grace as I can muster. There's something unsettling in the small quantity of clothing that stands between us.

'Because of your title. Do you need help?'

I wriggle into the tunic and lace it by myself, then go over to sit on a low stool. 'No, but I'm helpless with my braids. And I doubt you're of any use in that area.'

'Let's see,' he says, already frowning. I stare at a crack in the wall while he walks up behind me. His knee lightly presses into my back when he runs his fingers softly along my scalp and down the length of my hair. His touch grazes the sides of my face. I nearly tell him to stop when he bunches my dark locks into a single stream. 'What would you like me to do with it?'

What would I like him to do indeed. 'I could think of a few things.'

He says nothing.

My breaths come quickly as the silence stretches towards the edges of our bodies, so close together now. He twists my hair gently, as if it's a test, then arranges it over my right shoulder, letting it fall over my chest.

I'm too afraid to move.

I'm not entirely sure what I'm afraid of.

It occurs to me that I'm afraid of scaring him off instead of being afraid of what he's about to do.

His callused fingers touch the back of my neck. Gently. Just a whisper on my skin.

I gasp.

'I bathed in the river,' he says, his voice low. 'Since you asked. And I used soap.'

He smells a bit of weeds, a bit salty, and a bit of lavender. 'How rustic,' I say. Then, 'Don't stop.' My voice is not entirely my own.

'Humph,' he says, but his fingers are now parting my hair, starting from the nape.

I can't help arching into that, tilting my head towards him. 'Are you … trying to impress someone?'

'Like my brother?' he says quickly, his hands bunching my hair again. This time he twists a bit and my head follows into that move, sideways. Our eyes lock and his are burning. Absolutely burning, and so much intent is written on his face.

My mind clears of everything.

I press my back into him and then turn my head in the other direction, baring my neck. His hand slips to my waist while he drops to one knee, pulling me to him. His breath is hot and quick down my skin, and I lean into his chest. I can feel his rushing heartbeats that mirror mine.

He takes his time, trailing soft kisses up my neck, while his hands rove up and down my stomach, skimming my ribs, the underside of my breasts. It's astonishing what sorts of sensations he can awaken in me, going far beyond where his skin touches mine, trailing and pooling into my spine, and way beyond, into my limbs. It's with astonishment that I set to explore the feel of him.

I have been wondering for a while now.

But I kept this bottled up, like he said, like I do with everything that doesn't match the image of myself I want to present to the world.

And yet, I wondered what he would feel like, and whatever I've imagined cannot even compare to this, how I lose myself in the sheer size of his body, how small I am compared to him.

One of my hands travels up his thigh, my nails curling slightly into the fabric of his trousers, and he groans, driving his hips into me. His hardness presses into my back, and I arch into that, into the promise that it brings.

The bundle between my legs throbs, and I take his hand, guiding it there. But he toys with me. One hand clutches for the sensitive inner flesh of my thighs, and pulls my hips towards him, while his other hand reaches tentatively towards my face.

He twists my head towards him, placing a soft kiss on the side of my mouth.

My legs turn liquid.

'So tell me, Celine.' *Ssseline.* 'Is this the point where you push me away and run?' His voice is low and rough.

Our mouths are so close to each other that our lips are almost brushing. I breathe out, 'I'm afraid the farm is too small, I'm out of places I could run to,' before my fingers touch his lovely face, before I trace the shape of his mouth with my tongue.

Why should I run, anyway, when all I want is to be here with him?

We are suspended in time, Langly and Fort Cantor molten away by his touch. Mothers of the Forest, how I crave it.

And I'm drinking up every single moment of this, I drink up the look in his eyes, how I can't glance away from it.

I close that sliver of distance between our lips and kiss him. Everything fades away. My whole world is in this kiss, in the way we answer to each other, in the promises of tenderness and possession and heat.

His hands travel down to my hips now, and he twists me towards him, settling me in his lap. I wonder about the shape and the feel of his chest, of his shoulders, of everything underneath the shirt I'm tugging at.

He gives me a low chuckle, pulling me even closer to him, and my legs curl around him.

He hoists himself up, and me with him, and carries us the few steps to the bed. But his mouth doesn't leave mine, not until he lays me, gently, on the crisp sheets.

He pauses at this, his body still cradled between my legs, his fingers brushing my cheek, the corner of my mouth.

'What is it?' I ask.

Right now, I can't remember whatever stopped me from doing this. Precisely *this*. And more.

'It's just that—' he says, but I trace a finger from his collarbone down his chest and over every strong muscle. Down, down, down, until I meet the upper edge of his breeches.

He pants, but still grinds out, 'I didn't expect you to even notice that I was gone.'

I tug at the waistband of his breeches, and he places another kiss on top of my smile, his hand travelling up my thigh, crumpling my shift, revealing me to him, inch by inch. I gasp. I feel so many things that I can't think. I want him so much that it aches.

He lifts his head, surveying me. I drown in the look on his face. 'Celine, this is your last chance to run.' *Ssseline.*

'We've come so far, haven't we?' I tell him, pulling him towards me for another deep kiss. And whatever might come after that.

No, no more running today. No more running. Only, perhaps, running towards it.

HUNTING TRAILS

CELINE

*W*hen the edges of my vision have exploded into eternity, when my treacherous body has stopped shuddering, when he has finished moving inside of me, we lie there still tangled, my head on his chest, breathing all of him in. One of his fingers circles lazily through my hair.

I need to feel his skin on mine, I need to feel all of him, I need him close and the fact that we are still half-dressed is an annoyance.

'Well,' he says, 'this isn't how I imagined it would be.'

'Did you … spend a lot of time imagining this?' My voice comes out raw, and I know why.

There was no stopping the way I answered to *him*.

I lay my hand flat against his face.

His lovely face.

He turns and gives me a long, tender kiss and when I stop feeling his lips on mine, I can't help watching him.

With Philippe, too close isn't close enough.

I clear my throat. 'You didn't answer my question.'

He smirks. 'I'd rather not.'

I laugh with a lightness I haven't felt since a time I can't remember. There's nothing here except a dark room, a bed, him … and me. And it feels like there's nothing else I could ever want in the world.

I caress his neck, his chest, his back, learning the shape of him.

'Don't slip away from me,' he says.

And I reply, 'Don't let me.'

MAGALI

I stand by the open window in my chambers. My own, not Aurelie's. The chambers I have occupied for most of my life, for the entire time I lived here. In *my* castle. Of course, they're nothing now like they used to be.

They have been invaded by furniture I never wanted to lay my eyes on, a bed that should have been consumed by fire the very moment I cast Kylian away from Fort Cantor. I always say, it's better to do something and regret it than not do anything and regret that.

But have I done too much?

I squint—my eyes aren't what they used to be—trying to make out the shape of Castle Bencifert in the distance. Its shape is consumed by the falling darkness. I haven't set foot there since Julien died. Too much pain. Too many memories.

I try to imagine what Celine and Philippe must be talking about behind my back. Would he tell her anything? Would he tell her about me? My grip on Philippe is slipping, I can feel it. I never got to know him as well as I should have—I never had the time. Being two people at once can do that.

And when I think, when I think what I risked, what I gave up for him.

And when I think how he has turned his back on me…

He's on the brink of destroying everything I built so carefully.

I made him a duke and all he wants is his filthy farm.

Perhaps he will make a terrible duke after all.

Perhaps even I can sometimes be mistaken. Perhaps I have gone too far. Perhaps I struck too fast, too far, in the absence of Julien's wise counsel.

Perhaps there is something I can do to fix it.

Perhaps.

CELINE

Louis sends a carriage to fetch us, which is fine by me since I'm not keen to wrinkle my tunic and surcoat by hopping onto my horse. Philippe, in a better mood than I've ever seen him, points out to me the landmarks of his childhood: the farm; the village where the weekly markets take place; beyond it, the steep road that takes us up the hill to the castle.

The castle itself is made up of two sets of ramparts. The first rampart closes like a circle around the second, stone houses leaning against its wall. I see a blacksmith's, an armoury and a series of squat buildings that look like grain stores. 'This is where the villagers from around the castle retreat when there's any sign of danger.'

'In the houses? There aren't many of them,' I say.

'They raise tents in the space between the first and second rampart. Villagers sought refuge here for a long time here when Langly was in turmoil. When Frederic came back from war,' he says, tapping the large pocket of his coat. This is something new. It's a gesture I never noticed before. But how well do I know him, in the end?

I have time to know him better, I think.

I have time.

Philippe goes on. 'And, of course, when Hugo contested the succession again.'

A cold shiver goes down my shins. Hugo. Hugo, who sent me here. The mention of his name passes like a shadow between us. 'But there wasn't a war then, just a trial.'

'That's what you think.' He bites his lip. 'People had already started taking sides. It was said that even the Fallen Court was about to interfere.'

'The Fallen Court is a myth,' I say quickly.

Philippe studies me for a beat, then shrugs and says, 'In any case, Hugo and Magali started recruiting their men, each for their own side. I think we were lucky, five years ago, that it ended the way it did.'

Lucky? Not for Hugo.

My stomach lurches. Hugo again. Would I tell him about what passed between me and Philippe? I don't feel anymore that I owe him that explanation. Though he sent me, I came here with one thought in my mind: to bring back my ally, Philippe.

But I think it's more than that. Philippe was the one at my side while we fought the drought. It was Philippe earlier, helping me steer my Gift.

It was Philippe whom I chose, on that terrible night at Fort Cantor, when we'd been confronted by those thugs.

When his life was threatened, I didn't even blink, once I knew what I had to do.

The realisation spills out of me. I know why I came here, to the farm.

I came for my husband.

His face is half-turned away from me, looking at Castle Bencifert with apprehension. He had not been welcome here, I can see now, from how he stiffens when he is with his brother.

For some reason, Louis Bencifert did nothing for him, when Philippe was robbed of his farm.

And I...

Quiet dread poisons my blood.

If Hugo and I are to carry on with the plan, I would also cast Philippe aside.

Replace him at the helm of the duchy.

My heart quickens, surging against these new thoughts.

When all is said and done, at the end of the road, whose wife do I want to be? The duke's? Or the steward's?

'Are you all right?' Philippe brushes my arm. 'You seemed so far away, for a moment.'

I want so badly to take his hand in mine, but then I wonder what he would think if he ever found out that *I* stole my father's seal, that *I* forged the inheritance papers that relieved him of the farm.

I think I know the answer, but I need to hear it from his own mouth. 'Would you still have claimed your place as the duke if you still had the farm?'

Philippe sighs. 'When my father died, I was so terribly disappointed. To be left without anything, at all. And to hear that my father had approved of this scheme, with claiming the duchy, should something ever happen to Maël.' He pats his pocket. 'But I don't know what to believe anymore. Perhaps I should have been less trusting in anything except my own judgement, in anything anyone else said.'

Perhaps we should have all been. My blood heats again, for entirely different reasons. 'Did Hugo tell you to claim the seat?' I ask.

What I mean is, *Did Hugo tell you that you should claim* me?

Offering me up, as if I were his to give in the first place.

Not his equal, not his partner.

No, I may have never been that to Hugo.

Philippe seems to consider. 'I'm not sure. I think he might have. But it was odd; before my father died, I wasn't even told that the cat was magical. That it was—or ever had been— anything else aside from a cat.'

Again, the pieces in this castle of lies that I helped build don't seem to fit together.

Or they do fit together, just not for me, someone who doesn't know half of it.

'But there was so much I never knew,' he continues. 'I grew up on the farm and much of what happened at the castle, well, I never heard anything about it. There was this gap between me and my older brothers, always. I barely saw my mother, my entire life. I felt so lonely at the farm. So deserted by everyone in my family.'

And, until recently, deserted by me.

My chest is so full of all the things I feel for him. And I wish there was a way I could wipe the slate clean between us, start anew, so I could give him what he deserves.

Philippe says, 'It didn't surprise me that my father never left me anything, but it still pained me.'

I can hardly bear to keep my mouth shut for another moment about my betrayal. I slide closer to him on the bench of the carriage and lace my hands around his neck, kissing him on the cheek. His eyes widen in surprise, but he doesn't say anything; he just wraps an arm around my waist.

If only he knew. Right now, it's tearing me to pieces.

'My brothers, they were always… They always thought they were so much better than me. I think they were happy not to see me.'

This is precisely what I thought. Sadly.

'It must be … comforting that you're now a great duke?'

'Am I, Celine? Or am I just a puppet?'

He ruffles his hair in that way of his. 'I wanted to show my mother I was worthy, I suppose. That I can be more than a farmer. That I was worth more of her time than I received.' Philippe shudders and I lean my head on his shoulder. He *is* worth it. I wish he would believe it as well. 'I'm such a blundering fool. I'm pleased you came alone and didn't bring Aurelie with you.'

I look up. 'What does Aurelie have to do with anything?'

Philippe shakes his head. 'Look, we're entering the castle.'

As he says this, the carriage passes through the iron gates. The 'castle' is no more than another set of ramparts, the wall lined with a roofed gallery. Behind the gallery are entrances, sets of doors on two floors. I realise the rooms of the castle itself must melt into the ramparts. 'This isn't a castle; this is a fortress. Fort Cantor is a castle.' I roll my eyes. 'How rustic,' I say.

'Don't say that to my brother. I don't think it will help improve family relations.'

* * *

WE ARE LED to a set of communicating rooms on the first-floor gallery. 'My brother seems to have invited us to his private dining chambers,' whispers Philippe.

A liveried servant guides us through a green door to a sort of antechamber. A narrow window looks towards the valley, but it gives so little light that even at this hour of the early evening, all the candles are lit. There are a few low stools, carved from dark oak, and two tables. The walls are full of paintings of men in battledress, men in dinner clothing, men on horses.

'Your ancestors?' I ask.

Philippe nods. He points out a portrait of a rigid man in drab grey evening dress. His tight curls are cropped short, close to his head. 'This is my great-great-grandfather, the first Seigneur Bencifert. He was the one who built the castle.'

'Ramparts,' I whisper.

He nudges me. 'Shut up.' He moves forward to a portrait of a slim man on horseback. 'This is my grandfather. You might have heard about him.'

'Ah,' I say. 'Yes. The tale of the noble Seigneur Bencifert and the Red Maiden.' Their story, and the chain of events that it set into motion, changed for ever the fate of Langly and of our kingdom.

I chuckle. And then we stop in front of the picture of a man in a long coat. He is dark-haired and has an elegant, short beard clipped in harsh angles.

I'd know this man anywhere. There weren't many teachers at the Golden Pavilion, and I remember every single one of them. My heart thuds in my chest. I think, *I'm wrong; I must be wrong.* I seek the falcon-shaped pin at his lapel, the sign of every teacher of magic at the Golden Pavilion.

And there it is.

I see it, though its colour is faded silver, almost melting into the light blue of the man's coat. A person would have to look for it to know it's there. There's a knot in my throat as memories of the Golden Pavilion start rushing in: a sunny morning; the way I watched the man riding slowly up the winding mountain road; the anticipation.

Our teachers often had other obligations, worldly matters to attend to, so there were times when we were left to our own devices. Even Madame Hirondelle materialised in and out of the building.

And they often introduced themselves by other names than the ones they bore in the outside world.

'And this is?' I ask with a strangled voice. I hope he'll tell me anything but what I fear to be true—that he's a distant relative; someone who died a long time ago; one of his uncles.

But Philippe says, 'That is Seigneur Julien Bencifert. My father.'

* * *

WE SPEND the first part of the dinner in silence. Louis, the new Seigneur Bencifert, isn't the chatty sort, nor is his wife, a middle-sized woman, her hair an inconspicuous brown and streaked with grey. She can't be much older than I am. I take in the bare walls of the room, the simple table. My mind is busy absorbing the new piece of information I have just uncovered.

The good, straight-as-a-pole Seigneur Bencifert was not only a Magic-Binder, but he had also been my teacher.

He was strict, I remember. And if I look at Philippe and the way he carries himself, he does have some of his father's unapologetic manner of entering a room. At least, since he started slipping into his role as the duke more and more.

Seigneur Bencifert taught us all we ever knew about magic binding. He showed us simple techniques to avoid being caught up in it.

Seigneur Bencifert would have known Hugo's weak spots, since he'd been his student.

This twist seems a bit cruel. To teach him, only so he could bind him, later.

How interesting, though, that Hugo failed to mention precisely this. That I also knew the man who bound him. I prod in the depths of my mind, trying to look for a sensible explanation as to why my lover might have hidden such a thing from me, but I come out empty-handed.

'The quail is delicious,' says Philippe, jolting me out of my thoughts.

'Yes, thank you,' says the lady of the house. 'I asked especially for it to be cooked for you. I hoped it is what the princess might like?'

Philippe presses his knee into mine, a tinge of worry written across his face. 'I fear that the princess is a bit tired tonight, after riding all day.' He gives me a lopsided smile, which pulls me back here, into this room.

There's so much warmth in his thigh, next to mine. A pull in my chest. And I want him to win tonight. I want him to make a good impression on his brother. I don't want to show the humiliations we have inflicted on each other at Fort Cantor.

'I'm exhausted,' I say. 'But I love stuffed quail. It is indeed delicious.'

Madame Bencifert nods, pleased.

'I heard that there was a terrible drought in Langly,' says Louis. 'It somewhat touched us,' he says, 'but not as it touched you. It is odd that it barely affected us, when you come to think of it, because we're on the outskirts of the duchy.'

Philippe's expression darkens. 'You know what they say about the stories.'

'But you threw a ball, I heard,' says Madame Bencifert. 'To celebrate the rain that came afterwards.'

'Oh,' I say, 'We just needed a good excuse to throw a ball.' I take a sip of the wine, which I find to be a bit too tart on my tongue. Or maybe I'm just thirsty. It has, indeed, been a long day.

'I heard it was lovely,' says Madame Bencifert.

I detect a trace of regret in her voice.

'We wanted to thank the seigneurs for standing by us during a few difficult months,' I say, and Philippe touches his elbow to mine.

I turn to look at him, a question in my eyes: *What?*

He just smiles at me. And it's so genuine and brimming with happiness that it makes me feel even worse for all the things I'm keeping from him.

That I only married him with the intention to replace him, at Hugo's behest.

Hugo, whom I trusted above everyone else, who I thought trusted me with everything, in exchange.

'I heard it was a bit more unusual than that,' says Louis, in a tone far from neutral.

I hear what Louis implies, beyond his words—the lack of propriety of it all. And this is what I thought, too, at the ball. But perhaps I should try harder to see the world as Philippe does.

'Yes, unusual,' I say. 'But we had just come out of a most unusual situation.'

Next to me, Philippe stiffens. What his brother thinks matters to him.

'I think I would have liked to see it,' says Louis.

'Of course,' I say. 'The next time we have a ball for the seigneurs I'll make sure to invite you. It would be delightful to have Philippe's family there. But, of course, to be one of the Langly seigneurs, you'd have to swear him fealty first,' I say with all the innocence I can muster.

Louis chuckles. 'Falling to my knees in front of my little brother. I don't think so.'

Philippe takes my hand in his, under the table, and squeezes. A smile flutters to my lips. *You're welcome.*

'I hope you mean only that the Bencifert seigneurs have always enjoyed their status as direct vassals of the King, and that your words have no bearing on Philippe's qualities as a duke,' I say. 'Because I can assure you, Philippe is the best duke that

Langly has ever had. He cares for his people, and I can tell you that with all the authority I have as the king's daughter.'

Madame Bencifert still stares at me with wide eyes. But Louis raises his cup. 'Hear, hear.'

We turn to our plates again, nothing left to say on the subject.

'Are you leaving tomorrow?' asks Louis.

'No,' says Philippe.

'Yes,' I say.

All four of us exchange odd looks. We haven't yet spoken about the matter of Philippe returning to the duchy. We haven't even so much as touched upon it. But why would he not?

'I didn't think you could leave the duchy. Not now, when there's so much to do,' says Louis.

'And we should return,' I say.

'I was hoping to show Celine the surroundings,' Philippe says smoothly.

'Of course,' I say. 'We can talk about it later. I mean, make plans for the day.'

'Lovely. I'm happy to meet you tomorrow, too, at dinner,' says Madame Bencifert. 'It's such a pleasure to have you here.'

* * *

FINALLY ALONE IN OUR CHAMBER, I slip out of my embroidered surcoat by myself. My eye is caught by the view from the open window: the ruins of the Golden Pavilion, glittering in the distance. The golden-white absorbs the moonlight, reflecting it towards the Opal Mountain like an aura. Seigneur Bencifert must have had a short ride to the magic school.

I remember, as through a fog, what Count Goderic told me about Isabella, and where I might find her. Perhaps he's right.

Count Goderic isn't the sort of man to waste words—no, he's very careful with them.

For the first time in many years, I feel an urge to return to the Golden Pavilion.

'Should I help you?' he says, his hands on my hips, pulling me to him. An invitation.

We both look towards the curtained bed in the corner, and I have to smile. That we should have come to this point in a single day, where I wouldn't mind sharing a bed with him…

And then I think, *Hugo sent me here*. What would he say about all that has passed between us? The memory of him slithers between Philippe and me. As if there is such a thing as 'Philippe and me'. There would be no such thing, in any case, if he finds out the truth. And what can we build on lies? How could we ever trust each other?

I slip out of his grasp, facing him.

'Thank you for earlier,' he says, bunching the next layer of fabric and slipping it over my head in a quick move. His fingers brush my arms as he does so and the touch travels like lightning through my blood.

I shiver, unable to move. I want nothing more than to cup that lovely face, to kiss those lips again. I remember the feel of him inside of me and breathing becomes impossible, my chest tightening with so much longing.

And then, why not give in to this? To him?

What reason could I possibly have not to? He is my husband, after all. Leave building a future, whatever that might look like, for another day.

I have other plans for tonight.

Philippe says, 'This was most kind of you. And unexpected.'

'What was unexpected?'

'The fact that you were on my side of the barricade for once.

This day… It's as if you're someone else entirely.' He lays his hands on my back, nothing but a thin shift between us, and the pull is so strong that I raise my chin high, coming closer and closer, pining for that kiss.

But then he frowns, and something shifts in his eyes. 'Tell me something only you could know.'

He increases the pressure on my back.

'What?'

'Something only you and I would know. Something no one else would.'

I try to ransack my memory for moments that only he and I would have shared, but there aren't many of them.

'On that first day when I arrived at Fort Cantor,' he says. 'Into whose chambers did you lead me?'

'Magali's,' I blurt.

'And what did you take?'

I shake my head, unsure what he means.

'In the bedchambers you pocketed something, when you thought I wasn't looking.'

I almost gasp. Philippe does see and understand more than I give him credit for. 'The chain,' I say. 'An iron chain.'

He nods. I take a step back. Two. 'What is this about?'

'When we were in the … erm … your bedchambers. On our wedding night,' he says.

'I can't believe this. What do you want? Have you hit your head?'

'Just answer me,' he says.

'No,' I say. 'What's your point? Do you want to humiliate me now, after we've…' I think, *After we consummated our marriage? After I developed a soft spot for you?* 'Are you throwing in my face what I've said and done in the past?'

'The point is,' he says, narrowing his eyes, 'that there has been enough damage done by Shape-Shifters.'

I'm taken aback, unsure what he wants. Then it begins to dawn on me. 'So I can be nice to you only if I'm a Shape-Shifter? And how many Shape-Shifters have you met?'

'Plenty,' he says, slipping out of his surcoat and tapping his pocket. 'Magali, Maël, Hugo.' He counts on his fingers. 'Even my mother. They've all done lots of damage. And you mentioned Hugo's name earlier, in the carriage. I seem to recall that I specifically asked Celine about the cat not so long ago, and Celine told me it's just a funny talking cat.'

I think, *Hugo*. His shadow slips between us, widening that rift between Philippe and me.

'But how many Shape-Shifters have you met who can do water magic?' I say, hinting at what happened in the stables, earlier today.

He raises his eyebrows.

'I've been with you every single moment since I arrived at the farmhouse.'

Philippe seems to consider this for a moment, biting his lip. 'Not while I was bathing. I was away for a while.'

'Fine,' I say.

I head to the water jug on the table, touch the burnt clay surface and close my eyes. I raise my other hand in the air, then focus. The water splashes at first, but then builds an arc between the jug and the tips of my fingers. I swivel it in the air, then release, aiming at him. A jet of water brushes his arm.

'You missed,' he says, almost smiling. He pats the wet sleeve.

'No, it went precisely where I wanted it to go.'

He guffaws. The tension in his shoulders dissipates. 'I'm sorry. You can never be too careful. I can't tell who's lying to me and who isn't. Especially since you lied to me, too. About Hugo.'

I shudder at the thought of having to explain anything about Hugo to Philippe. Especially since I'm only beginning to glimpse how I might have been just a pawn in his game. And I'm so tired. By all of this.

I can't, and I don't want to face this today. So I turn on my heel and stalk towards the bed.

'I asked you something,' he says. 'I think we should speak about Hugo. Don't run away from me again.'

'I'm not. I'm cold.' I tuck myself under the quilt.

'Isn't it awful to live like this? With all the lies? You aren't honest with me, Celine.' He paces the room, up and down. 'Why did you even come here?'

It pains me that he has to ask. That he doubts it. But did I not doubt it, as well, until yesterday?

So I say to my husband, 'Because I want you to come back home.'

'Home?' He arches his eyebrows in that way of his that tells me that he doesn't quite believe me. 'You're nothing but awful to me at Fort Cantor.'

I huddle under the cover, terrified he might ask why I ever married him at all. Terrified he might make the connection with Hugo. What did I tell myself this afternoon, when I allowed us to grow so close?

There can never be anything between him and me after all I've done. *And* I've broken the promise I made to myself, that I will take no man but Hugo.

But I want Philippe. I wanted him earlier, and I want him now; I want him to sit down with me, and I want to touch him, and hold him, when it feels more impossible than ever.

I want him, and *I* ruined it.

And yet we would have never been together in this room if it wasn't for Hugo, and this certainly says something.

Probably about me.

Philippe mutters something under his breath and walks to the open window, his arms gripping the sill as if tearing it apart would get us all out of this situation.

And yet... Watching the way his shoulders tense, the straight line of his back, I find I can't think again. 'Come to bed. You must be cold.'

'Why?' he says. 'Why, Celine? Why do you want me in your bed?'

My cheeks catch fire. For many reasons. None of which I can explain to him.

'What is Hugo to you, Celine? I have been warned.' His back is still turned to me.

How appropriate.

I want him, I know this. But if Hugo is ever released of his cat form... I'm not sure if I would trade the duke for the steward, and this hollows me from inside out.

This is the sort of person that I am. And, in my heart, I know that Philippe makes me a better person.

Perhaps I'll feel different once I see Hugo in his true form again. Once we can stop pretending.

But perhaps I'll never want to let Philippe go—that is, if he should still want me. Maybe, maybe not. I wouldn't think so, considering how he challenges me now.

My life is a pile of lies and maybes.

So, for once, I tell my husband the truth. 'I don't know what I want, Philippe.'

'Do you know what Hugo told me, Celine? He told me that I could have you *if* I could get you. That day when he showed you to me, at the tournament in Langville, he said, "The princess can be yours, if you can coax her."'

My heart cracks and breaks like skin when it's been too much under cold water, too much under ice. Bloody rifts open across it. I try to tell myself, *Hugo lied. He was trying to persuade Philippe into the plan.* But my heart doesn't believe me, because my heart remembers the man I have loved for so many years. And he isn't quite the same as the boy who left the Golden Pavilion that night all those years ago.

'And tell me, Celine, who wouldn't want a princess?' With this, he stalks out of the chamber, slamming the door.

The reverberations that the quivering door send through my body shatter me to pieces. I bury my face in the pillow, trying to stifle all my tears, but there's no stopping the flow, no stopping the sobbing that takes over my entire body, no quenching the tears that soak the bed, no way to stop the pain, until sleep sends me into sweet oblivion.

THE GOLDEN PAVILION

MAGALI

I wake up, calling Julien's name. Looking for him. From across the valley, the silhouette of Castle Bencifert taunts me.

I walk up to the open window, taking deep breaths of fresh air. I have dreamed of him again. Dreamed of him wrapping his arm around my back, in that way of his. Planting a soft kiss on my cheek.

I have loved one man in my life and his name was Julien. I have loved one man, and all his life he did all he could to protect me. I have loved one man and when I remember the way he lay in the bed he died in, his lids draped across his eyes, never to open again, I can't breathe.

'Where are you?' I whisper into the night.

Julien was a Magic-Binder, but with his ideas about what was proper and what was not, he kept me fettered. And I trusted in his advice—how could I not trust the man who protected me and my son, when Kylian cast us out of Fort Cantor?

My son. I have done everything for Maël. But what have I done *to* him? And where is he now? Regret washes through me,

267

increasing the emptiness in my chest. We had quarrelled before. He reproached me that I tried too hard, tried to control all of his actions.

How it hurt me to see how blind he was to my wise advice. How it enraged me. And certain things passed between us, the last time I saw him, that should have never been said.

I kept them in my chest, safe, and they grew to the size of monsters, tearing everything apart.

In the night air, I let go of Julien's name, asking him if he thinks that I may have gone too far.

CELINE

When I wake up, Philippe is pulling on his trousers. He's slipped into bed next to me in the dead of night, his back turned, careful not to touch me. The mere presence of him made my eyes sting with tears.

I swallow them, bitter and unspilled.

'Where are you going?' I say.

'To the farm.' He shrugs.

'You can't go to the farm. It's not yours anymore.' He's just … tolerated there. I suppose. No one would contradict a duke if he wants to muck the stalls, would they?

'Come with me to Fort Cantor.'

'No.'

I wait for an explanation, but it doesn't come. He proceeds to put on the rest of his garments.

'That's it? You give up? You've done so much for the people, Philippe. I can't even begin to tell you how much you've done.'

He says nothing, but maybe, just maybe, I have his ear.

'How about making a difference?' I challenge him. 'How about everything you told me? Do you remember what you said when you wanted me to try harder? When did *you* give up trying harder?'

He doesn't even look at me. 'When I realised that what I do doesn't matter that much. That there are others who would do more harm, in my name, than good, and when you draw the line, there's much more damage than... You know what, I don't want to talk about this.'

He pats his pocket.

I have a thousand questions before I even begin to unwrap this statement, but I'm not sure if it would be of any use to ask them. Philippe can be stubborn, in that way.

And yet, I can't simply wait here for him to change his mind. I want to go back home, but not without him. I look away. The Opal Mountain glints in the distance. 'Then come with me to the Golden Pavilion,' I say.

'The Golden Pavilion? Why?' He frowns.

'So much happened at once five years ago. Hugo disappeared; the Golden Pavilion was destroyed; my mother died. Just like you, I'm being lied to. Just like you, I want some answers.'

He sits down on the bed, at a distance from me. Considering. 'It's a ruin.'

I take a deep breath. 'Count Goderic told me that's where your mother would be.'

Philippe seems dumbstruck. 'My mother? You want to speak to my mother?'

I bite my lip. 'We've been married for months, Philippe, and I haven't even seen her. She didn't come to the wedding. Why is this?'

There it is, a slice of truth that I'm offering him. A slice of my concerns.

Philippe's lovely face is twisted by a grimace of pain. 'Don't you think I'd like to know?'

Yet again, it cuts through me how callous his mother has been to him. 'I'm sorry. That's ... terrible.'

'Nothing surprises me about her anymore.' He begins pulling on his boots. 'The Golden Pavilion, you said?'

This is good, I think. Finally. We are touching on subjects we've always avoided; we are going into uncharted territory. 'Why were you never a student?' I ask.

He clicks his tongue, in supreme distaste. Straightens his jacket. But then he replies, 'My parents taught me all I needed to know. Between a Shape-Shifter and a Magic-Binder, I think I had rather a good magical education. I can control my magic, unlike you.'

I ignore the insult. 'Odd,' I say. 'I was told Isabella was a Storm-Caller.'

Philippe shrugs.

And if we are to be completely honest to each other... 'I realised last night that your father was one of my teachers at the Pavilion.'

By the way he stops in his tracks, I realise that I struck hard. That his parents should have kept him from the Pavilion, while his own father taught there.

He would have liked to be a student. He told me as much.

'How?' he asks, disappointment written all over his face.

'The portrait at Castle Bencifert, last night. The teachers introduced themselves with different names at the Pavilion. And I don't remember seeing your father at the Red Court.'

'No, he always sent my brother to represent him in Court... Oh.' He puts his face in his hands, rubbing it hard. 'By Lucius' Flaming Finger and Sabya's Darkblades and all the Mothers of the Forest, to the last one. He concealed this on purpose. From me. From his students.'

I'm frozen on the bed, aching to touch him, to give him

comfort. But I'm not sure if he would even want that from me, not after our conversation last night.

'What do we do now?' I ask instead.

Philippe straightens himself. 'We're going to the Golden Pavilion.'

* * *

IT'S A CLOUDY DAY, but rain does not ruin our ride. At a brisk trot, we cross the valley that separates Castle Bencifert from the Golden Pavilion. At the foot of the cliff, we stop to admire the ruins.

As I remembered, there isn't much left, except for a pile of white stones nestled upon a plateau, high above us. I still find it hard to believe that Madame Hirondelle took it upon herself to reduce the Pavilion to rubble after the Crystal of Power was destroyed. What harm would have been done if the ancient buildings stood?

'The road,' says Philippe. 'If no one has taken care of it, it might be unsafe. Parts of it might simply have slid down. And with two horses—'

I glance at the path winding at the edge of the mountain—a dusty white ribbon. Chipped here and there where rocks must have been torn from the mountain.

'Do you think we should leave the horses here? But we can at least try to see if we can go up on horseback. It's a long ascent.'

Philippe pats his pocket again. 'Fine.'

We start up the road at a steady pace. Neither of us says anything—we haven't exchanged many words during the day.

I suppose I'm grateful he agreed to come with me. The road is odder and odder as we ascend. As we look into the distance, we see a downtrodden, crumbling path. But the trail underneath the horse's hooves, as we move forward, is smooth and immaculate, just as I remember it.

I think of my mother and the power of her illusions, and I can't tell which is the greater lie: the clean path, or the broken one?

'Strange, don't you think?' I say.

Philippe looks down, and then at the ruins of the pavilion, drawing closer and closer. 'It might not be as deserted as we think.'

'Are you afraid?' I say, feeling my own heart drumming in my chest.

'I'd be a fool not to be.'

'Do you think we should turn back?' I ask, almost hoping he'll say that we should. I try not to look beyond the edge of the road. Whenever I do, I start feeling dizzy.

There used to be ancient spells in place to prevent horses and men from slipping from the path—for those who were welcome. There used to be other sorts of spells for those who weren't. A single wrong step and we'd fall into the abyss. No one would ever know what happened to us.

Where we went.

The art of weaving spells has been lost to us in the fog of time. But the Golden Pavilion held on tight to its old shields of protection. Until now, at least.

'Yes, I think it would be wiser,' says Philippe. 'But that doesn't necessarily mean that we should. What does your heart tell you, Celine?'

'I don't bloody know what my heart is telling me. It's beating much too fast.' And if I knew what my heart were telling me, perhaps we wouldn't be here today.

Philippe stops his horse. 'It was your idea to come here,' he says. 'Tell me, do you want to go back?'

I stare at him, a square, broad silhouette on the horse; the way he sits on his mount and stands behind every choice that he makes; the searching way he looks at my face. I think, *Perhaps what happened yesterday at the farm was just right.*

I could turn around now. Turn back to what I knew. To what I had. To what I thought I wanted.

Or I could move forward. With Philippe. 'No,' I say. 'Let's move on.'

* * *

THERE'S a bend in a road I don't remember, not far away from the ruins themselves. The pile of marble is ahead of us, so, so close, and then the road winds one more time around the cliff.

When we emerge from behind it, we find ourselves in the central square of the Golden Pavilion, which looks precisely as I remembered it. Yellow and white swirling patterns dance on the marble floor that our horses now tread on. Towers and turrets rise all around it, laced marble balconies and galleries connecting them.

'Philippe, do you see it as well?'

'I've never seen anything this beautiful in my life,' Philippe says as he dismounts.

'Everything ... everything is just as I remember it.' I swivel around, looking for the low building of the stables. They're empty, of course.

'What is this?' he says. 'It looks ... perfect. Unblemished.'

My palms break into a sweat. I think, *Illusions. Lies. We are surrounded by them.*

I look up at him as he takes in everything around us. He then glances at me and he must see something in my face because he lays a hand on my arm. 'Don't be afraid.'

'I'm absolutely terrified. I think I must be losing my mind here.'

'I see it, too,' he says. 'You're not mad.'

'Everything I've been told, it's been a lie.'

Philippe lays his hand on the back of my neck now, steadfast and reassuring. *You're not alone,* his touch seems to say.

'How can this be? So much magic is necessary to maintain an illusion like this.' Thoughts race in my head. There's only one person who could create this sort of magic, who could keep it up, but she died more than five years ago.

A loud clap sounds on the floor and we both turn to look towards the main entrance, at the mountain end of the square. A silhouette emerges from the shadows—tall, cloaked and hooded.

'Take your horses off the marble. They'll ruin it. Celine, you know the rules.'

My heart beats so wildly. I think, *This isn't possible. It will burst in a few moments.*

I remember this voice, this woman.

'Madame Hirondelle?' I say, barely a whisper.

'Mother?' says Philippe in a strangled voice.

The silhouette emerges from the shadows. It's a tall woman, with dark red hair cascading down her back that I've mistaken for a hood. She wears the same teal cloak she always used to wear while she was the rector of the magic school.

'Meet me in the Refectory,' says Madame Hirondelle. 'I assume you must be hungry. Celine, you can show him the way. And please do get those horses off the marble.' I hear the same clipped tone, the same command in her voice, that haunts my memories.

Tears are again close to the surface.

My hands are trembling as I tie the horses to a post. Philippe doesn't even move; he just stares at the place where Madame Hirondelle stood only moments ago.

Then, I realise. 'Philippe, that's Madame Hirondelle, the doyenne of the Golden Pavilion.'

'No, Celine, that's my mother.'

MAGALI

From the rooms that have always belonged to me, I stare into the distance. There is no sign of them. No sign of her, no sign of him.

No sign of Maël.

They have all deserted me.

I am finally in my castle, alone, on the lands that belonged to my family long before there was even such a thing as the Duchy of Langly, and yet, for all the joy that I expected to fill me, not a trace of it is to be seen.

I turn around to close the shutters, when I see *her*.

The Marchionessa.

Materialised next to one of the bedposts.

'Where is he?' she says, her skin almost translucent in the weak light. It's not her, it's not really her, I know as much from my brushes with the Fallen Court. It's just a projection, someone who can't touch me.

Though the rest of her tattered Fallen Court could. Can.

'I asked you something. Where is Maël?' Her voice is something you can't forget easily. Melodious, in spite of the commanding tone she's using now.

I cannot afford to forget. That's the sort of voice that could conjure a storm, that could make walls crumble.

That could make a king fall.

'I don't know where he is,' I say. I feel so drab in Aurelie's clothing, Aurelie's skin. Again, she has caught me on the wrong foot.

May Lucius' Fire burn her, and all her ilk.

'You don't seem crazed with pain,' she says, but I can tell that she is. Her projection is flickering, like the shadows thrown by the light of a candle, and there are dark circles underneath her eyes.

She always loved Maël so much, more than anyone else.

'I'm sorry,' I say brusquely. 'I have other matters to attend to.'

'I see.' She points at my threadbare cloak. I feel like I've been caught in the act of doing something disgraceful. I feel, simply, caught. 'You are up to no good. And if I find out that you had something to do with his disappearance, that your actions resulted in harm coming to him…' Her expression turns savage, her brown eyes burning with anger. 'Oh, Magali, how you will pay for it. You have no idea.'

I must not show fear, I remind myself. I must not show that I feel her eyes watching me. Counting my moves.

I prepare to say something to that effect, when she vanishes.

I remain in the dark room for a long while, trying to settle the beats of my rushing heart.

Hugo, I tell myself. She doesn't even know about Hugo.

No one in the Fallen Court does.

CELINE

We cross the square at a brisk pace. I can't think of anything to say. It seems that even my mind has frozen. That woman can't be Isabella of Langly. She's Madame Hirondelle. Isn't she?

'It can't be,' I mumble.

Philippe follows me through the light-flooded corridors to the Refectory, a vast room under a glass dome towards the mountain end of the Pavilion. I suppose I'd be dumbstruck to see my former school of magic looking precisely like it did more than five years ago, minus the students, if I wasn't so worried about this latest turn of events.

'Madame Hirondelle is your mother?' I can't imagine the doyenne as anybody's mother, let alone Philippe's.

My husband rushes after me, saying nothing.

Come to think of it, if it's true, it would explain any number of things. For instance, Isabella's 'travels' and her absences, both from here as well as from Castle Bencifert.

Our steps echo in the nearly empty hall of the refectory. The long tables with inlaid marble are the same as they used to be, as are the low benches. Madame Hirondelle—or Isabella—stands at the end of one of the tables, in front of three plates laden with food.

It's the usual fare we always had at the pavilion: fruit, a bit of bread with a chewy crust, and cold mutton. 'Sit down,' she says, pouring us water in the brass cups I also know so well.

'Madame Hirondelle, it's such a pleasure to see you again,' I say. 'I never thought I would.'

She gives me a thin smile. 'Nor did I, Celine. It is good to see you again, too. I don't have much company here.'

'Were you waiting for us?' I say.

'No. Why would I be? No one comes here. We made the pavilion look like a ruin especially so that no one would bother.'

So much for foreseeing the future and a higher purpose.

'What brings you here?' she says.

Phillip watches her, still in awe.

'An accident, I suppose? I am so glad... Well, we're a bit shocked. I never knew that you were Philippe's mother. I assume you know that he's my husband? That he's the new Duke of Langly?'

'News travels,' she says, 'even in the farthest corners.' She fiddles with her cape. 'But I had the pleasure of being at your wedding, so this isn't entirely a surprise.'

I shake my head. 'What?'

'The Lightsong,' she says softly, then pushes the plates of food towards us. 'Here, have something to eat.'

The Lightsong. The ancient wedding song, the quivering light in the dark.

'Are you a Light-Cantor?' I ask.

She motions with her hand. 'I don't have the Gift, like my mother, if that's what you're asking, but I learned the songs. And I sometimes sing at weddings.'

The commanding Madame Hirondelle sings at weddings. The thought is so absurd that I almost laugh.

Philippe grits his teeth. 'You're my mother. And what do you mean by "news travels"? You're the one who told me I should marry Celine.'

'It may seem that way to you, but I am not your mother,' she says.

'Really?' he says, his disappointment turning into fury. 'And who might that be?'

Madame Hirondelle looks down at his coat. 'I'm afraid it's not for me to say.'

He throws his hands in the air. 'This is ludicrous. Who are you, then? Are you also a Shape-Shifter?'

'I am Isabella of Langly,' she says, calmly. 'Also known to your wife as Madame Hirondelle. And I'm a Storm-Caller.'

I nudge Philippe. 'See? I told you Isabella was a Storm-Caller. Is.'

Philippe breathes heavily. 'A Storm-Caller. Perhaps the very Storm-Caller that had something to do with the recent drought in Langly?'

I whoosh my head around, appalled.

Madame Hirondelle tucks her hands in the sleeves of her cloak. 'I was led to believe it was the right course of action. Even I make mistakes.'

There's a cold fury in the way Philippe stands. 'Why should I believe you?'

Madame Hirondelle closes her eyes and lifts a finger, swinging it into the air. The winds pick up above the glass ceiling of the refectory, herding clouds together. Their colour changes from fluffy white to grey and a few drops of water plonk above us. She then opens her eyes and breathes sharply. 'See? Storm-Caller.'

Something clicks from what Philippe said earlier. About his mother telling him to marry *me*. 'You spoke to your mother about me? She told you to marry me? I don't understand a single thing,' I say.

'Obviously you haven't met my mother,' says Philippe. 'I should be shocked, but somehow, I am not.'

I watch pain rippling on his face, and even if the last statement I unwrapped unnerves me, the impulse to touch him, to lay a hand on his arm, is strong; to tell him that I am here, by his side.

But he wouldn't want that. I close my fist under the table.

'I am who I say I am,' says Madame Hirondelle. 'I do not lie. Ask Celine. I told you that there are some answers I cannot provide; you will have to ask someone else. But perhaps I can answer other questions you might have.'

I say, 'I wouldn't even know where to begin. So many things are afoot.'

Philippe is quiet, perhaps trying to get some kind of grip on what we have just discovered.

'I do have questions, about what's happening. There is a sort of...'

'Yes, things are moving, aren't they? This is the impression that one has, walking the kingdom right now,' says Madame Hirondelle. 'I don't spend all my time here. Sometimes I travel. You're lucky to have found me here today.'

'Yes, lucky,' mutters Philippe.

Madame Hirondelle says, studying him from head to foot, 'I hear you're rather ... unusual as a duke. So tell me, what brings you to the Golden Pavilion?' She looks to me.

I lace my hands on the table. 'If you've heard what's happening...' I don't know if I can trust her. The things she tells Philippe —they're more than strange. 'Maël disappeared.'

'Yes,' says Madame Hirondelle.

'And Philippe is the new duke. But matters are complicated.'

'How so?' she says.

Then I realise that, seen from a different perspective, matters aren't complicated at all. Hugo is attempting to regain his human form and his duchy, and I'm trying to help—but there's no reason Madame Hirondelle should know about Hugo and his difficulties.

In fact, if it weren't for Hugo, the situation would be quite straightforward. Philippe is the new duke, and I am his wife.

Unless...

'But if you're Isabella of Langly, and Philippe isn't your son, how come he is the new duke?'

She shrugs. 'Anyone can be the new duke, I suppose, as long as the king says he is. My father, the first duke, wasn't a duke until the King made him one. And my mother is so many things that...' She shakes her head. 'Why do you have to place such importance on what things are named?'

'I don't know,' says Philippe. 'Maybe because if things aren't labelled right, someone, somewhere might think it a good reason to start a fight? I only have to think of your brothers and your nephews to find plenty of examples.'

Madame Hirondelle waves him away. 'My brothers and their ilk... And people wonder why I chose a life at the Golden Pavilion.'

'But you destroyed it,' I say, my voice choking. 'You sent us all away, and made it look like it was in ruins. We all had a home here ... until we didn't. From one day to the next.'

Madame Hirondelle's eyes darken. 'And I'm so sorry I had to do things the way I did. I could blame your father, of course. Or the Fallen Court.'

My father, I understand... He was the one who wanted to destroy the Golden Pavilion, who wanted all magic erased. And he was the one who seized the opportunity to do so, after my mother died. But... 'The Fallen Court? What does the Fallen Court have to do with all of this?'

Madame Hirondelle's lips curl upwards. 'I may have said too much already.'

The Fallen Court. Creatures of shadows and whispers, with a finger in all kingdoms.

My mother warned me against them, against their plotting and throat-cutting. Over and over again. 'Why do they hate us so much? Why do they hate the mages?'

'Who said anything about hate?' says Madame Hirondelle. 'Your father isn't a man of passion. He had his reasons, and so did I.' She purses her lips, a sign that this conversation, at least, is over.

'But the Fallen Court—' I insist. They *do* hate us.

'The school gave the wrong sort of power to many people.' Her tone is definitive. 'Look at all the mayhem caused by the Shape-Shifters.'

'Through the Crystal? Is that still standing, as well?' But it cannot be. I felt my powers drain away that day. And so did everyone else.

Except her, of course. She seems perfectly capable of conjuring a storm or a drought whenever she needs it.

'No, the Crystal has been destroyed. Sadly.'

'Why do you still have your powers, then?'

Madame Hirondelle shifts in her place.

'Let's go,' says Philippe, who has been watching us until now. 'She lies, or speaks only in riddles.'

'Wait,' she says. 'Why did I always fail to teach you patience, Celine? And how to halt the flow of your magic?'

Philippe stops, perhaps persuaded by the mention of my poor ability to stop. He felt that on his own skin only a day ago.

'The Pavilion gave mages power because it taught them to use their skills, and it channelled that power back and forth, between the Crystal and the mountain.' Madame Hirondelle finally sits down, compelling Philippe to do the same. She taps her lips with her fingers, considering. 'A small number of mages chose to use their skills to do harm in the past and in the present, or to harness unjustified amounts of powers for themselves. They caused a lot of trouble. You see, the Crystal was just like a powerful weapon. You never knew who wielded it or when it was turned against you, against the others. And the doyennes of the Pavilion … in time, they forgot that.'

'Do you mean someone in particular?' I say, thinking about my mother. She had been a doyenne, too. For decades.

'You know what I mean.' Madame Hirondelle lies back. 'Hugo was about to start yet another war. We weren't prepared to stand by and wait for all of that to happen. Your father and I, we had to intervene. We couldn't allow it.'

'You closed the Pavilion because of that? But what did Hugo's trial have to do with magic?' As far as I remember, Hugo merely brought forward a witness to testify that his father, Kylian, was the first born, and not Frederic.

'And don't you think it's odd all of this didn't happen until after Frederic died? And that only one witness substantiated Hugo's claim?'

Philippe follows our exchange, his arms braced on the table, leaning forward. I throw him a glance that says, *This is important to us. Both of us.*

'I'm not sure what you're implying.' Hugo was terrified of Frederic. He always had been. 'Hugo had known this witness for a while, but he was afraid of what Frederic might do to the poor woman if she came forward. Frederic was like that. Ruthless. Like his father, the first duke.'

'Of course,' says Madame Hirondelle. 'Hugo would have told you this. And considering your ties to him, you would have believed him.'

I'm taken aback that she's aware about what went on between us. I would have wagered that she knew nothing, but it seems I am wrong again.

Philippe clenches his jaw, his face all angles and anger. 'Did he now, Celine? Did Hugo tell you all about his plans? All those years ago?'

I've hurt him, again. And Madame Hirondelle knows more about Hugo's machinations than I ever thought was possible. She says, 'There was never any witness.'

'What do you mean?' There is so much to absorb that I don't even know where to look anymore.

'Hugo was a Shape-Shifter, Celine. He *was* the witness, too. He made up that story and everything that was said in front of the Royal Court of Judges.' There's something steely in the way Madame Hirondelle sets her mouth.

'Hugo ... lied?' To me? Hugo lied *to me.*

All those years I wasted waiting for him, they were based on lies. And everything that I've done for him since he returned...

Am I entirely surprised? I only have to remember how he evaded answering the last time I asked him about shapeshifting. How he asked about what I did with Philippe, instead.

Philippe says, 'What do you mean, *was*? Hugo is very much alive.'

'Yes,' I say, boiling on the inside, 'he's at Fort Cantor now. He's been turned into a cat by Magali and Philippe's father, five years ago.'

Madame Hirondelle looks as if she's forgotten how to breathe. I stop myself, fearful that I've said too much. She takes us both in. 'Are you sure of this?'

'Yes,' Philippe and I reply at once.

Philippe says, 'He has been helping me. And helping Celine as well, it seems.' He gives me a sideways glance full of reproach.

Madame Hirondelle's nostrils flare.

She is livid.

'Did I say something wrong?' She still has the power to intimidate me. It seems that I haven't outgrown the Golden Pavilion just yet.

Madame Hirondelle lifts my chin with her fingers. 'Remember this, Celine. Remember the lies. The pain. I've made mistakes, too, and I'm still making them. It's always because of the people we care about the most.'

She turns to Philippe. 'It was never my intention to hurt anyone, but I simply cannot tell you what you need to know. However, I will say this: sometimes, people lie to protect themselves and those who they love, and other people help maintain the illusion because they care about the liars, and they can't help themselves.' She looks to me again. 'Consider yourself warned about Hugo. And if I were you, if he ever asks anything of you, I'd ask myself five times why he needs it. I've also made mistakes. Protected people I shouldn't have.'

'You've told me nothing,' says Philippe. He doesn't even look at me.

Madame Hirondelle lays a hand on Philippe's arm. 'You deserve the truth, for all the good that might do you. This is my advice to you: seek out Magali.'

'But she's gone,' I say. 'No one can find her. No one has seen her since Maël cast her out of Fort Cantor.'

'Not that you know of, at any rate,' she says, darting a glance at me. The calmness she radiated at the beginning of our encounter has dissipated. I can finally see that magnificent, ambitious Isabella of Langly whom everyone in the kingdom spoke about. But she's still protecting someone, still shielding someone by not telling Philippe the truth.

'Remember, both of you: there's nothing Hugo's done that hasn't already been done before by Magali. And if you truly seek answers beyond what I've already told you, they're the people you should ask.'

RUINS

MAGALI

I curl up in my bronze tub, though it is empty. A darkness unseen before envelops me. Philippe has left, and would have none of the gift that I had bestowed on him.

And Maël … he has done everything in his power to prove himself unworthy—drunken debaucheries, endless hunts, gold and jewels flowing into the hands of the lowest of brigands.

There has not been a time when the business of the duchy was better conducted than when I ruled it, hiding behind my son and my husband's shape.

Together, we became Illusionists, for almost ten years.

And yet. I could never speak openly. I was forever relegated to a smaller seat, my voice muted.

Wife of, daughter of, mother of dukes.

Never the duchess in my own right.

Even if I am better than all of them put together.

And Hugo promised me there would be a way. In that plan we forged together, at Castle Bencifert, in the days before Julien died.

Yet Hugo proves himself a burden. His true role may have ended long ago on the cliff opposite Fort Cantor. If he truly had

Maël, he would have produced him by now so he could join his silly princess.

And I should be rid of him before the Fallen Court finds out what happened to him five years ago.

With Philippe gone, there might be a way to move forward, without the cat and the princess. But I will need my Gift in order to do so.

Tilting, tilting. This way and that.

I remember what people say: where there's a will, there's a way.

And no one can accuse me of having no will of my own.

CELINE

We set off in the middle of the afternoon, back towards the castle, along a slow path descending towards the valley. There was nothing else that Madame Hirondelle would tell us, but there is enough to consider within what she has already revealed.

For instance, everything I thought I knew about the man I loved. And in this deep silence that keeps my husband and me more thoroughly apart than any physical barrier, I wonder if Hugo ever truly loved me. If he even knows what love is.

Does his heart ache for me, to think how lonely I have been in the past five years? Did jealousy tear his flesh when he sent me to fetch Philippe back? What kind of man does such a thing?

I'm the greatest fool in the world for letting his ambition shape my life. I thought I was nothing without him, but now I have so much more.

I am so much more.

Philippe rides in front of me, his shoulders hunched. I think of his pain. His confusion. I call out. 'Are you all right?'

'What do you think?'

What Madame Hirondelle said, the hesitations, the half-truths, will have thrown him even deeper into doubting everything. And if *I* am doubting Hugo now after what I've heard—

Why would Isabella of Langly tell him that she isn't his mother?

'I can't possibly imagine how you feel.'

'Humph,' he says.

'But I'm sure there's bound to be an explanation. A reason.'

'You'd think that I would know it though, wouldn't you?'

'Apparently there's a lot we don't know,' I say.

Most of all, about the elusive Magali.

'Madame Hirondelle said that you should ask Magali. I gather you're closer to her than you allowed me to believe. That, perhaps, you have seen her recently,' I retort.

Philippe might not be quite as naïve as Hugo made him out to be. But perhaps nothing good can come from looking back. Perhaps it is time to look to the future. To what can be done, what can be built upon these ruins where my dreams used to be.

'Magali was so angry. So, so angry. After all that she did for Maël...' He pats his pocket again.

I say nothing about how Maël had been kept in a cage in my own room for days, or about his mysterious disappearance.

I am such a terrible person. And then, I realise, I didn't come up with all of this. I just followed Hugo's guidance. Have I ever been more than a puppet? And I didn't expect that Philippe would have lied to me, too.

'And what about you and Hugo?'

My cheeks catch fire. I can't think of a lie quick enough. A lie to protect...

Madame Hirondelle said, *I've also made mistakes.*

Enough, I think.

Enough of Hugo. There is only one way to expose him, to untangle this web of lies. Comparing the lies he told to us both.

If I want an honest answer from Philippe, perhaps I should offer mine in exchange.

'Hugo, well ... I used to love Hugo. Yes, Hugo used to be my lover. And I had no idea that Madame Hirondelle knew. I thought we hid it well.'

Philippe stops his horse in his tracks and turns to look at me. Finally. His eyes are wide. He is beyond stupefaction. 'I should have known, I suppose. I always wondered why you would choose to play a part in all this. I kept asking myself why you would agree to this charade. What are you really hoping to achieve, Celine?'

The truth is a painful dish to serve, but I can't cook up a lie, not when my mind is positively ablaze with everything we have found out.

So I serve him half the truth. 'My father was determined to marry me off, and Maël, as the Duke of Langly, was the most logical candidate, but I couldn't bear the thought of that ogre ever laying a finger on me.'

'Ah. And what about me? Not an ogre, but you could persuade *me* to leave you alone, then?' He raises his eyebrows and urges his horse to break into a trot. I hurry to catch up with him.

'That's not how it was.'

'Then you tell me how it was.'

'You were the ... better option,' I call out after him, but some of my words are lost, fractured, in the valley beneath us.

'How so? Why didn't you just marry Hugo? If there's anything that doesn't add up for me today, that's it. You admitted that Hugo used to be your lover, so why didn't you just marry him?'

Tears sprout into my eyes, unbidden. 'But I couldn't, could I?' I could hardly marry a cat.

'I would have never agreed to this if I'd known that you loved him. He never said a word to me,' says Philippe, shaking his head.

Indeed, it seems he did not. In fact, Hugo told Philippe that he could have me. I believe now that this had less to do with Hugo's complete confidence in my faithfulness, and more to do with the fact that Hugo was prepared to go to any lengths to achieve what he wanted.

The ugly truth is, wrapped in these silk ribbons of lies, I don't matter. I never mattered. I was just a pawn on Hugo's board. A pawn on my father's board. My eyes fill to the brim and there's nothing I can do to stop my tears. 'But why did *you* do it, Philippe, if you're so against it? Why did *you* agree?'

'Because I had nothing, Celine. Nothing. My father died, I lost my farm…. All I had was this mad plan concocted by Hugo and Magali. And in my complete foolishness, I thought I could make a difference as the Duke of Langly.'

A shiver goes down my spine. Magali. Hugo has been working with Magali. Pretending all the while that we were looking for her.

He knew where she was.

He *knew.*

Does this mean…

Even the possibility of it makes me nauseous. Of how far Hugo's lies could have stretched.

I can't believe a single word he said to me. About Magali, Maël or Philippe. About what he wanted to achieve.

Everybody, everybody lied to me.

We reach the end of our descent and stop. The road here splits in three directions: one path leads to Fort Cantor, one to Bencifert Castle and one to Lafala.

I have a choice. We both do.

The tip of one of the towers of Fort Cantor glistens in the

distance. But I can't go there because I will have to face Hugo. Hugo and his coaxing, his cajoling, his charm. His lies.

He plays his games, and he plays all of them better than I do.

Where does that leave me?

I bite my lip, hard.

I wanted a partner to go with through life, a duchy.

And I had them both until a few days ago, and this simple fact knocks the breath out of me. I had everything I could have wanted, had I been able to see it. We could have been glorious together, had I not pushed my husband away.

Today, I have nothing.

For the first time I think, *I wish I had never met Hugo.*

As it is, I will have to confront him.

But not tonight. No, not tonight.

Tonight, I need safe haven.

I wipe away my tears. Philippe's silhouette distances itself from me, carried away by his palfrey's pace towards Castle Bencifert. I can't go with him, either. He wouldn't want me. Not after all I've admitted.

Fort Cantor might seem far away, but our afternoon at the farm together seems even farther. It was so beautiful but now it seems that it was no more than a dream. I never even knew that someone could make you feel like all the world has fallen away. It had never been like that with Hugo.

It was always about what we would do, not about what we had in that moment. But with Philippe... It was as if he had pulled me into the present and urged me to feel.

No more of that. Just a woman, alone, standing rooted at the heart of the crossroad.

I think, *I'll go back up. Up. I'll ask Madame Hirondelle if I can sleep in my former bedroom, just for one night. Or two. Perhaps longer.*

LILLY INKWOOD

I think, *Hiding in the shadows, that's something I've always done well.*

I turn my horse around. The road opens up underneath me, white and smooth. A road that doesn't lead forward, only back into my past.

SALVAGE

MAGALI

We eat in the Great Hall, the seats at the ducal table empty. No duke, no duchess, just the uncertainty that is always left behind when there is no one sitting on the dais; the body of people, writhing without their head.

After the Siege of the Twins, I made sure to show Frederic to the gathered crowds often enough to crush any buds of unrest. My husband is sick, I told them. He has gout. He cannot travel. He cannot come too often to the Royal Palace. He is often confined to his chambers.

There was not enough magic in the ring I now carry, to perform the trick for too long. Hugo's red pouch is bound to be much stronger. There was only so much I could do with what I had, and it was enough.

Yes, yes. For what I have planned, I will need to be stronger, and Hugo's pouch can make me so. If I can find a trace of that bloody cat. If he weren't doing his best to get out of my way, since Philippe and Celine left.

Look at the ducal table. If it is left empty for much longer, someone will try to grab it.

Better me than someone else. I must act upon this, and soon. And so I will.

CELINE

I've travelled a few steps back up the winding road, when Philippe calls my name.

'*Ssseline?*' There's the clop of hooves and whistling behind me. He stops beside me in a whir, nearly knocking me from my horse. 'Where are you going?'

'Back up. I can't go to Fort Cantor again.' There's a thread of snot dripping down my nose and I wipe it quickly with the back of my glove.

He whirls his horse around, taking me in. Up and down, down and up.

'I can stay with Madame Hirondelle for a few days. I need to think.'

He seems to consider this.

'Are you … are you going back to the farm?' My voice is clogged.

'No. As you kindly pointed out, there isn't a place for me there anymore. I'll go to the castle. To my brother. We've been invited for dinner, remember?'

'Yes,' I say. 'Well, tell them I had to go. And send my guards home.'

'Fine,' he says. He waits. And then he makes up his mind, and starts back down the track, away from me. But what did I expect?

I realise I didn't say goodbye to him. *Farewell*, I whisper. And I mean it. He deserves to fare well. He deserves it. Even though he probably lied to me about Magali.

I stand, rooted, watching him move farther and farther away

from me. Yesterday, at the farm, it all seemed so simple. He told me not to slip away from him again, and I told him not to let me.

And he's the one who is leaving me now.

Then he stops again. We take each other in for a long moment. There's so much in his eyes, that prying, that curiosity, that desire to untangle every single thought in my head. And there's so much hurt, on both sides, I suppose. As our inability to look away continues, because we can't seem to break our gaze, I feel a sudden glimmer of hope writhing in my chest.

'Home, you said?' he calls.

'Home.'

Together, yes, we might still make Fort Cantor our home.

He ruffles his hair in that way that is his. 'I'm sure I'm going to regret this, but I think you should come with me.'

* * *

OF COURSE we're late for dinner, but the Benciferts are probably too in awe of me to say anything. We skim through the account of our visit to the Golden Pavilion, saying that we found no more than ruins, while I push around my food, the boar in red sauce. I feel as if there's a heavy stone in my belly. There are plenty of things between me and Philippe that we yet have to unpack. Like Magali. And when her name drops in the conversation at the table—

Madame Bencifert says that she comes here often to brings sweets for their children. And, most interestingly, Louis tells us that the Dowager Duchess had been here as Philippe set off for Fort Cantor, when he lost everything.

But Hugo told me, after he went searching for her during the drought, that he followed her trail from Langville to Port Lang.

Lies on top of lies on top of lies. From everyone.

I give Philippe a sour look.

He presses his knee into mine, mouthing, 'Later.'

How much later? How long until we unravel this entire web of lies? I push my plate away. 'I'm so tired,' I say, getting up to my feet. The men follow suit. 'I am done here. Will you excuse me?'

I signal Philippe to follow me. Oh, he and I, we are not done yet, not by far.

MAGALI

Water. Food. My tongue is dry in my mouth. There's a jug on the table, but I can't move from the bed in the chambers that were my own.

I am the master of...

Day or night? Shutters closed, I lie in bed in my own shape, without knowing the hour. Tired. Too tired to shift. I forget how much it drains me. I touch the ring hanging from a chain around my neck. More. I need more. Hugo and his red pouch.

The red pouch. I must have it.

CELINE

We walk upstairs to our chamber in silence, but on the inside I'm boiling. I slam the door shut behind us. 'It's nice that you're on your high horse, while you lie to me, too. How can I trust you?'

'I never asked you to,' he says. 'I never asked anything of you.'

'Except that you've asked me to be your wife.'

'That wasn't quite how it happened, was it?' He stalks right up close to me. He smells a bit like himself, a bit like wine, and a bit like anger. 'What do you think I owe you?'

'You bang on about Hugo and his lies, and what do you do?'
It's stifling. The fact that I can't tell truths from deceptions
anymore.

I open the window to let some of the cool evening air rush in,
take a deep breath.

He says, 'It doesn't seem to me that you have the moral high
ground either.'

'There are things that we aren't telling each other,' I say. 'And
there are things that others aren't telling us. But even so, even if
we told each other everything, I'm not sure we could start piecing
all of the half-truths together.'

I plonk down on the bed and the ropes supporting the
mattress creak.

'I don't know if my mother is who I thought she was,' he says.

I don't want to feel sorry for him. Because feelings, they can
be used against us. As I have learned lately. 'That must be … terrible. But Madame Hirondelle said you should ask Magali. Why
was that?' I turn to watch his face as I ask the next question.
'When did you last see her, Philippe?'

I asked him earlier today, too, on our way down from the
Golden Pavilion, and he parried with a question about Hugo. It's
his turn to serve me some answers.

He bends down, his elbows on his thighs. He takes a deep
breath and sighs. 'Magali has been with us all this time at Fort
Cantor.'

I can't believe my ears. Where? And how could she have
hidden for so long, escaping detection? 'How can this be? We all
know what she looks like. The servants, her own nephews…'

'Magali is a Shape-Shifter. I've told you as much. Madame
Hirondelle has told you that today.'

'I thought Magali was a Storm-Caller—'

Philippe shakes his head.

Realisation dawns on me. No better place to hide than in plain sight. No better place to hide than in a different shape.

'Who is she?' My blood runs cold even before he tells me.

'Aurelie.'

My maid. The woman who has been closest to me, with unrestricted access to my chambers.

Magali has been right beside me all this time, while we've been looking everywhere for her.

'You slipped my most terrible enemy into my own bedchambers?' I'm numb with shock.

'Why would she be your enemy? Your mother was her friend. Why would she want to harm you?'

Because I never liked her. Because she never liked me. Because, ever since the newest debacle with Langly started, she never gave us a sign.

But she didn't need to, did she? She had been there, all along.

'You knew I was looking for her; that Hugo was also looking for her. He needs Magali to set himself free from his shape as a cat.'

That's what I thought. That's what I pray might still be true. Because if it isn't...

Philippe stares at me, more wide-eyed than ever. 'Is that what he told you? Is that why you told me today that you couldn't marry him, when I asked?'

My knees turn soft.

It's true.

What I had suspected today, since Philippe told me that Hugo had worked with Magali...

Hugo can change into his human form at will. He chose to keep his cat form, to trick me. He used it, so I would do his bidding.

This is why he told me not to mention to my husband that we used to be lovers. That I was 'in cahoots' with him. Not to protect what we'd done. No, just to make sure we never discussed *him*.

And I, in my endless foolishness, even sent Hugo to look for Magali. He claimed to have been away to Langville and Port Lang, while the drought ravaged Langly.

And he never said a word.

There had been a way out of the mess, to evade responsibility, and he took it.

And I'm the greatest dolt who ever walked the kingdom.

I grip the nearest chair to steady myself.

'You really love him so much that you'd believe anything he tells you?' Philippe shakes his head. Endless disappointment is written on his face.

'She's the one who turned him into a cat,' I say. 'He hates her.'

'Magali never turned Hugo into a cat. He turned himself into a cat,' says Philippe. 'And my father bound him to that shape. With help. But I wouldn't say it was all Magali's fault. Whoever told you that?'

I take a moment to remember. 'Hugo.'

Phillipe raises his eyebrows. 'See?'

I shuffle to the other side of the bed, as far away from Philippe as I can get. My legs won't hold me up anymore.

All this time, I've looked for the binding object. This is a betrayal so deep that I can hardly begin to grasp it. And even so, it brings me to my knees.

'What did he even tell you?' I ask, though I dread to know the answer. 'What did he tell you about the fact that he had to roam around the castle as a cat?'

'He said the time wasn't right. That we had to bring more stability into the duchy before he could stake his claim.'

The same lie, two different angles. Two sides of the same coin.

Philippe shakes his head. 'I always wondered… It all seemed too much of a coincidence. The way Magali told me that something was bound to happen to Maël, how she urged me to start towards Fort Cantor after my father died. And then, in one stroke, I was left with nothing. Except the bloody cat.'

I cradle my head in my hands. A dull ache begins to spread to my back and between my temples. 'It wasn't an accident.'

I feel him turning towards me, his body alert on the other side of the bed. 'What do you mean?'

'It was us. Hugo and me. He came to me in Langville and asked me to forge the inheritance papers your father left behind. And I did.'

Philippe is up on his feet in a scramble. 'That was you? *You* did this to me?'

I can't even look at him.

'Celine, tell me the truth. *You knew?* You *knew* this was the only reason why I staked my claim. Otherwise, I would have stayed on the farm and left Langly to someone else. And still, you—'

'But I didn't know you when I did it, did I? I had no idea who you were.'

'And still you stole from me. You stood there a moment ago and talked about moral high ground, and you, you—'

I swing around, watching him. The veins in his neck bulge.

'I'm sorry,' I say. 'But honestly, it didn't seem like I was doing much harm to you. Trading a farm for a duchy.'

'Yes, of course. Magali also thought it was better to push me onto this path. But no one asked me what *I* wanted. You all seem to know better.' He paces the room up and down. 'I don't want to hear you lie and claim you did this because you wanted to do me a favour.' He stops in front of me. 'You did it for him, didn't you? He convinced you to do it for him.'

I look away, towards the open window. In the distance, a few shadows fall across the Opal Mountain.

Madame Hirondelle said something today about being blinded by the people we love. And how we would do anything for them.

All my plans, my hopes and dreams, were based on lies.

A few weeks ago, when we made our way to the Mermaid's Lake, setting the plan in motion, I thought that I was breaking free. But I didn't. I simply exchanged one master for another, this one holding me even tighter in his clutches.

I was precisely like that falcon in Magali's story. She thinks herself free, and eats from her captor's hand.

The leash had always been in Hugo's hand. And I was so hungry for what he pretended he had to offer, that I never looked twice.

'I thought so,' says Philippe.

It feels as if the ground opens in front of me, a gaping hole, and I'm falling, falling, falling.

Philippe paces the room, ruffling his hair, thinking hard, while I stay quiet. It doesn't seem like there's much to say, anyway. And I don't want to cry in front of him.

'All right,' he says, easing himself down on the side of the bed. 'I thought about it.'

I almost dread to hear what he has to say.

'It's good that you told me because I can go back now.'

I sit up. 'What do you mean?'

'You can tell your father what you did. He can examine my father's will and the accompanying documents. He can make it all good again.'

The prospect of telling my father what I've done fills me with dread. 'But … leave? What will happen to me? You can't just leave.'

'But I have to, Celine. I'm so tired of it. What is the point of it, anyway? Now you know. You can replace Hugo with me, and I'll be out of your life. Everyone can have what they want.'

'I don't want Hugo,' I say. 'Not now, not ever again.'

Philippe's eyes are set on my face and I wish I could reach out through this space between us. 'What do you want then, Celine?'

The same as I always wanted. Someone to build a life with. I had been waiting for years for that life to begin, but only a few days ago, I realised that the life I'd wanted had already begun when I married Philippe.

I don't know if I can trust him—he lied to me, too, about Magali.

I don't know if we're still united by the same goals.

What I do know is that, perhaps, there is something worth fighting for.

'I want our life back,' I say.

'*We* never had a life. That's what became clear to me today. This is why I want to leave. Nothing was real.'

He is wrong. He is so wrong. 'It was more real than anything else, Philippe. You are a good duke. *We* are good together. Have you already forgotten what you told me? About how we complete each other? About how you want to make a difference?' My ears are burning as I say the next part, but it has to be said, nonetheless. 'How you won't let me slip away again?'

Philippe straightens. 'If we are so good together, you can come with me to the farm, then. But I doubt that you will. Because this isn't about you and me, is it?'

It is and it isn't. 'I am your wife,' I tell him. 'You can't make such a decision to turn our lives on their heads, without asking me if that's what I want.'

'But you made that decision for me when you forged my

father's last will, didn't you? And you suddenly seemed to remember only yesterday that I'm your husband, after all.'

Fine. Fair point. If it's anyone's fault, it's also mine. 'How about the duchy, then? Would you leave it to Hugo?'

Philippe bites his lip. 'What role do I have yet to play if Hugo reappears? His claim on the duchy is stronger than mine.'

'As far as everyone is concerned, Philippe, Hugo is dead. He would have a very hard time claiming the duchy if you opposed him.'

'Oppose him, and to what end? Frederic also reappeared after being presumed dead for years. If I oppose Hugo, we'd only repeat the story of the Siege of the Twins. Do you want me to ask people to take sides, to fight? You don't know me at all if that's what you think that I'd do.'

His words make me pause. He's right. Philippe opposing Hugo, that could only mean bloodshed for the people of Langly.

'Besides, it doesn't have to be like this.' He reaches into his pocket and pulls out a furry shape. It's a mouse. One with blueish fur.

I suck in a sharp breath. 'You didn't.'

The mouse gets up on his back paws, twitching his whiskers.

'Is this—' I ask, though I already suspect who it is.

'Yes, it's him.'

A hundred thoughts strike me, like a cascade of boulders toppling onto my head. 'But why? Why would you do such a thing? Everyone was looking for him like mad,' I say. Magali must have been looking for him. Unless she knew, too. 'What made you take him? He was perfectly safe in the cage.'

'Safe?' says Philippe. 'No, he wasn't. I didn't trust Hugo with him. I didn't even trust Magali.'

'But you don't realise the implications of what you've done.'

'Nor do you.'

'I can't believe it,' I say. 'And you've had him all this while?'

Philippe shrugs. 'It couldn't be helped.'

'Oh, yes, it could, and you bloody well know it.' I replay in my mind everything that's been said in the past few days, *and* back at Fort Cantor. Maël was part of it, the whole time. Even when Philippe and I were in bed… 'I can't even believe it.'

I think, *Hence the patting of pockets.*

'All the things… Urgh.'

'What was I to do?' he tries to defend himself. 'When Hugo admitted what they'd done to him, after we were married, I knew I had to keep him safe.'

'Lo and behold, someone is concerned over Maël's safety. Since when?'

'He was never unkind to me, Celine. Not even when we were children. We were always on the same side.'

'I can't believe you. Maël is a horrible person. I was so disgusted by the idea of marrying him that I did *all* of this just so I wouldn't have to.'

I throw the cover to the side.

'Be that as it may, now you know everything.' He sets Maël gently down on the floor. 'Do you want to run around a bit?'

The mouse scurries under the bed.

'Stop!' I say. 'How are we ever to get him out of there? What if we lose him?'

'No,' says Philippe. 'I do it all the time. He always comes back.'

I'm so upset I just want to scream. 'You're the biggest dolt I've ever met.'

Philippe shrugs. 'I couldn't have done otherwise.'

'Magali must have been out of her mind looking for him. We were all out of our minds looking for him.'

'Perhaps I would have mentioned it, if you'd have asked, Celine. Or any of you, for that matter. But neither you nor

Magali did, did you? Because it was easier to lie to me, or say nothing.'

I cross my arms, ready to shout at him, but then... His words latch onto my anger, suck all the life force out of it. No one bothered to ask him. Because no one saw him as anything more than a tool. Someone to be told what to do.

Understanding creeps on me slowly, like a fog lifting, and I begin to see why he would say now that he can't make a difference, not as long as all of us are caught in this web, pulling in opposite directions.

Perhaps it's time to look the entire truth in the face. Perhaps it's time to confront it, as ugly as it may be. 'Are you mad with Magali, Philippe? Are you mad with Hugo?'

He lifts his head and I can see that his eyes are streaked with red. The mouse scurries on the floor. 'What do you think?'

I sit down on the bed, gently, as if trying not to scare Philippe away. 'Will you come to Fort Cantor with me, then?' I point at Maël. 'If he is back... It still means that we have to face Hugo. And face *him* with his own lies.'

'No good can come of it. But...' He scuffs his feet on the floor, as if squashing an imaginary bug. 'I may not seem so, but I have my pride, too, Celine. I can't let them get away with what they've done. So yes, I will come to Fort Cantor with you. But don't read into it more than it is.'

It's good enough, I suppose. It's no more than I deserve. There will have to be a sort of transition, at some point, if Philippe is so bent on leaving. And I wonder if Philippe realises that Maël, when he breaks out of this form, will *kill* Hugo and Magali and possibly even me.

I don't know if he fully realises what sort of entanglement we are in.

I think, *Tomorrow, there will be another battle to wage.*

Yesterday, when Philippe and I lay in that bed at the farm together, I thought there was the possibility of a future together. I thought about picking *him*.

And today?

I'm falling, falling, falling and there's no one there to catch me.

THE ACTORS

CELINE

orning come, we say our goodbyes to our hosts and set off at a slow pace. I look into the distance, where Fort Cantor begins to take shape leaning against the cliff. My throat tightens in knots when I think that I'll have to make a choice soon: go with Philippe to the farm or return to the Royal Palace, covered in shame.

There are so many things I'd tell Philippe, if Maël wasn't listening. I'd ask him if he remembers the ledgers and the state of the duchy a few weeks ago, when we took over. If he's ready to deliver the people he tried to help so much back into Maël's hands.

But I cannot say anything—I've already made myself an enemy, I fear, and at the first sign of danger, Maël may yet run away.

I thought and thought and thought last night, until my head spun. It was Hugo who told me that Magali was our enemy, only for it to be revealed that they've been working together all along.

I tried to pinpoint the moment when I started thinking of her as a threat, and I realised that I could not. How skilled has Hugo been, driving a wedge between the four players in the game. To keep us from speaking to each other.

Who knows what lies he might have told Magali.

Perhaps it is time to listen to what she has to say for herself. To explain why she would replace her son with her nephew. Why she would do such a thing.

Perhaps she wants neither Hugo nor Maël released any more than I do.

MAGALI

'Would the princess like to change into different clothes?' I ask Celine. The smile on my face makes my cheeks ache. I'm so tired today, and the last thing I want to do is to serve *her*, but perhaps I won't have to keep this appearance for much longer.

She gives me a strange look while I help her out of her mantle. 'We were at the farm,' she says. 'I'd never seen it before. Quite a … cosy place.'

'It is, indeed,' I say. It is so tiring to remember the details of the lives of the different people I become. I can't remember if I told her that Aurelie worked at the farm or in the castle. Not that it will matter soon.

'Could you please take care of my hair first?' she says.

'Certainly.' I untie the careless weave she must have done herself. 'How would you like it?'

'Put it up in some way. Nothing too complicated.' We stare at each other, then she looks away.

'Is something amiss?'

'No.' Celine grins. 'I was wondering, Aurelie. How did you come to be in Philippe's service?'

'Oh,' I say, 'well, my parents lived here and there.'

'At Castle Bencifert, too?'

'I suppose you could say so.' These questions, always these dumb questions. How I ache not to have to justify my actions anymore.

A duke answers to no one—perhaps only the King. But even a duke can learn to stay out of the King's way.

There's a light rap on the door.

'Come in,' says Celine.

Philippe steps in. My heart fills with warmth when I lay eyes on him. He's such a good man. But then, perhaps it would have been better for him if he hadn't returned. He doesn't seem to thrive as the duke. Perhaps I should have assumed *his* shape. It would have saved us all a great amount of heartache. And, perhaps, the presence of the princess, which Hugo insisted upon.

Speaking of Hugo, he slips into the chambers behind Philippe. *Without* the red pouch.

'Take a seat,' the princess tells me. 'This will take a bit of time.'

I try to catch Philippe's eye, but I can't.

'So,' the princess says, more full of herself than I ever saw her before. And that's quite the feat. 'The joke's over, Magali. You can reveal yourself. And I suppose you already know that the cat is Hugo.'

The shock reverberates through my body in waves. I glance at Hugo, but he seems as stunned as I am.

'Magali, please, we need some answers,' says Celine.

'Philippe?' Has he betrayed me? After all I've done for him?

'Do as she says,' he tells me. 'Enough is enough.' He makes sure both the window and door are closed, then turns the key in the lock and places it in his pocket. 'The time for reckoning has come.'

Who does he think he is?

He's nothing without me. Nothing.

They will not make me waver. They have no idea. 'Yes, so? I am Magali. What of it?'

'You were here all this time, spying on me?' Celine's voice shakes, though she tries not to show it.

'I was keeping an eye on Philippe. And Hugo.'

'I needed to have an eye kept on me?' says Hugo. There's a cold glare in his eyes. 'Is that so?'

Celine looks to him. 'Your turn will come. For now, let me speak to her.' There's something savage in her voice.

It seems that the princess and I have something to discuss.

How interesting.

'I had to look after my son, too. Especially after he disappeared,' I say.

'Perhaps that wouldn't have happened if you hadn't turned him into a mouse,' says Celine.

Philippe is quiet, which is as good as a betrayal. I watch them both. They have conspired to face us today, together, I realise.

I could teach them a thing or two about pulling strings, then.

'It wasn't me who stole him from his cage,' says Hugo. 'Like I told you.'

'And yet,' I say, 'you were the only one who was interested in making him vanish.'

I look to Celine. 'Unless you did something to him? To my boy?'

'He's *your* boy now, is he?' says Philippe. 'That wasn't your tune when you came to the farm after he chased you away.'

'He needed to be put back in his place.' All he ever had, he owed to me. How I fought for him, how I taught him to wield his own power.

Yet he did his best to antagonise me, to destroy everything I've ever worked for. 'But I didn't want to harm him.'

'Yes,' says Hugo. 'You only wanted Philippe on the ducal seat instead.'

Celine's face distorts in anger. 'Hugo, you knew! You knew she was here the whole time and yet you never said a word to me. You made me look everywhere for her.'

This catches Hugo off balance. *Interesting.* Hugo made her look for me? I must say, his wickedness surpassed even my wildest imagination. Philippe and Celine are looking more at him than at me. If I play my cards right, then—

It should be easy. Show them I am on their side, and not his.

It should be easy enough, indeed.

'My dove,' says Hugo. 'It was in your best interest.'

'Don't call me that. And it's for me to decide, I think, what is in my best interest.'

'I only want the best for us. You have to believe me.' The slimy, slithering bastard. I'd laugh at how they corner him, if I didn't have my back against the wall too.

Celine catches fire. 'You acted some kind of cruel charade about looking for Magali and whatever Magali used to bind you to your cat form, and all the while you knew precisely where she was. I think this is more than a slip.'

I can't help but laugh. What a brilliant mind my nephew has. If only some good had ever come of it. 'So that's what you told her? That you were still bound?'

'Yes, and that he needed to find you in order to regain his human shape,' says Celine.

'Oh, the irony of it.' I chuckle again. 'That's devious, even for you.' I stare at Celine. 'Rest assured, since Julien fell ill, he has been able to transform at will.'

If looks could throw fire and brimstone, the one Celine is giving Hugo would have charred him alive. 'Show me.'

Hugo swishes his tail. He looks ... like a hart in the forest, facing a pack of hunters. 'My dove, it's not what you think. It was better this way.'

Dove, yes. She was a dove in a cat's claws. But now she wants to poke his eyes out.

'I'm not your anything!' she shouts. 'And tell the truth for once.'

Hugo winces. He *winces*. How it all falls apart for him...

'Show me,' she says.

'Celine, if you'll allow me to explain. You'll understand I was acting in our best interest. So that—'

Celine is beside herself with anger. How weak. *'Explain what? How you lied to me that you couldn't be a human until we carried out your little plan? That we couldn't be together until I found Magali? Show me.'*

Not that I want to say anything in his defence, but as long as I'm here, Hugo cannot make his bid for the duchy. I assume he had to tell her something to explain the delays. And I was the one who delayed even further, refusing to carry on with the plan, once Maël disappeared. Now I see how that would have worked against Hugo.

It's his fault. If he had issues with Celine, he should have trusted me, and told me about them.

'Hugo!' The princess points at the painted screen next to the bed. 'It's ridiculous to keep conversing with a cat. Change. Back. Now.'

Hugo studies all three of us, then makes a decision. He rises on all fours and disappears, unhurriedly, behind the screen.

'You know more than you led me to believe.' Philippe's words catch me like a stab in the back, especially since Celine is watching. 'You lied to me, too. You knew what they were plotting. You knew they intended to take the farm away from me.'

Hugo shouts from behind the screen, 'It was her idea. She said you'd never leave the farm otherwise.'

Hurt is written all over Philippe's face. But it was for the best —he just can't see it. I know better. I've done this for longer than he has.

'I trusted you, Magali. I truly did.' Philippe dishevels his hair. 'Did you have any idea about what Hugo was planning to do? That he planned to turn Maël into a mouse? You always spoke of something unavoidable. Did you know of his plan?'

I want Hugo to shut up, just this once, but he shouts, 'Of course she did. We were both there that day, on the cliff. Two Shape-Shifters were needed to catch Maël.'

Celine blanches. 'You worked together … and this was why.' Philippe puts an arm around her shoulder, and she shoots him a surprised look. Then she touches his hand.

Ah, and now I see it. This is why we have ended up in this comedy of errors: the children have taken a liking to one another. I was afraid this might happen, though I wonder what he sees in her.

'Can I have something to wear?' calls Hugo.

The two don't budge, so I toss him a clean chemise that belongs to Celine.

'What were you trying to achieve, Magali?' says Philippe. 'How could you do this to your own child?'

'Maël cast her out,' says Celine. 'And she's not used to not having a say in running the duchy.'

'That's not how it was,' I say, seething at the impudence.

'What I still don't understand is what kind of deal you and Hugo could have struck together so that both of you would get what you want,' says Celine.

'What do you think?' says Philippe. 'The kind of deal where they both double-cross one another.'

313

And then Hugo emerges. Honey-blonde locks fall on his fore-head; dark blue eyes sparkle. He is lean, yet strong, even in his lacy women's chemise. Celine appraises him and I watch clouds of feelings scud across her face. Philippe notices too and lets his hand fall from hers.

Celine's features twist. 'And what were you really planning, Hugo? What were you playing for?'

Hugo sits down on the edge of the bed. 'Magali knows what I intended. I meant for Philippe to be the duke, but I had some-thing else entirely in mind for you and me.' He gives her a sad smile. I can't tell if the feeling is genuine, or if he's trying to soothe her anger.

'What?' says Philippe.

Hugo says, 'I wanted Celine for myself more than anything.'

Philippe's fingers curl in a fist.

THE UNRAVELLING

CELINE

*T*he sheer arrogance of this statement. Hugo thinks that he owns me. But I was his, was I not? His little tamed falcon, sent on a hunt.

'That's a lie,' I say. 'We could have been together a long time ago. But you wanted more.'

I'm still taking in Hugo's features. The blonde locks, the blue eyes. That small button nose. The slight frame, and the power that it radiates, like heat from a fire. Hugo is a man who wants with burning intensity, and who holds himself as though he is about to spring into action and take it all for himself. I wish I could say I feel nothing as I look upon his face.

I wish I could tell myself that I feel nothing at all, but my heart starts to beat faster. How I longed to kiss those lips, only a few days ago. How I longed to lean into his chest and let him hold me.

Hugo is studying me, as if he can hear my thoughts. 'You deserved more, my dove. We both did.'

Tears are threatening to spill.

I am the master of myself.

'I didn't want more,' I say. 'You were enough for me.'

Hugo crosses his ankles. 'Was I, Celine? I remember we seemed to have wanted the same thing.'

I know what he means by this—all the plans we wove around Langly. Always that eye turned towards the future.

He could have had me, all those years ago. He could have married me, even without the duchy. I would have never refused him, and my father was so desperate for me to marry that perhaps he would have agreed. Even if Hugo had nothing.

But he never asked. Every single plan we spun, it was woven around Fort Cantor. 'I'll ask again: what were you really hoping for this time, Hugo?'

He lowers his eyes.

Magali shifts.

'It's too late to hide your intentions now,' I say.

'Magali,' says Philippe in a low voice. 'She's right. You might as well tell us.'

'The plan was,' says Magali, 'to force the King to change the law of succession.'

'What?'

'What?' says Philippe.

'You'll need to elaborate,' I say. 'This is mad.'

Hugo says, 'It was only what you deserved, Celine. Why do you think you shouldn't be queen? Why did you think you were less than your brother?'

I almost say, *Because I didn't want to be queen. Because not every woman would want to be queen.* But I see how this might have appealed to Magali. Why she would have agreed to play this game.

She says, 'You have to believe me, Philippe, it was for your own good. The plan was to settle you in as the duke, and then Hugo would reappear, claiming his birthright. In order to prevent this, the King would have had no choice but to change the law of succession so that the firstborn child, no matter its gender, would inherit the title. This would have put Isabella before Kylian or Frederic, you before Hugo.'

'But don't you realise,' Philippe says, 'how much turmoil this would cause in the kingdom? How many estates would have changed hands? How many people would have claimed inheritances they were never entitled to? It would have ended in bloodshed. It would have never ended.'

Magali goes on, apparently oblivious to Philippe's objections. 'And once the law was changed, Celine would have her marriage to you annulled.'

Philippe shoots me a questioning look. I close my eyes. *Yes. Yes, that's precisely what I would have done.*

Even last week.

I finally begin to understand why so much intricate and delicate plotting was required, because changing the inheritance laws would also change the succession in the kingdom, would put me in front of my little brother. At five years of age, he wouldn't even know what had happened to him. To his path.

The depth and breadth of their deceit is too large to fit into my head, and a dull ache takes hold of it.

The magnitude of it all. 'You wanted to become king. That was all you ever wanted me for,' I whisper to Hugo.

'Oh, yes,' says Magali. 'And he would have enforced his claim to the throne with the entire army of Langly behind him, if necessary. Philippe was bound to support him, wasn't he?'

My head feels so heavy on my shoulders and I can't listen to a single word more. The way that Hugo used me to feed his ambitions is beyond me.

I walk over to the door. 'This is too much.'

'Stop,' says Philippe. 'You can't go and leave him here.' He points at Hugo. 'We can't let him go free.'

Hugo tries to catch my eye. 'Celine? I can explain.'

I look past him. I wouldn't trust a single word that comes out of his lips. 'We need to confine him, until we find a more permanent solution.' Surprise glimmers on Hugo's face, as if he never expected such a thing from me. Revenge is a sharp, sweet thing in my belly.

Your turn to see how that feels.

I expect Hugo to break into a run, but he doesn't even move, still focused as he is on me. But it's not like him to hurry into anything.

'I agree,' says Magali. 'It's best to use a Magic-Binder. Tie him to an animal form.'

'I see you've given this some thought, dear aunt,' says Hugo.

'Of course I have. Anybody working with you would have done the same.'

'And where do we find a Magic-Binder?' says Philippe.

Hugo seems surprised. 'You too, Philippe?'

'Where do we find a Binder?' I ask, trying to remember who else is still binding magic in the kingdom. There aren't many mages left.

I don't remember ever having seen a Binder at the Golden Pavilion, except Seigneur Bencifert. 'I can't think of a single one.'

'It's not hard to find a Binder,' says Magali. 'And I wager he would help us.'

'Who?' I ask.

Magali chuckles. 'You might know him. It's your father.'

MAGALI

I tell the children about the containment spells, the ones that can be used to keep a person locked in a chamber. I just used them a few weeks ago, when Julien fell ill, but I am too depleted to perform them.'

Celine's face pinches. 'Spells? Where would you know such a thing? They're forbidden. We were never taught spells at the Golden Pavilion.'

'Just because they were never taught, it doesn't mean that they're forbidden, or they were lost. The doyennes always knew Spell-Lore.'

Celine gapes, her silly mouth open. 'The doyennes? But there would have to be spell books, knowledge—'

'They were hidden.' This conversation tires me and it's completely beside the point. 'Do you think you've seen even half of the Golden Pavilion?'

'Did you see them? The books?' asks Philippe, narrowing his eyes.

They are indeed exhausting since they started working together. 'And you have no idea what lies inside the Opal Mountain.'

'What lies inside the Mountain?' Celine's voice is a croak.

'No one knows.' That's a lie. The Fallen Court definitely knows. But no matter how close I ever was with Isabella, there are things not even she would tell me. 'And no one should look.'

I can tell Celine is too curious now.

I say, 'People have always made assumptions. The Mothers of the Forest said the Golden Mother is kept a prisoner there.'

'In the Year of the Red Maiden,' says Celine. 'That's why the people besieged the Golden Pavilion.'

'Precisely,' I say. 'Can we turn now towards the matter at hand?'

I explain to the children what they have to do, how to seal all the entrances with their Gifts. The words they have to sing, to pin them in place. They touch the window frames, the doors, the cracks in the floor, even. Celine's high, slight falsetto voice weaves with Philippe's. He sounds a bit like a donkey with a raw throat, but, somehow, they make music together.

It's their Gifts, even if they might not be aware, aching to tangle with each other.

Hugo watches us, pouting, his arms crossed. I'm amazed at his lack of action, but what can he do? He's not someone who rushes into things. After all, how long did he wait at the Golden Pavilion to come after the duchy? I'm more afraid of what he intends to do next.

No.

I have inhabited other shapes for too long. I fear nothing.

He tries to move closer to Celine, but she shoots him a savage look. 'Don't you dare.'

He takes a step back.

Celine says, doing her best to ignore him, 'I can't believe my father is gifted. I would have known.'

I laugh. 'But it makes sense, doesn't it? It was his responsibility to contain all sorts of errant magic. As a Binder and as the king. Of course he closed the Golden Pavilion. With so few Binders left, it was easier not to train people than contain the harm they would do.'

'Like the harm you've done, dear aunt?' says Hugo.

'I've only done what I had to do. Be quiet.'

'Does he even know, Magali?' Hugo glances at Philippe with the look of a lion pondering its prey.

'Shut up, Hugo.'

Philippe, his eyes closed, his hands rubbing the frame of a window, snaps to attention. 'What does he mean, Magali?'

'Tell him.'

'The window to the left doesn't close properly. Make sure you seal it well,' I say.

No.

Not my secret.

The one thing that I always kept closest to my chest.

'What do I need to know?' Philippe glares at Hugo.

'Perhaps how Frederic was well and truly dead, indeed, when my father returned from the Green Kingdom. Twenty years ago,' says Hugo.

I almost burst with relief.

This.

Not *that*.

'But ... Frederic came back, seven years later, to claim the ducal seat,' says Philippe. 'The seigneurs rallied. That was how the Siege of the Twins started.'

Hugo says, 'Frederic was dead.'

'And your father made sure of it, didn't he?' I might as well tell him how I sacrificed myself for them. If Hugo thinks this could sway them... 'I always knew from the moment Kylian returned and his Gift was gone. One mage cannot kill another without losing their Gift.'

'Yes, yes,' says Hugo. 'Do you want to ask Magali, Philippe, how your uncle reappeared?'

They all exchange looks. The harm's already been done. It's too late to turn back now. 'Frederic was indeed dead,' I say. 'As I said, his brother saw to that.' The level of deceit. The way Kylian never showed what his true ambitions were, fed by too much dallying when it came to whom the inheritance should be bestowed upon.

'Then...?' Philippe looks like he is bracing himself.

Better for them to hear it from me than from Hugo. 'It was Maël. I used Maël to take the shape of Frederic. Just for a few hours every day.' Between a boy and a ring, there wasn't enough magic for more.

'Maël?' says Philippe.

Celine straightens. 'You did this to your own son? But it must have ripped him apart. I can't even… It drains you, Magali. Magic drains you. Everyone knows this. How could you do this to a child? How old was he, even?'

How dare she judge me? 'It was the only way. I had to protect my children.'

Hugo says, 'Look at all the good it did everyone.'

Celine flexes her fingers. 'This is too much. My head aches with all of it.' She makes for the door.

How weak is this flimsy princess.

'Where are you going?' says Philippe.

'To your chambers. I need to lie down for a bit.'

Bon voyage. May you decide never to return.

CELINE

I hide under a bearskin that lies on Philippe's bed. I turn my head on the pillow, gritting my teeth because of how horribly my head aches. It makes me literally come face to face with the smell of him. How does he feel about all of this? It's been so crazy that we haven't even touched on half of what Madame Hirondelle revealed.

In this web of lies that tangles the fate of the kingdom, the matter of his own mother seems to pale into insignificance. I need to speak with him. If he chooses to leave me and Langly, we'll all be delivered to the machinations of Hugo.

It's uncanny how things can change so quickly and so completely. Uncanny how this is precisely the outcome I would have wanted a few days ago, and how this is now precisely what I want most to prevent from happening.

I hope Philippe understands that the most honourable thing he can do is to stand his ground.

Hugo must be contained and stopped at all costs. And not just because I want my revenge, but also because I want to hurt him as much as he hurt me. Philippe and I will have to speak later tonight. We'll have to dash to the royal palace and beg my father to help us.

It's funny how things turn on their heads.

It's funny how a part of me still wonders if Hugo truly loves me—but it would be madness to allow its voice to rise. It would be madness to fall back into a life of deceit and lies and hurt.

Who would have guessed that my father was a mage? Of all the secrets this kingdom hides, this must be the best kept. Not even I, his daughter, could have predicted it.

I take a deep breath. My head feels as if it's being pounded with a hammer. I draw the bearskin on top of my head and close my eyes. Magali, my father, Philippe and Hugo. No one is who they pretend to be. And then I also have to think about Maël, who was curled up in Philippe's pocket throughout our conversation. I think about what he had to endure as a child, and how that must have changed him for ever.

But Hugo is the one we need to take care of first. We need to protect ourselves, and the kingdom, against him.

* * *

THE CREAK of the door wakes me up. I don't remember drifting to sleep. It's dark outside, so I must have nodded off for several hours at least. Philippe steps hesitantly into the room. 'May I come in?'

I pat the bed to signal that he should come over, while I sit up. The fog around me starts to clear and when I realise what is still to be done, I feel like hiding under the bearskin again. 'Magali's here,' he says, 'but if you don't feel like coming down to dinner, I can make your excuses.'

'No, I should come, or someone might think that things are amiss.'

We'd agreed to send the false Aurelie away, so that she could return as Magali. She will play the pained mother who's mourning her son but who is still glad that her nephew is the one on the ducal seat. A united front is what we need to show today. To the seigneurs, to the people of the duchy and to my father, the king.

Even if Magali disagrees. She wanted to stay behind, with Hugo, but I pulled Philippe aside. I told him that I didn't trust her, that she had to come with us or none of us would go to the Royal Palace. Reluctantly, Philippe assented.

I touch his arm. 'You realise that you can't go to the farm now, don't you?'

'It seems that I'm trapped here, with you.' He laughs.

'I'm not so bad, as wives go,' I say.

'I think there is some room for improvement,' he says. 'When it comes to matters of loyalty.'

I punch him in the shoulder with a feigned easiness. It is good to have him here, in the same room with me, but we are not yet the united front we pretend to be.

He anchors me against things that I shouldn't feel. 'I hope you don't believe that I plan to release Hugo behind your back.'

He stares at his hands. 'I don't know what to think, except that now I believe anyone capable of anything.'

'Don't be like this. It will all be all right.' I say this to persuade myself of it as much as to persuade Philippe. 'You will see. One day, good things will come of it.'

'One day.'

'One day.'

I stare at his pocket, thinking about Maël and how we still have to decide what to do with him. For now, I think it's best if he remains in the form of a mouse. Philippe or Magali might disagree with me, so it's best I don't voice any opinions just yet, until we sort Hugo.

I am still struggling to believe he aimed so high that he thought he could become king, without even considering asking me what I thought of it.

Marrying the princess wasn't enough for his ambitions; he had to marry a future queen.

Philippe says, 'You're quiet.'

'Too much has been said already today, don't you think? I can't handle any more revelations.'

Philippe smiles.

'You didn't ask ... or did you? About what Madame Hirondelle told you?'

Philippe shakes his head. 'It never seemed to be the right moment. Compared to what Magali and Hugo had been planning... Celine, how did we become wrapped up into this? What happened?'

I rub my face, wishing it would all go away. 'I like to think that we were innocents swept up in a high-stakes game of chess, but a part of me ... a part of me wanted more. Wanted something to change in my life. I was lonely. I clung to Hugo as if he were the solution to all my problems.'

'And are you still lonely?' Philippe laughs and I wonder if it would be too strange to kiss him now, to ask him to hold me.

If it would be wrong to cling to *him*.

'What do *you* want?' I say in a low voice.

Philippe shrugs. 'I always wanted my mother to be proud of me. To see me. As I grew up ... she was never there.' For a moment, the hurt in the face of an abandoned little boy glimmers on the surface.

He wanted to be seen. And I wouldn't have seen him, either, if it wasn't for Hugo.

But today... In the way we confronted Hugo and Magali, in the way we wove our Gifts to seal the entrances... Perhaps, perhaps, there is still some hope for us, after all.

And what do I want? Looking at Philippe's lovely face, I know I want that chance to exist for us. To find a way to skirt Maël and his claim, for things to go back to the way they were, just a few days ago, minus Hugo.

A STAGE FOR THE DUCHESS

MAGALI

*T*he Great Hall seems quite different when you look at it from the raised seats at the ducal table, though I can't say that I agree with many of the changes Celine has made to the place.

In the destruction of its hearth, it has lost its soul. So much has been destroyed, of late.

I put this thought aside for tomorrow.

Tonight is dedicated to celebrations.

As soon as they hear the rumour, farmers trickle to the castle from all directions, to see with their own eyes the Dowager Duchess, returned.

Returned are my lavish surcoats embroidered in gold, from the trunks in which they had been hidden. Returned are the gemstone rings and the gold chain, hanging heavy across my neck.

Returned is the awe in the eyes of the people, waiting to hear the tale of my travels. To put an end to all sorts of speculation.

Before dinner commences, Philippe gets to his feet to make a speech. 'I speak for all of us when I welcome, with the greatest tenderness, the Dowager Duchess Magali of Langly. Fort Cantor has been her home and it will continue to be so. Each and every one of you can testify to her strength, wisdom and courage. We stand by her in these difficult times and give her the full support of the family.'

All the people gathered here hammer wildly on the benches. The uproar is unbelievable. They love me. I'm their mother, even more so during the past few years of difficult times with Maël.

I was the voice of moderation.

I was their shield.

I thank them quietly, bowing my head, overwhelmed by these signs of affection. I did, indeed, do good work at the helm of the duchy.

'Count Goderic,' calls the guard at the door, and I stand to attention at the entrance of this spindly figure I know so well, the man I can call neither friend nor foe. He strides on his long legs to my table and kisses my hand. Only after that does he acknowledge the presence of the other two.

Just as it should be.

Celine and I signal at the same time to the pantler that he should set another chair at the grand table.

'Your Grace, what an extraordinary surprise.' Goderic watches all three of us with his deep-set eyes.

'I was travelling when all of this happened,' I say. 'But I hurried back as quickly as I could to find out what happened to my son.'

'I'm so sorry for your loss,' says Goderic. 'We all regret Maël's loss terribly.'

'Thank you.' I gather my hands in my lap, shielding my eyes in case he sees the truth in them. It's never a mistake to be careful with Goderic. Celine gapes at me and I will her to stop, lest he notice something is amiss.

'Philippe and I were so pleased to see our aunt Magali,' says Celine. 'You do not know how my soul weeps for her.' She can barely refrain from smiling. 'She was so close to my dear mother. I hope she will feel at home here, with me and Philippe.'

'So you will stay here?' Goderic toys with the long stem of the goblet that has been set in front of him. 'At Fort Cantor?'

'Oh, yes, I think I will,' I say. 'But first, I'd like to pay my respects to our king. We leave tomorrow, at first light.'

'You're leaving already?'

'Yes, and my nephew and his lovely wife will be joining me,' I say. 'The duke wishes to report to the king.'

'Yes, yes,' says Goderic. 'But you have been travelling as well, Your Grace?' He raises his glass towards Philippe. 'I wished to speak to you yesterday and I was told that you were away.' In these moments, I can't quite read his expression.

This man is shrewd as a fox.

'Yes,' says Philippe. 'We went to Castle Bencifert. I wanted my wife to see my family.'

'Oh, so it was a planned visit? You didn't mention anything to me when we agreed to meet; we had planned to discuss the new plantations of hemp at the western limit.'

'Please accept my apologies.' Philippe's voice is steady, but his face is strained with the lies. 'It was an unexpected visit after the ball.'

Goderic studies us intently.

Celine leans into Philippe's shoulder. 'It can be quite overwhelming at Fort Cantor. My husband and I needed a bit of time for ourselves.'

Goderic watches them, then shifts his attention to me. 'So where have you been travelling, my dear? Please tell me. It's been quite a dull summer here in Langly. Nothing exceptional except a drought and then a ball when it was over.'

I feel the sting of this, the bee behind the honey. 'You forget my nephew's marriage,' I say. 'I was so sorry to miss that. But it all happened so fast.'

'Yes, fast indeed. The princess hesitated for a long time in choosing a husband, but once she had made up her mind—'

Celine leans closer into Philippe, the little witch. How has she managed to turn him around so quickly?

Well, I suppose even I know how. He was always a bit awestruck by her, though, really, as the Duke of Langly he could have had any woman he wanted.

'So where did you say you were travelling?' says Goderic. 'I was expecting you to come much sooner. It has been quite some time since Maël's disappearance.'

'The news took a while to reach me.'

'Months? I wager there wasn't a nook in this kingdom where two toothless old hags didn't talk about what happened to Maël.'

'Oh, no...' I play with a linen napkin. The man simply doesn't know when to give up. He pushes and pushes. 'I'm sorry, but I'm too distraught to even think of it. That I could have been enjoying myself at Crane's Harbour, when all of this...' I dab the napkin to my eyes. This should silence him.

'No, no, I didn't mean to upset you, Magali,' says Goderic kindly. 'We mustn't speak of it if you do not wish to.'

Finally.

CELINE

Philippe and I withdraw to his chambers once the dinner is finished. We send Magali to check that Hugo is where he should be. Once we set our protection spells in place, it's better if we don't pass through them ourselves.

330

The duke's chambers are larger than mine, but there's much less furniture, just a cave of a hearth with a roaring fire and two simple armchairs in front of it. There's also the bed covered in the bearskin, and a solid table with two massive chairs. I hadn't noticed much when I came here this afternoon. I'd only wanted a place to hide.

'Have you changed the furniture?' I ask, leaning back against the table. 'I seem to recall this differently.' From the day when I dragged an unwitting Philippe across Fort Cantor.

It seems as if it was ages ago.

It seems as if it happened to a different person.

My husband taps the plain back of one of the chairs. 'Yes, this is much more to my taste. This is the first duke's furniture. Magali found it for me in one of the upper rooms. Maël's furniture ... well, it wasn't quite what I would have chosen. But I kept the bearskin.'

I roll my eyes. 'I don't even want to imagine.'

We're only a few steps from each other and the impulse to close the distance is pulsing in my feet. The safe haven of his chest is a lure—his lips, my mouth on his, the promise of losing myself in sensations and not in the maze of my own mind.

He can do that to me.

I take in all of him as he stands there, imagining how it would be to help him slip out of his outer garments and untie his chemise. What if he were to lift me on the table—

'What is it?' he says. 'You're gaping at me.'

I scramble for a decent thing to say, instead of *I want you, all of you, just to escape from* this *for a few moments*, when he pats his pocket, extracting Maël and scratching his head.

'I'm sorry I hated the furniture,' he says, setting him down.

Maël. Bloody Maël.

I lean back, stamping down all of those filthy thoughts. Sadly.

'Perhaps it's time to give him to Magali. She might have a good idea what there is to be done with him.'

'You might be right, but I don't know if I can trust her.'

The door creaks and Philippe picks him back up and hides him swiftly in his pocket, just in time before Magali marches inside as if there are at least a dozen people following in her wake. I rise on the tips of my toes to check but no, she's alone.

'All in good order,' she says, unapologetic as usual.

Philippe moves slightly away from me and his mood changes. He's a bit like a hound whose hairs on his back stand on end. He must have been irked by her lies. If he had never quite trusted Hugo, he must have trusted her instead. We were both fools, weren't we?

'Is everything in place so we can leave at first light?' she says.

Philippe nods.

'Good.' Her shoulders loosen, and she almost crashes into one of the armchairs by the fire. She stares into the flames. 'So much depends on the next few days going as planned. Then we can all be free to live without fear.'

'Is this one of your games again?' says Philippe. 'I saw the performance you gave at dinner. Brilliant.'

'What do you mean?' says Magali.

'Telling everyone how sorry you were about your son.'

'But I am sorry about him. And worried,' says Magali. Her features crumple and she looks very, very tired. 'I wish I could find him and I hope he's not in pain. But he's alive—I think I'd know if he wasn't.'

Philippe and I exchange a look and I nod. 'Yes,' I say. 'Yes, please.' I'm tired of Philippe carrying Maël around with him. And before we go any further, we'd better lay all our cards on the table. I'm not sure what I'm expecting from Magali, but I hope that, once Hugo is contained, we might live together in peace.

Though I don't know how much peace there would be, with both of us roaming Fort Cantor. But then again, I don't even know what my future might look like, beyond the next two or three days. Everything I thought I knew about the world I live in has been upended.

'Magali, I have something for you.' Philippe reaches into his pocket, gingerly takes out the mouse and hands it to its mother.

'Maël?' says Magali, and I hope that the excitement written in her wide eyes and in her smile aren't pretended. 'So he was with you ... Philippe?'

'Yes, I took him. I didn't trust Hugo with him. And I didn't trust Celine, either, that she wouldn't harm him.'

That's not the story he told me. He said he didn't trust Magali. But I suppose we both have to play the game now, by Magali's and Hugo's rules.

'You've done well,' says Magali. She rubs her finger along the mouse's fur and it squirms in her palm. 'Where have you been, my boy? It's unlike you to hide in dark holes. I've been so worried.' Her voice takes on a sweet tone. 'But you deserved it, didn't you?' she says. 'You brought this upon yourself. I'm so sorry.' She drops him into one of the wide pockets of her dress and holds it shut. 'Where's the cage?'

'What cage?' says Philippe.

'The golden cage,' says Magali.

'Oh.' Philippe reaches under the bed and pulls it out.

So this is why he had the cage removed from my chambers. I should have paid attention.

With one hand, Magali opens the door, and with the other, she extracts Maël from her pocket and pushes him inside. Her features relax. 'Are you hungry, Maël, dear?' She looks up to Philippe. 'Where have you been keeping him? In the cage?'

'Partly,' says Philippe. 'Partly in my pocket. When I was away, for instance.'

'I gather he has heard much of what we've been saying?' Magali rubs the sockets of her eyes. 'Philippe, you should have told me. A long time ago. Didn't I make it clear enough that I wanted him to be safe?'

Philippe and I exchange a look. So he is still on my side. I think.

'Can we trust you?'

'Darlings, I've done nothing but protect your best interests. You offend me.' Her jaw is now set. I think of everything I know about this woman—what a powerful mage she is, and all the manoeuvring she has done behind closed doors.

I shift.

But then, don't I always allow myself to be manipulated and intimidated?

I'm not that person anymore.

'Don't feel so offended,' I say. 'If you were in our shoes and had even a grain of wisdom, you'd be wary. What do you mean to do with him?'

'Nothing,' says Magali in an icy tone. 'He has what he deserves. And so does Philippe.'

'Not yet,' I say, tilting my head in the direction of my own chambers, hinting at Hugo. And Count Goderic, tonight, has me worried. I wonder where his allegiances might lie. 'How do we know we can trust you?'

'*I* know,' says Philippe. He leans back on the table, just like me, but the action seems to make him taller, as if he is taking up more space in the room. 'How about you tell us how Hugo managed to do this?' he says, pointing at Maël in the cage. 'Hugo was never particularly forthcoming with the details.'

Magali takes a deep breath. 'It was easier than you think. Do you remember the lion that's been rampaging through the duchy, over the years? That was Maël. When I turned into a lioness and roamed about too, Maël was bound to go out and investigate. It was easy to draw him to the cliff.'

'I can't say I'm surprised. But how did he have the power to shapeshift, since most of our powers faded when my father destroyed the crystal at the Golden Pavilion? And for that matter, how do you and Hugo do it?' My own powers are just a fraction of what they used to be.

'There are objects that can help enhance magic.' Magali reaches into the pocket of her dress and draws out a signet ring. It is the signet ring of the Duke of Langly. The lioness. 'I took this when Maël and I quarrelled. It was too dangerous to allow him to have it. So yes, when I left the Duchy of Langly, Maël hadn't thrown me out. I escaped ... with this.'

'That's when you came back to the farm. To Castle Bencifert.'

Magali nods, twisting the ring.

'Then Hugo must have an enhancer as well,' says Philippe.

'Yes,' says Magali. 'I could never find out what form his takes.'

'So before we bind him, we'll have to take from him whatever that object is,' I say.

'Or not,' says Magali. 'If he's bound, it will make no difference.'

'You still haven't answered my question,' says Philippe. 'How did Maël turn himself into a mouse? Why? It doesn't make sense. The stableboy who was with him that day said he was attacked by the lion.'

'The stableboy would say that,' says Magali.

'Oh,' I say. 'Then who...?'

Magali scoffs. 'Ah, darlings, you still have so much to learn.'

'Magali,' says Philippe. 'You're not answering my question.'

She lays her hands in her lap. 'Someone was there who knew exactly how to provoke Maël. Who knew how to coax him.'

I draw in a sharp breath. Philippe watches her with wide eyes. None of us dares to speak the truth out loud, except Magali. 'I pretended to be the lioness, to draw Maël out, and Hugo shifted into the stableboy. It was that simple.'

I think, *The stableboy*. Hugo was right under my nose that day when the steward brought him to our breakfast. He looked directly into my eyes and lied to me.

Suddenly, I feel nauseous.

And yet, still not everything fits together. 'But you and Hugo, you're both Shape-Shifters. You must have needed a Magic-Binder to keep Maël tied to his form.' Seigneur Bencifert had died, and hadn't approved of the plan, as far as I can gather. 'Who helped you to do all that?'

Magali shrugs. 'Your father, of course. The last Magic-Binder.'

THE LAST MAGIC-BINDER

CELINE

*W*hen I greet my father in his throne hall, I don't feel the same respect for him that I once did. Nor fear. He isn't the man upholding the right and wrong in our kingdom. Because he, too, has been lying to me.

I can barely wrap my head around the fact that he has played a part in this mad plan that involved Philippe and the Duchy of Langly.

We file in front of my father to pay our respects—or whatever's left of them. I watch with a cold glare the way he accepts the assurances of our loyalty and how he flinches when he sees Magali with us.

It turns out that my father, the king, is afraid of something after all.

I am impatient to catch my father alone, but he has to give audiences, it turns out. He doesn't have time to speak to his own daughter. I wander the halls of the palace I used to know so well, where I lived for such a long time. A cold fear grips my chest. I remember my life in shadows. Langly is home now and I start to grasp the lengths to which I would go in order to protect it.

At the royal dinner, my father is more than courteous towards us. He pays very special attention to Magali, studies from the corner of his eyes what she's saying, who she's speaking to.

I wonder how I could have missed this, his fear of her. All the times when Magali has visited us, and not once had I caught a trace of it.

But nor am I the same person I was back then. I'm reborn. Emerging from this web of lies that he has spun around us, emerging from the shadows, determined never to return again. I watch Philippe, how he observes everyone, moves little, says even less.

I wonder where he will want to be in a few days' time, once Hugo has been taken care of. If he will leave me. Magali moves with such ease in this world of the Royal Court, and an alliance with her is just as dangerous as one with Hugo.

I think, *What's done is done. Onwards.*

I'm the one who approaches him, as he rises from the table. 'Father, I must have a private word with you.'

He waves me away with his hand. 'Perhaps tomorrow. You must be tired now.' He glances at Magali, standing behind me. Philippe is at my side.

'No, Father, today. It must be today.' He disappears through the door behind the dais, and I follow him closely.

'I have business to attend to.'

'I promise, no business is more important than this. The fate of Langly is at stake.'

He envelops all three of us in a wary look. He must see something in our faces because he eventually concedes. 'Fine. Follow me to my solar.'

He leads us through the wide, airy corridors of the Royal Palace. The place I grew up in isn't a fortress-turned-residence. Its only purpose is pleasure, with its wide, glazed windows, the blue marble that clacks under our shoes, its generous spaces opening into arched courtyards and terraces that overlook them. We walk in silence towards his royal chambers, to the airy solar where he receives his private guests.

This used to be my mother's favourite receiving room.

Magali finds her place quickly on one of the wide turquoise-silk sofas. Philippe stands in the middle of the room, as if unsure what he should do with himself. I take the seat under the window.

'We need your help,' I say without preamble.

'I reckoned,' he says, clasping his hands behind him.

There is no time for niceties and polite openings—we have burnt through them all.

'Hugo is loose,' I say. 'Free to shapeshift. We need to bind him.'

My father stares at Magali. 'I thought you had taken care of that. That's why I gave you the cage.'

Magali shrugs. 'The plan ... hasn't gone accordingly.'

'Why is that?' Fury narrows my father's eyes. 'The plan was simple: the ties around Hugo were loosened by Julien Bencifert's death. You were meant to use the cage to bind him to his bird form. That's all there was to it.'

I think, *So Magali lied to my father, too.* She didn't even tell him what form Hugo had taken. This is why he allowed himself to be persuaded by the cat at Mermaid's Lake. I search for signs of treachery on Philippe's face, but he seems as surprised as I am.

'The plan has changed,' says Magali.

'When?' says my father. 'Why now? It's been weeks since I gave you the cage. What happened?'

Magali stares at her fingernails. I think, *She lied to you.* The events take shape in my mind. Instead of binding Hugo, she decided to use him, to change the law of inheritance in this kingdom.

I can see now, even clearer, why Magali would think she would have a claim upon Langly. Why she always did—through her own mother, of course.

And in this moment, in this stifling room, I begin to understand why my father would want magic banished from his kingdom. It causes too many complications. It makes a handful of people far too powerful and dangerous.

'Magali?' he says, his tone as cold as a bar of iron in the snow.

'We... I... We used the cage to bind Maël.'

'Maël,' says my father. He looks at me. 'Did you know?'

'Not until recently,' I admit. 'And I had no idea that you were involved. You never thought to tell me that you have magic.'

My father lifts his head. 'There was no need to.' He turns to Magali again. 'Hugo is free? To shift as he pleases? Of all the things you've ever done, Magali, this might be one of the worst. How could you? You know what he's capable of.'

'I had my reasons,' she says. She meets his gaze, unflinching.

My father paces the room. 'If you think that saying *I have my reasons* will make me give away binding objects so you can do with them as you please, as you've done before, you'll have to think again.' His voice rises. 'If there's someone who needs to be bound, that person is you.'

'I can't say I disagree.' Magali smooths her gown—red velvet entwined with black lace. 'But we can discuss that later. Our priority now is Hugo.'

'That's what you said before,' says my father.

'He's at Fort Cantor for now, with powerful protection spells keeping him locked in one of the chambers. I'm not sure for how long they will hold,' says Magali.

'You left him alone? At Fort Cantor?' he roars.

'We didn't know what else to do,' I barge in. 'He's dangerous.' *And we didn't trust Magali to stay behind*, I think to myself.

340

Magali says, 'If you want the truth, he played a part in what happened to Maël. He was the stableboy who went out with him to hunt.'

I notice the slick way in which she shifts the blame onto Hugo, when I know perfectly well that she was also on the cliff on that day. She's such a skilled liar that my blood runs cold. Yet, I find myself unable to contradict her. What would my father think of us then?

My father's face turns white. 'The stableboy I spoke to? Who told me the story about the lion?' He strokes his beard. 'I need to sit down.' He fidgets on one of the ottomans.

'And that terrible lion, the one that terrorised Langly from time to time, that was Maël,' says Magali, twisting the truth again, so that it would fit her purpose. 'Your Majesty.'

My father looks stricken. 'Where would he find the kind of power to transform himself, and hold the shape for that long? I always assumed the lion was a sort of pet that Maël brought to the castle through Port Lang. I never knew what to expect of him next—the debaucheries… A lion fit right in.'

'Would your daughter have fitted in, then?' I say.

'Maël was never as bad as everyone thought. I wasn't worried—'

'Perhaps you should have been.' My father quietens. I think this might be a good time to push him. 'Did you know about the Golden Pavilion?'

'Ah.' My father taps his lips with his finger. 'Did Magali tell you that, too?'

Philippe and I both whip our heads around towards his aunt. 'You knew of this?' he says. 'That the Golden Pavilion still stands?'

Magali shrugs. 'I had no idea you were interested in the old magic school.'

'No, Your Majesty, the dowager duchess didn't tell us a thing,' I say. 'We saw it with our own eyes.'

'It was Celine's idea,' says Philippe.

'More of an urge to see for myself. A call.'

For a moment, a sad smile flits on my father's lips. 'Your mother's call. That's why I never travel close to Castle Bencifert.'

The meaning of his words escapes me. I mean to ask, but Magali is the centre of attention. Again. 'None of this matters now,' she says. 'We have to save the duchy from Hugo.'

'Where's Maël?' says my father.

'In the cage, in Magali's chambers,' says Philippe.

'Ah, yes,' says my father. 'Of course. It serves you perfectly to see both Maël and Hugo removed, doesn't it, *Duke* Philippe? To be the next male heir to Langly?'

'It's not his fault,' I say. 'It's our fault.'

'Whose?' says my father.

'Hugo's and mine. He … he promised… I just had… I had to take care…'

'Speak clearly, girl. Don't babble,' says my father impatiently.

'Hugo persuaded me to forge the papers that declared Seigneur Bencifert's intentions after his death—the last will and the inheritance of his estate. I took your seal and wrote a new one that left Philippe with nothing but a cat.'

There's a sharp intake of breath behind me, but I don't dare look. I already told Philippe. But it's another thing to twist the knife in the wound, to remind him of it. But I must do this; my father cannot believe Philippe is of the same ilk as Hugo and Magali.

He's made of a different mould entirely.

'Girl! You plotted with Hugo, too?'

My chest burns, and so do my eyes. I don't dare look at Philippe as I did a moment ago. I have to confront my father on my own. 'Hugo lied to me, too. He lied to everyone. The worst part is that he almost obtained what he wanted. He is dangerous, Father. This is why he must be contained.'

He looks at Magali. 'Then why didn't you contain him when you told me you would?' He turns to me again. 'And you forged documents? Why, Celine?'

I can't tell him, *Because I didn't want to marry Maël.* I wasn't even meant to know about this. So I say, 'Because Hugo led me to believe it was the right thing to do. He's one of those people who can twist the truth in so many ways to their own advantage. I was foolish to trust him.'

'And now you believe *this* is the right thing,' he says.

Philippe clears his voice. 'I do understand your doubts, Your Majesty. I have no love for the ducal seat, and both my wife and my aunt can tell you as much.'

My father pricks his ears when he hears the words 'my wife'.

'Leave Hugo be, then,' Philippe continues. 'If you think it is right. Let him become the Duke of Langly.' My husband stands straight, his eyes blazing. He's not a man of many words. He's a man who can cut through to the heart of the matter.

And the heart of matter is this.

'But what about Maël?' says my father. 'What of him?'

MAGALI

The King throws us out soon afterwards, saying he wants to speak with me and only me in the morning; saying he needs more time to consider. The conversation went perfectly well: much to-ing and fro-ing, and the endless coaxing that our indecisive King needs in order to reach any sort of decision. Of course, Philippe had to ruin it all by confronting him.

Today, though, I don't have the heart to tell him what he did wrong. And by the way his eyebrows knit, I suspect this wouldn't be a good time to do so.

To be reminded that Hugo, Celine and I all plotted to take the farm away from him… Philippe is so much like Julien, his father. He knows how to hold a grudge.

'I'll have to tell your father the whole truth tomorrow,' I say to Celine.

'I'm sure it will be awful for you,' she says. 'To have to tell the truth.'

The little snake. 'The truth wouldn't have brought us very far in the past twenty years.'

Philippe marches ahead of us, quiet. I give up trying to catch up with him, so I stop to turn into one of the side corridors. 'I'll see you both tomorrow.' No point in fighting a battle today that I'm bound to lose.

But Celine has yet to learn that lesson. I watch her quicken her pace, calling Philippe's name, softly.

'Not now,' he says, looking over the top of her head.

'Philippe,' she says. 'What happened?'

He gazes at her, all the disappointment in the world in his eyes. 'I don't think I can trust you, Celine.' With this, he stalks back towards his chambers. Celine stands rooted, a lonely silhouette in the middle of the marble corridor. Her hands make a half-move, then fall to her sides.

It serves her right. Perhaps she will learn something from it.

DEFENDER OF THE CASTLE

CELINE

J wake in the middle of the night, trying to catch the rushing beats of my pounding heart. I dreamt of battlements and a lion above me, surrounded by men with raised swords. I ran. I ran, but my horse buckled beneath me. I saw Philippe and cried out for help, but he looked into the distance, at a point above my head.

A stout redhaired woman sang, 'Twist, twist, twist in my heart. What I carved out of the earth has exacted its price in too much blood.' The light in the sky flickered. 'Tell your sister the Morningstar is with Veliara. The Shadow Queen must pay a visit to the Goddess of the Edge. And tell Magali the Court will make *her* pay.'

I wake up in the middle of the night, the shapes of my old chambers familiar and yet so strange—the cloudy veil of the curtains around the four-poster bed, the window looking towards the city at its feet.

A feeling had been weighing on my shoulders all day, a feeling clinging to the very bricks this place is made of. It's in the fibre of my sheets, in the thread of the embroideries. In the carvings of the heavy furniture in my room. A feeling that has been my companion for the five years since I returned from the Golden Pavilion, since my mother died.

Loneliness.

A wisp of the dream clings to me. I think, my sister. Anne-Mihielle. I haven't seen her in so many years.

I never used to be lonely. Not before they took her away from me.

No, with Anne-Mihielle on my side, I never used to be a lonely child.

My Mihi, who has now also turned away from me.

* * *

AFTER A TOO-LOUD, too-busy breakfast, my father swoops Magali into his private chambers, as promised, while I corner Philippe in one of the inner gardens of the palace. It was my mother's favourite. It has blue, white and red tiles on the floor, and a tall fountain at its centre; two white marble statues of women grace its corners, women in the cloak-and-hood of the teachers of the Golden Pavilion, the silver pin with the falcon fastening it together. My mother once told me why the silver pin is the sign of our order—because we hold it all together. And that's what I have to do today.

Philippe leans against the back of one of the statues instead of sitting on a bench, like I am. This is such a Philippe thing to do, but this is not a time to concern myself with courtly manners. His face looks drawn and his eyes are red.

'Did you sleep well?' I say.

'No. All of this. It's … too much.'

I shrug. 'The palace?'

'No. All of this bloody situation.' He avoids my gaze. 'I talked to Magali last night.'

'And?'

He stares at his toes. He looks quite the proper gentleman now, with his velvet doublet and the thick chain around his neck. Such a far cry from the Philippe who was up to his ankles in manure a few days ago.

'Lies, lies, lies,' he says. 'We've all been lied to.'

I chuckle. 'Tell me something I don't already know.'

'But you don't know,' he says. 'Let's see how this entire business with Hugo turns out.' He runs a hand through his hair, ruffling it. 'Which reminds me. I need to ask you a question.'

The ground shifts under my feet.

'Why aren't you trying to free Hugo now and make him duke?'

I turn this over in my head. Years of love—or infatuation, perhaps—don't disappear overnight, and the situation we find ourselves in is complicated. To think about spending my life with Magali at Fort Cantor still sends shivers down my spine.

I can hear my voice, but it isn't the *sound* of my voice. It's an avalanche, falling on our heads. 'Because the Hugo in the castle isn't the man I fell in love with. In fact, I think the man I fell in love with never actually existed.' I look up at Philippe. His arms are crossed so tight. There's anger, and there's something else, as well. 'We were young, Philippe. We were close at the Golden Pavilion in a way ... and then he disappeared.'

'You waited for him.' The way Philippe says this, it's not a question.

'I did,' I say. 'But I feel so stupid now. If I had known where his plans were leading... I told him that. Five years ago. I would have married him back then even without a duchy, but he never asked. He said he wanted me to be the wife of a duke.'

'And you are, aren't you?' Philippe shifts uncomfortably.

I can see the lack of trust, tearing at us both. 'Philippe, I'd never ask my father to change the law of succession. I don't want to be queen. I don't want to push my brother aside.'

'What do you want, then, Celine? There seem to be a lot of don'ts.'

I think, *I want to be more like you. To take responsibility, and do some good, like we did during the drought. And it does not come down to just a title, though a title might be an interesting tool to achieve what we want.*

I want to be with you in the way we were on that day at the farm. I want us to weave our Gifts, whether they're magical or non-magical.

I want to see what we could do together.

I know what Magali thinks, that she is better than me, or Philippe.

She *is* better than me, better than Philippe. But not as good as we could be together. I know enough about the duchy now to realise that the tangle in the ledgers, the taxes imposed on the people were not all of Maël's doing in the last few years. Those were wrongs that stretched back for decades, through Frederic's, Kylian's *and* Magali's rule.

Magali wants power for the sake of it. I also dreamed about how I would rule, but I'm beginning to realise that I had no idea, in fact, what that ruling might look like, before Philippe came into his role as the duke.

I've been reminded, of late, about the Year of the Red Maiden and everything that happened then.

It happened because the seigneurs forgot what they were meant to do, forgot about the people.

The Mothers of the Forest teach us that the land belongs to the people, and that the seigneurs are there to protect. To unite the people in the face of greater threats, to show them the way through drought and pestilence and wars.

Not to thrive on the people's hunger, on their hard work.

How easily we could forget that it was on the ruins of the principate of Anselme that Langly rose. How easily we could forget what had been at the heart of it all.

But Philippe knows. Philippe ... he is something else. And with me steering him among the seigneurs and their alliances, with him steering us towards what Langly needs...

Together, we could be unstoppable.

But I'm not sure how to begin to tell him all that, without seeming that I'm just like Magali, manoeuvring him for my own ends.

Philippe looks at me intently, and I am struggling to find a way to say what I need to say, when I hear my name being shouted from the corridor.

There's the sound of rushed steps, almost like running.

'In here,' I call.

A maid appears in the covered gallery around the garden. 'Princess Celine, it's your father. He asks you to join him immediately.'

* * *

WHEN WE ARRIVE in the private chamber, my father is red in the face. Magali sits on the couch, the golden cage with Maël at her feet.

'Yes?' I say, the beats of my heart rushing and rushing. It's quite clear that something has gone very wrong.

Philippe closes the door softly behind us.

'What's happened?'

'We've had word from Fort Cantor.' My father's voice is choked. I've never seen him this ... furious. 'It seems that Maël turned up. In the castle. And he's rallying his minions. He's sending word everywhere.'

I stare at the golden cage. 'How can that be?' My mind can't wrap itself around the facts.

Philippe kneels and takes out a piece of carrot from the pockets of his doublet. The mouse comes to him and nibbles from his palm. 'This is Maël,' says Philippe. 'This is him. What you say can't be true.'

'I know,' says Magali.

'Do you?' says my father. 'How do you know that? Did he tell you he's Maël?'

Magali pales.

'I think,' says my father, swiping his gaze over all of us, 'at least one of you is lying.'

'Are you sure?' I say. 'It might be a rumour.'

'Celine, dear, if Count Goderic says he has seen Maël, and that he's at Fort Cantor, then I will go ahead and believe Count Goderic because he has never lied to me. Not that I know of.'

My knees turn soft. Next to me, Philippe's face drains of blood.

'But if that is Maël, who is this?' *And what about Hugo*, I don't say. 'Who have we been keeping in the cage?'

'Who have I been carrying around in my pocket?' Philippe wipes his forehead.

'There must be an explanation,' I say. 'There must be.'

'Explanations be damned! Maël has seized Fort Cantor,' says my father. 'He's rallying his troops.'

I crash into the nearest armchair I can find. 'Then...'

'Then I am nothing,' says Philippe. He throws Magali a look. 'Maybe it's for the best.'

'How can you say that?' I intervene.

'We plotted against Maël,' says Magali. 'All of us. And now he's gathering an army.'

'Philippe, you must rally the seigneurs,' I say. 'Quickly. See who is faithful to you. I wager plenty of them are. Plenty will want you on the ducal seat, and not Maël.'

'Why?' says Philippe. 'What right do I have? He's the duke, not me.'

I shift in my seat. 'But you're Isabella's son. You have a claim to the duchy. If the law favoured the first-born, no matter if they were man or woman...' I give my father a quick glance. 'Father. You can't allow this to happen. You can't allow Maël to take over the duchy. You can't—'

'Celine, my dear, I can and I will allow this,' he roars. 'Not just because your husband now has nothing to his name. Think of the implications. Think of what this would mean to the kingdom one day.'

Queen, I think. *If my father changes the law to give today Philippe precedence over Maël, this will also give me precedence over my brother.*

I will be the next queen, which is precisely what Hugo wanted. I shudder. How neatly it all plays into his hands. Yet again.

'There's a way we can find out who is in the cage,' says Magali.

'Don't you even dare,' says my father. 'And what difference does it make?' There's a hint of something in that, words that he can't bring himself to speak out loud. 'I can't believe you all. The position you have put me in with your lies. The last thing I need now is to have Maël marching on the Royal Palace because he believes I had a hand in this,' my father shouts.

I flinch. My indecisive father, who always defers confrontation; who loathes it.

My hands are clammy. I never imagined something like this would be possible, not even in my worst nightmares.

'It will be fine. Philippe and I will stay here, at the Royal

Palace. Things will calm down.' I rub my temples. All of this feels so unreal.

'You will not stay here, Celine. You absolutely will not,' says my father. 'It would be a provocation to Maël.'

I look up at Philippe. 'It's fine,' he says. 'It will be fine. I know what I have to do.'

'I tell you, there must be a simple explanation,' says Magali, 'if we could only check.'

I take in the cock of her head, the way she avoids the king's gaze. There *is* a simple explanation, and I know why she doesn't even suggest it to my father.

Because if it is true, then we are the most imprudent dolts in this entire kingdom.

And I, for one, am not ready to suffer the entire brunt of my father's wrath.

So I say nothing, chewing on my swirling thoughts.

'You will not check. And you will not raise a single finger against Maël!' screams my father. 'Not one of you. I'll sort this. I'll sort this mess out, but I don't want to see any of you right now. Get. Out. Of. My. Chambers.'

MAGALI

Now this is quite a turn. I hold up the golden cage carefully. You never know what the mouse might do. As I swirl it around, the blueish fur of the creature catching the light, I *think* this is the mouse I carried in my pocket for a few days.

But how can we be sure what mouse ended up in the cage in Celine's chambers?

I could scream at my foolishness. I went to look for the red pouch after the children wove the containment spells. Later, when I asked him about it, Hugo just laughed mockingly. He didn't carry it with him when Philippe and Celine confronted him.

He must have sensed something, because, without the pouch, he can't hold another form for long.

I didn't have the time or means to squeeze the truth out of him, and I didn't want Philippe or that nosy princess, both watching me so closely, even now, to catch a whiff of what I wanted.

I thought I'd have time.

What a fool I've been.

'This is mad,' says Celine. 'Mad.'

For once, I agree with her. 'There must be a simple explanation. There always is.'

'You always have an explanation, Magali.' Philippe narrows his eyes and for a moment I doubt whether it was wise to tell him what I told him last night.

It's not the first mistake I've made.

I sigh. If they'd only listen to me. I have no other way to proceed than to do what's right, in this instance.

Philippe turns away from us. 'Some things are best left to rest, the way they are. Now, if you'll excuse me.' He leaves, the clop of his steps echoing further and further from us.

It was certainly not a good idea to tell him.

* * *

By noon, the King orders us to pack our bags and leave. I'm already looking for Philippe, who is missing, and though I hate doing it, I must look to the person who managed to bring him back the last time.

The princess sits on her bed, a wild look on her face as the royal botler tells her she must leave.

353

'And where must I go?' demands Celine. 'Fort Cantor?'

'No, not Fort Cantor, your father said.' The royal botler is quite red in the face when he conveys this to the princess. 'Fort Cantor least of all.'

Celine seems on the verge of crying. I almost feel sorry for her. I, too, know what it is to lose everything.

I approach, still holding the cage. 'Did the King say anything about Castle Bencifert?'

'He did not,' says the botler. He seizes the opportunity to bow and withdraw. 'If you'll excuse me.'

I lay the cage on a table, unsure how I should break the news to her. Not to spare her feelings, but to make sure that she will be compliant and do my bidding.

It is the wisest course of action, of course.

'We should go to Castle Bencifert,' I say simply. 'I think that's where Philippe has gone.'

The princess's face dissolves in shock. 'Philippe has gone? He didn't say a word to me. I must … I must tell my father. To reverse the…' Celine wipes her face. 'I can't believe he didn't say a word. He barely came back, and now he's gone again.'

'I think he didn't want to wait for your father to tell him to leave. Philippe is proud that way.'

'And what will we do at Castle Bencifert?' Celine is so dumb-struck that she looks to me for advice. Good. 'Rely on the hospi-tality of Seigneur Bencifert? I'm not sure he has any left for us. What will Maël think of that?'

Oh, how tiring. She has an opinion. 'We lick our wounds. Come up with a plan.' That's what I've done in the past and it has worked miracles.

Celine says nothing for a long while, just stares at her hands.

'I don't think there is much more we can do,' I say, eventu-ally. If only she would budge. I'd leave without her, but something tells me that Philippe might be more willing to speak to *her*.

'This is why everyone fears you so much, isn't it? Because you don't know when to give up.'

Ha! *And you don't know when to give in.* 'I do want what's best for you. For you and Philippe.'

'Why? Why don't you run to Maël now and make amends? What are you after? I don't understand.'

But how could she? She never had to fight for anything. It seems a gentle approach is necessary with her. What a stubborn creature she is. I sit down on the bed. 'As I've said, there's an explanation for everything, but it's not my explanation to give to you. It's Philippe's. He'll tell you, if he thinks he should.'

Celine gathers her knees under her chin. It's unbecoming for a young woman. 'I'm nothing but a pawn to all of you, aren't I? I have to do as you bid me and shut up.'

'I want what's best for you,' I repeat.

'Says the woman who keeps her son locked in a cage.'

She understands nothing at all. 'You can't even imagine what it is to be an outcast from one day to the next. Today a duchess, tomorrow a supplicant.'

'I know precisely how that feels. It's happening to me as we speak.'

'Kylian wanted to kill us, Celine. All of us. Isabella, me, Maël. He wanted to erase us from the face of the earth. Magic was the only thing that kept us alive. The magic around Castle Bencifert. And Julien himself.'

'Philippe's father?'

'Julien Bencifert sheltered us, hoping Kylian would leave us alone. But he wouldn't. I had no other choice but to do what I did. To thrust Kylian out. Otherwise we would have never been safe. Sometimes, the only way is to cut the evil from the root.'

'You're talking about felling your own son.'

'I don't believe that's my son at Fort Cantor. We didn't leave my son there.'

The little witch narrows her eyes. 'No, we left behind some-body else entirely.'

I'm amazed that she had the sense to grasp this. How the easiest way for Hugo to finally become the duke would be to assume Maël's shape. In the end, people think he's been dead for a long time.

'Yes.' No matter what, it does me good to see that someone nurtures the same suspicions as I do. Even if it's just Celine. 'There *is* a way to tell. But it's risky.'

'But we could know for certain. We could ride to Fort Cantor.' The princess rises to her feet. 'We should find Philippe. Hugo... we can still catch Hugo. We can make him disappear, if only Philippe would help us.'

'Like I said, we need to go to Castle Bencifert. I know Philippe; that's where he will be.'

CELINE

I pack my bags at an alarming speed but I can't leave without speaking to my father, so I roam the chambers of the castle, looking for him. He's in one of the council rooms, speaking to a handful of noblemen.

They stop and stare as I step in. 'Father, I'm leaving,' I say quickly. 'If I could just have a word with you.'

My father waves his hand, signalling to get out. *Does he mean me?* I wonder. Then he says, 'Thank you, my seigneurs. We shall convene later.'

They leave the room in a rather displeased shuffle.

'Any parting words?' he says.

I take a seat at the large table next to him, unsure where to begin.

'Yes?' he says.

I take a deep breath. If I want any genuine help, I need to be truthful with him. 'I think Hugo might be at Fort Cantor impersonating Maël.'

'That's what we all think, isn't it?' he says, taking me completely by surprise. 'But what difference does it make, in the end? They both have a better claim to the duchy than your husband.'

I lean back in my seat. 'So that's your plan? Let them fight it out over the duchy, keep your hands clean, and see who comes out the victor?'

'I can't give you what you want. I can't change the succession laws. Celine, it's not that I think you wouldn't make a good queen. Perhaps in time, if you learn to … stand up for what you believe in. You're clever, and kind. You could make a good queen. But this isn't about what *I* think. It's about the Red Kingdom, and the people in it. And they're definitely not ready to be ruled by a queen. These aren't the times we live in. Don't think I haven't considered changing the succession laws, myself. But I think no good could come of it.'

What he says strikes me with full force. 'You think I'd make a good queen?'

'I think you make a good duchess. I think it's up to you to keep that position.'

I pause, catching a loose thread—something that visited me in my sleep. 'How about Anne-Mihielle? What kind of queen would she make?'

My father shifts uncomfortably in his seat. 'Anne-Mihielle… She has her own battles to wage.'

Ah, yes. I'm not sure if she would want to come back—I heard that she's become the Haute Chausseuse of the Mage-Hunters this year, though I have no idea how that might have come about. News travels between the kingdoms, especially when it comes to such positions of power. The Green King seemed to have been just as surprised in the letter he wrote to my father.

The Mage-Hunters, of all orders.

'So. Langly,' says my father, indicating that the conversation about my sister is over.

I know better than to pursue it. 'But right now I can't be the duchess. Remember? Maël? Hugo?'

'No, right now, Philippe can't be the duke, but you can still be the duchess. That was your plan in the beginning, wasn't it?'

I feel a flush creeping up my chest and into my cheeks. 'Are you suggesting I should marry Hugo? Like you betrothed me to Maël, without telling me?'

My father is taken aback by this. 'You were never betrothed to Maël. Besides, what's with all this talk about Maël? He would have never married someone who was unwilling. Who told you this?'

Hugo.

Of course. The very thing that made me desperate to help Hugo. To want this as much as him.

My father, mercifully, goes on. 'And I'm not suggesting anything. I'm saying that what you do now is up to you. I will not interfere.'

This strikes me so hard that I can't think of anything to say. And then I realise he's dodging his responsibilities again, indecisive as usual.

'You're a grown woman, Celine. You make your own choices.' He dips a hand into his pocket and extracts something. It is a silver pin, shaped like a falcon. He hands it to me carefully. 'This is a binding object, the strongest I've ever created. The moment I inherited the throne, I made this. I've never used it before—my reign has been dedicated to something else entirely, as you well know.'

Yes, erasing magic from the kingdom.

He says, 'I think the time for magic is gone. I have my reasons for saying this, and one day ... perhaps...' He scratches his beard, considering. 'Step by step, we must make the future we wish to inhabit. The choice is in your hands, Celine. And so is the pin. Use it, or don't. It's all up to you.'

RALLYING CRY

CELINE

*A*s I expected, we aren't exactly welcome at Castle Bencifert.

'Duchess,' says Louis, staring at both Magali and me.

She's clutching the golden cage—she carries it everywhere—but now she avoids my gaze because during the carriage ride here, we had the opportunity to talk.

'You have to trust that I want the best for you,' she said.

'I don't think so,' I replied, the power of the silver pin burning in my pocket.

The plains rolled under the carriage's wheels, wheat and rye rippling in the hot breeze. There was a ripe smell of late summer in the air, and we inched forward on our path between two castles.

'Everything I did, I did for Philippe's sake,' she said. 'Who do you think placed Hugo with Philippe, when Julien fell so ill? Who do you think laid the groundwork for all of this?'

'It was you?' I said in disbelief.

Hugo told me we had to save Philippe from Magali's clutches. What a despicable, elaborate lie.

'Yes. After I escaped Fort Cantor, I went to my refuge. My safe haven.'

Indeed. Magali had been at Castle Bencifert when everything happened.

'Why didn't Maël look for you there?'

'Maël is imprudent, impulsive, but not a complete fool. He wouldn't have started a fight with the Benciferts, when all he wanted was to see me gone from Fort Cantor. I assume he was pleased that I had stopped nagging him.'

'You nagged Maël?'

'I never gave up hoping that he'd become a better man.'

'But you did give up. You plotted his downfall.' The mouse grew uneasy in its cage. 'And, as his mother, you can stand by and watch this happening to him? Trapped in the body of a mouse?' I shuddered.

'I hope it won't be ... permanent,' she said. 'I'm looking for other ways.'

'Well, anything short of this, and my husband abandons the ducal seat.'

'Your husband has already abandoned the ducal seat.' She seemed dejected as she said this.

'Yes, all that plotting and it has come to nothing.'

'I'm pleased, at least, that nothing truly bad happened to Maël. I was so worried while he was missing. I had no idea what Hugo might do to him. I'd put nothing past Hugo.' She extracted a cube of sugar from a little box and passed it to the mouse. Maël. 'But now it makes sense that Hugo was so frightened when Maël disappeared. I threatened to do all sorts of things. This is why Hugo couldn't reveal himself earlier, not until we found Maël again.'

This particular last piece of the puzzle sickened me even more. Hugo sent me on a treasure hunt, keeping me busy. I was searching for the magical object that bound Hugo—which didn't even exist—while he was searching for something else altogether. For some*one* else.

I said, 'So Philippe actually kept us all together without even knowing it.'

Magali smiled. 'I suppose so.'

'You have no heart,' I said. 'And no scruples.'

The truths that were coming to light were nauseating. She had plotted with her sworn enemy, to ensure the downfall of her own son. Just to maintain an illusion of control. Did she think she would be able to sway Philippe as she wanted?

And then, I remember what my husband said. About not being able to make a difference as he would have wanted, when he left the first time.

Perhaps he meant *her*. 'I need some air,' I said, and signalled the coachman to stop the carriage. I continued on horseback for the rest of our journey, just so I wouldn't have to speak to her again.

And yet now, the end of our journey doesn't seem to be much of an end in itself. Louis bows again. 'How may I be of service?'

'Seigneur Bencifert,' I say. 'I was hoping we might be able to abuse your hospitality again, as my husband is.'

'Philippe is also with you?' Louis peers behind me.

'No,' I say. 'I thought he was already here?'

Next to Louis, his wife shakes her head, her lips a thin line.

'I'm afraid not,' says Louis.

A ripple passes over Magali's face, but she controls herself too well to let anything show. 'We expect him to arrive soon, then.'

'The farm,' I say. 'He must be at the farm.' I turn around, ready to hop on my horse again. Magali makes to follow me. 'I think, Magali, it would be best if I go alone. I think there are some things we must say to each other in private.'

'I don't think that's wise,' she says.

'You can still speak to him if I fail to persuade him.' I mount my horse. Magali would only be in my way, and I've had enough of her meddling.

My father said I have a choice, but it all depends on what Philippe has to say. I think, somewhere on the road between the Royal Palace and Castle Bencifert, I made mine. In fact, I think it was there, already made—I only had to rise up to meet it.

'Seigneur Louis, I hope I'll be able to enjoy your hospitality a bit later.' I turn and signal two of the guards to follow me.

'Is it true what they say about Maël?' cries Louis behind us.

'I'll leave the Dowager Duchess to give you all the details. She is so thoroughly acquainted with them.'

I gallop to the farm in a flurry. I don't mind that Philippe wasn't at the castle. I don't mind having left Magali there.

We stop our horses in the space between the farmhouse and the stables and Albertine, the tenant, emerges from one of the side buildings. 'Duchess,' she says, making a clumsy curtsy. 'We weren't expecting you.' She wipes her red swollen hands on her apron.

'I came to find my husband,' I say.

The woman looks crestfallen. 'The ... duke?'

'Yes, my husband, Philippe.'

'Duchess, the last I saw the duke was days ago. When you went to the castle.'

There's a sharp sound in my ears. I hope I haven't heard her right. 'Days ago?'

'Yes, when you left together to go to the castle.'

I climb down from my horse, reeling. I didn't even consider that he might not be here. I have no idea where he would otherwise go. I tap the flank of my mare, absent-mindedly. 'Do you mind if my men take a look? Maybe he came here and you didn't see him arrive?'

'No. Yes. No, I don't mind,' says the woman. 'But I don't think I could have missed him if he came here.'

I give my guards a silent signal and they start the search. I lean into the horse, my legs soft and trembling. I must be even more tired than I realised. I look around at the farmstead, the shapes of the stables and the house a blur.

The people in Philippe's family have a bad habit of vanishing. Magali. His mother.

This gives me an idea. 'Say you, good woman, might you have seen Isabella of Langly?'

The woman blinks. 'Today?'

'No. Lately. In the past few weeks. Or months.'

The woman shakes her head slowly.

I try to plant my feet firmly into this moment. 'Did you live on the farm before, too? When Philippe still owned it?'

'No, my lady, we had a smaller farm, that way.' She gestures into the distance. I raise my head and far, far away I can see the shape of the Opal Mountain, the cavernous rock where the Golden Pavilion used to be—where it still is, but hidden from view. 'But we came to the farm often, to trade. I never saw Madame Isabella. She was never here.'

My mother was never at the farm, Philippe had said.

I did all this so my mother would be proud of me.

If I can find his mother, maybe I can find Philippe.

My men return. 'I'm sorry, my lady, but there's no trace of him.'

They assist me in remounting the horse. 'To the castle,' I say.

While I hunt for my husband, it seems that I'll have to spend the night there, whether Louis likes it or not.

MAGALI

In the three days since we arrived, there has been no sign of Philippe. Weak, he is so weak. Much weaker than I expected.

He does not understand the size of the responsibility that has been bestowed on him. He does not understand that it cannot be shaken off like a dirty shirt.

Nevertheless, the people have been trickling in, hearing that we are here.

It must be my name that makes them set up camp within and beneath the walls of Castle Bencifert, to the increasing unrest of Seigneur Louis.

There are rumours of Shape-Shifters in our midst that have begun to spread—that the real Maël is dead, that the stableboy, the only witness, is nowhere to be found.

I have not lost my touch.

As dusk sets in, I stop in the camp outside the walls. Carts and wagons have been drawn up in a circle, with the men and women and children sitting around fires. A young man speaks, a man who grew up on the farm with Philippe and who fled from Fort Cantor today. 'It is no clean business with the master Maël, I tell you, Madame. I looked into his eyes and they were wild. The eyes of an animal.'

The eyes of a cat? The eyes of a lion? Perhaps. But the lion should be trapped in the cage that I carry with me everywhere.

'Do tell,' I say to the man, and the others lean in to listen.

Stories told around a fire, plans being forged in the fading light… In the darkness across the other side of the plain lies Fort Cantor.

The unrest rustles and grows, and I have a decision to make, unless we want Fort Cantor to be lost to us for ever.

At dinner, Louis says, 'It won't be long until Maël attacks.'

It's just the four of us in the private chambers—me, the princess, Louis and his wife. His manners are wearing thin, showing the hardened man underneath, the steel his father was also made of.

'I know,' I say.

'These are farmers; this isn't an army,' says Louis. 'Maël has summoned the seigneurs to Fort Cantor; he recalled his mercenaries from Port Lang, and Count Goderic's third son has apparently been strutting around the castle as if he owns it.'

'Philippe will come,' I say, with an assurance I don't feel, of this boy who runs away at the slightest sign of unrest.

Maël is made of sterner stuff.

'We don't have any more time,' says Louis. 'Aunt Magali, don't you realise?' His long, sharp face is drawn. 'When he rallies the seigneurs and marches towards Castle Bencifert, nothing will stop them. No amount of carts and forks and axes. They will march straight through them.'

'And by what right do they march?' I say. 'Castle Bencifert is the King's fief, and does not owe fealty to the Duke of Langly.'

'They march by the right of the sword,' says Louis. 'That's all the right Maël needs.'

'That's not Maël,' I say, with all the certainty of which I'm capable. This much is true … I think.

Louis prepares to contradict me—we have had this conversation many times in the past few days—when Celine says, 'Then send word to the King that he should provide an army to protect you.'

'On what grounds?' says Louis.

His wife sips her wine quietly, staring at a point on the table between the goblets and the plates.

'As your liege, he must protect you,' says the princess. 'It's part of the oath.'

'But don't you see, Duchess?' he says. 'If the King gathers an army at Castle Bencifert, it could be used as grounds for Maël to attack. He will take it as a threat.'

'Is there any truth to what they claim?' says Louis's wife, surprising us all with the scratchy tone of her voice. 'About the Shape-Shifters.'

'More than you'd think,' says Celine.

'I think we should rally the seigneurs, too,' I say, to silence her.

'If there is anyone who can rally the seigneurs, it's Philippe,' says Celine. 'At least, those who are still faithful to him.'

Philippe, who may be far, far away by now. I don't know why she still expects him to return. It becomes clearer and clearer to me, as the days pass, that he doesn't mean to come back. Not after what I told him about his parentage. No matter. He was bound to find out the truth. If not from me, then from Hugo.

'This is madness,' says Louis. 'And it smacks of rebellion. I can't allow you to stay here anymore. I'm sorry but you need to go. I have to look after my own lands and my own people. I hope you understand.' Louis's voice quivers and he avoids our gazes. I can tell he's not happy to have to say it. I can tell he's been thinking of this for a long time.

'Fine,' I say. Suits me just as well. 'I'll go and rally the seigneurs myself.' If not, there is something else I can still do.

'And why would they follow you?' says that little snake.

Louis seems on the verge of telling us something, but nothing comes. He knows, he must know, that he cannot stop me.

I bid everyone a good night and start to prepare.

CELINE

The night is sweltering and I suffocate in the small chamber, tossing and turning in the bed. Rallying the seigneurs? This is madness, indeed. How many would follow the two duchesses? And why?

I reckon Magali has done a good job of seeding doubts and rumours to weaken the position of the Maël at Fort Cantor, but how many would dismiss them as old wives' tales? As far as they're concerned, magic is gone from our world. At least, that's what they prefer to believe.

In the darkness, it's hard to trust that our chances are anything but feeble. I get up and open the shutters that seal the windows. Tepid air flows into the room. I stare at the stars shining in the sky, at the half-moon nestled between them. We need Philippe, and he is hiding; he might never come out, not if he doesn't want to be found. Louis said today that he might be halfway across the Glittering Sea, if he took a ship from Port Lang.

Magali insists on rallying the seigneurs. Asserts that Philippe will come when he hears. But what if he doesn't hear? What if he's so far away that he never does? A tide of anger ebbs and flows. Philippe, who has left again.

Hiding where no one will ever look for him. The false remains of the Golden Pavilion twinkle in the distance, while the Pavilion itself must gleam golden-blue in the moonlight, in reality. I remember how it shimmered on nights like this.

I remember that night with Hugo five years ago. When he left. When he promised he'd come and find me when all of it was over. When he'd become the Duke of Langly, a worthy husband to me.

It seems that Hugo kept his word, finally. He is there, across the plain, at Fort Cantor. It would be so simple to ride over and seek him out. I could easily find an explanation for what passed between us a few days ago.

Hugo is there, following through on his plans, while Philippe has run away, where no one can find him.

The ruins shimmer in the moonlight. The ruins that no one would disturb, because no one would think that something is still there. Not Isabella, who hasn't been seen at Fort Cantor for years, because she was too busy being Madame Hirondelle. But why would she say that she wasn't Philippe's mother?

What is the Golden Pavilion if not the perfect place to hide if you didn't want anyone to find you … because no one would think to look there. The idea knocks the air out of my lungs. It is so simple, and it's been right before my eyes this whole time. I peer through the half-lit night, wondering if he's been watching us.

I turn quickly to write a message for Magali.

Do as you said – rally the seigneurs. I'll meet you at the camp before Bencifert Castle, when the time is right.
    Celine

I charge out of the room and saddle my mare in the dark. I tell no one about where I plan to go now.

* * *

BY THE TIME my horse weaves its way up the path towards the Golden Pavilion, a pink sunrise lights our way. Not that we need it. The road is in the same impeccable state as it was a week ago – sleek and soft and clean. Kept in place by threads of forgotten magic.

I have made my decision. I am rolling the dice. There's no way back now, if I find what I'm looking for. And my heart thumps because I don't know if this is the right choice. In any case, it's the hard choice. Nothing would be easier than to have ridden to Fort Cantor instead and begged for Hugo's forgiveness. I'm sure there's more than one use he could put me to.

But, for better or for worse, this is the path I have chosen.

And just before I reach the ruins, there's that twist in the road, that bend. And when I round the corner, I stand again at the edge of the square, just like the last time. Except not quite like the last time. On the first-floor balcony, leaning on the delicate marble rail, Philippe is waiting. 'Celine!'

He disappears into the shadows and my heart starts thumping even faster in my chest. The merest glimpse of him has made my belly fill with warmth. I slide down off my horse and prepare to tie it to a post when I hear the sound of rushed steps behind me.

'I thought it might be you,' says Philippe, taking the reins from my hands. Our fingers touch and all I can think about is that I want him to hold my hand. 'I saw you were coming. Across the plain.'

He ties the horse in the stables. He is wearing a shirt, the hem hanging over a pair of tight riding trousers. The plain clothing becomes him. I have so many things I mean to tell him and I can't think of a single one.

He was looking out for me, just as I've been looking for him.

'You were watching? From above?'

'Of course,' he says.

I know what he'd see from the balconies or from the towers. The carts, streaming across the valley on their way to Castle Bencifert. On a clear day, he might even see the camp. 'So you stood here, watching what was happening in the valley, and you did nothing? Do you know that Maël or Hugo, or whoever it is, is rallying the seigneurs? Do you know that all these people who are gathering at Castle Bencifert are coming to look for you? And you disappeared without saying a single word.' I don't mean to scold him by way of a greeting, but here I am.

His jaw is clenched. 'I was afraid this is why you'd come, Celine. What did you expect?' He shakes his head. 'You don't understand. I had no choice.'

'Of course you had a choice. You still have one. Magali has been spreading rumours about Maël, that he isn't the real Maël. We can still...' I think about the pin in the pocket of my dress. 'We can still trap him. We can still make him go away. But I can't do it alone.'

'Celine.' *Ssseline.* He proceeds to untie the horse. 'I can't. If this is the only reason you came, you might as well turn around and go back.'

'At the first sign of trouble, you run away? What about all the work we've done at Fort Cantor? All the improvements? Hugo will undo everything. What about—' *Us,* I nearly say, but hold back. 'You have to return and claim your right to the duchy.'

'Celine.' He locks his arms in front of his chest. 'I have no right. None at all.'

'You're still Isabella's son. The blood of the Duke of Langly. If you would just stand and fight—'

He shakes his head, and turns to go back to the Pavilion. As I follow him with my gaze, I notice Madame Hirondelle standing in the shadow of the covered gallery.

'May Sabya's Lightsong brighten your day, Celine,' she says. 'We weren't expecting you.'

I stalk after Philippe. 'Magali is rallying the seigneurs,' I say. 'But so is Maël ... who is really Hugo.' I look into Madame Hirondelle's face, trying to glean how much she knows. How much Philippe has told her. 'Please, help us. Hugo must be stopped.'

'Hugo will stop at nothing,' says Madame Hirondelle. 'This is what I try to tell Philippe too, but he won't listen to me. Perhaps he will listen to you.'

Philippe throws his head to the side. 'Leave me alone, both of you.' He passes Madame Hirondelle and stalks up to the inner garden of the Pavilion. Golden light floods it from all directions.

'You must tell her, Philippe. You must tell her and let her decide. There are ways. Hugo can still be contained.'

'We can bind him,' I say, grabbing the hem of Philippe's shirt, stopping him in his tracks. His shoulders rise. 'My father ... he gave me something. We can bind him if we choose to.'

'And for what? Why would we do that? Hugo is the duke, Celine. Or Maël. We don't even know who is who anymore! I'm tired of these games. One of them is the duke; I have no place there.' He unclenches my fingers. 'It's done. I'm done with it all.' He stalks up onto the stairs that lead to the first-floor gallery.

'Are you now? Would you let them rule, then? What did you make of Maël's rule, when you saw the ledgers? And what sort of duke do you think Hugo will make?'

'It doesn't matter,' he says. 'Even if I wanted to make a difference ... too much blood has to be spilled so I could start making that difference.'

Nonsense. If Hugo or Magali or Maël are allowed to go down that path... We will live through another Year of the Red Maiden.

But I have one more card to play. 'And what about me?'

He stops, a hand on the marble banister. 'You can do as you please. Consider me dead. Go and marry Hugo. I have nothing to give you.'

I look into Madame Hirondelle's face, a face I know so well. A woman I thought I knew. 'Are you truly Isabella of Langly?'

'I used to be called that.'

'They said you were ambitious. They said Kylian banished you when he took the castle because he was afraid of you.'

On the stairs, Philippe has stopped, listening.

Madame Hirondelle says, 'Yes, he was afraid of me. But not because I wanted the duchy for myself. That life wasn't for me. Marriage, and what it entailed.'

'Why was he afraid of you, then? Why did he banish his own sister?'

Shadows shift in Madame's Hirondelle's eyes. The past. The emptiness of the Golden Pavilion. 'Because I was more powerful than him. And if Hugo is allowed to have what he wants, if he thinks he needs to take his revenge upon you—'

'Isabella,' says Philippe. He's watching us from the stairs. 'Leave her alone. She needs to go.'

'No, you need to tell her.'

'Tell me what?' I look from the one to the other, but their faces betray nothing. 'Madame Hirondelle, back then, when your brother banished you, what did you do?'

'I didn't want Langly. You know who I am—I'm the doyenne of this school. That's who I wanted to be.'

I think, *But Philippe? Your son?* And then I say, 'Your school is empty. You have no students.'

She laces her hands in the wide sleeves of her cloak. 'There's a different sort of work that I do now. It was for the best.'

'And when you closed the Pavilion, didn't you feel it was all for nothing?'

'Things had been coming to a head for a long time. This is why your mother enclosed the illusion spell around the school, a short time before she gave birth to your brother.'

'You mean, before she died.' And then it strikes me. 'What do you mean, my mother enclosed the school? This magic, all of this—'

I remember what my father said. How he couldn't bear to

travel close to the ruins of the Pavilion. I remember my mother's call.

And then I think, *A part of her, a tiny part of her, might still be here. Giving me courage.*

What would my mother think if she saw me for the past five years of my life, hiding, making myself small, just a puppet?

What would she think to see me here today, taking a stand for what I believe in, for what I want, and losing?

'Your mother, Celine, is still here. Her magic was bound to the school only a short time before she was gone. It's your mother's Gift that keeps the Pavilion hidden.'

It's as if the world turns dark for a moment. Everything I ever thought about my parents, about my family... 'You're implying ... that my mother knew what my father meant to do? But she loved the school. She was its doyenne before you. She encouraged me to use my magic. She would never have—'

Philippe comes down a few steps, hesitating. 'Why do you need to tell her all this, Isabella?'

'Larger forces were at work. Higher stakes. She finally saw the sense in closing the school,' says Madame Hirondelle, ignoring him. 'And she supported it. There is no place for magic in this world. It must be used only to bind the rest of it. There is no more balance, Celine. There used to be balance between the mages and the Binders, but the Crystal became tainted... The pain and sorrow that could come are endless. My life's work isn't the school. Not anymore.'

'Is it, Isabella?' Philippe's voice sounds raw. 'Tell her what you did, then. Tell her how you helped my mother.'

I snap my head so quickly towards him that it nearly hurts. His mother?

'I told you both that you sometimes do the most foolish things for love,' she says. 'And sometimes the bravest.'

'So much for undoing the harm.' Philippe snorts. 'Who helped put my mother back into the ducal seat, when Kylian was the duke? Tell her, Isabella. What, you suddenly have no more wisdom to impart?' He's thunder itself.

And what he says is frightening me.

Because the pieces are beginning to slot into place.

Everyone had a place. From the very beginning.

And in order for it to work, some people had to be in more than one place at the same time.

And some people were never together at the same time, in the same place. Because they were *one and the same* person.

Leaving a boy who knew too much isolated on a farm.

'Should I tell her? Should I tell her about Magali? How you let Magali pretend that she was you, so she wouldn't have to sneak around at night with my father, so that they could be happily married? Should I tell her how you tricked even me, my whole entire life? So I wouldn't tell? Should I tell her that I didn't know my mother's true face until a few days ago?'

The truth. The truth is so ugly that I have to turn away from it. The truth makes everything crumble to pieces.

Pain twists Philippe's face. I see a darkness that I never knew in him before. I want to touch that stubble on his cheeks. I want to kiss his forehead, which is creased in anguish. I want to smooth it all away from his face, and from his heart.

'Go away, Celine. I have no claim to the duchy at all because I'm the son of Magali and Seigneur Bencifert. The true Isabella of Langly was never married to my father. I'm not at all who you thought I was.'

PERSPECTIVES

MAGALI

*M*orning comes and Celine is gone. If there was any boon I could have wished to be granted, it is this.

Her, out of my way.

I must act fast.

I must act swiftly, lest she should return.

There is only one more thing I can do.

I place the cage on the floor and prepare the necessary spells.

CELINE

Trust me not to be able to control myself around Philippe. He stalks to the left tower, where the students' chambers once were, and shuts himself in one of the rooms.

Madame Hirondelle promptly takes me by the arm and leads me to him. 'The two of you need to speak. In private.' She knocks on his door, in the unapologetic manner she was famous for, and ushers me inside. 'She needs something to eat. I doubt she had any breakfast.'

Philippe looks me up and down. All I see is the sadness etched upon his face. 'I *am* hungry,' I say. 'Don't make me eat my own horse.'

Madame Hirondelle vanishes. I plonk myself down on one of the low stools, the room so familiar and yet unfamiliar at the same time—the arched windows that look across the valley, the escritoire underneath, the simple furniture made of polished wood, the narrow bed screwed to the wall. I used to squeeze into a bed like that with Hugo, when I thought no one was watching. Urgh.

So much for looking to the past; despite our current woes, the present is far easier on the eyes.

I walk up to Philippe, as if to make up for the dumb trespasses of youth and take his hand with a self-assurance I don't feel. 'How do you feel since you found out, with only Madame Hirondelle to speak to?'

He looks at me as if I've grown three heads. I kick a stool closer with my foot and sit next to him. I feel a rush to clasp my hands around the back of his neck and dig my nose into his skin. But I'm terrified he'd push me away.

We exchange a long, long look.

He leans forward.

Yes.

Please.

But then he gets up and moves to the window, his back turned to me.

'Why are you here, Celine?'

He rests his hands on the windowsill and I take in his wide back, his strong arms. I want to curl myself around him.

'Because I want us to go home.'

'Fort Cantor is *not* my home,' he says. 'I don't have a home, and I don't care to be a pawn in anyone's plans anymore.'

'Yes? Then what are your plans?'

A long silence settles around us, and between his turned back and the awful days I've had at Castle Bencifert—the humiliation of being left behind, again, just like five years ago, without a word, without a sign—all the pain floods my chest, drowning my heart.

'You *left* me,' I say. 'We were in the middle of this catastrophic situation, and you just left. Without saying a word.'

'Can you blame me?'

'Yes, of course I can. Even Hugo said goodbye, five years ago.'

He turns around in a whoosh. 'Don't compare me to him.'

'Of course not,' I say. The anger, the pain, they flush through me, unchecked. 'At least Hugo has the courage to fight for what he wants. You don't even *know* what you want.' And then I realise, *Yes, I'm ready to fight for it, too; to do whatever I have to.*

'I know what I want,' he says. 'If it's also good for me, that's an entirely different matter.'

'Your mother is starting to rally whichever seigneurs are still faithful to you at Castle Bencifert.'

It all makes so much sense now. Why she would replace Maël with Philippe. Not with a nephew. But with her *other* son.

Her *children*, she said on the day when we confronted Hugo. That she did it all to protect her children.

It also explains why Isabella was neither at Fort Cantor nor at Castle Bencifert: because the real Isabella was at the Golden Pavilion, while a false Isabella—Magali, shapeshifting—married the late Seigneur Bencifert.

'Then she is mad,' he says.

'Tell me something new.' I pause, gathering my thoughts. 'Did your father know who your mother was? I mean, that she was Magali, and not Isabella?

'Of course,' he says. 'Always. He'd been in love with her ever since they were both students at the Golden Pavilion.'

'By Lucius' Flaming Finger, they studied here?' I gasp.

'Yes, does the story sound familiar?' he arches his eyebrows.

I prefer to gloss over this. I don't wish to discuss Hugo anymore. Hugo is in the past, and in the present we must battle. 'But then ... is that why Magali went to your father after Kylian threw her out of Fort Cantor?'

He says, 'He was the only one who took her in. And Isabella came, too. And then ... I assume my father and Magali started some sort of affair, but it would have been a scandal. I think Magali didn't want to admit that Frederic was dead, either. It would have gone against what she was aiming for. Isabella was unmarried, and it was much easier to pretend, she said, especially when Magali became pregnant... She took Isabella's form in public, and married my father, while they continued to act out the fairy-tale in private.'

'This is madness,' I say. 'The levels of deception. The lies. To everyone.'

'To me, first of all. She never showed herself to me as Magali. She was afraid I'd *tell* because I was just a child.' The depth of hurt in Philippe's voice breaks my heart.

That's why she was never there. Because she was two people at once, and she had to steer Maël into Frederic's role and guide him as the new duke.

I remember how much Philippe strove to please this woman. How much he wanted to make her proud. The forgotten son, showing her how good he was.

But Philippe is good perhaps largely *because* she had little to do with his upbringing. 'That's why she sent you to the farm.'

'Yes,' he says. 'So she could be in two places at once and pretend that she was with me.'

'She is … something else,' I say. The amount of coldness and calculation required to be able to pull off something like this. So much like Hugo. 'You'd think she was Hugo's mother. They are cut from the same cloth.'

'And you know what the worst is? That my father, whom I thought to be the most honest, righteous man alive, also lied to me all his life. *All his life*. The secrets he kept from me: Hugo; my own mother.'

'Do you remember what Madame Hirondelle said, about the things that one would do in the name of love?' What I've done. What Julien Bencifert did. What Madame Hirondelle herself has done to protect Magali, though I can't fathom why she would. What my mother and my father have done. 'Can you imagine?' I say. 'That my own mother should have worked to close the school, binding her own magic to it. But here's the crux of the matter: if we step aside, if we don't act now, then everything everyone has ever done, all the lies that have been told and the pain that has been caused, will have been in vain. Hugo will stop at nothing to become duke, and we are the only ones who can stand in his way.'

'That is none of my business.'

'Do you think that if you simply step aside, all the problems of this land will disappear? If so then you must be more naïve than I thought.'

'Of course not, but I swear to you by the Mothers of the Forest that I won't play a part anymore in plotting and backstabbing. I won't have anything to do with it, with all the harm they've caused.'

I open and close my mouth. He's more stubborn than a mule. 'So you intend to hide here for the rest of your life, do you?'

'I'm sorry that I'm not willing to march an army of unprepared farmers and stableboys into battle, just so you can keep calling yourself duchess!'

'Well, I'm sorry that I thought you would do more than stand aside and watch Hugo destroy every good thing that you've ever achieved!'

'And I'm sorry that I don't need to order thousands of people around in order to be happy. Unlike you!'

There's a tap on the door. Philippe shouts, 'Come in,' while I mouth, 'We're not done here.'

The door floats open and Madame Hirondelle stands in the threshold. 'You need to feed her, Philippe. She's always in a foul mood when she's hungry.' She turns around and disappears down the corridor, beckoning us to follow her.

Philippe seems more than happy at the interruption, but I'm certainly not. He's the first to follow her. I'm dumbstruck at how well Madame Hirondelle knows me, even after all these years. How she notices these details. It couldn't have been a coincidence, then, that my punishments for trespasses or for lack of skill were often having to skip a meal. Or two. Let's say that her teaching methods were strict, to say the least.

Madame Hirondelle leads us to the Refectory again, to a table set with three places and a platter of food. There's cheese and grapes and apples and a lump of old bread. 'I don't really cook,' she says apologetically. 'I never needed to, not for one person. Do you cook, Celine?'

I shake my head, already gnawing at the bread.

'Of course,' says Phillipe. 'I would hardly expect either of you to be able to,' he says sourly.

'And you can?' I retort.

'I can make a decent stew, a soup or char some meat, if I have to.'

'Good for you.'

Philippe pops a few grapes into his mouth, leaning back. 'See? You'd wither and die if you didn't have an army of servants at your beck and call.'

'Sometimes, strength resides in being able to survive on one's own, not having to depend on anyone; and sometimes, strength is being able to lead, to depend on the many who depend on you,' says Madame Hirondelle.

'Another piece of wisdom from the bottom of the barrel of pickles,' says Philippe.

I expect Madame Hirondelle to scold him, but she only laughs. 'Do with it what you will,' she says. 'My own father didn't have a single magic bone in his body, and yet his brood are the most powerful mages in the kingdom.'

'How is that possible?' I ask.

'Through marriage. He married the most gifted mage he ever laid his eyes on. But it was never about the Gift, with the two of them. She was the light of his eyes. His sun, and moon, and stars, every lit torch in the kingdom, every blazing fire.'

That's certainly not what I heard. But Madame Hirondelle—Isabella of Langly—should know, shouldn't she? They were her *parents*.

'He was devastated when she vanished. He would have stopped at nothing to get her back.' Madame Hirondelle stands in front of us, her hands hidden in her cloak, like she always used to do, when I was a student here. I'm mesmerised. I want to hear more about the legendary first duke and duchess.

'But I digress. What was I speaking about? Power. Gold helped buy that power, or, at least, find two magic enhancers. Magali has one of them.'

'The ring,' I say.

'Yes, the ring.'

'And the other one?' says Philippe.

382

'A red velvet pouch.'

I gasp.

'What?' says Philippe.

'That bloody pouch. That was how Hugo was able to change his shape, even without the Crystal of Power.' I feel like an idiot. Of course it was the damn pouch. He carried it everywhere.

'That red pouch?' he says, choking on a grape.

I thump him hard on the back. Perhaps harder than I needed to. He coughs and gives me a strange look.

I tear at a bit of cheese. 'But where does it end? What prevents him from pretending to be the king, one day? If he can't marry a queen, like he intended to.' I shudder. That particular thought is unsettling.

'*You* can stop him,' she says. 'Both of you, together.'

Philippe looks annoyed. 'The two of you, you talk of starting a war like this as if the people who would be pulled into it don't matter. Do you know how many lives would be lost? And for what? Maybe you're ready to take that risk but I'm not.'

'Plenty of lives will be lost, too, if Hugo gets what he wants,' I say.

'Wasn't that precisely what you wanted to achieve even last week?' he says sarcastically. 'And how do you know that?'

'Hugo won't give the farmers the fair terms that you've given them. If anything, he'll return to the taxation that existed in Maël's time. I can promise you that.'

'It still won't kill them like battles would. Burnt villages, burnt crops, a winter of famine and death. You do realise what it means when the seigneurs start taking sides, don't you?' he says.

Madame Hirondelle says, 'There are other ways.'

'Don't tell me,' says Philippe. 'A horribly complicated plan that involves a lot of lying. You are truly a Langly, Isabella. But I am not. I never was.' Philippe gets up from the table and I wonder whether I should follow him. But I'm tired. I'm tired of him stamping on every single one of my ideas.

I'm tired of him running and giving up, when I still want to fight.

The sounds of his receding steps drill into my skull.

'What other ways?' I ask Madame Hirondelle, in almost a whisper. 'I wouldn't… I'm not sure if I'm ready to … *murder* him.' Greater good or not.

'Oh, this complicates matters a bit.' Not a muscle moves on Madame's Hirondelle face.

The hairs on my arms stand on end.

She chuckles. 'I was only jesting. What must you think of me! I never worried much about what other people thought. That's why when Magali suggested she wanted to pretend she was me, I didn't mind. I knew what I wanted to do, and if there was a reason for me to vanish and continue here at the Golden Pavilion, then it was fine by me.'

'This is more than a little … unusual.'

'Maybe,' she says. 'I never bothered too much with it. In any case, what I meant to say is that, no matter what you think of me, I'm not the sort who would be able to murder her kin without batting an eye. I'm not my brother Kylian.' She frowns as she says this. 'But binding? I'm not sure if your Gift is strong enough. Binding is a different thing altogether, and it arises from absences, more than anything else.'

'You can help me,' I blurt. 'You have powers, don't you? You can help me.'

Madame Hirondelle wrings her hands, which means she's restless.

Madame Hirondelle is never restless.

'I shouldn't be involved. As the doyenne of the Golden Pavilion … and there are other matters—'

'The Golden Pavilion is dead,' I say. 'What is a school without students? And the plan is that there should never be any students again at the Pavilion, if I understood this right. I think this might be the time, if any such time exists, to set aside such scruples.'

'I promised not to interfere.'

'And yet you did, only a few weeks ago.' The drought. That terrible drought.

She paces up and down the Refectory, up and down. The clip-clop of her shoes fills the empty hall. She stops next to me and extracts something from her tunic, a medallion on a thin golden chain, then places it in my palm. The medallion is round, like a button made of white stone, but with a thousand tiny shards stuck to its surface. I turn it over and it seems to catch all the light around us. 'What is this?'

'It's made from the last shards of the Crystal of Power.'

I close my hand around it. I can feel its warm, pulsing energy. It's the same feeling as when Philippe touches me and channels his magic through me. 'You made an amulet. A magic enhancer.'

'I did. A long time ago.' She taps her lips with her fingers. 'But it won't be enough. You will need another enhancer.'

'Magali's,' I say. 'If we ask her, she'll give me hers.'

'I'm not so sure about that. And you have to think… *We* have to think what to do about Magali, too.'

I'm not sure what she means, but I have to wonder what bonds her so closely to Magali. Perhaps sharing this great secret together for so many years, watching out for one another?

'You will need to take Hugo's enhancer,' she says. 'You'll need to take it away from him, so he won't be able to transform anymore. But the cost…'

'The cost?' I say.

'Oh, yes. It will cost you.' Madame Hirondelle sighs. 'You need to cast the sort of spell that will survive even you, like the magic your mother put in this place to keep it hidden.' She gestures all around us, at the hidden splendour of the Golden Pavilion. 'To do this, Celine, will cost you a part of your own Gift.'

I think, *I don't mind. It wouldn't be much of a sacrifice.*

I know how to live without my Gift, I had to do without it for a long time. My future does not hinge on it. Nor does my heart.

I think, *If this is what it takes to restore the peace, then it will be more than worth paying the price.*

MAGALI

I lose myself in Julien's portrait at Castle Bencifert, begging him to lend me strength, as he did during his lifetime. I might have made the most terrible mistake of my life, and everything I've ever done comes down to the choices I'll make in the next few days.

I've never needed strength as much as I do now. I hold the lioness ring tightly in my hand. I hope there is enough power in me to achieve what I need to achieve. To finally claim what is mine.

This skin should serve. It has done so well enough in the past.

There's the sound of steps behind me, coming closer. Two silhouettes, pale and drawn. Goderic and Louis, side by side.

'Madame Isabella,' says Goderic. 'How may I be of service to you?'

CELINE

I finally corner Philippe in the evening. The Golden Pavilion might be large, but there's a limited number of places where he can hide. I find him in the library, a hall-like construction with a gallery going around the two-storey room to allow access to the higher shelves.

He paces the ground floor, his hands clasped together behind his back. 'Look at this place,' he says. 'I've never seen so many books. How do you even begin to choose one?'

'You think about what you'd like to read and you get started.'

'But,' he says, still taking in the shelves, 'how do you know if it's the right one?'

'If it's not, you put it back and take another.'

'Yes, of course.' He squares his shoulders. This makes him looks even larger and I just want to step next to him, wrap myself around him, indulge in the way he towers over me. 'That's what *you'd* do. If something doesn't fit your requirements, you toss it aside and find something better.'

I say, 'I'm not sure we're still speaking about books here, but yes, I see no reason to persevere with something that doesn't meet my expectations.'

Philippe raises his eyebrows in that way that is only his. 'Then perhaps it is, indeed, for the best if you and the unsatisfying book part ways.'

He drives me mad, I swear.

When I arrived at the Golden Pavilion, when I saw him for the first time, I felt a certainty in me that everything would be just fine; that if a man made me feel that way from the moment I laid eyes on him, then everything would turn out all right. Because all we need is already here between us.

He still makes me feel that same way when I look at him now, as he stands in the library. All the light is behind him; he is no more than a dark, broad silhouette in the middle of this hall. I'd like to touch his face. When I think about even the possibility of it, I feel a pit in my stomach.

Something holds me back, pins me to this place.

'You had a choice, though,' I say. 'What did you say, when Hugo pointed me out to you at the yearly fair in Langville? You said you wanted the princess, and now you're turning away?'

'What we think we want, Celine, and what we need are two very different things. And the princess I saw that day at Langville and the person standing in front of me now are two different people.'

This strikes me hard. That I should prove to be someone's disappointment. And not just anyone's disappointment.

His.

'But—' *But the drought,* I want to say. *The time we spent at the farm. How close we felt to each other. What we can achieve.* I want to say, *Was none of that real? Was it all in my mind?*

'This life isn't for me. Don't make me into someone I'm not. And I see you are offended. That wasn't my intention. I just meant that the Celine I created in my mind isn't at all like the real Celine. I don't even know the real Celine. You keep everything you feel to yourself, and then, when you explode, it's with the fury of weeks of anger and frustrations. It's the same with every decision you make. You're so intent on wrecking Hugo now … I'm not sure if you can see clearly.'

He is right, I feel this in my heart. I need to do better at setting boundaries for myself. For what I want to achieve.

But, yet again, I don't know how to say this. 'Do you know what, sometimes, people not meeting our expectations is the best thing that can happen to us. You made a terrific duke. Even if you're … rough around the edges.'

His eyebrows twitch. 'Celine, I wasn't born to lead.'

'And yet people follow you. How many came from the farm when you moved to Fort Cantor? Nobody made them go with you.'

'I was never happy at Fort Cantor. It felt like I was trying to fill shoes that were too large for me.'

'But so was I. Too large or too tight, sometimes this shoe will have to fit the wearer, and sometimes the wearer will have to learn how to walk with an imperfect shoe.' But then I think—

He doesn't want this. He never did.

If I truly loved him, even a tiny bit, wouldn't I let him go? Isn't it awfully selfish to require all of this of him?

Sorrow clutches my chest. The humiliations, all of Hugo's manipulations ... this can't all have been for nothing. I can't face being pushed aside again, like a broken toy.

The road forks in front of me, and I am shocked to realise that the safer path might be the one that leads towards Magali.

* * *

IT's TOO late to leave—I don't want to ride at night, with the camps encircling Castle Bencifert growing thicker and thicker. The ant-like movement I can spy from here around Fort Cantor grows every hour. I can't make out clearly what it is—troops? Tents?—not from this distance, so it will have to wait until tomorrow until I find out.

Madame Hirondelle has disappeared without a word, but this hardly surprises me. Philippe and I stalk the halls, avoiding each other. Not only the halls. The terraces, too. I stand on the balcony of the main building, trying to make out what's happening in the distance.

A group of riders snakes across the valley, moving between two smaller castles at the borders of the duchy. Philippe wanders the narrow slip of terrace around the tower where I used to sleep as a student. He swivels around, sees me, and then is gone without a word.

There is a crack in my heart, a chasm widened by all the unrest in the duchy, by all the feelings that are smouldering inside of me. I've fallen in love again, I realise. And he doesn't want me. I twist and turn and re-evaluate every one of his gestures today, every word. He dismissed all I said, all he thinks I stand for.

The worst of it is that he's just feet away from me. I want to be with him so much that I ache with it, and yet we could be half a world away, for all that it matters.

Enough.

I'll leave tomorrow. I'll never see him again. He'll go his way, when all of this is over, like he said, and I'll go mine. I can't defeat Hugo and Magali all by myself, so I'll have to strike a deal with the lesser of two evils.

And then forever live in her shadow.

But.

Maybe if I stand by Hugo, become his wife like I always wanted to, maybe I'll be able to change him for the better. Or, at least, contain some of the damage.

And then I think, I'm not a hero. I am not capable of sacrificing myself, of living in doubt and fear in a nest of lies and vipers for the rest of my life.

The doubts. I must overcome the doubts. I must be brave enough to take a risk. I must not be afraid of making a fool of myself. Ridicule is nothing, faced with the prospect of a bleak existence.

As of tomorrow, what happens tonight won't count anymore.

So before my courage deserts me, I run up to the second floor of the tower, where my husband is. When I thrust open his door and it crashes against the wall, I'm breathless. He turns around in a sweeping move.

'Celine?'

'Yes.' I try to catch my breath, to find a way to ask him what I need to. But there is no simple way to say, *Do you love me, even a little bit?*

I say instead, 'Do you think that if I were to go to Hugo, if I was his wife, I'd be able to ... contain him? I mean, prevent some of the damage. Do you think I'd be able to do enough good to make it worth it?'

Philippe stands up straighter, feelings shifting on his face. I want to run to him. I realise how everything I've just said came out backwards.

'Yes? No? I don't know. I have no idea. Hugo ... I don't know him at all. He was a cat for five years, remember? I have no idea what he was like before. I never knew him. But you did.'

My cheeks are on fire and I don't think it was only the run up the stairs. 'I'll go tomorrow,' I say. 'I will go. You don't have to worry about me.'

He ruffles his hair again. 'All right. If that's what you want.'

'Obviously I don't want any of this. I didn't want things to turn out this way at all, but what can I do? Tell me. One way or the other, I can't stand aside. I either have to go to Hugo, beg him to forgive me and try to be a ... good influence, or I have to defeat him. Which I can't do alone. I just can't.'

I walk a few paces towards him. Anger fills my belly. I came here with a purpose and here we are, still tiptoeing around what I truly want to know.

'I assume that if you can't defeat him then you'll have to play along? And be a good influence, like you said?' Uncertainty glimmers in his eyes. And something else. He lifts his chin when I approach.

'Why don't you...' This close, I can smell him. Like something fresh, something new that has just broken out of the earth. And yet we might as well be speaking a different language. 'Do you have any opinions of your own? Because all you've done is repeat what I said to you. Philippe, as of tomorrow, we don't have to see each other again. Ever. I can see it's all the same to you, whatever I do.' I throw my arms into the air. 'You say you never know with me, but nor do I. I have no idea where we stand. Do you even care about me at all? What do you feel when you look at me? Because when I look at you—'

Surprise is written on his face. A small grin starts in the corner of his mouth. He comes a tiny step closer. 'Yes?'

'I can't explain it.' Now that the moment has come to tell him how I feel, fear grips my chest. But then I think, I may never see him again. This moment is all that matters, and then it won't matter at all. 'I just want to be with you. I want you to touch me.'

We're an arm's length away, so he stretches out his hand, gripping my fingers. 'Like this?' he says, and that warm feeling spreads through me, like it does when he channels his magic. Like I am full. Brimming with light.

I stop a moment to take it in and close my eyes. 'Like this, too. But also, the other things.'

'What other things?' he says, smiling.

He stops the buzz of energy coursing through me, but his fingers are now stroking my palm and I'm filled with another sort of tingling. One look into his eyes, seeing the intent written there, and my body strains against the layers of clothing around it. Especially in certain parts.

I draw a sharp breath, and take a step towards him, and then I lose myself in the sheer delight of his body enveloping mine. Each breath I can feel in my own chest comes from his warmth. And I want time to stop now, so I can revel in all of this, in the way his hands go to my hips and pull me even closer to him, how my mouth seeks his, how it's the line that makes me feel so, so alive, burning and wanting.

Closer, closer, under his skin, I want to be under his skin. I want to be under him, over him, all around him.

I feel it in my blood, in my chest, in all the parts that tighten and throb.

His tongue slips into my mouth, stroking gently, and I give myself over entirely to this kiss, opening up more for him, tilting my head back so he can claim it all, so I can claim him, too.

Not enough. Not enough, by far.

I grab him by the shirt, taking a step back, pulling him with me until I feel the edges of the escritoire digging into my backside. 'Here,' I say, relieving him of his shirt.

He braces his arms on the desk and just the sight of those muscles flexing starts me whimpering. He drives his tongue from my collarbone and all the way up my neck. I lay my hands flat on his chest, knowing that I will want to remember this, precisely how his skin feels on mine, with that powerful body behind it. 'Wherever you want,' he whispers in my ear, while his hand sneakily encloses my backside, lifting me onto the escritoire.

'Now,' I say, melting into another kiss.

His hands go to the laces of his trousers, opening and releasing, and at that sight, at the shush of fabric on the stone floor, my knees grow soft with what I know is coming.

'Not yet, Celine. Not just yet.'

OF LESSER LIGHTS AND DARKER CAVES

MAGALI

I am skilled, but I fear I am losing my touch. I thought they'd come to me as Isabella, the daughter, mother and sister of dukes. But none have—not Goderic, not the other seigneurs. The mistake I made was ripping my flesh apart: they have run to take the other side, the other side of my creation. The one I set free last night.

And he must be seething.

There is nothing between me and the two Maëls but a pathetic shield of farmers, children and creaking carts.

Where is that little witch when I need her?

CELINE

When I wake in the morning, my back is aching. These beds are definitely not made for two people to sleep in them once the exciting antics are over. I'm wedged between him and the wall, his arm slung around me.

So close, and yet, not close enough. I take in his lovely face, so peaceful when he sleeps. I can't resist tracing a finger down his temple, his cheekbone, his jaw. He opens his eyes, foggy with sleep, but he smiles. I twist and press my lips to his, softly.

A question.

He answers by tugging at mine with his own and my mouth opens for him. His hands travel up my waist, pulling me slowly on top of him. I lean into his chest, listening to him breathe, to his heartbeats.

He coils a finger around one of my locks, twisting it lazily. 'I wouldn't mind waking up this way every morning.'

I snigger.

'Why couldn't you have been this lovely from the first day of our marriage?' he says.

'We have time,' I say.

'Do we?'

I look up. Something has changed on his face. Our worries have caught up with us—there was only so long we could escape them.

I untangle myself from him and sit up on the edge of the bed.

He takes my hand, laces his fingers through mine and lets his magic flow. I raise my other hand and lift the water from the jug on the table into a very crude shape of Philippe. He laughs and lets me go. 'You're getting better at it,' he says.

I have yet to tell him about the medallion which Madame Hirondelle—Isabella—gave me. I splash his shape onto the window.

He laughs, a deep, wicked laugh. 'Yes, that's how I feel right now too.'

I cradle my knees, hiding my face. Today, I know that he will leave, and I will leave, and we will go on our separate paths. I might never see him, even after our night together, and that feeling is a fracture in the ground after an earthquake, threatening to split me in two.

When did I fall between the cracks of my desires and of what I thought I must do?

My desires, tucked away so far that I didn't even know them when they looked me in the face.

We will part, but perhaps not just yet. He comes up behind me, enveloping me with his warmth, his arms slung over mine. I am in a cocoon, I am with him, there is no place in the world I'd rather be. He dips his head to my neck, breathing warmth down its length, settling with a kiss on the dip on my shoulders.

Yes.

More.

I lean back into him, feeling him awakening, too, just as heat blazes through me, nothing to separate our burning skin but two flimsy shifts.

Yes.

This, again.

His hands start roving over my waist and hips and the underside of my breasts, each move more urgent as I rub myself against him, demanding, coaxing, teasing, and the Celine I know, that Celine who would look from the outside, she would be shocked and ashamed at such behaviour. But I am not a Celine outside of myself anymore; I'm the Celine who inhabits her own body, who is here and now in her own skin, clinging to all these sensations. And when he tilts me gently forward, and I come down on all fours, I have no shame, no past, no future.

I give in completely.

Not just to him, but to myself, to what my body wants.

To what it needs.

And that is him.

Philippe, Philippe, Philippe, over and over again.

* * *

We do leave the bed, but only because my body starts craving food, also. We find ourselves alone in the Refectory. There's no sign of Madame Hirondelle, and no sign of food left out for us. 'She told me last night that she was going down to the valley,' says Philippe, intertwining his fingers with mine.

Mothers of the Forest and Sabya's Morningstar and Lucius' Flaming Finger, every single one of his touches is delicious.

But I'm still hungry, and for more than he can offer.

I pull him towards the Pavilion's old kitchens, an annexe built into the mountain. It's dark and cavernous, but a shaft of light ensures that the room is bright enough and that smells might have somewhere to escape. It doesn't smell like anything today, however. We see only the scrubbed surfaces of tabletops and a hearth with a chimney in the centre of the room. A spotless cauldron hangs in the middle. Philippe peers inside. 'Just dust. Nobody has used it for ages.'

'We aren't going to start now.' I open a side door, which leads to a dim corridor. I've never been so deep in the heart of the Pavilion. 'This way, I think.'

Magali said something a few days ago, about the horrors, or the wonders, trapped inside the mountain. This is a good time as ever to start exploring, to start moving outside the cage I've assigned for myself.

For this is what I've been doing, haven't I? Weaving the cage around me as much as Hugo did. I've been an accomplice to my own entrapment.

Philippe's brows furrow in a sweet, perplexed way. 'To what?'

'To the larder. I can't imagine Madame Hirondelle keeps all the food in her chambers.'

The corridor leads into the heart of the mountain, gradually narrowing, its walls closing in around us.

'Are you sure?' says Philippe.

'No, but we can always turn back.'

We can turn back. We can set ourselves on a path, and then change our minds.

We walk a few dozen paces, hand in hand, until we reach two doors—one to the side and one in front of us.

We stop before the door to the side. He touches the intricate, forged iron handle, but I pull him back.

'Where will you go?' I ask. 'When I leave?'

He ruffles his hair, in that confused way of his. 'To the Blue Kingdom, probably.'

'Ah. Your mother's relations then.'

He seems to hesitate at this, as if he's still trying to grow accustomed to the fact that his mother is Magali, a princess of the Blue Kingdom. 'Yes,' he says eventually.

'And what will you do?' The princess, the wife in me is awakening, pushing away Philippe's bedmate.

'I don't know. Magali seems to think there will be work for me.'

I think, *Another farm? Or work at the Bluefort? Crane's Harbour?*

Philippe unwraps his hand from mine. 'You will still leave, won't you? It doesn't matter what... It doesn't matter.'

Will I leave? The part of me that's Philippe's bedmate seems furious.

I grin at my husband.

Will I leave?

I'm not sure. For now, I'm pleased to contemplate the what if's.

Philippe's eyes are ablaze now, but I don't flinch from that look. I face it with all I have in me. With the princess, the wife, the chatelaine, the bedmate. And mostly, with *his* duchess. 'I'm asking because I want to know what my options are. Don't you think it's only fair?'

'Options?' He cocks an eyebrow. What he must think.

But I don't know, don't know, don't know.

What if, though?

How would it feel to give in again, let go of everything I *thought* I wanted?

What we think we want, that can also be a cage.

I push open the door behind him.

I might still be looking for answers, but at least we found the larder. A room as tall and wide as the library, with shelves stacking up to the ceiling. They're mostly empty. Cold foods are crowding the lower shelves, and demijohns of wine are stashed high on the wall to the left.

'Of course,' says Philippe, picking up one of the wine containers. 'The famous cellars of the Golden Pavilion.'

'Not much of a cellar, though. More like a cave.'

We skirt around the difficult subject.

I don't have to make a decision yet, I tell myself. I can go on exploring.

Philippe starts picking up something for our breakfast, but I'm still drawn to the other door. 'Where are you going?' he says.

'Expanding my horizons.' I smile and tug at the handle and, contrary to my expectations, it gives way. The view beyond takes my breath away.

The chamber that opens is so vast that I can't even see where it ends. There are small openings in the high ceiling that let in sunlight, which is reflected in the mesmerising waters of an inner lake. It's milky white, with a blue-and-gold irridescence toying like silk on its surface. This is the infamous Opal Lake, which gave the mountain its name.

'What is this?' says Philippe. 'Oh.'

I can't believe what we just stumbled upon. 'This is the place where the mages of the Golden Pavilion withdrew to during the darkest days in the Year of the Red Maiden, when the Golden Pavilion was besieged.'

The first time in living memory that the people rose against the mages. The Fallen Court had had a hand in it somehow, it was rumoured.

And look at us today; we haven't learned anything.

'The siege at the Opal Mountain,' says Philippe.

'The mages still had the Crystal of Power then.'

Philippe starts walking around the vast cave. The sound of his steps echoes, broken into a million shards of sound.

'That's where it used to be,' I say, pointing at a pedestal rising from the middle of the lake. 'At least, that's what I've heard. I'd never been here before. I thought the Opal Lake was just a legend, even though my own mother told me the story.'

'Everyone tells this story,' says Philippe.

'Not like my mother.' I walk down to the surface of the lake, feeling the thrill of its water on my fingers. There must be power still in it from the shards of the crystal that was shattered—like the shards that are part of the medallion I'm wearing around my neck. 'She was here on the day of the siege.'

Philippe walks up to me. I can see his handsome face reflected in the waters. 'But that can't be. The siege was such a long time ago. If my memory serves me, it was my grandfather who broke the siege. He brought his troops to the foot of the mountain and sided with the Pavilion.' He sways on his feet. Of course, the ground beneath him is still settling, after what his mother has told him. 'He's not actually my grandfather, though. I keep forgetting.'

'The first Duke of Langly. Yes, not your grandfather, apparently. The outlaw who carved himself a duchy. But my mother's story is a bit different. She says that the mages were preparing a spell amongst all of them, something so dark and terrible that it would have wiped out the besiegers altogether. In fact, when the duke scattered the assailants of the Pavilion, he only did them a favour.'

'But I still don't understand. This makes your mother as old as my— as the first duke. How can that be?'

'Older than him, in fact.' I try to catch the water, but it slips through my fingers. 'She was an Illusionist, my mother. Her Gift was illusion. This is why she was able to hide the Golden Pavilion. That was her strength. Illusionists ... well, they maintain the lie around their own person.'

'She was an old woman who managed to look younger?'

'Not exactly. They are older than they look, but they also live longer lives. So when she had my brother, five years ago ... I don't think she should have. Her body was already depleted from maintaining its illusion, and from giving birth to me.'

Philippe lays a hand on my shoulder. 'But this means she must have had a very good reason to have another child, Celine. She must have believed, too, that it was important.'

'She told me so,' I say. 'She said the kingdom had had enough squabbles between the people and the mages, enough fighting over Langly. She said the kingdom needed peace, and she could give it peace.'

She had been on my father's side, I begin to realise. The illusion around the Golden Pavilion, everything they did... Even if he'd betrayed her with Anne-Mihielle's mother, that did not deter her.

I think, *You knew who she was.* She must have had her reasons. Perhaps going far beyond what I believed.

And yet, everything seems to go back to Langly.

Must I, too?

Philippe says, 'This is why you don't want to ask your father to change the succession.'

'This is why I'm pleased that my father refused to change the succession. He might have quenched a small fire now but started a blaze that would flare out of control in ten years.' His words ring in my ears, about how the people aren't ready to be led by a woman. Also, they might not be willing to be led by mages anymore. This is why he hid his Gift.

The time for magic is fading. Perhaps.

Perhaps it would be good to present Philippe with his options, too.

At the edge of the lake, I tell Philippe of Madame Hirondelle's plan.

* * *

WE'RE in the middle of a heated conversation as we finally lay our supplies on a table in the Refectory. 'I will not interfere,' says Philippe. 'I've had enough of Langly.'

'Even if Hugo is the alternative?'

Philippe sets down two plates and a knife we swiped from the kitchen. 'The alternative is bloodshed, as you well know.'

Haven't we already had this argument? For trying to avoid that bloodshed, he would make a better leader than Magali, or Hugo. Because he is aware of the cost. Because it makes him pause.

'Do you not see? That whether you are there or not, blood will be spilled in *your* name? Do you not see that we're already tangled too deeply in this?'

I break the bread in clumps while Philippe starts chopping the smoked ham. 'I will not be a pawn,' he says. 'Not again.'

I just lay a hand on his wrist, settling him. 'That's not what I want for you,' I say.

I want us to be partners. Equals. And to be whatever we were this morning. Ourselves, unburdened.

I'm preparing to tell him that, when I hear the clop of hurried, assured steps. Madame Hirondelle comes into view. 'Children!' she calls.

'Lucius' Flaming Finger,' mutters Philippe.

Madame Hirondelle crosses the floor of the Refectory with uncharacteristically quick steps. Her face is drawn and she seems ... frightened. 'There have been some developments in the valley,' she says.

'I don't think I want to know anything about this,' says Philippe.

'You will, believe me. Isabella of Langly is trying to rally the seigneurs to her son's name. Did you look outside today?'

'Not yet,' I say. We were inside the Pavilion, and then deeper inside—much deeper than Madame Hirondelle would perhaps want to know. She glimpses the food on the table.

'Knights and soldiers are rallying at Castle Bencifert too, but there aren't many of them. There are rumours that the Maël at Fort Cantor will march upon them tomorrow morning.'

There's something that bothers me terribly in what Madame Hirondelle has just said and how she said it, but I can't quite pin it down.

'What do you mean, you are rallying the people? You said Isabella is rallying the people. *You're* Isabella.' Philippe frowns, absolutely bewildered.

Madame Hirondelle tucks her hands in her sleeves, avoiding our eyes.

'See?' I say. 'You should go back. Things are moving that way whether you want it or not.'

'It's Magali,' says Philippe, before Madame Hirondelle has

managed to put in another single word. 'She's pretending to be you.'

'And rallying the seigneurs in your name.'

'Because you wouldn't,' I say. My Gift stirs within me. We should be the flood that washes away those who would stop at nothing in the name of power, the blade of grass peeking in the spring sun, full of hope.

We should weave. Sing a song of a bright future.

Madame Hirondelle lifts her hands in the air, trying to calm us. 'Don't squabble; things are much worse than you think.'

'Worse?' Philippe and I say at the same time. 'How can they be worse?' I ask.

'Your father, Celine, is marching on Castle Bencifert with a small army.'

I feel the blood draining from my face. My father will come. And he will expect me to have chosen sides by the time he arrives. The falcon pin in my pocket weighs heavy, holding me back.

If Phillippe leaves … I can't go with him, as much as a part of me might want to.

'This isn't good news,' I say.

'If you think this isn't good news…' says Madame Hirondelle. She's pale and her hands are almost shaking. Almost. 'There's another Maël at Count Goderic's castle, since last night. Count Goderic is also rallying his knights; they left the camp at the foot of Fort Cantor last night. Fabien joined them, too.'

I have to sit down because I can't stand anymore.

'Why did she have to go and do that? Release him?' says Philippe, cursing. 'Why? What did she think? The wrong son on the ducal seat is better than no son at all?'

Madame Hirondelle lets her hands hang by the sides of her body. I've never seen her so miserable.

'Is Philippe right?' I say. 'Did Magali release Maël?' The implications are so huge that I can't even begin to grasp them. Three armies, rallying under different banners. The valley will be a bloodbath by tomorrow.

'Tell me, Isabella. No one knows her better than you. Why did she release Maël?'

Madame Hirondelle looks away. Shifts her weight from one foot to the other.

'*Tell me!*' Philippe screams.

'Because she needed to be sure who was at Fort Cantor. But it doesn't matter. This makes matters easier—'

'She released one son and is rallying troops in the name of the other? It makes nothing easier, Isabella. Everything is now set for slaughter.'

THE THREE ARMIES IN THE VALLEY

CELINE

The first thing I do is eat something and chew on my thoughts. I feel like there isn't enough room in my head for all of them, but at least one thing is clear: we are out of time. I have to act. Now.

I can't turn away from what is happening—I'm tangled in too deep.

'I have to go,' I say, looking at both Madame Hirondelle and Philippe.

Maybe this time, if I go, he will be the one to follow.

'Yes, we must go, Celine,' she says. 'There is no more time.'

I turn to Philippe. 'This is where you make a choice.'

He says without blinking, 'You know my answer.'

'And you know mine,' I say. Philippe grimaces and something ugly twists in my chest. Something that makes it harder for me to breathe. I can't leave without an explanation. 'When we first met, when I was searching through Magali's chambers, you told me something. That you don't want power for its sake, but because of what you can do with it. You taught me that.'

He changed me. I wanted power, and yet wouldn't have

406

known what to do with it. I can see now what there is worth fighting for. What there might be. 'If you feel that you must leave, I have to go back.'

Philippe's face twists with pain. Yes, pain, which bolts through me. His fingers twitch, as if trying to grasp something that isn't there, or that never was, in the first place. 'So what we are to each other—whatever that might be—it doesn't matter?'

I ask him, 'Does it matter? To you? This is it: we each make our choice, and we go our different paths?'

By the way he clenches his fist, I know I have struck something. But what *does* matter, in the end?

Not the games we play in the grab for power; it's the aftermath that matters. So I tell him, 'Every end is a beginning. It will end, in the valley, one way or the other. Something will come after. Do what you must, and—'

I trail off, but he seems to understand. 'If I leave, I'll let you know where I am, Celine.' My name is still a song on his tongue, calling me to him. 'So you will have your options. Later.'

If *I leave.*

I nod, and it's all I can do to keep the tears from my eyes. 'I can't make promises.'

'I wouldn't want any that you don't intend to keep.'

Brutal in his honesty. I knew what he was, how he was, from the first moment.

I think to myself, *Yes, I could live with this.*

We could build anything, if the foundations are strong.

It's all the goodbye I can muster before I march out of the Refectory. From the corner of my eye, I make out how he tries to stand, to come after me, but changes his mind.

MAGALI

I'm parading around the camp, followed by my retinue of knights and petty seigneurs—much smaller than it should be—when I see her hurtling towards me. Celine.

'Madame Isabella, so wonderful to see you again. I'm sorry for my absence, but there were matters that needed tending to.'

I jolt, startled by her presence, by her tone. 'Celine?'

'I was wondering if we could have a quick word? In private?'

Perhaps it isn't her at all. Perhaps Hugo has decided to solve the problem in the valley in a swifter and more devious manner. There is no way I can trust this creature.

'Please?' she says, taking my arm, already pulling me away from my retinue.

'Of course, darling daughter,' I say, calculating. With her here, the King might be inclined to help us … perhaps. It's worth finding out.

'Lead the way. I'm sure you know your way around the camp much better than I do,' she says sweetly.

And I lead her.

Like I lead everyone else.

CELINE

I take her arm, feeling nothing of the reverence I feel towards my former teacher, the real Isabella. I look to the distance, towards the Opal Mountain, where the false ruins of the Golden Pavilion glimmer in the sunlight. Madame Hirondelle and Philippe might be there, watching, but it all amounts to the same thing.

He turned his back on me.

It's my curse, to give more than I want to, but I can't say I don't understand. For Philippe to have done otherwise, it would have meant to betray all that he is. All that he ever wanted to stand for. You cannot claim a duchy based on a betrayal of yourself—it's almost like marrying a man for all the wrong reasons, which I did.

A kingdom of lies, a kingdom of many kings and queens.

The false Isabella of Langly, Magali, leads me to a larger tent, erected at the foot of the hill.

I stand alone here, again, but for the first time I would rather do so than with the wrong person beside me to guide and help me.

No, if I must stand alone, then so I will.

It helps to know, though. That perhaps there will be something to fall back upon. That perhaps there will be options.

Even if there will be loose ends and loose arrows, I have no choice but to go forward, because whatever happens today on this field, I'm partly responsible. Wasn't I the one who helped Hugo take Fort Cantor?

I am afraid, and yet I will not baulk at what lies ahead. I will try not to, at least.

My Gift twinkles within me. *I am the master of my own power.*

I am the master of myself.

Not Hugo, not Magali, not my father. Not even Philippe.

And the person beside me bears the same responsibility for the consequences—even more perhaps. Much more, if I think about what she let loose when she released Maël. So when we find ourselves alone in the cool darkness of the tent, the first thing I do is break away from her and find a stool to sit on. The flaps are still swinging behind us.

'You wanted to speak with me?' she says.

My jaw clenches. I'm tempted to break out in anger, to ask her what she could have been thinking when she released one son and started posing as Isabella, but this isn't who I am. No. 'I found Philippe,' I say.

Relief is etched into the face that looks like Madame Hirondelle's. But the grimaces don't belong to her. It makes me curl my fingers into claws. 'Magali. Please. Stop pretending. I just saw Isabella, and if we want to have even a half serious conversation, I want to look you in the face. *Your* face.'

'Fine. But if you don't mind?' She points at the tent flaps.

I walk out into the sunlight again. It smells of fires and onions and too many people crammed together. I take in the camp—it feels like I've walked as if I were in a dream until now, more inside my head than a part of my surroundings. It isn't much of a military camp. A few tents, a handful of carts with whatever the people could pile on: chickens and turkeys with their legs bound; pigs tied to the carts; pots and pans and hay for the animals; sacks of grain, probably, or flour, or whatever these poor people had in their larder. And, of course, whatever might serve as weapons: forks and sickles and axes.

A few soldiers in chainmail thrown over well-worn shirts weave around groups of barefoot children who mill about small fires with cauldrons above them. If Maël's armies get here, or Hugo's, for that matter, it will be a short battle. My armpits moisten in an unpleasant way and my heart thuds. I'm responsible for what is happening here.

I belong here, today. And Philippe does, too. I can't help glancing at the mountain again. He could help set it all right, innocent or not as he was when he was swept up into this mess.

'Come in,' says Magali, this time in her own voice.

I step back into the tent. Even in the faint light, I can see that the rings under her eyes have deepened. 'Where is Philippe?' she asks.

I think of all the reasons why I shouldn't tell her he's at the Golden Pavilion.

'Far away from here by now, probably,' I say.

She doesn't seem shocked by this. In the end, Philippe said that it was Magali who told him he might go to the Blue Kingdom. Who knows what plans she has hatched, in my absence.

'He thinks that if he disappears, all the problems that were born out of his claim to the seat will disappear as well.'

'How naïve,' she says. This is what I also think, but I don't let on. 'It's impossible to stop any of the forces that are at work now.'

'Like Maël, for instance? At the head of the largest army in the duchy?' I shiver when I think of it, and it isn't just anger. There's a large dose of fear mingled with it all.

'Maël can't take Fort Cantor, not even with an army that size. Hugo has gathered too many people inside the walls.'

'But will Maël ride to Fort Cantor?'

Magali bites her lip. 'We can stop him. Together.'

'How?'

'With your father's army.'

I scoff. 'That is your solution? My father, who can't stand you?'

'He doesn't have to know Philippe won't return.' She gives me a meaningful look. 'We can pretend you are expecting an heir. It might persuade him.'

So, all of it, it comes down to this. The last sleight of hand.

A plan where she needed, of all people, *me*.

She must think me so silly, so frail. Her perfect pawn. I can't believe the audacity she has to suggest something like this. But I need something from her today: the ring. I'll have to play the game by her rules, pretend to agree. And yet I have to be mindful not to seem too eager to give in. 'What could you have been thinking, Magali, when you released your son?'

Magali picks at her fingernails. 'It was a mistake. It happens. But I had to be sure before I went against the Maël at Fort Cantor.'

'Yes, and look where you are as a result.' I shift on the low stool. 'Or was it because you thought that it would be better to have a son—any son—on the ducal seat, rather than Hugo?'

She throws me a savage look. 'No, that wasn't it at all. When I released him … Maël overpowered me and he ran.' She lifts her wimple to show me the thick blue line that spreads across her temple. 'Though, I assure you, this was an accident. I tried to stop him. To speak to him. He would have none of it.'

'If something worse had happened, he would have lost his powers.'

Magali chuckles. 'Out of all of us, Maël needs them the least. He doesn't need to change his shape to be the duke. He already is the duke and wouldn't mind being anyone but himself, for the rest of his life.'

'If people believe that it is truly him.'

'If,' says Magali. 'Yes, that is, indeed, the question.' She clicks her tongue. 'More people will flock to Philippe's cause once they realise how dangerous it is that there are two Maëls. We need to give them time.'

But do we have time? Maël might realise it too. He might realise that he needs to act quickly to secure his position; that all he has to do is march into our camp. He has many swords under his command—he only needs to bring them down on us. Half of his problems would disappear.

His grandfather did the same, once. He marched on a ragtag army of desperate people. And made himself a duke.

'All that matters is that we destroy their following from the inside,' says Magali.

'No, not quite. All that matters is that we save these poor

people from certain death. They are here because of us. Because of all we have done in the past few months. And it's our duty to protect them. No one else will. Does it really matter who ends up on the ducal seat if the people are all dead?'

Magali takes a deep breath. 'Yes, yes.'

I have to give it to her, it is tempting. Crushing the uprising with my father's aid—if he is willing to give it. But I'd have to lie to him. And what would happen afterwards, when he realises there is no child?

This imaginary child, who would become the heir presumptive to my brother.

I dread to think what she plans to do afterwards to smooth out this little wrinkle.

There isn't room for both of us at Fort Cantor.

No. I must stick to the task I have set myself.

Hugo would surely be the better option than ... this.

And yet.

What if, after the storm settles, if Magali and I secure the seat for him, Philippe would consider returning?

My chest tightens.

What if.

And then... 'What will you do if Philippe returns?' I ask, unable to pretend that I simply agree with her. Unable to hold my tongue.

She smiles in a maternal way. It smacks of lies and betrayal. 'That would be the happiest outcome, wouldn't it, Celine?'

I think, *This is who she is. This is what she wants. This is who she always was. It was never about her children. It was always about what she believed was owed to her.*

But what if Philippe actually returns? Am I ready to spoil this chance for him? For us?

I think, *If I go through with the plan, the plan laid out by Isabella...*

I don't know which is the more dangerous of the two. I don't know who it's more important to contain: Magali or Hugo. Who is more of a menace for the duchy.

The flaps of the tent are torn aside and a tall silhouette steps inside. My breath catches in my throat—it didn't even occur to me that someone might have been listening. The woman removes her hood and I recognise Madame Hirondelle—an even more worried version of her than the one I saw earlier at the Golden Pavilion. 'Philippe is gone,' she says.

'I know,' says Magali. 'We've been looking for him for days.'

'No, he's gone, gone.'

The meaning of Madame Hirondelle's words begins to pierce through. I take in her sunken shoulders, the wringing of her hands, the way she avoids my gaze. This can only mean that whatever morsel of a plan we might have had, it has just been crushed to pieces. The kind of pieces that crunch under your foot, glass dust that doesn't even sting anymore.

It's as if the ground is shaking, resetting the very foundations of my life. Of what I thought that my future could still be, in spite of it all. And with this quake, I realise that I was still holding on to a shred of hope.

'Maël will march on the camp,' says Madame Hirondelle. 'That much can't be avoided.' Finally, we catch each other's eyes.

My part was to secure Magali's ring. I hadn't even got that far. For some reason, I have doubts.

I don't trust myself.

'Which Maël?' says Magali. 'My son or Hugo?'

'Both,' says Madame Hirondelle. 'I think you see how it cannot be avoided.'

Between hammer and anvil, there is less and less room to move. We must think on our feet.

Adapt.

Survive.

'Count Goderic is mustering his troops,' says Madame Hirondelle. 'They can't be allowed to reach our position here. If they do, we all know how this will end.'

Magali's hands tremble slightly. 'It wasn't meant to happen this way. It's too fast. We have no time to—'

'We don't have any time for anything,' I say. 'Except to try and save the people who have come here seeking shelter.'

'But how do we even begin to sort this?'

'We proceed. With caution,' says Madame Hirondelle, holding my gaze with a curious look.

We proceed with caution.

We proceed.

How can we? It's madness.

Magali bites her lip, a faraway look on her face. Then she turns towards the makeshift bed in the corner of the tent and pulls the cover aside. She hums, displeased.

She looks to me. 'Will you at least do what must be done?' The lie about the heir, she means.

'Stop, sister, please,' says Madame Hirondelle, laying her hand on Magali's shoulder gingerly, as if she's afraid Magali might break. 'Don't be rash, as usual. Let us think of what we can do.'

'Sister, I'll do what I always do, which is what needs to be done.'

She shakes Madame Hirondelle's hand off and pulls out a pair of riding boots. I'm amazed by Madame Hirondelle's uncertainty, by her lack of authority. Magali goes through her like a plough, opening wounds of vulnerability, cutting through every small gesture.

'Did I not always take care of you?' says Magali.

She's out of the tent quicker than any of us can say anything. I go to run after her, but it's Madame Hirondelle who stops me.

'Stay,' she says. 'You're wasting your time. You won't change her mind.'

'So I sit here and wait while she goes off to… You know what she does. She's a destroyer.' Magali never bothered to build. Just to defend what she always thought was due to her. 'Can you imagine? With everything Maël knows about what's happened, what we've all done to him?'

I shudder to think how much he has heard, especially while Philippe carried him around in his pocket. Not even Philippe has done him any favours—even though he's been kind to his cousin, he didn't try to release him from his shape.

'We are his sworn enemies now. And although I don't know Maël well, I can't begin to imagine what he'll want to do to us.'

'Indeed, Maël will want to take revenge. On everyone,' says Madame Hirondelle. 'On every single person who sought to replace him with Philippe.'

I bite into the flesh of my fingers. 'How can we stop him? He has an army behind him. And there's only two of us.'

'Alone, we have no chance in stopping him. Celine, I do not ask this of you easily, but the way we have positioned ourselves … and considering that Hugo might not have the same thirst for revenge … he might be the lesser evil.'

CONFLUX

CELINE

*I*t's not hard to gain access to Fort Cantor. Not alone, as I am, just me and my horse. The guards at the gate wave me inside and the captain himself leads me to the Great Hall, where Maël-Hugo presides at the ducal table over a gathering of his thugs.

'Princess, what a surprise,' says Maël-Hugo, assessing me from head to toe.

He might be tall and broad, with the skin stretched taut on his cheeks that reminds me of Magali; his hair might be curled in fashionable locks away from his face and his hands might be half the size of the plate he eats from, but this is not the real Maël. Certainly not Maël in the way he tilts his head or brings his fingers to his chin. This little gesture painfully reminds me of the Hugo I once used to love. The Hugo of my dreams.

That Hugo never existed, I remind myself, while wondering if these small gestures truly escape the notice of his band of thugs, who fill the rest of the ducal table and the tables on the either side, seated in order of precedence according to the seigneur's favour. I wonder if they feel that something isn't quite right about him, isn't quite as it used to be. I wonder what story he told them about his reappearance. I wonder if the rumours about the Shape-Shifters have reached Fort Cantor, and what he had to say about the other Maël, the one who rides with Count Goderic.

The one whom Magali went to meet.

'Where is your husband?' he says, tapping his fingers on the table. There's hope in the way he can't tear his gaze away from me.

'He left,' I say.

There's a rising murmur in the hall as men's gazes wash over me. I stare straight at Hugo, trying to ignore the fact that, aside from the serving girls, I'm the only woman in this room. I try not to let this overpower me.

'He left?' says Maël-Hugo. 'The last I heard, he was down in the valley, surrounded by beggars and farmers. And women.' He tilts his head when he says this and the hall erupts in laughter.

So Magali's ruse worked. Some think that it is Philippe who is rallying the people.

'If I may have a word,' I say. 'In private.'

He examines me for a long, long time and the chatter in the hall dies down. So much depends on this moment.

So much is at stake.

And yet he's clever enough to know he has no reason to trust me. None whatsoever.

But does he need my allegiance, my help, my power? That remains to be seen.

'What of your father, Princess? We hear he's heading towards Langly with an army. Why does he need an army if he comes only to visit?' he says.

A murmur of assent rises.

'That I cannot tell you. My father has always been little

418

inclined towards giving me lengthy explanations.' The choice is in my hands, he told me. I can make or unmake the next duke.

How little choice I had, since Philippe turned away from me.

A guard bursts into the room. 'My lord, Count Goderic's army. It is in motion.'

Maël-Hugo's lips twitch in anger. 'Is that so? How interesting.' The rustle in the hall is growing. 'And where might they be heading? Fort Cantor or the camp at the foot of Castle Bencifert?'

'Too early to tell, Your Grace. Just heading in this direction.'

'Well then, what are you waiting for? Arm yourselves and to the battlements!' He unfolds himself from his seat to his towering height. Maël had always been a tall, strong man. 'To arms!' he calls, heading towards the gate, not giving me another look.

My heart thumps wildly in my chest. What has Magali done? And how did I ever believe that I could stop it?

Without any warning, as the crowd starts filing out towards the battlements, Maël-Hugo grabs my wrist and drags me towards the entrance hall, and from there pulls me into a small side room. I don't even try to protest—the speed at which everything is happening overwhelms me.

It's a small office that Philippe and I sometimes used to speak to the steward without having to go to his tower.

'What game is this?' he says, circling the room. 'Did they send you here?'

'This is no game,' I say. 'Isn't this what we always wanted?'

'Yes. Except that the last time we spoke, you said how I disgusted you, then used your Gift to seal me in a room. So that I couldn't get out before you found a way to bind me again. Forgive me if I don't see how that was part of our plan.'

'I had to bide my time,' I say. 'Philippe was furious.'

'I think *you* were furious, my dove.' He walks up to me, towering a head taller than me. His smells are all wrong, like wild game and blood and horse. But these are Hugo's words behind the mask. 'How do I even know it's you?'

'Ask me something that only I could know.' I remember. When Philippe asked. So many Celines, just one skin that is now prickling with goosebumps.

He leans back, just an inch. He is so close. Almost close enough for me to find what I am looking for.

'You have a birthmark on your inner thigh, shaped like a tree.'

'No, Magali knows that, too.'

He rubs his chin in that Hugo way and it strikes me again how the person standing before me has Hugo's gestures. And yet he's not the Hugo I loved. 'Where did I take your maidenhead?'

I blush to think of that night. How I was sure that he was the only man I could ever love. 'In the library,' I say, my throat dry. 'You said no one was going to come in at that hour. There was a glass dome in the corner, and an ottoman underneath it. You said it was a spot worthy of a princess, under the starlight.'

'I did say that, didn't I?' He grins. 'And it was so true, as I stand and breathe in front of you.'

Except that he stands in the form of someone else.

I close the distance between us, inhaling the strange smells of his body. Maël always repulsed me. I dreaded him. What he could do. It's hard for me to find traces of Hugo when he looks like this.

And yet the real Maël, especially one with a taste for revenge, would be worst of all, I remind myself. Hugo is, indeed, the lesser evil.

'Did you ever love me?' I say. 'Or was I just a means to an end?'

He lifts my chin with one finger, searching my eyes. But he won't find lies there. The pain of being betrayed after I waited for him for all these years is still real. It still breaks me apart.

His breath is in my face. 'I loved you more than anyone and anything in this world. We would have been a wonderful ducal pair, Celine. We would have made an even better king and queen. I'm sorry you chose to turn away from me.'

'But I'm here,' I say. A part of me wants to believe him. Most of me, betrayed, knows that it can't. It never will. 'I came to you. All is not lost. It can be real, all of it. It's still within our grasp.'

He slips a hand around to the back of my neck, bringing my head closer to his, and then he kisses me. It's a kiss that acts like a stamp, that marks his me as his possession, all searching tongue, looking for submission on my side. I lean into him, my hands on his.

I try not to hesitate. I try not to shrink from what I must do.

He breaks away, breathing hard. 'See, I still have a weakness for you, Celine. You can still do this to me.' He pushes me away, just slightly, and seats himself on the desk behind him. 'This is why I must not give in to my weakness. So tell me, Celine, why is Maël coming to pay me a visit? With Count Goderic's army.'

'I don't know,' I say. 'He might be going to Castle Bencifert to attack the camp there.'

'Don't toy with me, Celine,' he says, raising his voice. 'Don't lie to me. I couldn't bear it.'

And yet, that's all that you did.

My heart thumps so hard that it threatens to break my ribs. 'I don't know what Maël is doing here. I have no idea.'

Maël-Hugo curses through his teeth. 'Philippe?'

'You don't need to worry about Philippe.'

Maël-Hugo purses his lips. 'Well, that makes things a tad easier. And where *is* that dolt of a husband of yours?'

'Too busy being a dolt,' I say. 'He fled so that blood wouldn't be shed on his account.'

Maël-Hugo considers this for a moment. Perhaps he is waiting to see if I have more to say.

I don't.

'It does sound like something Philippe might do,' he concedes. 'But I still don't believe you're here out of love for me.'

'Do you believe instead that I was in love with that dolt?' I say, scoffing.

I think, *I was. I am?*

I think, *I'm not quite giving it all up for love, am I?*

Something will come after this, I tell myself.

Once I finish what I have to do. This is why I came here, isn't it?

But that's not quite true. After giving it all to Hugo, I wasn't prepared to give everything to Philippe.

I kept something for myself: the responsibility for all the things I have done. For what Hugo had turned me into, the schemer and the pawn.

Maël-Hugo scoffs. 'You and Philippe? Never.'

How little he knows me. How little he can see into my soul.

'But then ... why *are* you here?'

This is it. This is the moment. This is the time to step up. To roll the dice and see what happens. If I can't have what I want ... at least I can still do the right thing. I can keep the real Maël off the ducal seat, and this is also my move against Magali.

I walk up to Maël-Hugo and lay my hands on his shoulders. 'Because I still want to be the duchess of Langly. Because Fort Cantor is my home. I made it my home. This is what I've dreamt of for so many years.'

'This sounds more believable, when you don't say you do it all for love.'

'What do you know about love? I waited for you for five years. Can you blame me that I felt betrayed when I found out what you were doing behind my back?'

He slips his hands around my hips.

'Don't, please,' I say. 'And I draw the line at being kissed by you in this shape. Never do that again. I worked hard for five years precisely to avoid being this close to Maël.'

He chuckles, and for a moment, for a single heartbeat, he seems like the person I know. Someone I used to know, at least. 'Fine,' he says. 'I'll give you that. I was also thinking that I wouldn't want to be with you in this shape.'

I think, *Not all is lost.* 'So you did think about me? Did you know I would come?'

He shuts his mouth abruptly, as if fearful that he has already said too much. I think, *Yes, there is hope. He may not love me, but that doesn't mean that I'm nothing to him. Or that he doesn't think I can be useful.*

I can see into his mind now. How he believes that with the princess by his side, he has a better chance of winning the Battle of the Two Maëls, or whatever it might be called one day.

And then there's the sound of trumpets outside, sharp and clear, like a knife through fog. And after that, the call of a horn, low and guttural—more of a grunt.

Maël-Hugo lets his hands drop. 'We have to go to the battlements. Now.'

* * *

BEFORE THE WALLS of the castle, there's a group of riders in battledress. The bulk of Count Goderic's army, foot and horse, are gathered at a distance behind, perhaps two hours' march from Fort Cantor.

'How did they get here so fast?' yells Maël-Hugo. 'Why didn't anyone tell me?'

'We tried to find you,' says one of the thugs, a bulky man carrying a short sword. 'But we couldn't.'

423

'They marched at great speed,' says another one. 'As if the wind was behind them.'

I think, *Wind*. I think, *Madame Hirondelle*. I think, *But I have her magic enhancer, the medallion made of shards. I never gave it back to her, not even after our plan self-immolated before we even started to set it in motion.*

'Stand ready!' says Maël-Hugo. His entire body is tense, watching.

The group of riders starts moving slowly towards the castle, carrying the red standard with the lioness of the Duchy of Langly and the golden standard of parley.

'Parley!' shouts one of the brigands. 'They want to parley!'

Maël-Hugo and I exchange a look. 'What is this?'

I walk up closer to him and whisper in his ear. 'They might try to kill you at close range. They might try to cleave you with a quick cut. Take care. Maël is sure not to have any magic enhancers left.' I watch Maël-Hugo's hands intently as they feel for his breast pocket, squeezing it.

I think, *How ironic that the smallest gesture can betray the biggest secrets.*

Maël-Hugo barks at one of the thugs. 'Tell them I don't parley with traitors. Tell them that Count Goderic should forget this madness and bow to the true Duke of Langly.'

The thug, who has a very penetrating voice, I realise, conveys this to the nearing group. They slow their pace before one figure breaks away from the dozen riders and charges for the castle. It's an unusually tall and wide silhouette, brandishing a spear. 'Duck,' I hiss at Maël-Hugo, taking him by the elbow and pulling at him. 'You know who that is.' He cannot be mistaken.

Maël-Hugo takes a step back, as if evading a punch, then plants his feet wide on the stone of the castle. 'He can't hit me with a spear. Not from down there. Not even he has such good aim.'

The wind ruffles my hair and a stray strand blinds me. By the time I've brushed it away, the real Maël is underneath the castle walls. He gallops at the side of the castle, scratching the tip of his spear on the walls in an unbearable sound. 'I, Maël, Duke of Langly, call the traitor and the Shape-Shifter to a parley. Come out from behind those walls, you rat. Come out here and speak to me.'

Maël-Hugo wavers.

The thugs mutter under their breaths, looking between the two Maëls.

'Should we shoot him?' asks one of the captains.

Hugo lifts his hand so quickly that he almost slaps the man in the face. I know what the matter is. If Maël dies by his hand or by his orders, the Gift will drain out of Hugo and he won't be able to keep Maël's shape any longer, which would surely see him killed by his own crew.

I see the conundrum, and I see how we can use it. Underneath, the real Maël continues with his taunts. 'What, are you afraid, Shape-Shifter? I thought talking was your best ability. Come, come, I only want to talk.'

I draw Maël-Hugo to the side. 'You can't let this go on. You have to speak with him.'

'I don't have to do anything,' he hisses. 'We can last for months under siege. You saw to it that Fort Cantor was well provided for. I have to commend you for that.'

'The men will grow restless,' I whisper. 'How confidently can you rely on them? How long until they start to doubt you, now that they have seen the real Maël with their own eyes?'

'I'll handle the men,' he says.

'We can trap him. I can help you.'

'Trap who?' Maël-Hugo gives me a wild look. If there's anyone who is trapped, it's him.

'Maël,' I say. 'My father gave me a little gift.' I extract the brooch from where I keep it pinned on my dress, covered with my cloak. It glints a blueish sliver in the grey sunlight.

Maël-Hugo runs his finger over it. When I feel his fingers curling, I take a step back. 'He gave me the spell, but don't even think about trying to take it for yourself. You have to trust me. If I wanted to use it on you, I have had several opportunities to do so. I'm on your side.'

'Do what?' He squares his shoulders.

'You're not my enemy. *He* is.'

From below, Maël starts calling the men by their names. Calling them to action. For him. There's a rustle of uneasy movement amongst the thugs.

A long look passes between us both. 'Do it,' I say. 'We can trap him. We can be rid of him. For ever.'

Maël-Hugo considers me for a long time, probably trying to decide if he should trust me. If he can afford not to.

'Do it. Do it now, before your own so-called followers slay you.'

Maël-Hugo leans over the parapet. 'Get back to your puppets, you dog. I'll parley. One hour. Outside the castle walls.'

* * *

WE MEET near the stream that flows down from Fort Cantor into the valley, the stream that I made flow when there was a drought. When I used my Gift, with Philippe's help.

I ride in the middle of the group, by Maël-Hugo's side. Our following is twice as large as the group we're about to meet, but

426

this could go both ways—if the thugs decide the real Maël is the one riding with Count Goderic, this might work against us.

Two knights ride out from the opposite side: Maël and Count Goderic. Our guards fan out to make room for us to meet them, but we keep a safe enough distance from them.

'Princess,' says Count Goderic, bowing his head.

'I believe the last time we spoke I was the duchess,' I say.

'That remains to be discussed.' Count Goderic takes off his half-helm and gives me a tight smile. Next to him, Maël tosses his helm to the ground altogether. The thugs murmur and gasp.

Next to me, Maël-Hugo tenses again. 'Count Goderic, I demand that you swear fealty to your true liege, the Duke of Langly. Me.'

'That remains to be discussed,' he says.

'I am the duke,' says Maël-Hugo.

'No, I am the duke, you snake, and I'll make sure you'll pay for everything you've ever done for the rest of your days,' says Maël. His nostrils flare. And then, just like that, he fixes his gaze on me. I'm petrified at first. This bulk of muscle and rage is indeed a sight to behold.

He knows. He knows everything.

I must remember why I'm here. I must remember the medallion and the pin. Remember to get close enough to him. I look to Maël-Hugo, for support, but my heart fails to sing. Yet again, just like the day of my wedding, I find myself next to a man who leaves me cold.

I want Philippe, and only Philippe.

'The two Maëls stake their claim,' says Count Goderic. He makes a gesture with his hand and a few more riders step forward, falling in line with them.

Our group closes their lines around us.

427

'Knights and lords, who is here to support the claim?' says Count Goderic.

'Seigneur Champy.' He takes off his helm and bows his head. His forehead is beaded with sweat. I wager this isn't the way Seigneur Champy dreamt of spending his afternoon.

'Isabella of Langly.' Madame Hirondelle takes off her hood. Maël-Hugo twitches, perhaps in response to a memory of his time in the Golden Pavilion, when we all feared her. But she completely ignores him. When her gaze passes me, she briefly closes her eyes.

Is this truly her? I wonder. And if it is her, what does she expect of me now?

And then, it might not be even her. If it's Magali behind this shape, how she must loathe me.

But the true Madame Hirondelle said something to me about the lesser evil.

I try to sit straighter on my horse.

I had to make a decision, one I didn't want to make, and now I have to stand by it.

I think, *No, this can't be the true Madame Hirondelle. The true Isabella of Langly.*

She would have never joined the real Maël.

'Seigneur Peneric of the Mermaid's Lake.' When he removes his helm, he drops it to the ground. These men are frightened.

A tall, lean lad on the largest horse I ever saw also steps forward. 'Fabien of Goderic Castle.'

'Now that's a surprise,' I snort.

'Duchess. Always a great pleasure to see you. Though in such company…' He sucks in air through his teeth.

'Pleasure is certainly one thing you could call it. I have other words in mind.'

Fabien guffaws.

No wonder he is here, I think. It was clear from the beginning whose side Count Goderic was on. The evasive answers. The fact that he brought Fabien to the castle in the early days to investigate Maël's disappearance. The way he had distanced himself from his third son's actions have been nothing but a charade.

And then another man, on a red horse, steps forward, taking off his helm slowly. The wind kisses his dark hair. His jaw is squared in what looks like anger. I catch the beats of my racing heart. *It can't be him. He left.*

I think, *Shape-Shifters.*

I think, *It can't be.*

No.

'Celine,' he says.

Ssseline.

I open and close my mouth. It's uncanny what effect the very shape of him has on me. Chills cut through to my knees.

But he's gone, I think.

He left.

He left me.

Maël-Hugo pokes me in the ribs. The pin, I remember. This might be a good time to use it, before this escalates to a point of no return.

I am not, by a long shot, close enough to Maël for this to work. And with everyone watching... The courage drains from my chest.

I can't take my eyes off Philippe. He drives his hand through his hair and I catch something in his eyes, anger and hurt at the same time.

'Phillipe?' I croak. My voice is leaving me.

Because I realise, this is Philippe. This can be no one but Philippe.

That's when another rider steps forward, a woman with deep

wrinkles around her eyes and skin stretched taut on her cheeks. And when I see Magali, every trace of doubt is erased from my heart.

Philippe is on Maël's side. And so is Madame Hirondelle. And Magali.

I find myself on the wrong side of the barricade. Yet again, I have made the wrong choice. There's a gaping hole in my stomach and as I hold Philippe's disappointed and reproachful gaze, I want to leap off my horse and run over to the other side. To him.

But the events unfold too quickly.

'Seigneurs of the duchy,' says Magali, 'on this day, who is your liege? Who will you answer to?'

Around us, everything suddenly grows quiet. Not even the stream snaking at our feet dares to disturb us.

And I hope. In this heartbeat that seems to stretch on and on and on, before Count Goderic and his armies declare for the real Maël, the Maël who had been the duke for longer than anyone else, I still dare to hope.

Count Goderic steps forward, throwing me a quick glance. 'The seigneurs of the Duchy of Langly answer to Duke Philippe and Duke Philippe only.'

My head pounds, and I don't dare believe what he has just said. Is it my imagination, playing a cruel joke? By the look on Maël's face, it is true enough. And this is not what he was expecting.

Philippe's cheeks drain of blood, but he sits straighter in his saddle, while Maël turns almost purple. He draws his sword. 'Traitors! That's what the lot of you are!' he aims at us, and then everyone draws their swords: our thugs, the Langly seigneurs, every man with a weapon. Fabien gallops to Philippe's side to protect him, and the helms are jammed back into place. Maël rushes bare-headed, his helm forgotten.

Only Magali draws something else—a golden cage from under her cloak—and races towards her son, not away from him, like everyone else.

Magali cries, 'Now, now, now!' and the entire party of seigneurs charges towards her son.

I watch as if in a dream as the real Maël is unhorsed by his own mother with a knock of the cage; how the seigneurs, Fabien foremost, hold him down. Magali places the cage on top of his head and closes her eyes, murmuring. I know what she's doing. It is what I was supposed to do before she released Maël, before she started strutting around as Isabella.

Philippe. Our gazes cross again and there's so much pain in his, but also a question. *What will you do now, Celine?*

And then Madame Hirondelle calls for my attention with a little cry. From the sleeve of her wide cloak she extracts a small object, which glints in the sickly sunlight.

A golden ring.

This explains the wind that brought Count Goderic's army so quickly to the doorstep of Fort Cantor.

Magali has given her the ring and is binding her own magic to tether Maël's Gift.

Madame Hirondelle trots up to Philippe's side and places the ring in his palm. Maël writhes on the ground, roaring, trying to escape his ties, while Magali is focused on her binding spell.

The future that I had dared to dream for myself is again within my grasp.

I turn to Hugo. 'We can still do this,' I say breathlessly. 'Take them both, Philippe and Magali. We can still do this. You can still be the duke.'

'What are you talking about?'

'I need your pouch. The magic enhancer. I have my father's brooch, I have the spell, I have the power. Magali is binding her own powers in order to keep Maël contained for ever.'

'I don't know what pouch you're talking about.'

I pause as I realise that everything comes down to this one moment. I cannot fail. I must not fail.

'Hugo, do you want to be the duke or not? Give me the pouch.'

I hold his gaze for what feels like an eternity. Maël's writhing subsides and I feel Philippe's stare drilling into the back of my neck, but I can't look. Not now.

Hesitantly, Maël-Hugo reaches into the pocket of his coat and passes me the velvet pouch.

I clasp it in my hand. I unpin the brooch and put it in the pouch, closing the mouth tight with the string. I give Hugo one last look and kick my horse hard in the belly, making it rear and then charge through the thugs gathered around us, and to Philippe's side.

'Now!' I say.

'Celine.'

'Now!'

I jump down from my horse, the golden medallion around my neck, the pouch at my waist. It's so easy now to call on the water to lift, to rise, to push Hugo towards Magali, horse and all.

I am the master of my own power, and what a power that is. The Gifts coils and rises within me, drawing merciless waves from the small creek. Hugo, Maël and Magali tumble down in a scramble of limbs. She looks up at me, drenched, while I call for the seigneurs to bind them, too.

Without the pouch and in the heat of it all, the false Maël's shape trembles into Hugo's features. Magali remains to the side, unscathed. The thugs start to come forward to free their master.

I cry, 'Don't you dare! Don't you even dare!' and they step

back. I hold the pouch and touch the medallion, but I don't know if I can wield enough power to bind both of them while Magali is still free, no matter how much anger I might have bottled inside.

I look into her eyes and think, *I should to be rid of her, too.* For how long has she been the bane of my existence? For how long have her plotting and lies cast a shadow over my life? For how long have I dreaded the moment she would return to Fort Cantor?

No, as long as she looms above me, I will not be able to live my life as I wish. As I could. And on this moment, everything else depends. If I will ever be free of her or not.

MAGALI

Who does she think she is? A long silence passes between all of us. Hugo and Maël, writhing on the ground, held down by the knights. Me, a bit to the side. I can see what she wants to do. I can see what she tries.

She'll never succeed.

She doesn't have it in her.

'Don't you even think of it. They would never,' I say, tilting my chin at Goderic. He would never dare touch me. None of the seigneurs gathered here would.

The little princess has played her hand and she has lost.

Hugo grows smaller and smaller into his own size, the power of his shapeshifting fading.

I have to end this. Now. I point a finger at Celine. 'Seize her! Seize the pouch! Strip her—she may yet hide something else, too.'

Goderic blanches. What is he waiting for? Get the deed done and we will never have to worry again. I look to Isabella and signal her to throw me back my ring. I need it.

But she looks away.

Even her. Even Isabella.

I shake off the edge of dread. Be that as it may. Today, one of us, Celine or me, will fall. There isn't room for both of us in the Duchy of Langly.

And then there's the sound of steps, dragging through the mud.

CELINE

I do believe I can do the binding alone, but I don't think I can fight Count Goderic too, who fidgets, perhaps wondering which side to strike. Which of us might win, so he can position himself accordingly. Though I have to hand it to him, he gambled a great deal to support Philippe.

I can't fight the seigneurs.

I can't fight my husband.

And then I think, of course I can. The Gift courses and surges through me, the water calls.

I have enough anger bottled for everything. For every single time when I was slighted or used.

For every moment when I rose my voice, and it wasn't heard.

I am the master of my own power. Waves crash within me now, eager to be released into the world.

I could bind them all. The red pouch, the medallion, together, they're much more powerful than I would ever have imagined.

I can do this alone, but I don't want to. All my life, this is all I have been: alone. If I'm not wanted here, then why bother tying Magali alongside them?

There's the sound of steps behind me, a clop in the mud, and someone takes my hand. I don't have to look to know it's Philippe —the feeling of warmth that surges through my entire body is unmistakable. The feeling that I'm powerful and that there's nothing that can stand in my way, not even Magali.

'Seize her!' I say. 'This must end here, now, today.'

Philippe tightens the grip of his hand around mine and I feel every callus in his palm, every single patch of scorched skin on his fingers as the warmth of his hands pumps through me.

'Do as my wife says.' Philippe sounds exhausted. 'She's right. All of this must end today. It's gone on for far too long.'

Count Goderic looks to all of us in turn and something clicks into place within him, because he nods and lays a hand on Magali's shoulder. 'Don't make me tie you. It would be unseemly for us both.'

Shock is written across Magali's face but before she can say anything, Philippe and I step forward. I lay a hand on Hugo, who now looks more and more like himself and less like his cousin. Philippe places a hand on his own mother's arm. I pass him the pouch and then we begin to say the spell.

Together.

I reach deep within myself to find the strength in my own Gift to channel the power of the pin, of the medallion, of the pouch. Of Philippe and me. The air begins to shimmer around all five of us, tied by this binding. It flickers and shudders, like wind around a fire, distorting the shape around us. And I feel the power draining from within me, tied into the water in the ground, on the ground, above the ground.

The flow of Philippe's powers through mine wanes to a trickle and I make myself ready for the hardest part.

Because it isn't enough to see Magali and Hugo with their hands bound, unable to wreak more havoc by changing into any shape that suits them. I need them gone from my duchy, gone from my sight. I never want to see them again. I never want them to cause such chaos as they nearly have today—the clash of the three armies.

'I bind you by water,' I whisper. 'I bind you out of the boundaries of this kingdom. May the water find you and carry you away if you try to put a foot on the ground of the Red Kingdom, wave your hand into its winds, sink a single strand of hair into the streams. May the water bind you and banish you.'

Philippe turns to me, slowly. The stream behind us trickles and sways out of its way to engulf Magali, Hugo and Maël in its grip. Water encloses like a dozen arms around them.

Behind me, Isabella dips her fingers into the brook, strengthening the spell, as we'd agreed this morning, though Magali hadn't been a part of that settlement.

'Untie them.' I'm barely able to summon the strength to say the words. I feel like the powers have departed from me, flowed into the last rise of this stream, intent on carrying the three away from the borders of our kingdom, and keeping them out.

Count Goderic extracts his dagger, the sheath studded with precious stones, and cuts the ties binding Hugo and Maël. The stream drags them away towards its main riverbed, from where it will take them to the sea. While the cousins struggle to return, slashing their arms uselessly against the rage of the waters, Magali eases herself onto her back and floats with her eyes to the sky, letting herself be carried away.

MAGALI

You have to pick your fights, and you have to know when you've been defeated. You have to do this in order to summon your strength so you can come back one day and strike harder.

Maël mouths the foulest insults I have ever heard and Hugo is livid with rage. 'By the Dark Mother, you haven't seen the last of me!' he yells as the current carries him away.

Not a word passes my lips. There's nothing more to say as we drift, the water bearing us downstream, kindly making sure that we float, across the valley, between the farmhouses and towards the sea.

CELINE

The stream twists and bends, and that's the last any of us sees of them.

A stony silence reigns amongst those gathered here. Philippe lets go of my hand, breaking the last of our bond. He shakes his head slightly at me. I know why. While we discussed with Madame Hirondelle this part of the plan this morning, I was met with the most resistance from his side. *But why do we have to do this?* he said. *We could take care of them, make sure they live a comfortable life under our gaze.*

Not while both Hugo and Maël are alive, I said. And we were speaking back then about tying the two to their animal forms—so I think I'll consider myself merciful today.

We never once spoke about banishing Magali, as well.

His own mother.

'It had to be done,' I whisper to Philippe. 'We would never have been truly free, if they were here.'

I turn to the gathered seigneurs and thugs. Even the thugs might prove useful one day, so I give them the explanation that will forever be the world's version of events.

'On this day, we have prevailed against evil and magic. On this day, I, Duchess Celine of Langly, bound the last of my powers to ensure that the three Shape-Shifters who had assumed the shapes of the ducal family will be forever banished from our kingdom.'

They all turn towards me, drinking in my words. There's a tinge of fear in their eyes, and I have to speak to that fear, to soothe it, so that it doesn't, one day, turn into a monster. 'The Dowager Duchess Magali has been dead for weeks. Messere Hugo, as we all know, perished more than five years ago. And Duke Maël was taken from us this spring by a terrible beast. Those responsible will be brought to justice, I can promise you that.' I raise my voice. 'And today, your duchess has given up her Gift to make sure that such intriguers and liars and shifters never lay a single foot in Langly again.'

I try to prevent my voice from wavering. Philippe is quiet, sombre, a castle that has closed its gates.

'Today, we welcome a new world, free of the treacheries of magic. An age of trust. An age where we help and support each other. An age in which we seek not power, but the well-being of one and all.'

Loud cheers erupt from the seigneurs. It almost sounds like relief and it makes my ears ring.

'Today, every man and woman who wishes to live honourably is welcome in the Duchy of Langly.'

The men stamp their feet on the ground, their armour clinking. I will have to repeat this speech later, in front of the assembled soldiers. I will have to drink the brew of a day that has not gone as I had planned but, in the end, better than I could have expected.

For now, I have to find Phillipe's gaze.

It will all be fine in the end, I tell myself. They will believe this story, because it makes more sense than the intricate truth, and because they will want to believe it.

But I'm more interested in what Philippe believes. I lean in and whisper in his ear. 'It will be all right. You will forgive me, one day.'

He blinks, his shoulder moving ever so slightly away from mine. 'Celine, I will have to forgive myself first. I've played my part in the banishing spell.' He touches his hand briefly to mine. 'My Gift has all but left me.'

Hope flutters in my chest and there must be traces of it on my own face, because he adds quickly, 'Do you think I'll ever forgive myself for banishing my own mother? Do you think I'll ever be proud of what I did?'

I think, *Of course you will.* I think, *One day, we'll be very happy, when you'll allow yourself to.* I think, *One day, you'll see how this was the only way. And you will know, in your heart, that she won't be able to bear you any ill will.*

All that I say is, 'One day. One day, when the world looks back upon what has happened today, it will seem to have been a very, very different story.'

FLOTSAM

MAGALI

*T*he river rushes us down, down, down, and then upstream along smaller confluences. We ride on its waves as if it's a terrible underwater creature. Like the Nightdragon of the Dark Mother. By now, even Maël and Hugo have stopped quarrelling with each other and with the magic that carries us forward.

Plains with small villages scattered around them give way to hills, fields of wheat give way to willows, and then to forests of pines. Ah, so it seems we're not being dumped into the sea after all. We travel past dumbstruck merchants, peasants returning from the day's work, women doing their laundry.

It all passes by me in a blur. All I can think about is how Isabella betrayed me, too. How all of this must have been the Marchionessa's doing.

She must have wanted Maël back, in her clutches. Who knows why.

Oh, yes, if Isabella would betray me for anyone, that would be *her*. What I can't fathom is how the Fallen Court would accept Philippe as the duke, with Maël exiled.

I'm sure the Marchionessa has something in mind.

If I were her, so would I, and we have always been so much like one another. Too much for anyone's good.

We travel through murky waters and clear streams into cliffs and even beyond borders. I have given up looking for landmarks. We are not in the Red Kingdom anymore and I wonder about Celine's Gift that could compel water in this way.

We travel up, up, up into smaller streams until the brook is so narrow that we could be in water no deeper than our knees, should we be able to set our feet down, should we not be carried by its merciless flow.

And then, just as suddenly as we were lifted from the earth, we are set down on a mossy bank. The three of us are so shocked that for long moments we can think of nothing else but the grass under our feet and the solidity of stone.

Maël is the first to come to his senses and gets up on wobbly legs. He draws himself up to his full, towering height and looks at us with murder in his eyes. Water is still dripping off him, streaming down his face. 'If I ever lay eyes on either of you again, I swear I'll kill you.'

Hugo stands up straight, wringing water out of his cloak, and has the decency to avoid his gaze.

I sit up, panting. *Where are we?*

'They're here!' comes a sharp shout from the pinewoods.

A horn begins ringing, resounding through the forest, its sound clear and bright like the sky after storm clouds have scattered.

They start emerging, one by one, from the line of trees.

Soldiers in chainmail. The blue cloaks of the—surprise!—Blue Kingdom. Maël grapples for his sword, but only finds a dagger in his boot. And Hugo looks like he's ready to jump back into the water.

The soldiers draw themselves into a perfect line, mere feet from us. Maël is wet and bristling, ready to go down fighting.

'Stand down, Maël. Don't be a fool.' It's a woman's voice, sharp and commanding. 'Put that knife away.'

The soldiers part to allow a single person to pass. Her steps are small and full of purpose. She wears a white fur mantle on top of a trailing blue dress. A crown sits on top of her head.

'Bow to Queen—' a soldier's voice booms.

'Not now,' says the woman, exasperation in her tone. 'Let them breathe, by Sabya's Morningstar. They can do the bowing later.'

Maël's face wobbles into a smile. 'Auntie. What a pleasure to see you.'

Valerie simply nods and strides towards me, stretching out a hand. 'Welcome home, sister. I wasn't expecting *you*.'

There is a certain bitter aftertaste to being back here, after so many years, carrying with me the sting of defeat, but I take her arm and rise to my feet, still swaying. 'How did you know where to find us?'

Valerie shrugs. 'The Marchionessa told me, as it was agreed with Isabella.'

I smile bitterly. Celine might have thought she won the day.

She would be wrong.

As always, the winner of the day is the Marchionessa of the Fallen Court.

I remember her promise.

'Isabella?' says Hugo. 'But it was Celine who performed the spell.'

'I know,' says Valerie, an odd gleam in her eyes. Of course. Celine would have done what Isabella told her. What they had planned together. 'Isabella added a little extra something to make sure that you ... arrived safely at your destination. Though I wasn't sure who I would find, to be honest. That was still an open matter.'

Maël growls, shaking the water out of his hair.

'The princess picked the other one,' says Hugo, pure venom in his voice. 'Bencifert's son.'

'That's not how it was. The *seigneurs* picked Philippe,' I cut in.

'*She* thought it might be a possibility,' says Valerie.

Of course she did. The Marchionessa.

My sister studies Hugo for a beat and he shrinks from her gaze. 'Isabella let us know that you might bring your pet, but I simply couldn't believe he'd have the cheek to come here, after all he's done.'

They knew. How long have they known about Hugo? About what I'd done to him?

'Maybe you can kill him,' says Maël. 'You would be doing everyone a great service.'

Unlikely. What Maël is to the Marchionessa, it's the same with Hugo. As much as she wants to forget it.

'He may still have his uses,' says Valerie, angling her head in that way that our mother always did. She was always so much like our mother. 'I'll deal with you later,' she says to me. 'We have some reckoning to do.'

Ice stabs my insides, from my chest to the depths of my belly. It will not end well.

She reaches then for Maël's arm, and he offers it, as if he weren't soaking wet, as if he hadn't just become an outcast from his own duchy. As if they were two perfectly well-mannered people at a ball. But before they take another step, she says, 'I have something for you.' She extracts a mark of the Fallen Court from her pocket and lays it in his palm.

A contract, then.

A mission from the Marchionessa.

Maël's eyes glitter.

Valerie says, 'I'm glad you're the one who arrived. She has work for you.'

AUTHOR'S NOTE

Dear Reader,

I hope that you enjoyed *The Kingdom Is a Golden Cage* and that you're curious to untangle the complicated history of the Red Kingdom. I hope that the ending has provided as many questions as it has provided answers, and that you're as excited as I am to embark on the next stage of this journey. If you made it all the way up to here it means that you understand that many of my characters are chronic liars, and they often have their own version of the truth. I hope you'll have fun unravelling that very truth over the next books in the series, and that you'll make up your mind which version of the fairy tale you believe, Celine's or Magali's.

Or neither...

I wanted to talk to you a bit about the inspiration behind the book. There were two main sources for me when I began writing this novel: European folk tales and history. I used to write historical fiction before I took up fantasy and I think old habits die hard.

When it comes to myths, there are some motifs that have

floated into the novel from Eastern European fairy tales—for instance, the Mother-of-the-Forest is often the literal mother of the villain, also called the Zmeu. While depictions of the Zmeu vary, it's often identified with a dragon (more about this in later instalments!).

But many motifs in the novel were inspired by the classic folk tale *Puss in Boots* (did you guess that already?). When reading the story of the wily cat in his little boots, I always wondered: what would it look like if it was seen through the eyes of the Princess and not the male characters in the story?

As for the historical bit… You know, I stepped into writing fantasy naively thinking that I wouldn't have to do research.

Wrong.

I read a lot, from life in medieval castles to knights and knighthood, the internal power struggles in the Holy Roman Empire and, and, and. But I'd say that I had two historical sources of inspiration for this book, both revolving around inheritance, how it was legislated in the Middle Ages, and the devastating effects that power struggles within the nobility had upon the entire population of those kingdoms.

A crucial historical event that inspired the series is the War of the Roses. The women were often pushed to the background (well, until Margaret of Anjou, at least), and they were often 'vessels' for an inheritance claim. This inspired me to write Magali's reflection on how she is 'the mother of, daughter of, sister of dukes', but never the duchess as an entity within herself.

As for the world where everything takes place—the Red, Blue and Green Kingdoms are imaginary spaces that are at the confluence of Germanic, Celtic, and Roman-Italian elements. This, in turn, has been inspired by the *Agri Decumates* territories at the edge of the Roman Empire, but they have more to do with antiquity than with the medieval-inspired world this novel takes place in. The *Agri Decumates* space, is, historically to the Kingdoms, more relevant to Sabya's own story and her parentage (yes, I *do* have something in mind).

The confluence itself also draws on history, and specifically on the fact that the medieval kingdom of France had formed under the rule of the Franks, which are, in turn, a Germanic people that settled in a space of predominantly Celtic population, which had been ruled by the Romans for centuries. Confused? I guarantee you that, as complex as the story of the Red, Green and Blue Kingdoms is, it doesn't even come close to how complex and confusing European history is.

Do you know what the best thing is about writing fantasy instead of historical fiction? I don't have to stick to the facts. I can draw from them, but this is an entirely imaginary world, so congratulations, you live in my head as well!

It's a very busy place, as you can see.

You will have noticed how important the rules of inheritance are to the people of the Red Kingdom. The rules in the book aren't invented, as such. As Celine describes the inheritance law in the beginning of the book, they are similar to the Quasi-Salic law. This is also like the male-preferred primogeniture (I think the name says it all).

The Salic Law is the code of law of the Franks, which has been in use in the Middle Ages.

To my novel it was relevant how the Salic Law encoded the succession—which meant that women were excluded from it. In *The Kingdom Is a Golden Cage*, I was interested in exploring how this reverberated in the lives of the women, how they would regard it, and how their perception of their own roles would be impacted by these restrictions.

And to those who are, perhaps, disappointed that the laws are the same at the end of the book—I will tell you two things: please

447

remember that this is a book series, and revolutions do take time.

Also, I do promise you a Queen.

But you haven't met her yet. Not face-to-face, at least.

Love,
Lilly

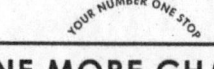

ONE MORE CHAPTER

The author and One More Chapter would like to thank everyone who contributed to the publication of this story...

Analytics
Emma Harvey
Maria Osa

Audio
Fionnuala Barrett
Ciara Briggs

Contracts
Georgina Hoffman
Florence Shepherd

Design
Lucy Bennett
Andrew Davis
Fiona Greenway
Holly Macdonald
Liane Payne
Dean Russell

Digital Sales
Laura Daley
Michael Davies
Georgina Ugen

Editorial
Arsalan Isa
Charlotte Ledger
Federica Leonardis
Lydia Mason
Ajebowale Roberts
Jennie Rothwell
Tony Russell
Kimberley Young

International Sales
Bethan Moore

Marketing & Publicity
Chloe Cummings
Emma Petfield

Operations
Melissa Okusanya
Hannah Stamp

Production
Emily Chan
Denis Manson
Francesca Tuzzeo

Rights
Lana Beckwith
Rachel McCarron
Agnes Rigou
Hany Sheikh
Mohamed
Zoe Shine
Aisling Smyth

**The HarperCollins
Distribution Team**

**The HarperCollins
Finance & Royalties
Team**

**The HarperCollins
Legal Team**

**The HarperCollins
Technology Team**

Trade Marketing
Ben Hurd

UK Sales
Yazmeen Akhtar
Laura Carpenter
Isabel Coburn
Jay Cochrane
Alice Gomer
Gemma Rayner
Erin White
Harriet Williams
Leah Woods

**And every other
essential link in the
chain from delivery
drivers to booksellers
to librarians and
beyond!**